praise for
o solo homo:

"This collection is a joyous public service—like those Irish monks who preserved previously evanescent performance works. And it beats *Beowulf*."

—kate clinton

"It's hard to believe that some of the fearless and gifted writer-performers represented in this anthology had to defend their very right to bear witness to their lives, but we should all be glad they persevered. They do nothing more dangerous or threatening than tell the truth, and their tales are hilarious, moving, thrilling. We are lucky to be able to read them."

—anthony rapp

"*O Solo Homo* represents the most significant and vibrant cross-section of queer solo performance since the gospels. A must-have field guide for the amateur and professional alike. Ten thumbs up!"

—the five lesbian brothers

o solo homo

o solo homo

THE NEW QUEER PERFORMANCE

*edited by holly hughes
and david román*

Grove Press   New York

Published simultaneously in Canada
Printed in the United States of America

FIRST EDITION

Library of Congress Cataloging-in-Publication Data

O solo homo : the new queer performance / edited by Holly Hughes & David Román.
    p.   cm.
   ISBN 0-8021-3570-6
    1. Gays' writings, American. 2. Lesbians—United States—Drama.
3. Gay men—United States—Drama. 4. Gays—United States—Drama.
5. Monodramas. 6. Monologues. I. Hughes, Holly. II. Román, David, 1959– .
PS627.H6702 1998
810.8'0920664—dc21   98–5203
                                                        CIP

DESIGN BY LAURA HAMMOND HOUGH

Grove Press
841 Broadway
New York, NY 10003

98 99 00 01 10 9 8 7 6 5 4 3 2 1

Contents

Acknowledgments

We would like to thank the following people for helping make *O Solo Homo* happen: Malaga Baldi, Amy Hundley, Rosemary Weatherston, Jessica Smith, Jackie Gares, Morgan Jenness, and Jim Moser.

Greg Mehrten's advice, support, and trust proved indispensable to our project. We would also like to thank Gary Indiana and Penny Arcade for their permission to publish Ron Vawter's *Roy Cohn/Jack Smith*.

Thanks also to Ellie Covan, Alisa Solomon, José Muñoz, David Drake, Sue-Ellen Case, Dona Ann McAdams, Jill Dolan, Steven Drukman, Lenora Champagne, and C. Carr.

David Román would like to thank everyone at Highways Performance Space, Diane Rodriguez and Luis Alfaro at the Mark Taper Forum, and his colleagues in the Department of English at USC for making room for him and his work at these different institutions. Special thanks to his Los Angeles friends: Chay Yew, Judith Jackson Fossett, David Joselit, Dorinne Kondo, Tania Modleski, Tim Miller, Joe Boone, Teresa McKenna, David Rousseve, Conor McTeague, and, as always, Richard Meyer.

Holly Hughes thanks her bevy of spiritual advisors and emotional spin-doctors: Minnie Bruce Pratt, Eileen Clancy, Madeleine

Olnek, Alina Troyano, Gerry Gomez Pearlberg, and, as always, Esther Newton. And let's not forget Velveeta, Flynn, Tabouli, the Cookie Monster, and Mr. Pierre for important services rendered.

We especially want to thank all of the book's O Solo Homos; we are deeply honored to be associated with their work.

Anyone lucky to have seen performances by Danitra Vance and Ron Vawter, two of the most important artists working in the theatre before their lives were cut short by breast cancer and AIDS respectively, will know why this book is dedicated to them.

O Solo Homo:
An Introductory Conversation

DAVID ROMÁN: Queer solo performance is booming. The field is so diverse—diverse in terms of its artistic form and content, and diverse in terms of the identities of those performing—that it challenges any effort to define it. Queer solo performers work in a variety of different and quite distinct traditions—autobiographical, character-driven monologue, stand-up, "classic" performance art—and artists embody and perform from a wide range of political identities defined by race, ethnicity, HIV status, class, gender, and sexual practice. The boom in queer performance is compelling to me for a number of reasons. It's one of the few areas in public culture that is immediately understood as multiracial, cogendered, and multisexual. It's also one of the few forms of artistic expression that registers as democratic: nearly anyone can do it and nearly everyone does. It's for these reasons that solo performance also seems to be such an easy target to attack. Concerns about artistic quality and political content, when combined with the larger cultural anxieties about queers in general, push queer solo performance right into the national spotlight. The fact that so much of this work sets out to articulate some of the most pressing issues of our day—queer families, HIV and AIDS, breast cancer, race relations, the role of the arts—contributes to these attacks and may begin to account for the reason why such a diverse range of queer artists are driven to do solo work in the first place.

HOLLY HUGHES: Boom. The queer solo performance boom . . . is that what's going on? Perhaps I'm having trouble with the "boom" model because it suggests a "bust" will follow. But I can't come up with a more precise word that describes the growth of this form. A "proliferation"? No, sounds like the arms race. "Explosion" . . . too reminiscent of Mel Gibson movies, and he is one person who has no place in this book. The critics of this form—and there are naysayers on both the Right and the Left—have called it a "glut." Of course, these are the same people who'd label an audience of five hundred white people and two Latinos "diverse." So boom it is. But I think that the bust isn't going to follow the boom; it's happening simultaneously. It's a bust caused by lessened arts funding and the encroachments of corporate entertainment on the cultural margins.

There is a relationship between the boom and the urgency of those problems we as queers in this country are facing and the development of solo performance. Why are so many theater artists choosing to explore these issues by making solo performance pieces rather than creating ensemble works or even plays? (You remember them, right?) I'd guess that 75 percent of that question can be answered by looking at the economic situation of most theaters in this country. Solos are all they can (barely) afford to produce. In 1997 the National Endowment for the Arts ended all funding for individual artists (except fiction writers). Memoirs are described as "hot" forms, meaning they've found audiences that are sometimes larger and more enthusiastic than the audiences for theater and fiction. But at the same time, memoirs and solo performances are frequently dismissed by critics as "self-indulgent" and artless, as though there were no art involved in rescuing images and metaphors from the flotsam and jetsam of daily life.

I believe a lot of this work is rooted, consciously or not, in a particularly American tradition of testifying, of witnessing history in the first person. It's a tradition that's entwined with this country's social change movements. Two prime examples: the testifying in African American churches, where the modern civil rights movement was born, and the consciousness raising that was central to second-wave feminism in the sixties and seventies.

Witnessing has its less overtly political manifestations as well: the American literary world got its knickers in a major knot when confessional poetry appeared in the fifties and sixties. In this country you have to either make something up or cloak your experience as fiction to have your work accepted as "high art." Two of this century's most acclaimed thespians—Eugene O'Neill and Tennessee Williams—wrote work that was clearly autobiographical. They threw something over the sofa that made it acceptable, even if the fabric was so thin, you could see the stuffing coming out underneath. Williams, for example, had to translate his experience into women's voices. But suddenly there were writers like Sylvia Plath and Anne Sexton, who were refusing to speak obliquely, who were telling tales that hadn't been told when all the women in literature were ventriloquist dummies for their male authors. These writers led to a boom of autobiographical work in the sixties, which is part of the American lineage of autobiographical performance.

Not all of the work in *O Solo Homo* is autobiographical. And none of it is mere reportage. Tim Miller begins one of his other performances, *Sex/Love/Stories*, by saying that all of this is true and some of it even happened. The late Danitra Vance, Michael Kearns, Kate Bornstein, and many other soloists channel a variety of voices. Perhaps the most celebrated nonautobiographical solo is Ron Vawter's performance of *Roy Cohn/Jack Smith*. The script includes a fictitious Roy Cohn speech as imagined by Gary Indiana and an abridged excerpt of a Jack Smith performance. But I would argue that this work can also be understood as autobiographical. Certainly Ron is not absent; he doesn't merely disappear into these other characters, although they are marvelous characterizations. Vawter framed the piece by making a brief curtain speech—as Vawter. He comes out as a person with AIDS and tells us directly what these two men represented for him so that interdiction is always informing the way we see the piece.

When we attend a solo piece it's knowing that there is a good chance the performer is also the writer and the stories we will hear "really happened." There is some level of safety that disappears for the audience: we can't hide behind "it's only art." Susan Miller's exquisitely written *My Left Breast* ends with her exposing her chest. This is not a fiction. Breast cancer is not something that happens only to other people. The fact that these are "real stories" has something to do with their critical reception, which for the most part has not been good. Oh yes, the pieces in this collection have won Obies and grants and have often gotten raves. But queer solo work is not in any danger of being welcomed into the canon; it's often pointed to as symptom and even cause of decline, a landmark in Robert Hughes's *Culture of Complaint.*

DAVID ROMÁN: Autobiographical work is an especially popular form for queer writers and performers and for their readers and audiences. In part, this is because autobiography fits into the model of identity politics on which lesbian and gay liberation is founded. In other words, autobiography is perhaps the most immediately understood form of queer self-representation, and it is also often part of a larger collective and ongoing process of revisionist history. Its premise is generally based on a certain political investment in visibility; queer autobiography furthermore contributes to the "we are everywhere" mantra of seventies lesbian and gay liberation. But queer autobiography is far from trapped in the seventies or tied to an outmoded model of queer representation and politics. This work has remained vital and viable even as the form itself grows and changes. And I, for one, still find it politically useful and necessary to assert a gay identity—again and again. I am also very drawn to work that comes out of this identity politics model. Not only is it invigorating to be sitting with other queers at a queer solo performance event, but I also believe that the form itself is inexhaustible and therefore exciting. And the categories "gay," "lesbian," and "queer" are themselves dynamic, subject to the shifting historical forces that help shape these terms and subject to the personal histories that mark any queer individual's life. Queer solo artists can't help but bring this mix into their performances, animating their work within the context of the larger culture and history in which they live. More to the point, there are still voices and experiences that have yet to be heard in queer culture. I will always remember the thrill I experienced when I first saw Alec Mapa's *I Remember Mapa*. Alec is a terrific performer whom I had admired ever since I first saw him perform in the national touring company of M. *Butterfly* and in *A Language of Their Own*, Chay Yew's stunning play about gay Asian relationships, at New York's Public Theater in 1994. Alec's talent is irrefutable, but it was his story—his experiences as a gay Filipino—that especially interested me. The fact that Alec takes such an irreverent tone to identity politics makes his work all the more complex. Except for the work of Han Ong, I hadn't seen many performances that explored gay Filipino lives. I don't want to suggest that performers like Alec Mapa or Han Ong—or other artists like Noel Alumit or Joel Tan, whose work I've since seen— are interesting simply because they are queer and Asian; however, I do think it is important to stress that their work contributes enormously to the multiple overlapping worlds that compose queer public life. In this sense, queer solo work is usually pedagogical. All of the artists in this anthology, for example, have something to teach us about what it means to be queer and how that aspect of their identity intersects with various other identity factors such as race—including whiteness—ethnicity, class, gender, and region. Queer performance serves to educate queer audiences of all backgrounds even as it entertains us or mobilizes us politically. And this applies not just to queer audiences; I first saw *I Remember Mapa* as a work in progress at East West Players, Los Angeles's Asian American theater. This performance was commissioned and produced by the Mark Taper Forum's Asian Theater Workshop.

Queer people know well that identities are dynamic and contingent—and queer solo artists perform this fact and do so generously. Queer solo performance comes out of a sense of community and thus helps inform and shape our understanding of identity and community. Queer solo performers trouble the comfort of community even as they invest in it, and this tension is what I find so exciting. One could even argue that queer solo performers are often at the frontiers of new social identities and more inclusive community formations.

This sense of pioneering new identity formations is evident in the history of the form. Consider that in the pre-Stonewall era and to a lesser extent in the immediate years following it, there were very few queer performers creating solo work and even fewer doing autobiographical work. Figures such as Pat Bond, a lesbian performer whose *Murder in the WAC* was among the first of this genre, and Stuart Sherman, a New York performance artist who began creating solo pieces in the 1970s, were the exceptions and not the rule—O Solo Homo indeed. A history of queer solo performance begins in the context not only of the lesbian and gay movement, but in the subcultural world of queer bars, cabarets, and drag revues and in the public context of lesbian and gay people negotiating personal safety with outright defiance.

Queer people have a rich history of solo performers entertaining queer audiences in the bars and nightclubs, and this, of course, is still true. And here we must stress the significance of drag and other forms of gender performance in shaping a certain kind of queer aesthetic that lives on in the solo work of such diverse "drag" artists as Charles Busch, Everett Quinton, Shelly Mars, Diane Torr, Lypsinka, and Peggy Shaw. But as the work of these artists powerfully and consistently makes clear, "drag" is not only a form of entertainment, it is sometimes a queer survival skill as well. While this pertains to many gay male drag artists, I find Peggy's work one of the most profound explorations of this issue. In Peggy's performances, drag always seems to signal both a peculiar form of gender acquiescence *and* a specific form of gender resistance. It can also be, as *You're Just Like My Father* explains, an erotics. In this piece, Peggy performs the formations of her butchness. Performers such as Peggy Shaw help us see the crucial role that drag has played in queer life. I don't think it's too much of a stretch to suggest that all of us who are queer can loosely be described as solo performers insofar as we have had to fashion an identity around our gender and sexuality, drag being only one manifestation of this process. Consider, for example, the way in which nearly all gay men and lesbians had to "perform" some version of normative heterosexuality before "coming out." Even out queer people often retain a sense that gender and sexuality, including heterosexuality, are performative.

The performative nature of queer lives involves a continuous negotiation between our sense of private and public selves that does not always amount to seeing these two areas as discrete. The friction between the private and the public self brings me back to the issue of the personal and the autobiographical. Not only does autobiographical work bring into representation the diversity of queer life, it also provides a space where queer people can themselves rehearse key issues and concerns. Take, for example, the heated issue of queer families. Various solo performers tell stories of kinship, but these individuated stories extend beyond the lives of the artists and provide their audiences both an affirmation of our own struggles around kinship and an expansive identificatory grid from which to consider our own realities and possibilities. Michael Kearns and Susan Miller, two of our most accomplished queer performers, ruminate on queer parenthood in the pieces we've included here—Susan on being the lesbian mother of a teenage son; Michael on the charged issue of gay adoption. *Clit Notes,* in part, reflects on our relationships with our parents, and Carmelita's *Milk of Amnesia* takes kinship one step further to confront the politics of home. I wouldn't want to reduce these works to these familial themes, but I wouldn't want to refute this intervention, either. All of this is to say that the autobiographical—and each of these performers pursues the performance of the personal differently—is a vital contribution to queer culture.

HOLLY HUGHES: Prior to 1990, few Americans outside of the big-city art ghettoes had even heard of performance art, much less seen it. Then the likes of Reverend Donald Wildmon, Ralph Reed, and, of course, Senator Jesse Helms latched on to it. On TV, through mass mailings, and in full-page newspaper ads the leaders of the religious Right served up soundbite-size descriptions of performances they usually had not seen. The NEA was bleeding the American people so that artists could show off their privates, smear themselves with chocolate, cross-dress, and splatter the audience with HIV-positive blood. In 1990 the Christian Coalition brayed in *USA Today:* "They teach your children how to sodomize each other." In response, the Save-the-NEA forces sidestepped the issue of public funding for provocative work, instead conjuring up images of fingerpainting preschoolers and well-heeled audiences enjoying the ballet. Frequently they disowned the work under attack, bragging about how little controversial work the endowment had funded or even admitting that "some mistakes had been made."

In the wake of this debate even people who'd never seen a show began to get a sense of what performance art is: "queer." When I travel to schools in parts of the country where there's little chance to see this work—and that's most of the country—students do have a sense of what the work is about: art about bodies, particularly bodies that were othered by race, by gender, by sexuality, by illness. But wait, aren't there plenty of performance artists who may not be poster children for family values but are at least undeniably heterosexual? Just think of the form's most feted practitioners: Spalding Gray, Laurie Anderson, Guillermo Gomez-Peña, and Eric Bogosian. These artists—who do very different kinds of work— have been so well received that nobody calls their work "performance art" anymore; they've been promoted to making "theater." There's a pejorative connotation to the term "performance art," a sense that it is a junior achievement art form, a warm-up to making real art, or just a phase some of us had to go through.

Sometimes students are disappointed to discover that most performance artists keep their clothes on most of the time and there's much less gratuitous spilling of blood and chocolate than Bob Dornan would have you believe. What they often find most shocking is not the work, but the intention that informs it. Performance artists are often folks for whom "the personal is political" remained a vital challenge, rather than a piece of seventies' kitsch or an excuse to pass off attending Twelve Step groups and aerobics classes as contributions toward social change. Consequently, few performance artists—no matter how skilled or funny—intend simply to entertain: they mean to provoke, to raise questions, to implicate their audiences. While Ellen DeGeneres is allowed to carve out a gay identity on prime-time TV because she insists that "we" queers are no different from "you" straight people, the artists in this book don't even attempt to gain acceptance by masquerading as your average Middle Americans who just "happen" to be homos.

In these narratives we are called to meditate on difference, not merely on what distinguishes us from what performance artist/film-maker Jack Smith called "the pasty normals," but also on the divisions, the inequities, that divide the queer sphere. Transgender poster girl Kate Bornstein demolishes the two-party gender system by introducing us to new galaxies of gender and sexuality. In *Virtually Yours* she invites us to boldly go where no man or woman has gone before without having his or her sense of what it means to be male or female seriously challenged. Tim Miller's *Naked Breath* stages a new chapter in gay male eroticism with its portrayal of a relationship between an HIV-negative and an HIV-positive man, describing the way the push/pull between these individuals echoes in the larger community. Lesbian and gay phobias of bisexuality are at the heart of Denise Uyehara's *Hello, Sex Kitty,* a work that calls into question the queer commitment to inclusivity we so frequently proclaim.

The volatile fault lines of race and ethnicity crisscross American culture, causing as many temblors and aftershocks in gay life as in straight. In the work of Tanya Barfield, Craig Hickman, Luis Alfaro, Alec Mapa, Carmelita Tropicana, and Denise Uyehara, queerness and ethnicity are woven together so tightly that white audiences can find their eyes starting to cross. I've taught both Tanya Barfield's and Carmelita Tropicana's work in gay and lesbian theater classes enough times to know that my mostly white upper-middle-class students will appreciate their work as theater but will give me a hard time about presenting it as lesbian performance. Yes, they agree, there is some lesbian content in their work, but not "enough" to qualify. Their insistence that sexuality must be always foregrounded over other aspects of identity in order to be truly gay is unfortunately not unique to undergrads; it's part of what keeps the emerging canon of queer literature mostly male and quite white. And, they say, what in the hell can Craig Hickman be thinking when he punctuates his queer-coming-of-age story by channeling Jeffrey Dahmer, the white Milwaukee serial killer whose favorite prey was young men of color? Hickman is placing his coming out within a larger narrative; he's saying you can't understand his life story without looking at the way white America has historically viewed African American male sexuality.

The idea for *O Solo Homo* grew out of our frustration with the gap between the Right's distortions of queer work and the so-called Left's apologies and disclaimers. Performance art tends to be ephemeral; it's seldom well documented. A few exceptions exist, notably *Caught in the Act*, a collection of the work of photographer Dona Ann McAdams that was published by *Aperture* in 1996. For years Dona has sat in the front row at Performance Space 122, where she is the staff photographer, capturing in black and white many of the most influential artists in their natural habitat—that is, in performance. C. Carr's *On Edge: Performance Art at the End of Twentieth Century*, a compilation of columns she penned while covering this scene for the *Village Voice* in the eighties and early nineties, is an invaluable and accessible cultural history. Some of the texts of the more well-known artists are anthologized in two collections: *Out from Under*, edited by Lenora Champagne, and *Out of Character*, edited by the artistic director of Performance Space 122, Mark Russell. Still, much of this work exists only in the memories of audience members, memories that are probably clouded by not enough sleep, possibly by drugs and/or alcohol, and certainly by loss. And if the Right is going to smear this kind of work, they could at least get their quotes right! I'm tired of having Pat Buchanan confuse me with Karen Finley, turning us into one big two-headed femi-Nazi he calls "the chocolate-covered lesbian."

DAVID ROMÁN: Such distortions of queer performance all too often circulate as representations of that performance for people who have never seen the work in question. Think, for example, of the various misrepresentations that fueled the controversy around Ron Athey's 1994 Minneapolis performances of the "Human Printing Press" scene from *Four Scenes in a Harsh Life*. Athey, who is HIV-positive, was falsely accused of putting his audiences at risk for HIV. In one carefully choreographed moment, Athey carves an African scarification on the back of Daryl Carlton, an HIV-negative performer from his ensemble, and then blots the incision with absorbent medical towels, which are then hoisted above the aisles over the audience. The hysteria resulting from Ron's piece not only misrepresented his work, it also demonized him to such an extent that hosting venues were reluctant to present his work. The issue of the documentation of queer performance is part of a larger debate already under way among theater and performance scholars. Two questions are at the heart of this debate: What happens to performance once it is translated into a different medium such as video, photography, or published script? and is this translation still "performance"? *O Solo Homo* clearly invests in text as a privileged means of documenting queer solo performance. And we do so for specific reasons. First, as Holly already suggested, *O Solo Homo* sets out to make available in print for the first time many of the performances that have been at the forefront of the American culture wars, including debates around the future of the National Endowment for the Arts. Our goal is that the book provide larger cultural access to this work and place this specific artistic practice within its broader cultural context.

The publication of the scripts of queer solo performance also serves another purpose. It lessens the burden of representation that some of these artists have had to carry. Most, but not all, of the artists we've collected in this anthology have had their work censored, slandered, or derided. The work has been singled out and attacked. This burden goes both ways. It not only places undue burdens on specific performers who are extracted from their specific communities and who are then expected to bear the brunt of a phobic culture alone—O Solo Homo yet again—but, from a completely different angle, it also plays into the rules of exceptionalism. Isolating one queer solo performer from the field, even when this selection involves a form of recognition, positions the recognized solo performer as the exception to the rule rather than as a representative of the field. By placing these works in relation to other work by queer artists, we might begin to understand queer solo work a little differently. When Luis Alfaro was awarded a 1997 MacArthur Award, for example, he was adamant about accepting this prestigious honor as a validation of the various communities that compose his world. Luis made clear that his work was part of something bigger than himself. He made great effort to call attention to the many other talented performers he has collaborated with, been influenced by, and who have fed his own work throughout his important career. Luis, who happens to be one of the most generous performers I know, understood that solo performance is never really solo work. His work, like all the work we have collected in this anthology, is enabled by a larger cultural collaboration not just of presenters, directors, and tech artists, but also of spectators and the political movements that make this work possible in the first place. Luis knew this because he's lived it. *O Solo Homo* supports this notion and sets out to help articulate it more forcefully.

Many of these performers here have worked together or collaborated with each other. Carmelita Tropicana, Peggy Shaw, and Holly Hughes have all worked together in the early formative years of the now legendary WOW Cafe, a space that gave us not just these three important artists, but such nationally recognized lesbian performers as Lisa Kron, the Five Lesbian Brothers, and Reno. Luis Alfaro, Michael Kearns, and Denise Uyehara often present their new work at Highways Performance Space in Santa Monica, a performance venue cofounded by Tim Miller in 1987. Some performers are also affiliated with performance companies or ensembles, while others appear together at benefit fund-raisers, raising money for queer organizations and helping mobilize public attention to a variety of issues of interest to queer audiences. All of this is to say that queer solo performers—although they may perform solo—participate in a more encompassing collaborative effort that advocates for a queer public culture. *O Solo Homo* only begins to provide a glimpse into this vibrant community of queer performance.

HOLLY HUGHES: I got through the Reagan administration by hanging out at the WOW Cafe, which describes itself as a "home for wayward girls." On a stage not much bigger than a g-spot, I got to see many of the artists who've become homo household words develop their work: Split Britches, Lisa Kron, Marga Gomez, Terry Galaway, the Five Lesbian Brothers. Reno had a weekly Friday night cabaret, giving lesbians and the occasional straight feminist the chance to do the material they could do nowhere else. One night an artist I'd heard a lot about but had never seen—Danitra Vance—performed with her backup singers, the Mellow White Boys. Men weren't supposed to perform at WOW, but all the rules at WOW then were made to be broken, and nobody wanted to stop this show. Danitra's act was formally similar to something you'd see in an uptown place with a two-drink minimum: she sang, she did characters with exaggerated accents and attitudes. But the material was something you'd never see in a straight club: here she was performing Shakespeare, showing us her acting chops, then translating into hip-hop for a group of African American teens. The next thing you knew, she was morphing into the Lesbian Recruiter, challenging stereotypes by trying them on and turning them inside out. Hey, I feel a song coming on, a Barry Manilow tune: "I Write the Songs," rewritten by Vance as "I Play the Maids," a musical salute to the racism of casting directors everywhere.

I saw Danitra perform several times after that: at BACA Downtown, a now closed haven for experimental theater in Brooklyn, and at the Club at La Mama. I'd leave the show with my laugh muscles aching, but in Danitra's shows comedy was as much about subversion as it was about entertainment. The audiences were always huge and appreciative, but potential backers for extended runs were always saying she should either be *more* like Whoopi Goldberg or *less* like Whoopi. The position of "funny African American female" has been filled, thank you, and we simply can't use another, especially if she's lesbian. Danitra's talents weren't unrecognized: she was on *Saturday Night Live* for a season, and she was in several plays at the Public Theater, notably *Spunk* by George C. Wolfe. She was scheduled to do another show of her own at the Public when she died of breast cancer.

David and I had hoped to include one of Danitra's pieces in this collection. Unfortunately, most of the work exists only on tape, and we were unable to get the rights to transcribe it. Of course, she is not the only important performance artist we've lost—with AIDS and cancer rampant, there are too many to count.

DAVID ROMÁN: Not only have we lost Danitra Vance, but we now run the risk of losing her life's work. This concern returns us to the issue of documentation. While many of us carry memories of profound and life-changing performances, and these memories, like all memories, have their own distinct shelf life, I'm finding it more necessary to establish some sort of archive of queer performance. It's simply not enough for me to think of performance's legacy as being *only* its ephemerality.

The artists selected for publication in *O Solo Homo* are representative of the new queer performance, but they do not—by any means—exhaust it. Simply stated, there are more solo performers out there than this collection could begin to accommodate. We selected work that spoke to and from the diversity of contemporary queer life. We also selected works that would reflect a diversity of performance styles. Holly and I both share an interest in providing a forum for the artists to speak for themselves here. Therefore, each performance is prefaced by the artist's personal statement, which begins to situate the work more specifically. One of our goals for the book is to provide a space for queer solo artists to present their work in a friendly and supportive environment and to see their work championed in a venue that already sets out to advocate for them.

HOLLY HUGHES: This book isn't a canon, and as far as I'm concerned, it's certainly not *the* canon. Perhaps *O Solo Homo* can serve as a theatrical pu pu platter, whetting appetites all around. I'm hoping that other platters will soon circulate and there will be many requests for seconds, even thirds.

DAVID ROMÁN: Our title—*O Solo Homo*—plays off the anxiety often associated with the initial self-recognition of homosexuality, that moment when you think you are the only queer person in the world. Such laments are often the initial registrars of queer identity. These notions of the sad young man, the lonely old queen, or the lesbian dropped into a well of loneliness still haunt public and private impressions of queerness. *O Solo Homo* sets out to trouble these stereotypes even as we, in part, invoke them through our title. The solo artists in this collection speak out against imagining queerness as pathos or as lamentation. They defiantly take to the stage, queering the spotlight: O Solo Homo!

milk of amnesia – leche de amnesia

CARMELITA TROPICANA

PHOTO: DONA ANN McADAMS

Notes on *Milk of Amnesia—* *Leche de Amnesia*

Once upon a time, two days after I had a fire in my house, I was eating brunch and Karen Finley, performance artist, said: "Oh, Carmelita, I'm sorry about the fire, but I can't wait to see your next show." The next show was a multimedia play, a collaboration with Uzi Parnes and Ela Troyano called *Candela* (*Flame*). Could it be true that artists don't suffer from broken hearts, we just get material?

In October 1993 I was invited to attend the International Theater Festival in Cuba. I had not been back since I was a kid. Both Lillian Manzor Coates, an academic theater critic, and Ela Troyano, a filmmaker (and my sister), encouraged me to go. At the time I needed a new show, and a trip to the homeland seemed perfect grist for the mill.

Milk of Amnesia—Leche de Amnesia was the result of that trip. The piece allowed me to experiment with a different style of writing. In *Milk* I combined the campy stylized satire with a more personal autobiographical style. In this solo, I was able to let my schizophrenia surface, turning it into art. I could have the voice of the writer with the voice of my Carmelita persona, and sprinkle that with assorted animals.

In January of 1994, Lillian Manzor Coates invited me to the University of California at Irvine to present the work in its infancy. I was surprised to see during that presentation that the slides of Cuba worked really well. In taking those photographs, I had questioned myself, Would people really want to see slides of my house, my bathroom?

In the spring of 1994, I was asked to do a piece for the New Museum of Contemporary Art's exhibition entitled the *Bad Girls Show*. I commissioned Uzi Parnes to design a Cuban hat as part of that piece, and the hat was later integrated into *Milk*. I now had one prop/costume piece for the show.

The text was completed. Now it was time to lift it off the page, to lift and separate like a good brassiere. Enter director and designer for supple shaping. Ela Troyano, whom I often collaborated with, acted as dramaturge and director for *Milk*. She wanted the piece to look minimalist in contrast with earlier, colorfully flamboyant work. The images of milk and childhood memories in the text had to be a part of the visual style. Ela suggested that we hire Kukuli Velarde, a sculptor, to create the look.

When the three of us discussed childhood images, Ela suggested a piñata. Kukuli created a six-foot-long papier-mâché pig with blue tiled mosaics painted on its back. The pig has the expression of one who is about to be slaughtered. One of my favorite moments in the piece is when Carmelita regains her memory and remembers her tonsil operation. The pig tells of his operation where his vocal cords were cut. Both operations took place in a clinic with blue tiles. At that moment, Carmelita pulls on a string attached to the pig's neck (a tampon acts as a cork or stopper), and when she does, a stream of red glitter flows from the pig's throat, forming a puddle of red glitter "blood" on the floor. (Ela, who had worked with Jack Smith, had seen his adaptation of Ibsen's *Ghosts,* where a little stuffed animal appears and glitter comes out of the animal. The red glitter in *Milk* is a stolen homage to Jack Smith.)

Milk, as produced in October 1994 at Performance Space 122, had a white cube, white linoleum floor, white wall, and a six-foot-long pig. When touring, some of these visual elements change. A theater will not let its floors or wall be painted white, so a screen and white tape will often form the spatial cube. The pig, though magnificent, is too big to travel. Improvisation is necessary. In Barcelona the pig substitute was a whole ham—*jamón Serrano,* with hoof and everything. In London it was a can of Spam. The last pig sighted was a two-foot-long Mexican piggy bank used at the *Milk* performance at Highways in Los Angeles in 1997.

About Carmelita Tropicana

Alina Troyano, a.k.a. Carmelita Tropicana, is a writer/performance artist who has received fellowships from the CINTAS Foundation for her literary work and from the New York Foundation for the Arts for screenwriting/playwriting and for performance art. Her solo Milk of Amnesia *toured extensively. She has co-authored numerous plays with Uzi Parnes, including* Memorias de la Revolución, *which will be published in the spring of 1998 in* The Latin Theatre Anthology: Puro Teatro. *The film* Carmelita Tropicana: Your Kunst Is Your Waffen, *co-written with Ela Troyano, won Best Short at the 1994 Berlin Film Festival.*

milk of amnesia - leche de amnesia

CARMELITA TROPICANA

(STAGE HAS A MINIMAL LOOK. IT IS DIVIDED INTO TWO
HALVES. THE LEFT IS THE WRITER'S SPACE AND IS DIMLY LIT.
IT HAS A MUSIC STAND WITH MAKEUP, COSTUMES, HATS. THE
RIGHT SIDE IS PAINTED WHITE, RESEMBLING A WHITE CUBE.
THERE IS A MIKE AND MIKE STAND AND A CHAIR THAT GETS
PLACED THERE DEPENDING ON THE SCENE.
    PIECE BEGINS IN DARKNESS AS AN AUDIOTAPE WITH THE
VOICE OF THE WRITER IS HEARD.)

Years ago when I wasn't yet American I had a green card. On
my first trip abroad the customs official stamped on my papers
"stateless."

When I became a citizen, I had to throw my green card into a
bin along with everybody else's green cards. I didn't want to. I was
born on an island. I came here when I was seven. I didn't like it
here at first. Everything was so different. I had to change. Acquire
a taste for peanut butter and jelly. It was hard. I liked tuna fish
and jelly.

I used to play a game in bed. About remembering. I would
lie awake in my bed before going to sleep and remember. I'd remember the way to my best friend's house. I'd start at the front
door of my house, cross the porch. Jump off three steps onto the

sidewalk. The first house on the right looked just like my house, except it had only one balcony. The third house was great. You couldn't see it. It was hidden by a wall and trees and shrubs. Whenever I'd look in, the German shepherd sniffed me and barked me out of his turf. I'd continue walking, crossing three streets, walking two blocks until I came to my best friend's house. I did this repeatedly so I wouldn't forget. I would remember. But then one day I forgot to remember. I don't know what happened. Some time passed and I couldn't remember the third block, then the second. Now I can only walk to the third house. I've forgotten.

I had a dream when I was a kid. (SOUND OF FOOTSTEPS RUNNING ON TAPE) I guess because we were refugees. Me and my cousin were fugitives running away from the police. We had to escape. We were running through the streets. We saw a manhole cover and it opened up. (SOUND OF METAL DOOR SHUTTING) We went down. We were in a sewer. (SOUND OF DRIPPING WATER, ECHO) We were safe. But it started to get hot. Stifling hot. And as it happens in dreams one minute my cousin was my cousin and the next she was a peanut-butter-and-jelly sandwich. The heat was making her melt. I held her in my hands. She was oozing down. I was crying: Don't melt, Pat. Please don't melt. I woke up in a sweat. (ALARM CLOCK)

In the morning I went to school. Our Lady Queen of Martyrs. That's when it happened. In the lunchroom. I never drank my milk. I always threw it out. Except this time when I went to throw it out, the container fell and the milk spilled on the floor. The nun came over. Looked at me and the milk. Her beady eyes screamed: You didn't drink your milk, grade-A pasteurized, homogenized, you Cuban refugee.

After that day I changed. I knew from my science class that all senses acted together. If I took off my glasses, I couldn't hear as well. Same thing happened with my taste buds. If I closed my eyes and held my breath I could suppress a lot of the flavor I didn't like. This is how I learned to drink milk. It was my resolve to embrace America as I chewed on my peanut-butter-and-jelly sandwich and gulped down my milk. This new milk that had replaced the sweet condensed milk of Cuba. My amnesia had begun.

(PINGALITO, A CIGAR-CHOMPING CUBAN MAN, ENTERS AS A TAPE OF MAMBO MUSIC PLAYS. HE GREETS THE AUDIENCE. HE IS ON THE CUBE AND BRIGHTLY LIT.)

PINGALITO

Welcome, ladies and gentlemen, to the show de jour, *Milk of Amnesia*. I am your host, Pingalito Betancourt, the Cuban Antonio Banderas. For those of you who are from Cuba, you may recognize my face. I was the conductor in 1955 of the M15 bus route, the route that go from La Habana Vieja to El Vedado. And it was in that bus that I meet Carmelita. There is a Streetcar Named Desire for Stanley Kowalski. For Pingalito this was Destiny on the M15 bus route.

When I heard of Carmelita's tragic accident I rush right over, hoping a familiar face can trigger something in her deep recessed cavities of her cerebro, cerebellum, and medulla oblongata. You see people, the doctors have their methodologies for curing amnesia, and I have mine.

I make my way through the hospital corridors, saying hello to all the nice Filipino nurses, and I enter her room. She is asleep, looking like an angel, mouth open, pillow wet, making puttering sounds of a car engine. And I think of a childhood memory she used to tell me about. Her grandfather, who smoke a cigar, would take her for a drive in his Chevrolet, driving with a foot on the brake, stopping and starting, stopping and starting, stopping and starting. She would get so carsick. So I decide to simulate this memory. By blowing smoke in her face, playing with the controls of the hospital bed, making the legs go up, the head go down, up and down, up and down. I am playing her like a big accordion when a doctor comes in and says I gotta go. Something about my cigar and an oxygen tank.

But I don't give up. I return the next day. I think, What above all is Carmelita? I tell you. Cuban. One hundred fifty percent. So

I decide to tell her some facts about Cuba. See if it jiggles something. (SHOWING TO AUDIENCE A MAP OF CUBA) I have here audiovisual aid number one, a placemat I pick up in Las Lilas restaurant of Miami titled "Facts about Cuba." Ladies and gentlemen, upon further examination of this placemat, you can see that the island of Cuba is shaped like a Hoover vacuum cleaner with Pinar del Rio as the handle. How many of you know Cuba is known as the Pearl of the Antilles because of its natural wealth and beauty? And the first thing we learn as little children is that when Christopher Columbus landed in our island, kneeling down, he said: *"Está es la tierra más hermosa que ojos humanos han visto." This is the most beautiful land that human eyes have seen.* The majestic mountains of la Sierra Maestra. Our mountains, not too tall. We don't need high. If we get high, we get snow, then we gotta buy winter coat. And the beaches of Varadero. But, ladies and gentlemen, none can compare with the beauty of the human landscape. *Oye me mano. Esas coristas de Tropicana.* With the big breasts, thick legs. In Cuba we call girls *carros* and we mean your big American cars. Your Cadillac, not Toyota or Honda. Like the dancer Tongolele. I swear to you people, or my name is not Pingalito Betancourt, you could put a tray of daiquiris on Tongolele's behind and she could walk across the floor without spilling a single drop. That, ladies and gentlemen, is landscape. For that you give me a gun and I fight for that landscape. Not oil. You gotta have priorities.

Fact two. Spanish is the official language of Cuba, and it's a beautiful language. You talk with your hands, you talk with your mouth. My favorite expression, when you want to find out the color of someone, you say: *"Oye, me mano ¿y tu abuela, dónde está?" Tell me, brother, where is your grandmother?* Which brings us to fact three.

Three-fourths of all Cubans are white of Spanish descent, and a lot of these three-fourths have a very dark suntan all year round. When they ask me, "Pingalito, and where is your grandmother?" I say, *"Mulata y a mucha honra." Dark and proud.*

Well, I look at Carmelita and she is not blinking, and I have fifteen more facts to go. So I decide to change my route. If the M15 bus doesn't take you there, maybe the M21 does. So I ask you people, what is Carmelita above all? Eh? Above all, she is an art-ist. One hundred fifty percent. So maybe a song and a poem will do the trick. Poetry is something we Cubans have in our souls. It is our tradition. I don't know how many of you know that our lib-erator Jose Martí, our George Washington, is also the Emily Dickinson of Cuba. So I recite for Carmelita and for you today "Ode to the Cuban Man."

Ode to the Cuban Man (Pingalito)

Spielberg forget your assic park
Some say the Cuban Man is disappearing
Like the dinosaur
I say que no
The Cuban Man
This specimen
Will never go away
We are here to stay

Like the Cuban crocodile
One of a kind in genus and species
You find us in the Bronx Zoo
The swamps of Zapata
Calm in the water but also volatile

So don't bother the crocodile
Because we got big mouths
We open up and swallow a horse and a cow
That's why we have the Cuban expression
Te la comiste mi hermano
You ate it bro

The Cuban Man is persistent, stubborn
Like the mosquito, always buzzing around
Why you think yellow fever was so popular

The Cuban Man is the apple in his mother's eye
Even when he is a little dim of wit
To his mami he is still the favorite
And at eighty she calls him baby

The Cuban Man has no spare parts
Nature did not create any excess waste
She made him compact
Not tall in height, but what street smarts
Suave, sharp, slippery, and sly
Like yucca enchumba in mojo greasy pig lard
Or like the Yankee from New England say
Slicker than deer guts on a doorknob

The Cuban Man has a head for business
He combines the Jewish bubbullah with the African babalu
And that's why they call him the Caribbean Jew

Above all the Cuban Man is sensitive, sentimental, simpático
With sex appeal for days
And this is where our problem comes
Our hubris, our Achilles' tendon
It is our passionate and romantic side
We love women too much
Too many women, too many kids

But when you tally up
The good the bad
You too will decide
He is like a fine Havana cigar
The one you gotta have
After a big heavy meal with an after-dinner drink and
Coffee on the side
Because he is the one that truly, truly satisfies

(PINGALITO EXITS. AN AUDIOTAPE WITH THE WRITER'S VOICE
COMES ON.)

In high school I was asked to write an essay on the American
character. I thought of fruits. Americans were apples, healthy, neat,
easy to eat, not too sweet, not too juicy. Cubans were mangoes,
juicy, real sweet, but messy. You had to wash your hands and face
and do a lot of flossing. I stood in front of a mirror and thought I
should be more like an apple. A shadow appeared and whispered:
Mango stains never come off.

I didn't write about fruits in my essay. I didn't want them thinking I wasn't normal.

In the eighties, that's when my amnesia started to show cracks.
As I joined the ranks of Tchaikovsky and Quentin Crisp—I became a civil servant and a thespian on the side.

As a teen I had gone to the Circle in the Square Theater, but
my thespianism had been squelched the day the teacher announced
the Puerto Rican Traveling Company was holding auditions and
needed actors. When she said the Puerto Rican Traveling Company
everyone started to laugh. As if it was a joke. Like a Polish joke,
only a Puerto Rican one. I was the same as a Puerto Rican. Maybe
the island was bigger, but same difference. I guessed I wouldn't do
theater.

Until I came to the WOW theater and got cast in Holly
Hughes's *The Well of Horniness.* We were asked to do it on the radio.
I had a dilemma. Would my career as a civil servant be stymied if
people knew I was the one who screamed every time the word "horniness" was mentioned, or that I was playing Georgette, Vicky's lover
or Al Dente, chief of police? Maybe I needed a new name.

As if by accident the pieces were falling into place when I
entered the WOW theater and a comedy workshop was to take
place. The teacher would not give it unless four people took it.
There were three signed up for it, and with me the body count
would be four. I said no. No. No. But the teacher, she was cute.
So I took it.

But it wasn't me. I couldn't stand in front of an audience, wear sequined gowns, tell jokes. But she could. She who penciled in her beauty mark, she who was baptized in the fountain of America's most popular orange juice, in the name of Havana's legendary nightclub, the Tropicana, she could. She was a fruit and wasn't afraid to admit it. She was the past I'd left behind. She was Cuba. *Mi Cuba querida, El Son Montuno* . . .

(CARMELITA IS SITTING ON A CHAIR INSIDE THE CUBE, WEAR-ING A HAT MADE OF HELIUM BALLOONS. A SQUARE SPOT-LIGHT RESEMBLING A FILM CLOSEUP IS ON HER FACE. AS THE SCENE PROCEEDS MORE LIGHT BATHES THE STAGE.)

CARMELITA

The doctor said hypnosis might help. I said, "Anything, Doctor, anything for a cure." So he started to hypnotize me, but in the middle of it he said I had to count backwards. Backwards. I got this sharp pain in my throat and I felt these blood clots inside my mouth and I said, "No, Doctor, I can't count backwards. Don't make me. Count backwards. I never count backwards." The doctor writes in his chart: "Subject is mathematically impaired." They wanted to know what other impairments I got. So they connected these wires to my brain, my computer, my mango Macintosh. The doctors, they monitor my every move.

This (POINTING TO DEFLATED BALLOONS) is connected to my organizational skills, this to my musical memory, and this to my housecleaning ability. This big one (POINTING TO AN EXTRA LARGE BALLOON) is linked to my libido. When I think of Soraya, my nurse, giving me a sponge bath or rubbing Keri lotion on my chest, it (POPS BALLOON) pops uncontrollably. And this one (POINTING TO A REGULAR-SIZE BALLOON) is for languages. *Schpeiglein Schpeiglein on der vand. Wer is di schonste in ganzen land* . . . What language is dis? Is this the language of Jung und Freud? Oh, *herren and herrleins*, pierce me with your key. Let me not be a question mark anymore. Open up Pandora's box.

The doctors, they tell me my name is (PRONOUNCING THE NAME WITH AN AMERICAN ACCENT) Carmelita Tropicana. I've had a terrible accident. I hurt my head when I was chocolate pudding wrestling. I don't remember a thing. (SINGS) Remember, walking in the sand, remember her smile was so inviting, remember . . . I don't remember the lyrics to this song. So much flotsam and jetsam inside my head. And I want to remember so much, I get these false attacks. In desperation, I appropriate other's memories.

The doctors try to control these attacks by surrounding me with familiar things. (SHOWS BOTTLECAP NECKLACE) This beautiful bottle cap says "Tropicana, Shake Well"—I don't know. Then they tell me to eat the food they bring, because the French philosopher Proust ate one madeleine cookie and all his childhood memories came rushing back to him. (PICKING UP A CAN OF GOYA BEANS) Goy . . . Goya? Black beans. (PICKING UP BEVERAGE BOTTLE) Malta Hatuey, or is it Hatuey? The H aspirated or not aspirated? And is he the chief Indian Hatuey or the Native American Hatuey? Oh, these labels are so confusing. (PICKING UP A YUCCA) Is this a yucca or a yuucka? Do I eat it or do I beat it? Oh, to be or not to be. But who, that is the question.

That short guy with the cigar—what was his name, Pingalito, the one who made me throw up on the bed—he tells me I'm from Cuba.

Maybe there is only one way to find out. To go back to the place I was born in. My homeland, the place that suckled me as a newborn babe. In the distance, I hear the clink, clink, clink of a metal spoon against glass. It is my mami stirring condensed milk with water. She holds a glass. The milk beckons me. I feel a song coming on.

How would you like to spend the weekend in Havana?

I won't be the same anymore. (CARMELITA TAKES OFF BALLOON HAT)

(LIGHTS CHANGE, CARMELITA SPEAKS INTO THE MICROPHONE.)

My journey begins at five A.M. at the Miami airport. I am so sleepy. Crazy to be at the airport at five A.M. I don't know where I am going; I hear "Follow the Maalox, follow the Maalox" and then I spot a multitude. The Cuban diaspora that's going back, holding on to plastic bags with medicines and the most magnificent hats. I am so underdressed. These people are so dressed: skirts on top of pants on top of skirts. The gentleman in front of me, an octogenarian, has his head down. I don't know if it's age or the weight of his three hats. I discover my people are a smart people. They can weigh your luggage and limit you to forty-four pounds, but they cannot weigh your body. The layer look is *on*.

The excitement mounts when I enter the plane. The doctors told me to be careful. Too much, too soon, can cause attacks. In only forty-five minutes I will cross an ocean of years.

When we land it is scorching hot outside. People desperately rip off the layers on the tarmac. I see a field in the distance. Palm trees, two peasants, and an ox. It reminds me of Southeast Asia, Vietnam. I never been there. But who knows where memories come from—movies, books, magazines.

I go to the counter in the airport, holding on to my Cuban passport, my American passport, and a fax saying my visa is waiting for me here. Names are called for people with visas, but mine is not one. The immigration guy says I gotta go back. Say what? You know who I am. He says, "Who?" *Yo soy Cecilia Valdés* . . . Oh, my God. I started to sing an operetta, a zarzuela. The guy thinks I am making fun of him. I say no. I'm sorry. I say I hurt my head and it has affected my vocal cords. He don't care. I am returned. Back to El Norte. But I don't care because I have determination. I go back especially now that I know how to dress. I go in style. I make myself a magnificent hat. Check it out. (CARMELITA MODELS HAT)

Soy una tienda ambulante. I've my Easter bonnet with toilet paper on it. I'm a walking Cuban department store. Tampons and pearls, toilet paper, stationery supplies. What a delight. (LEAVING THE MICROPHONE TO SPEAK DIRECTLY TO THE AUDIENCE) Now this is the part where you think it's performance art, a joke. Truth is stranger than fiction. *The New York Times* in 1993 had a photo essay of women with these hats. And when I went back the competition got tougher. Next to me was a woman with a pressure cooker on her head. A pressure cooker. These people are going to survive.

(RETURNING TO THE MICROPHONE) When I go back, the immigration guy is so friendly, so I give him a couple of tampons. "Back so soon? I like your hat."

I take a taxi to the Hotel Capri. I tell my driver, Francisco, I want to see, touch, feel, hear, taste Cuba. All my orifices are open. Francisco says: *"No es fácil."* *It's not easy.* I have come during the Special Period. The Special Period—that's what the government calls it. No gas, no electricity, no food. I look out the window. Cubans are all on bicycles. They look like skinny models. Francisco says when there is no gasoline and the buses are not running, he fuels his body with water with sugar. Water with sugar. The great Cuban energizer. *Agua con azúcar*, and then he can walk for miles.

When I arrive in the Capri hotel I go to the dining room. I can tell who the Cubans are with relatives here. They are the ones wrapping up food. I meet Maria Elena, who is here for a conference and is wrapping chicken, bread, cheese. I ask her, What about eggs? Don't forget the eggs. She says, "Eggs. *Qué va.* Yesterday I had to give a lecture on the poet Julian del Casal, and when I took the paper out of my briefcase there was egg yolk all over. Egg yolk all over. *No es fácil.* It is not easy."

(THE TAPED VOICE OF THE WRITER IS HEARD.)

WRITER

Sometimes New York is too much. So is Havana. I toured the colonial part of the city. Kids flocked to me for candy, gum. Two decrepit mangy dogs limped along the cobblestones. Two guys tried to sell me a potent drug, PPG. Makes the man potent, satisfy your woman. A girl about fourteen asks me for my *pinta labios.* I part with my Revlon #44 "Love that Red" lipstick. I eat at La Bodeguita with two Cuban artists, a meal of fried yucca, fried pork, fried bananas. Cholesterol is not a problem. I take a ride to my hotel in a private vintage Chevrolet circa 1955 rumbling as it plods through streets darkened except for a building blindingly bright, a beacon of light, the Spanish embassy. And the new currency is the dollar: five dollars for the ride, five dollars for the beer at the hotel lobby. And who do I see coming in, Pinta Labios, Revlon #44, looking good with a man. What is she doing with that man and my lipstick? She looks down when she sees me. I'm pissed, but with a swig of beer, reconsider, maybe the lipstick got her a steak dinner. And I go to my room, place a call to New York and put the TV on. CNN news. And the call comes through, and I switch channels. A movie is beginning, *The Green Berets*. I am in Cuba watching *The Green Berets*.

(CARMELITA GOES TO THE CEMETERY. A CUBAN SONG, IS PLAYING AS CARMELITA ENTERS THE WHITE SPACE.)

CARMELITA

I have been in Havana for three days and I don't have any flashback, not even an attack. I decide to go visit my relatives, the dead ones at the cemetery. Maybe they'll talk to me from the grave. *El cementerio de Colón* is a beautiful cemetery with big trees that give shade and lots of statues and mausoleums. I start to look for the Tropicanas, but find Menocales, Menéndez, instead. Menéndez? I see four seniors hanging out by the tombstones. They look like they're in their seventies—two men and a couple. I go ask if they know the Tropicanas. They don't, but they are very curious about me and start to ask me my name, what I do, where I live. When I say New York, they all say "¡*Nueva York!*" The woman, Consuelo, looks at my nose.

CONSUELO

José, mira que se parece a Luisita. De la nariz pa abajo. Exactica. You look like my niece Luisita. She's a very smart girl, a painter. She went to New York last year. Went to all the museums.

She was fascinated, fascinated. All those restaurants you have! Japanese, Chinese, even Filipino! She said the food, that was the real art. She came back twenty pounds heavier, and her work changed. She went from abstract to realism. I have a new painting hanging in my living room. It's a triptych of desserts. There's a strawberry cheesecake, crème brûlée y cake de chocolate. *Está lindo, lindo.*

JOSE
(GRADUALLY BECOMING MORE AND MORE DISTRESSED) Carmencita, you don't know this, but Consuelito here used to be obese. Obese. A diabetic with a sweet tooth. *¡Imaginate!* Now in nine months of the Special Period she has lost ninety pounds. *No es fácil. No es fácil.*

CONSUELO
José, your blood pressure y *el Stress.*

JOSE
Chica, déjame hablar. How am I going to get rid of *el Stress* unless I talk? *Mira,* Carmencita, people here are doing everything to survive. They are keeping roosters, chickens. Animals right here in Havana. *¡Animales! Pa que contar . . .* (SOUND OF CRACKLING FIRE)

CARMELITA
(ON TAPE THERE ARE THE SOUNDS OF A STAMPEDE, HORSES NEIGHING, AND FLAMENCO MUSIC.) I was born in Badajoz, España. *Todo era tranquilidad. Un sueño dulce.* The sky clear, not a cloud in the sky for miles except for the clouds of dust me and Dulcinea made as we galloped across the dry fields. The sun was strong. One day it rained and the mud spattered from our pasterns to our forearms. When I turned two my master told me I had been sold to a Conquistador. A Conquistador, what a strange and exciting sound. The day came when I had to leave Spain and become a stallion. The stallion of a Conquistador. But I was too excited that night

to sleep. (WHINNIES) We horses are a bit high-strung. I stayed up with my mother, counting stars. At daybreak she gave me her *bendición*. "Arriero, from now on you will be counting stars in the New World."

I was one of the first horses to set hoof in the New World. And I should have known from the voyage from Spain to Cuba what was to happen. All of us animals herded into a tiny ship. The roosters that climbed on my back, the rats I had to stomp on. But the worst was the boredom. Nowhere to go. Couldn't stretch my legs. Always fed the same thing, hay and oats, hay and oats, for variety I ate my own dung. I thought the voyage would never end. I started counting the days. *Uno, dos, tres, cuatro.* I gave up. I fell into such a depression, and there was no Prozac in those days. (SINGING) *Quiero escribir los versos, más tristes esta noche* . . . Then somebody yelled: "Land. Land!" It was the island of Cuba. I couldn't believe my three-hundred-and-forty-degree peripheral vision. Grass everywhere. And trees with fruit: guanábanas, mangoes, mameys. And the natives were so friendly, they walked around smoking, offering us cigars: Partagás, Panetela. Camel Light. No, thank you. I don't smoke. But I will have some of that yucca barbecue. Yucca barbecue was my favorite. I hated the guinea pig. I'm a vegetarian.

Havana in those days was teeming with life, especially the mosquito kind. I couldn't swat them fast enough with my tail, which is why I hated Gonzaga the priest, that kept plucking the hairs out of my tail to make hair shirts, hair shirts to give to the natives as gifts. Gonzaga was not my master—it's just that I was given to him for a little while. I was on loan because of my name, Arriero: the one who can carry much weight. And *joder*, that priest was fat. It took three men to put him on my back.

That day we were delivering the hair shirts is when we saw the chief Indian, Hatuey. There was smoke in the distance. I didn't want to go because I know where there's smoke there's fire, but Gonzaga saw some of his fellow priests and we had to go. There was a crowd gathered, so much commotion we couldn't hear, but I rotated my left ear and heard a priest say to Hatuey, "Repent,

repent, and if you will—you will go to heaven. If not, hell." Hatuey looked at the priest and said, "If heaven is where the Spanish Christians go, I'll take hell." And the flames took Hatuey. Right there. I saw it. And so much more. I saw so many Indians die, so many. So many dead Indians from disease and working in the mines. I thought of my mother's farewell words: "Arriero, from now on you will be counting stars in the New World." No mother, not stars.

CARMELITA

Ai, my head. I must have fallen into a CUMAA. A Collective Unconscious Memory Appropriation Attack. I need an aspirin. When I take out the Bayer aspirins, the four seniors yell, "Bayer!" Like they have never seen an aspirin. So we decide to divide the one hundred and thirty-five aspirins into four seniors. Some fall on the ground. It is too much, so the men take the ones that fell on the ground and Consuelo takes the bottle. As I am leaving José Miguel says:

JOSE

Do you pray? Do you believe? I do. Every day. If I didn't I'd be dead.

(SLOW FADE TO BLACK.)

(AN AUDIOTAPE IS HEARD WITH THE FOLLOWING JOKE.)

Did you hear the one about the eggs and the fried steak? There are these eggs running through the Malecón Boulevard in Havana. And they're running because they are being chased by a million hungry Cubans. And these eggs are running and the Cubans are after them, and as the eggs are running they pass in front of a fried steak that is sitting on the wall of the Malecón, very relaxed. And the eggs yell at the steak, "The Cubans are coming, the Cubans are coming! Aren't you afraid they'll come get you?" The steak says, "No way, these Cubans don't know what a steak looks like."

(STAGE IS DARK AS SLIDES OF HAVANA ARE PROJECTED ONTO A SCREEN. THE WRITER READS INTO THE MIKE, AND WHEN THE SLIDE OF HER OLD HOUSE COMES ON SHE STOPS READING AND SPEAKS INTO THE MIKE, POINTING OUT THE DIFFERENT PARTS OF THE HOUSE.)

WRITER

(SLIDE OF CUBAN COUNTRYSIDE.)

As I go sight-seeing I try to strike up a conversation with everyone I meet. But when people ask me where I'm from I have a certain trepidation. How will I be received? I lie. I begin by telling them my father is Puerto Rican. After five minutes I feel comfortable enough to tell them I was born here, but don't remember much.

(SLIDE OF CUBAN PLAZA WITH FLAG.)

I am like a tourist in my own country. Everything is new. I walk everywhere hoping I will recall something. Anything. I have this urge to recognize and be recognized. To fling my arms around one of those ceiba trees and say, "I remember you from the park when I went with Cristobalina, my nanny, who had Chinese eyes, kinky hair, and used to sing '*Reloj, no marques las horas.*'"

(SLIDE OF CEMETERY.)

I want a crack on the sidewalk to open up and say, "Yes, I

saw you when you jumped over in your patent-leather shoes, holding on to your grandfather's index finger." But it doesn't happen. There is no recognition from either the tree or the sidewalk. So I do what Ronald Colman did in the movie when he had amnesia and what Cubans do when they go back. I visit the house I was born in. . . .

(SLIDE OF AERIAL VIEW OF HAVANA.)

319 de la calle 8 entre 5ta y 3ra. The address pops out as if I'd been there yesterday.

(SLIDE OF CENTRO GALLEGO.)

I'm nervous. Why? It's just a house.

(SLIDE OF HOUSE.)

Oh, my God. There it is. The house I was born in. (POINTING TO VARIOUS IMAGES ON THE SCREEN) There was a patch of dirt here, and in this corner there was a slug. I used to poke him with a stick. The slug, he's gone. And on this side I planted my mango tree. We had invented a new game, "agrarian reform" and had to cultivate the land. It was by the mango tree that I had an epiphany. I was poking at the ground to see how my mango tree was doing when I heard her footsteps. She had long hair tied into a ponytail, red lips, and dreamy eyes like a cow. I ran to her and jumped on her and kissed her creamy cheeks. "Okay, okay," she said, putting me down. We looked at each other for an instant. I ran and hid by my mango tree. My heart was beating fast, I was sweating. I knew then that that was no ordinary kiss. That kiss would mean a lot more in years to come.

And it was in this balcony that we played with our live Easter chicks. Live chicks dyed purple, pink, and green. We left my cousin Teresa with the chicks while we went to make skirts for them from plastic ruffled cookie wrappers, and when we came back Teresa was throwing the last chick from the balcony to its death. And in this porch we used to play Tarzan and Jane. I begged for a human part, but I was told I had to play Cheetah or the elephant. I was playing Cheetah when my father came. I called him the stranger because he had been away fighting in the revolution. He gave me and my sister gold bullet shells.

(SLIDE OF STAIRS.)

I couldn't wait to go inside. Those are the stairs, the stairs I fell from when I was six months old. I bolted upstairs to my bedroom.

(SLIDE OF WRITER BY DOOR.)

Two men are in the middle of a business meeting. I interrupt. I'm sorry. I used to sleep here. The woman who has been following me, the secretary, tells me I can't just barge in as if it's my house. You don't understand, I say, this was my house. She opens the door to the bathroom.

(SLIDE OF BATHROOM.)

Oh, my bidet, my toilet. She says, "Hey, you're not one of those Cubans who plans to come back and take over their house." I say, "Oh no, we only rented." The moment I say this I feel like I'm not like one of those Cubans who left—who never would have said they rented. Are you kidding me, we owned the whole block.

(SLIDE OF CONSTRUCTION.)

My house is now a construction company. Privatization entering Cuba right through this, my house.

(CARMELITA ENTERS THE WHITE CUBE. A BALLAD PLAYS.)

CARMELITA
It's the middle of the afternoon. There's music playing. From the window I see the Hotel Nacional as it sits on a rock and over-

looks all of Havana Bay. I think of having a *mojito*, the favorite drink of Papa Hemingway. It could also be mine since I don't remember what it tastes like. I walk to the renovated, four-star Hotel Nacional, smelling the delicious grass. The sun is trying to come out. It just rained. I walk to the entrance of the hotel. The doorman winks. I say, *"Buenas tardes."* Inside it is cool and beautiful. There are potted palm trees, Spanish leather chairs, and blue tile. Blue tile. How I hate blue tile, especially with yellow squiggles. It doesn't go with anything. Bad decorating choice. A hotel employee looks at me. The blue tiles are making me sick. I'm holding tight to the potted palm frond.

DOCTOR
Carmelita, suéltala. Let go. Let go of your mother's hand. You have to be brave. *Hay que tener coraje, mucho coraje en la vida.*

CARMELITA
No. Mami. No, Mami. Please don't let go of me. I'm your child. I want to be with you, Mami. I don't want to go with the green man.

MOTHER
Carmelita, it's just a green uniform. *Mi hijita.* Don't be afraid. It will be over soon.

HOTEL EMPLOYEE
Señorita, if you don't let go of the palm frond, I'm going to have to call security.

CARMELITA
I'm sorry. Yes. I don't feel well. I need to eat. I'm hungry. I have to sit down in the dining room and eat. I go into the dining room like a somnambulist, following the song "Lágrimas Negras" played by a trio. Where have I heard "Lágrimas Negras" played by a trio like this? Oh yes, last week in Gloria Estefan's Miami restau-

rant. At least the short-term memory works. I should try to remember a lot. The more I remember, the more I will remember. Let's see, what did I learn today? Ochún is the goddess of the sea. No, that's Yemayá. And if you want to get the love of your life, you have to leave honey on a plate under your bed for five days. You get the love you want and the *cucarachas* you don't. And the slang word for dyke is *bombera*, firefighter. So maybe if I yell, Fire, *fuego*, would all the dykes come out now? I feel much better. So much better I order a *mojito* and pork sandwich. "La Ultima Noche que Pasé Contigo" is playing. The waiter brings me the sandwich. He has a green jacket on. I try not to look at his green uniform. Trembling, I pick up the sandwich. A slice falls—no, it jumps.

(PIG FLIES IN AND HANGS ABOVE CARMELITA'S HEAD. ON TAPE IS THE SOUND OF A SQUEALING PIG.)

PIG

(SNORT, SNORT) The horse thought it was bad in colonial times, he should talk. I was a pig in the Special Period. *Cochinito Mamón.* I was just two weeks old, lying under my mother's belly, sucking her sweet milk with my brothers and sisters, when I was yanked off her tit by a man who put a blanket over my head and took me from my farm in Santiago to live in an apartment in Havana. It was so quick, I couldn't even say good-bye to my family. The apartment was on the second floor. My legs were too short. I couldn't go up the stairs. Señor, I am no goat. I went into the apartment. I looked for mud, but everything was so clean. The woman in the apartment, the wife, cradled me in her arms, calling me *Nene*, boy. She fed me milk in the bottle. Hey lady, I'm not into rubber. I want real nipples. The man complained about my smell, so every day she had to give me a bath in the tub.

WOMAN

Nene, sit still. *Nene*, don't splash. *Nene*, let me wipe your nose.

PIG

I'm not a boy, I'm a pig (SQUEALING), I'm a pig! One day the man came in walking funny. He had been drinking with his brother, who worked at the Hotel Nacional. He smacked the wife on the rump and made her get the tape measure from her sewing kit. He put it around my belly.

MAN

¡Coño, *qué gordo está este puerco!* This pig is fat.

PIG

I could smell the rum on his breath. She should give him a bath. The phone rang. It was long-distance, the relatives from the United States. The man said something about showing me to them. The next day was Sunday. I didn't know what was happening. The woman put a hat on my head. It was a gift from a cousin in New York. A baseball cap. It kept falling off, so she tied it with another gift she got from New York: a bungee cord. The cord was tight around my neck. She was sitting on a chair, holding me on her lap, lifting my head to look up. The man quickly got behind us when a flash went off. I got scared. I didn't know it was supposed to be a family portrait. I jumped down. My hoof ripped her panty hose. I tried to run, but I had put on some weight. I slid behind a table and knocked over a lamp. It broke. The man went after me. He was screaming:

MAN

¡Puerco, puerco de mierda!

PIG

She was screaming:

WOMAN

¡Nene! ¡Nene!

PIG

I was squealing: ¡*Mami!* ¡*Mami!* With all the noise, the neighbors, they knocked on the door.

NEIGHBORS

¿*Qué pasa?* ¿*Qué pasa?*

PIG

The man flew across the room and tackled me. He whispered in my ear.

MAN

Coño, puerco de mierda. You are going to be roast pork, but before that we are going to cut your vocal cords so you don't squeal and disturb the neighbors anymore.

PIG

The next day I was put in a box. The woman was crying as she punched holes in the box so I could see. We got to the place. I could see blue tiles.

DOCTOR

Carmelita, relájate. Estamos en la sala. I'm going to put this on so you can breathe deep. *Respira profundo.*

CARMELITA

No. I don't want to breathe.

DOCTOR

Déjate de tonterías, niña. Carmelita, quiero que cuentes. I want you to count backwards. Count backwards: one hundred, ninety-nine, ninety-eight . . .

PIG

When I got out of the box, I saw a man in green. He had a shiny knife. I squealed, ¡*Mami!* ¡*Mami!* (SILENT)

(SHE PULLS A STRING FROM THE PIG'S NECK AND A STREAM
OF RED GLITTER GUSHES DOWN, SPILLING ONTO THE WHITE
LINOLEUM.)

CARMELITA

My vocal cords, my tonsils. The pig and I, we had our operations at the same clinic. The clinic with blue tiles. I remember.
We are all connected, not through AT&T, e-mail, Internet, or
the information superhighway, but through memory, history,
herstory, horsetory. I remember.

(SHE SHADOW-BOXES AS SHE RECITES THE POEM.)

I remember
Que soy de allá
Que soy de aquí
Un pie en New York (a foot in New York)
Un pie en la Habana (a foot in Havana)
And when I put a foot in Berlin (cuando pongo pata en Berlin)
I am called
A lesbishe Cubanerin
A woman of color
Culturally fragmented
Sexually intersected
But I don't esplit
I am fluid and interconnected
Like tie die colors I bleed
A Cuban blue sky into an American pumpkin orange
Que soy de allá
Que soy de aquí

(LIGHTS UP BRIGHT.)

Hello, people, you know me. I know you. I don't need no
American Express card. I am Carmelita Tropicana, famous nightclub entertainer, superintendent, performance artist. And I am so

happy to be here with you today, because ever since I was a little girl I ask my mami, "When can I do a show called *Milk of Amnesia* at PS 122?"* And here I am. I am so lucky. Lucky I can dance *un danzón, cantar un son, tener tremendo vacilón.* Thanks to *El Cochinito mamón, sandwich de lechón.* I got to exit with a song, *sabrosón* like the *sandwich de lechón.*

(SHE EXITS SINGING AND DANCING.)

> *Cochinito mamón*
> *Sandwich de lechón*
> *Cochinito mamón*
> *Sandwich de lechón*

(LIGHTS FADE DOWN. AUDIOTAPE WITH WRITER'S VOICE COMES ON.)

WRITER

September 1993. I met an American lawyer who is here in Cuba to witness a period of "transition." It seems in 1993 anything can happen. In the theater festival there were plays that were critical of the system and played to packed houses. I thought by coming to Cuba, I would have answers. Instead I have more questions.

These are *Star Trek* glasses. They form rainbows around everything you look at. Am I looking at Cuba from an American perspective? *No es fácil.* It's not easy to have clear vision. In seven days I can only get sound bites. Cuba is a land of contradictions.

No one is homeless in Cuba, although homes are falling apart. Everyone gets health care, but there is no medicine. There is only one newspaper, but everyone is educated. No conspicuous consumerism. The dollar is legal, but there's the U.S. embargo. The clothes are threadbare, vivid colors now turned pastel. So much food for the soul, none for the belly.

---

*Performance Space 122 is where *Milk of Amnesia* premiered. When performing the piece elsewhere, the name of that space is referenced instead.

I don't want to keep score. It's not a competition. Cuba vs. the U.S. When the Olympics are on I'm at a loss as to who to root for . . . No, not really. I root for Cuba. Why? Is it that I'm for the underdog and that if I'm in the U.S. I am more Cuban and if I'm in Cuba I'm more American? Is Cuba my wife and America my lover or the other way around? Or is Cuba my biological mami and the U.S. my adopted mom?

(LIGHTS GO UP BRIGHT.)

CARMELITA

My journey is complete. My amnesia is gone. After so many years in America, I can drink two kinds of milk The sweet condensed milk of Cuba and the grade-A, pasteurized homo kind from America.

My last day in Cuba I spend at an artist's house. We sit, ten of us, in a circle, all sipping our one bottle of rum. I turn to the man next to me and tell him I have one regret. I didn't hear any Cuban music, and to me Cuba is music. He smiles. He is Pedro Luis Ferrer, famous composer, musician. He will play me his songs, but first he tells me, "The embargo is killing us."

(STEPPING OUT OF CARMELITA CHARACTER AND ADDRESSING THE AUDIENCE.) I agree with Pedro Luis, and I want to leave you with a song by him called "Todos Por lo Mismo," a song that says it best:

> *Everybody for the same thing*
> *Between the pages of colonialism*
> *Capitalists, homosexuals, atheists, spiritualists*
> *Moralists*
> *Everybody for the same thing*

(THE TAPE PLAYS SEVERAL CHORUSES AS CARMELITA EXITS.)

naked breath

TIM MILLER

Notes on *Naked Breath*

I wrote *Naked Breath* because I wanted to write a piece for performance that was full of the raw and intimate stickyness of blood and cum. I began working on it in 1992 shortly after getting beaten up by the Houston police during my visit there with ACT UP during the Republican National Convention. This came on top of several years of being batted around as a First Amendment poster boy as one of the NEA 4. A bit the worse for wear, I created *Naked Breath* at a time when I had begun to doubt some of my own slogans and my in-your-face street activism that had fueled me for a number of years. My response to how AIDS was hitting my life began to be really intimate and full of memory and sex and sorrow. This set the scene for this work. Also during this time my partner, Doug Sadownick, and I were primary caregivers for singer and AIDS activist Michael Callen. Michael and I planned to collaborate on this performance and in fact were awarded a Rockefeller grant to bring it to life. Sadly, Michael died before we had a chance to complete the songs for *Naked Breath*. I felt haunted by the loss of Mike as well as other friends and lovers. I was surrounded by bodily fluids and I wanted to get wet in *Naked Breath*. I felt drawn to the day in my life when I had bled the most, a day in 1981 that ended walking down East Sixth Street in New York with my boyfriend of that time, John Bernd. This seemed to me to be a day full of portent, humor, and twenty-eight stitches on my right arm and hand. Somehow I threw this story in the blender with another day that ended walking down that same street in 1992. Eleven years later, and a little spent from the culture war and onslaught of AIDS, I wanted to write a sexy and highly personal story about how two men managed to connect, one HIV-negative, the other positive. After several years of shouting in front of government buildings or being dragged by cops down the asphalt on the streets of Los Angeles or San Francisco or Houston or New York, I felt called to really honor the quiet human-size victory of remembering what has happened and being ready to connect with another man there in the swirl of blood within and the cum on our bodies.

Naked Breath premiered in Portland, Oregon, in 1994 at the Echo Theater. It has been presented in performance spaces and theaters in dozens of cities around the world, including Performance Space 122 in New York, the Institute for Contemporary Art in London, Actors Theatre of Louisville, the Center for Contemporary Art in Glasgow, the Boston Theater Offensive, and Highways Performance Space in Santa Monica.

Naked Breath is dedicated to the memory of the fierce spirit and voice of Michael Callen.

About Tim Miller

Tim Miller, performer and author of the book Shirts & Skin (Alyson Books), is best known as an internationally acclaimed theater artist who has delighted and shocked audiences all over the world. Miller's creative work as a writer and performer strives to find an artistic, spiritual, and political exploration of his identity as a gay man.

Hailed for its humor and passion, Miller's performance art is dedicated to trying to make sense of sex, life, and love in a tumultuous world. He has tackled this challenge in such pieces as Postwar (1981), Cost of Living (1983), Democracy in America (1984), Buddy Systems (1985), Sex/Love/Stories (1991), My Queer Body (1992), Naked Breath (1994), and Fruit Cocktail (1996). Miller's performances have been presented all over North America, Australia, and Europe in such prestigious venues as Yale Repertory Theater, the Institute of Contemporary Art (London), the Walker Art Center (Minneapolis), and the Brooklyn Academy of Music.

Miller, who is currently a visiting assistant professor at the California State University in Los Angeles, has taught performance art at UCLA and New York University and was an adjunct professor in religion and theater at the Claremont School of Theology. He is a founder of the two most influential performance spaces in the United States: Performance Space 122 on Manhattan's Lower East Side and Highways Performance Space in Santa Monica, California, where he is currently artistic director.

Miller has received numerous grants from the National Endowment for the Arts. In 1990 Miller was awarded an NEA Solo Performer Fellowship, which was overturned under political pressure from the Bush White House because of the gay themes of Miller's work. These artists, the so-called NEA 4, successfully sued the federal government with the help of the ACLU for violation of their First Amendment rights and won a settlement, where the government paid them the amount of the defunded grants and all court costs.

After a nine-year stint in New York City, in 1987 Miller returned home to Los Angeles, California, where he was born and raised. He currently lives there in Venice Beach with his dog.

naked breath

TIM MILLER

(THE STAGE IS BARE EXCEPT FOR A GIANT SUNFLOWER IN A
HEAVY GLASS VASE. TIM ENTERS FROM THE BACK OF THE
HOUSE, BREATHING IN AND OUT VERY LOUDLY. HE CHECKS
TO MAKE SURE THE AUDIENCE IS BREATHING, TOO. HE
STOMPS ON STAGE, AND THE LIGHTS COME UP.)

I'm breathing. Are you? How about you? Everybody take a
breath. Let me hear. . . . That was good. Now take a nice breath
through your anuses. Here. I need to do a spot check.

(TIM APPROACHES SOME AUDIENCE MEMBER WHO IS PROB-
ABLY DREADING JUST SUCH AN EVENT.)

Would you breathe on my wrist? Would you breathe on my
heart?

(TIM LOCATES A SPECIAL SOMEONE FOR THE NEXT BIT.)

On my dick? I fear I get ahead of myself. Time for a tattoo, I
think.

(TIM PULLS A MAGIC MARKER OUT OF HIS POCKET AND SITS
ON THE LAP OF AN AUDIENCE MEMBER AND ASKS HIM/HER
TO DRAW ON HIM.)

Could you tattoo my arm, please? Just write "NAKED BREATH" in bold Virgo clear letters and then put a heart around it and an arrow through the middle. Here's a Magic Marker. Ya know they say that with every breath we take we breathe in a couple of molecules that Leonardo da Vinci once breathed. I have always believed this. I choose to believe this because it makes life more interesting. But that also means that with each breath we make we also breathe in some molecules from Attila the Hun. Mary Tyler Moore. Poppin' Fresh? A coupla molecules from Jesus on the cross. A coupla molecules from the guy I had sex with last week and he breathed so deep. His skin so beautiful. A coupla molecules from Bill and Hillary and what I hope is still their loving bed. A coupla molecules from each of us gathered here. Thanks for the tattoo. Wow. I'm gonna breathe you in.

I'm gonna breathe in your warmth and miracle of human presence in this room. You all got here! No one got hit by a car on their way to the theater! I don't take it for granted, believe me.

I'm gonna breathe in the colors and ages and sexes and haircuts and fashion choices in this room.

I'm gonna breathe in the multiple piercings and even the presence of the butt plug this gentleman in the third row chose to insert before coming to the theater tonight. (Not much gets past me, doll!)

I'm gonna breathe in the wish that some of you have that tonight you'll meet someone, go home together, have sex, and become life connected.

I'm gonna breathe in the sadness. Oh, it's here, too. Sometimes hiding there in the seams of our trousers and the hems of our dresses.

I'm gonna breathe in the joy. It's different for each. The joy of the morning cup of coffee! The joy of the blow job! The joy of the favorite song! The joy of the touch that matters.

I'm gonna breathe in the heat that is reflected from that time last summer when you lay in the sun as naked as a short-haired cat.

I'm gonna definitely breathe in the voice of Mike Callen. He was a singer, activist, and the ultimate diva I've ever met. His songs are with us here tonight. I'll float with his breath.

I'm gonna breathe in the memory we carry of the others that have died.
Some of our lovers. Some of our mothers. Some of our brothers.
I'm gonna breathe in the blood and the wood and the sacred beds in Gramercy Park that are in this story tonight.
I'm gonna breathe in the grace of each beat of our pulse. Each snap of our fingers. Each rise of our chests. Each breath we make.
I'm gonna breathe you in and I'm gonna let your breath carry me down a street. You know, we all have a street inside us. (It's the first metaphor of the show. I'll give you a moment.) It's a place where some things happened. I'm gonna let you carry me down that street now to a time that was a time for building.
As my hand reaches down behind the upstage left black curtain (you're not noticing this) and grabs my very special . . .

(TIM CRAFTILY GRABS A HIDDEN ELECTRICAL CIRCULAR SAW AND GETS IT GOING. LOUD!)

Of all the approved boy activities of childhood, the only one I was really good at, other than beating off fourteen times a day, was carpentry. I loved this shit. It was the one place my dad and I had a slim chance of connecting, where his expectations and my homo predilections could look each other in the eye and exchange a manly handshake.

Under my dad's watchful eye, I built bookshelves, napkin holders, birdhouses that no bird thought were safe to go into, and glamour-filled split-level treehouses decorated with throw rugs! I'd invite my little friends into my treetop lair, pull up the rope ladder, and try to convince them that we should cover ourselves in corn oil and play naked Twister.

I loved going to the lumberyard with my dad. It was like church. Better. More authentically spiritual. Sackett & Peters Hardware and Lumber in Whittier, California, was a gothic cathedral of two-by-fours, a delicate abbey piled high with a maze of construction-grade plywood. The sunlight slipping in between the spindly fir strips dappled our bodies as my dad and I searched for just the right piece of maple wood. Most important, lumberyards were staffed by sexy men in sleeveless orange fluorescent vests showing their great arms. Their job was to meet your every woody need. The lumber workers sauntered godlike as they led you into dark hallways to offer you their mahogany. They'd turn the plank over in their hands, show you the wood's true line, stroke the smooth sides, measure out in inches exactly how much you needed.

Then they would take the wood to an enormous table saw, a fierce machine that could rip and tear the wood. In an explosion of grating sound, the sawdust covered your body. The sensation tickling your skin and the earthy smell of a shower of sawdust made me shiver with pleasure. I breathed it deep inside me.

In my life journeys through teenage blow jobs, synth/pop music, the Reagan/Bush years, and the rise (and fall) of the Queer Nation goatee, I have always tried to stay close to my carpenter roots. When I was nineteen I moved to N.Y.C. and began the usual scoreboard of crummy jobs.

First I was a bellboy on Central Park South. Every Tuesday the retired dentist on the fourteenth floor (it was really the thirteenth; could that fool anyone?) would push his bourbon-drenched face into mine and try to kiss me. "You can't kiss me in the elevator, Mr. Rothbart!" I would say, trying to tame his octopus arms. "Think of your wife! Your grandchildren!"

I spent two weeks as a falafel maker on MacDougal Street. The owner, a Hungarian with a heavy accent, criticized everything I did: "You stupid boy, you must put hummus evenly on *inside* of pita bread. You would have been worthless when Russian tanks rolled into Budapest!"

I worked with my new friend Mark, who shared my interest in performance art, as juice boys at a busy midtown healthy eatery called the Curds and Whey Café. The unctuous manager explained my precise time schedule to me: "From 9:05 to 9:08 you collate juice filters. From 9:08 to 9:11 you take the carrot inventory."

Now my parents did not raise me in the Golden West to become alienated labor back east. Finally I gathered my tools, chisels, saws, hammers, sexy carpenter belt, and I started my own carpentry business. I became a builder of beds. With a newfound entrepreneurial zeal, I designed an advertisement which I Xeroxed that had the look of a kidnap note: CARPENTER-PERFORMER-HOMOSEXUAL AVAILABLE TO BUILD LOFT BEDS THAT WILL CREATE A NEW YOU! The phone started to ring almost at once. I built hundreds of beds for the people of N.Y.C. Now, in New York no one really has space in their apartments to sleep properly, so most folks with tiny apartments more sensibly decided to have special raised sleeping shelves in their apartments that were called "loft beds" whether they were in a loft or not. Somebody had made up the word in an effort to make it sound glamorous, like we were in Paris: "Darling, let's retire to the loft bed, have a cappuccino, and bump our heads." Clearly there would be a market for my loft bed construction business.

No solution to the space problem was too bizarre for me: I'd build my loft beds anywhere. I'd build beds in hallways. In closets. A bed built out over the stove in a studio apartment's kitchen was very practical in a Lower East Side tenement without heat. You could make some potato latkes and keep yourself warm in bed at the same time. One loft bed I craftily hung from the ceiling by chains attached to meat hooks in a bedroom painted slate gray. This bold design became very popular on certain streets in the West Village and Chelsea. The reassuring stability of the chains provided numerous secure places for bondage toys which solved that age-old problem that has confronted mankind, "Where do I attach my handcuffs or wrist restraints so I don't have to pretend I can't escape?"

I would build hundreds of beds for the people of New York City. Beds for people to sleep on. Beds for people to fuck on. Beds for people to get pregnant on. Beds for people to get sexually transmitted diseases on. I had found my vocation. I was a husband of sex! A maker of sleep!! I took Manhattan to bed!!!

Okay, running your own carpentry business when you're a young fag performance artist takes much too much work. Trust me on this. The burden was too great, Manhattan too vast, the money too meager. So, in the summer of 1980 I gathered my saws and hammers and chisels and sexy carpenter belts (I had two now, one for day wear, the other for evening), and I found a contractor named Frank di Martini who needed an extra hand. He hired me, and my life as a Brooklyn construction worker began. I now became a part of the subculture of a small construction company in Brooklyn. It was such an intense testosterone scene on the construction jobs, a mix of carpenter jocks, ex-hippies, intensely butch dyke union wanna-bes, and one fag. All of us shared one thing: we were all good with wood.

Frank di Martini was a good-natured, compact, ponytailed, rippling-muscled sensitive New Age guy. He insisted on having at least one sweet and emotionally tuned-in gay man on every construction crew. I suppose that was me. This was Frank's version of a sort of queer Affirmative Action. I think he mostly wanted to have someone to talk to at lunch about things of mutual interest: metaphysics, love trouble, the latest Sondheim opening on Broadway. Frank would share with me the feelings that crosscut his life. Drilled into hidden places. Chiseled into his sense of self.

There was a darker side to this, though. I think Frank also wanted to have access to my Homo Sensitivity Gold Card. We were all given those plastic cards at birth, whether we know it or not. Frank thought he could borrow it from me if things got bad. It might help him meet his emotional payroll. We would use it to divide our feelings into lines on our lunch break over foot-long submarine sandwiches.

Okay, I know there are some people who would criticize me for idealizing this male universe I had landed in. They would say to me, "I think you are giving too much energy to a basically oppressive heterosexist job situation!" They might have a point, and I may be destined to end up on the Oprah Winfrey's "Queer Carpenters Who Give Too Much on the Job" episode.

Sure, I was giving, but I was also getting. I was getting the vibe of a world of workingmen in Brooklyn. Part of me had always wanted to be accepted by these guys who reminded me of my brothers and cousins. It was sexy, too, being surrounded by all these straight men and their tools all day long. Mostly I was out on the construction sites, except, of course, when hardened union guys from Queens were around. I was honored that in some way my queer gifts were being acknowledged and honored there amid the whir of the saw and the bam-bam-bam of the nail gun.

That first day on the job with Frank we did eight hours of demolition in an ancient basement on Adelphi Street. Yuk! The Pleistocene dirt of Brooklyn covered me from head to toe. This grime was made up of the grit of the writing of Walt Whitman and Hart Crane. At the end of the day, covered in their poems and black soot, I sat on the D train heading over the Brooklyn Bridge back to home on the Lower East Side. I caught a glimpse of my face in the shutting subway door. I didn't recognize myself. I was filthy from the day's work. There was a raccoony splotch of white where my face mask and goggles had been. I looked like those Welsh coal miners in the classic 1941 film *How Green Was My Valley*.

At the first stop in Manhattan, some artist friends got on the train and sat across from me. As they chatted amiably, they had no idea who I was. They didn't recognize me. I had become the invisible worker, someone who earns his keep with the sweat of his brow.

(OVER THE SOUND SYSTEM WE HEAR, NATURALLY, THE RED ARMY CHORUS SINGING "THE INTERNATIONAL.")

This realization of born-again working-class identity went straight to my head. Before too long, in that crucial summer of 1980, I became the head co-foreperson carpenter at the People's Convention in the South Bronx, a protest shanty town designed to expose the hypocrisy of the middle-of-the-road Democratic Party, who were having their convention in New York that summer. My partner foreperson carpenter was a fabulous dyke named Marty. She is a performance artist today, too! Marty and I were Dyke and Fag Carpenter People's Heroes, ready to build a new social experiment there in the bombed-out South Bronx. Later on in that summer, Marty and I would march with thousands of others in defiance of the corrupt Democratic Party convention at Madison Square Garden. I took off my red plaid sleeveless shirt, the one I always wore on the construction sites, and waved it over my head to show my politics and attract the cute man with the trust fund representing the Socialist Worker's Party. We poured past the Garden as we manifested our demands for social justice! Economic empowerment for all workers! We will seize the means of production!

(I do miss communism every now and then.)

But my friends on the subway couldn't see any of this. They probably thought I was just some working grunt on my way back to the wife and kids in Washington Heights. Had they only looked closer, though, they would have noticed the Manifesto Red nail polish I was wearing that particular day. I had crossed over from my art life, and I now dwelt in a different world. I was now part of this realm of dirt and dust and beer and . . . blood!

Earlier that afternoon, while the jackhammers had pounded, Mike from deepest Brooklyn was starting to space out after his five-foot-long submarine sandwich lunch and four Budweiser and two Amstel Light (because he was dieting) beverage break. His blood sugar was not doing well at all. At about two P.M., he slipped on a rock and his Sawzall, which was on at the time, tore a hunk of meat from his leg. Screaming in pain, he was hustled off to the emergency room. Those of us remaining exchanged nervous glances as Frank picked up a bucketful of sawdust and threw it over the spreading red pool of blood and said, "Back to work."

Now, every carpenter knows this is the tightrope we walk. These tools that can cut through brick and wood can also cut through our meat and bones. It is a blood contract, and nobody really knows the terms of it.

While I was going to Brooklyn to rebuild brownstones throughout 1980, I was also seeing a man, this guy named John. I met John because I saw a postcard up in the Laundromat on Second Avenue for a performance art piece he was doing. It caught my eye during my spin cycle. John was so beautiful, with his mess of androgynous curls glowing in the photo. His dancer's arm was held extended out to the side, fingers reaching all the way to New Jersey. I had to meet him. I got his phone number.

"Yes, in Manhattan," I said to the telephone operator. "I'd like the number for the attractive man on this postcard doing minimalist dance." (Directory assistance is amazing!)

I called John up. "You don't know me," I said, "but I think we should get together and talk about the new directions for gay men's performance in the eighties. I'm putting a festival together at PS 122." Okay, so it's been a recurrent pickup line in my life.

"It sounds interesting." John said cautiously. "Why don't you come over and we can talk about it."

On my way to John's apartment in the East Village, I walked down East Sixth between First and Second. This is the block with all the Indian restaurants. Shagorika. Kismoth. Taste of India. Passage to India. The Gastronome Ghandi. Ghandi to Go. They're all there! I used to imagine that all these restaurants shared the same kitchen. I was sure there were block-long conveyor belts delivering huge piles of poori and papadam like stacks of laundry to each small restaurant. In those soon-to-arrive delusional paranoid days with the election of Ronald Reagan, I was convinced that one of his operatives (Ollie North, perhaps) was going to sneak back there with his clutch purse full of plutonium and dump it into the common vat of mulligatawny soup. In one fell swoop he would wipe out all the queer performers in the East Village because these cheap restaurants were where we ate.

I got to John's house, 306 East Sixth Street. He buzzed me in.

"How many flights is it?" I shouted as I climbed the many stairs leading to John's apartment.

"Just keep on coming," John called down. "You've almost made it."

"Whew," I gasped. "That's quite a hike."

John extended his hand.

We had tea. We ate cashew chicken from the one Chinese takeout restaurant on the block. I was very drawn to John, so I cast my net wide and tried to pull him to my shore. John resisted me. I think he knew I was going to be big emotional trouble, so he struggled to avoid the coastline of my side, to miss the shoals of my chest, not to get pulled down by the undertow to my dick and butt.

John tried, but it didn't work. Sorry.

Who's the fish and who's the lure, really, in all of this? I don't know. I know we sat on wood boxes. John and I shifted near each other, and the inevitable thing happened, the only thing that could have happened between John and me: we began to fall toward each other, obeying the law of gravity and the even greater law that governs falling bodies. It was like when NASA's Sky Lab was going to fall from outer space and crash to earth. They could try with all their might to keep it from falling, but down it came anyway. Nobody really knew who the debris would hit when it plunged into western Australia. What if a big piece had hit a future boyfriend of mine, then a little boy in Perth dressed in a Catholic boys' school uniform? I didn't care as long as it didn't hit me or anyone I love *personally* in the head.

That kiss with John happened as we hit the earth's atmosphere. Then came the opening of clothes and the rush of feeling as we entered each other's undiscovered countries.

"Can we go into your bedroom?" I asked, a little uncomfortable on the wood boxes.

"You want to?" John asked, rubbing my close-cropped hair.

"I think so."

There was a voice inside of me that was telling me to wait. I wasn't sure if I had a passport for this journey. *My papers probably aren't in order. I'd better turn back. I'll just leave now. Well, on second thought, maybe John and I can just sneak over the frontier at night. Hope for the best.* So we kissed. And ate each other's butt holes, of course. And fucked each other.

That night as I slept next to John, I dreamed so vividly the dream came with specially composed dream-sequence music. I dreamed I was in a graceful world, rolling fields of grass extending as far as the eye can see. Feeling John in bed next to me, it seemed that this was a world we might get to live in together. On these fields of grass was humanly designed architecture, like the perfect college campus, the University of Iowa, maybe. It was all the colleges I never got to go to. I walked through this grassy dream looking for John, while strange and beautiful music played from hidden speakers in my head.

John didn't want to love me. He had been burned by men many times and was cautious about opening himself to me. But I forced him to. For a while it gave him a lot of pleasure. Later it would give him a lot of pain. But for now, for a few powerful months together, how we loved to fuck each other!

I should get back to work. The first weeks I was seeing John, Frank di Martini and Company was doing a job in the Fort Greene section of Brooklyn. We had undertaken a massive renovation, and now I was working all alone on this site, doing the finish work on some doors and parquet floor. Most people don't know that I am an expert door hanger. (I know, it's a fascinating subject.) Now, door hanging is a very useful skill because everybody needs doors. We need doors to go from one room to the other, sure. But we also need doors to go from one time of life to another. So if you know how to make a doorway, you'll always have work.

I had framed out a door at this brownstone and had left a space above for a transom. I was waiting for the stained-glass artisan who was late (as artisans will be). Finally Gene, Mr. Stained-Glass, arrived with his wide grin and wider shoulders. His long hair and two-day stubble made him look like one of the cuter of Jesus' disciples just fresh from a workout lifting rocks in the desert. He stripped to the waist as he installed his piece . . . of glass. I pretended great interest in how he was deftly placing his work of art. It gave me a reason to be close enough to him to sniff the aroma coming up from his shucked-down overalls. The stained-glass commission he had fulfilled was a sort of reedy-lake-mallardy-duck-on-the-wing thing. We admired it. Then, out of the corner of my eye, I saw he was admiring me quite obviously. Then Gene the Stained-Glass Hunk spoke.

"So . . . uh . . . do you like being a carpenter?"

"It's okay," I replied, flinging a slug an electrician had left on the floor.

"You really seem to have a knack for it," he said, examining my rather skillful work on the doorjamb.

"I'm good with wood," I replied, looking him in the eye.

Well, with that line, he had to make eye contact, right? So he glanced up and moved slowly toward me, brushing a fleck of wood off my cheek. His hand reached around my shoulder, and he pressed his body onto mine as we leaned against the door frame. The heat of his body made my face turn red like a bursting cartoon thermometer.

"You really know how to hang a door," Gene said. "Let's see if it swings."

Suddenly we were kissing and grabbing and poking. Soon our cocks were in each other's mouths as we stirred up the sawdust below our feet. The smell of the wood was in my nose and on my skin. It took my breath away. We offered each other our mahogany. We turned each other over in our hands. We showed each other our true line. We stroked our smooth sides. We measured out in inches exactly how much we needed.

It was clear to me that Stained-Glass Man was about to come on my pricey birch-veneer clamshell molding. I breathlessly said, "Not there! Shoot on the inexpensive knotty-pine door saddle!"

We both came by the door hinge. Lazy dollops of cum, like a dentist's office abstract expressionist painting, meandered slowly down the length of the wood. At that moment life seemed like a graceful and interesting place, where I could work hard and then mark what I had created with sex. The ab-ex look was quickly turning very Francis Bacon as the cum lost its shape and melted to the floor. We looked at each other and laughed, brushed each other off, and we pulled up our pants. Stained-Glass Man chuckled, hoisted his tool bag, pecked me on the lips, and went off to his next delivery.

I grabbed some sawdust and threw it on the dripping splooge. I got down on the floor and rubbed the queer cum into the arrogant pride of these rich people's brownstone. Put that on your croissant, class enemy!

For the last part of my job that day, I needed to shave one thirty-second of an inch from the back of some of the pieces of parquet floor to fit flush around the door. For this job I was going to use my hand electric planer. A hand electric planer has eight to twelve razor-sharp blades whirring five million times a second. It's basically a death machine. Now, this was not exactly a case of using the right tool for the job. In fact, it was completely the wrong tool. But since I'd enjoyed an unplanned sex break, I was in a hurry and needed to finish up.

I carefully held the first piece of parquet floor between my fingers. Errrrrh! One thirty-second of an inch off. Good. Glued and installed. I gripped the second piece and carefully brought it close to the whirring blade held in my lap. Careful. Careful. Careful . . .

Now, if we were looking at this scene from outer space, what would we see? We would see a young queer carpenter in a hurry about to make a grave error. From space we would see the swirl of sawdust from where their bodies had recently been, the lingering heat of these two men's mingled breath as visible as any nebula's gases on the opening credits of *Star Trek: The Next Generation*. From outer space we would see that in 1897, the Italian workman in the Bronx who had fashioned the piece of parquet floor had noticed a hard little oak knot there on the underside. Uh-oh. I want you to all watch that oak knot very carefully now as it moves toward that leering blade. Closer. Closer. Closer . . .

The knot hit those blades, the machine jammed, and my hand is pulled into the planer's teeth. Blood spurts everywhere: a tidal wave of gore. I have cut off my entire arm, I think. No, my arm is still there. My hand. No, my hand is still there. My fingers. No my fingers are still there. Wait, the end is gone. I've cut off the end of my finger.

What could I do?

On automatic pilot I decided to go to St. Something-or-Other, the Catholic hospital by the De Kalb entrance to the subway. Now, I believe whenever you cut off a part of your body, you should first find it, then put it in a teacup of ice, and then remember to bring it with you to the hospital. They can do amazing things with these cut-off parts. (I've seen the John Wayne Bobbitt penis restoration video.) I picked up the bloody tool and poked through the blades. I found the cut-off piece of finger, but it seemed like it wasn't going to be much of a help. It didn't look so good: sort of like a little spoonful of steak tartare. I left it in the electric planer.

I tore off my red workshirt and wrapped it around my squirting finger. Bursting out the door, I ran down the street, leaving a trail of blood behind me. If anyone was looking for me, they'd know where to find me that way. Each drop of blood there on the pavement was for someone in my life. This one, for John. This one, for Frank di Martini. This one, for me. All these, for everyone here tonight.

As I ran down the street, I remembered all the jobs I'd done in this neighborhood. I put two doors in that brownstone for a Wall Street stock analyst. I made the cabinets in a bathroom in there for this fuck buddy of mine who did public relations for the Brooklyn Academy of Music. I was proud of the window sashes for the yuppie family across the street.

I finally arrived at the Catholic hospital and rushed breathlessly toward the emergency room, my hand clutched to me like a relic of the one true cross. I burst through the doors and screamed, "I've cut off my finger! I'm bleeding to death!"

Everyone in the emergency room was screaming, too. The nurses and orderlies were weeping and throwing themselves on each other. This seemed an extreme response to my, admittedly, bad problem. But they weren't paying any attention to me. They crossed themselves and said "El Papa" this, "El Papa" that.

Finally, a formidable nurse with a faint mustache and the name RAMIREZ on her breast screamed over the loudspeaker, "The pope has been shot in Rome! Let us all pray." They all fell to their knees.

My mind took this in and quickly made a checklist of the situation: I have cut off the end of my finger. I have run bleeding through the streets of Brooklyn. I have come to a Catholic hospital emergency room six minutes after Pope John Paul has been shot at the Vatican! Is this fair, God, really? We have to talk.

An old woman with cataracts was weeping uncontrollably next to me as she grabbed at me, thrusting her rosary into my bleeding hand. I had never felt more like a WASP in my entire life. Finally, the commanding Nurse Ramirez glided toward me. She gathered me unto her and put me in an examining room. Capably she placed my whole hand, red shirt and all, into a metal bowl and poured a bottle of antiseptic on it. She began to peel the cloth away, unwrapping my finger like the Mummy revealing himself. My finger was chewed up pretty seriously. It looked like I had stuck it into a garbage disposal and then dipped it in a bowl of salsa ranchera.

Nurse Ramirez remained calm. "Young man," she told me, "we're going to cut off some skin from your arm and sew it onto the end of your finger."

My eyes replied, "Yes! You're beautiful, Nurse Ramirez."

She grabbed a scalpel and neatly cut a nickel-sized piece of skin from my upper arm. After peeling it off like a Band-Aid, she flopped it onto the end of my finger and sewed it on with deft strokes. The exposed flesh on my biceps looked like a science project, like a cow I saw at the county fair with its stomach exposed so you can put your hand in it. The flesh winked shut as Nurse Ramirez stitched the wound closed.

"Sit!" she ordered me. "Keep your finger extended over your head. Wait here for twenty minutes, then call someone to bring you home."

The woman with the rosaries sat next to me. She was calmer now. Patting my shoulder, she said, "I will pray for you even as I pray for the pope." The TV news reported to all assembled that the pope would live and so would I.

I waited exactly nineteen minutes and then walked slowly to the pay phone on the wall. I called John and hoped he was home.

"Hello," John said sweetly after the fifth ring.

"I'm in a Brooklyn emergency room," I panted. "I cut off the end of the finger. I'm lucky I didn't die. Please help me." I felt the tears start to come.

"I'll be right there, okay?" John knew to say the right thing. "I'll get there as soon as I can and I'll bring you home."

I don't think any words had ever soothed me so much in my life up to that point: John will bring me *home* to the East Village.

"Okay." I stifled a sob, wanting to be a big boy. "Hurry."

A half hour later John walked into the emergency room. I can still see him now, this most confusing man in my life. How much I loved and resented him for his gentleness. I can see him like he is in front of me. John's beautiful face, so generous with his smile.

His brown curls tumbled down his forehead and made a place that I would have liked to hide in. John had on his old winter coat even though it was May. It was cinched up with a wide belt.

"I guess my finger slipped," I said, holding up my enormous bandaged hand. "Do you think we can use this in a performance?"

"Don't think about that right now," John cooed. "Let's get you home."

John helped me up from the plastic seat, which was damp from my nervous sweat. We went outside to Flatbush Avenue, the afternoon light making Brooklyn look good, and John hailed a cab. This was a luxury not usually indulged. Feeling special, I nestled down into the seat like it was a stretch limo and leaned my face against the window as we crossed the Manhattan Bridge. The suspension cables framed my view of New York, chopping New York's skyline into little shapes, like the slices of pizza John and I loved at Stromboli's. These bits of Manhattan visible through the thick bridge cables were manageable bite-size pieces, just like the end of my finger back in the electric planer.

The cab left us at St. Marks and Second by the Gem Spa newsstand, where I often browsed in the porn magazines. John quickly bought a half dozen bialys for us to snack on from the woman at the Second Avenue bakery who loved us and pretended we were yeshiva boys.

Walking quietly down the street, I felt so old. I leaned on John. I felt scarred and scared by this day in my life. I looked up at the buildings of the Lower East Side. I had built beds in so many of these buildings. And I'd had sex in all the rest. I knew their insides. I knew where the studs hid under plaster walls, waiting for the nail. I knew which brick would take which exact spike. I knew what dwelt there in the mystery under the floorboards, the dark places between the joists that we walked on every day of our lives.

I had sawed and screwed. I had nailed and pounded. I had opened my body, and the blood had started to pour. I would try, but I would never be a carpenter again. I might even build another bed or two, but I would never *really* be a carpenter again. But I would always know, inside me, that there had been a brief time in my life when I *was* good with wood.

We walked on to East Sixth Street. I felt the sticky blood still on my arm. On my pants. On my shoes. I felt this blood on Sixth Street. It was slippery under my feet. It was hanging over my head. I saw my boyfriend John that day in May of 1981 on East Sixth Street. I looked to the East River. For an instant I saw the blood that was about to rise up from that river. I saw a wall of angry blood that would sweep away so many, that will sweep away John. I saw this for a second, a deluge about to come.

John nudged me and asked, "Are you okay?"

"Oh, yeah, I'm fine," I replied. "Can I stay at your house tonight?"

"Sure."

We walked into his building and climbed up the stairs very slowly. We went into his apartment. John carefully took the clothes off of me and helped me into the bathtub in his kitchen. He took his clothes off too and then got in behind me. The water surrounding us both, John washed the blood from my body.

(THE LIGHTS FADE TO A DEEP BLUE. TIM CAREFULLY SLIPS HIS CLOTHES OFF UNTIL HE IS NAKED IN THIS LIGHT. WE HEAR MICHAEL CALLEN SINGING THE SONG "THEY ARE FALL-ING ALL AROUND US." A PERFORMER WHO HAS BEEN SEATED IN THE FRONT ROW SLOWLY RISES FROM THE AUDIENCE AND WALKS TOWARD TIM. HE CARRIES A BUCKET WITH WATER AND A WASHCLOTH. HE SETS THE BUCKET DOWN AND HE SLOWLY WASHES TIM'S BODY AS MICHAEL CALLEN SINGS. HE HOLDS TIM CLOSE WHEN HE IS FINISHED AND THEN QUIETLY RETURNS TO HIS SEAT. AS THE SONG ENDS, TIM SPEAKS.)

We're walking down East Sixth Street. In December of '92. Eleven years later and eleven years into the plague. How many times in my life had I walked down East Sixth Street in New York? How many times had I walked down this street with blood on my clothes from the cut-off end of a finger, with groceries in my arms for a dinner with friends, with a new man at my side for a night's work? How many times had I walked down East Sixth looking for sex? Or Indian food? Or both?

(TIM PULLS HIS PANTS UP, SHIMMYING THE WHOLE WAY.)

Sometimes I would sit afterwards in an Indian restaurant, beloved Kismoth or tasty Shagorika, snuggled into a booth with a man I was seeing. The cum would be still marking our bodies, crackly on my neck or sticky between his legs. The Bengali waiter would arrive with his freshly starched, white-shirt smile.

Waiter, I'll have the mango chutney and a large Wash'n Dri, please.

How many footsteps have walked here before me, the memory of their soles wearing that East Village concrete into sand and dust? How many footprints of the dead who came before us are layered beneath our striding feet? They ate their bagels, wept in their beds, and read the newspaper with great interest long before I had gulped in my first breath. Right now I might be stepping on the tiny footprints of my boyfriend Doug's dead grandma. As if I was crossing a river on a series of slippery stones, I can follow her path as she walked up to Fourteenth Street from Delancey in 1912. She walked uptown to buy a book or a piece of meat. Maybe she was window-shopping for a dress she'd never be able to afford for the new year.

Our feet joined that throng.

Am I being sentimental here? Well, I'm sorry, but I listen to doomy and gloomy music frequently and this makes me remember the footfalls of the dead. I hear that music loud in my head. I do what it takes to keep the memory alive of each slaughtered queer poet on each battlefield or immune suppression ward. I remember every dyke and every faggot erased by this culture. I spend hours looking at the photos of my dead lovers on my altar at home. I touch my first SILENCE=DEATH button with a nostalgia I can't help but feel for 1988, my first tour of duty with ACT UP. I jab that SILENCE=DEATH pin into the palm of my hand. I hope for blood. I hope that the blood might actually mean something.

The light . . .

(RIGHT ON CUE, A FIERCE DIAGONAL OF LIGHT BISECTS THE
STAGE.)

. . . pours in.

I had met him earlier that day, this man I'm walking with down
East Sixth Street. We had become acquainted at Performance
Space 122 during a performance workshop I was leading. The space
was wall-to-wall ghosts for me. I heard my nineteen-year-old self
laughing at me from one of the dark corners. The faint echo of
past lovers and past performances almost made it impossible to stay
in the room. I stood on the exact spot in the space where John
and I had sucked each other off in front of the tall windows on
Ninth Street until we saw a balding man across the street looking
at us with binoculars.

The light poured in through those same tall windows as I opened
the curtains and swabbed the deck to get the room ready for the
workshop. One by one the two dozen guys arrived, bundled up
against the even-for-December cold. Some of the men knew their
way around 122, changed into their comfy warm-up clothes, and
started stretching. Others came into the room and only by exerting
the greatest will kept themselves from fleeing the building.

As the workshop got rolling I invited the men to breathe
deeply as we walked among each other. We were in a room full of
queer men who had chosen to overcome their fears of each other
so that we could spend some time discovering who we actually are.
We gathered to tell some stories about our lives. I hoped the warm
breath of our raised voices would keep us toasty. The weak four
P.M. sun spread long and low on the floor as it shined through the
somber stained-glass window that had preached to generations of
immigrants this inscribed poem:

> Every waking hour we weave,
> whether we will or no—
> Every trivial act or deed,
> into the warp must go.

That "party on" message spread its soft glow on the group of huddled-together faggots eleven years into the plague. In our own way how much like immigrants we were, too. We had left our families and our places of birth to come and be in the New World together. We, like them, had also discovered the terrible sadness that comes when you see the streets are not paved with gold. Arms around each other's shoulders, sweaty and swaying. We're close enough to smell each other. We're close enough to listen to each other as our stories weave together. I look for these circles. Conjure them, too, sometimes.

"I'm Andrew," he had said as we went around sharing our names. This was the man I would walk down East Sixth Street with later that night. Andrew was broodingly dark and handsome, a Heathcliff on Houston kind of thing. He broadcast a sweet generosity that I wanted to know more about. On account of his trendy East Village haircut, buzzed on sides and rock 'n' roll jet black up top, I guessed his age at twenty-eight, though he could easily pass as twenty-four. That octopus ink hair made a dramatic curtain across his forehead while he swooped through the space.

I know you, I thought to myself.

Andrew and I rose to our feet even as the workshop's tales of sissy boys and first loves swirled about us. I looked at him, and he met my gaze. The glance lasted only a second or so, but the daring look was enough to get the wheels turning. I noticed how we began to orbit each other as the men in the workshop improvised some movement together. A flurry of gestures containing the little boys, wild animals, and angry men that dwell inside us exploded from the workshop participants. I saw Andrew slip like a cobra through a tangle of men's arms and legs.

Andrew and I were wearing almost exactly the same outfits (how unusual). We were boldly duochrome in our bear-up black sweatpants and white sleeveless T-shirts with crosses and religious medals dangling from our necks, sort of a City Ballet meets St. Mark's Place kind of look. It was like we had spoke on the phone to decide what to wear to the first day of East Village High School!

"How long have you two known each other?" someone asked me, commenting on our similar getups.

"Not long enough," I whispered to myself as I maneuvered my way nearer to him. The generous Hula Hoop action in Andrew's hips showed me his Generation X cool exterior was balanced by a more than nodding acquaintance with his Big Queen Within. In fact, he *was* pretty big! Tall, I mean, a bit taller than me. I hated that. It meant that if we kissed later, I would have to twist my neck up and around to reach him. I would be sure to get a neckache. I should probably just call my chiropractor right now and make an appointment. Andrew wore a religious medal I didn't immediately recognize. What was it? A petite St. Peter and Paul medal. Understated yet boner–producing.

Who was Andrew anyway? I had taken in the signs and symbols he displayed of queer urban culture, but what does the presence (or absence) of a nipple piercing really tell you about someone? Can that Tom of Finland tattoo or Superman pompadour haircut let you in on the secret of what books a man reads or whether his father beat him when he was a kid? I knew one thing for sure: Andrew's dark eyes and black hair reeled me right in. I could fight that tight fishline, try to get that hook out of the soft flesh of my cheek, but I knew the story would end up with me flopping around on the deck.

We snuck a look again, longer this time.

The workshop ended after three hours of creating performances about the secret powers we held as gay men and PS 122 was bursting with metaphors and hormones. Andrew and I hung around the room till almost all the participants had already left. We stood by our shoes, which had ended up next to each other (oh, fate!) on a well-worn seating platform. Those black boots waited for us to get our act together. They engaged in Doc Martens gossip.

The size 10½ wide muttered, "I just wish they'd go talk to each other."

"I just wish they'd go fuck each other!" the 11 narrow complained through the sock that was suffocating him.

Finally, to shut the boots up before they said something really embarrassing, Andrew and I grabbed those Doc Martens and stuck our feet in their mouths and flattened their shoe tongues as we threaded every last eyelet. These were the eleven-hole, *not* the eight-hole variety, so this trying activity took a little while. Each diving swoop of those shoelaces drew Andrew and me nearer and nearer. Face-to-face while we waited for the last person to leave, we tugged the laces tight and made a knot. Everyone was now gone. One of us had to do something quick. I crossed my fingers and stepped into the void.

"I'm glad you came to the workshop," I said with false confidence, sounding like my football coach uncle.

"It was great. I had a really good time," Andrew responded with a friendly look. "It's been a while since I've done this kind of thing."

"Are you a performer?" I asked. "You look like you've done a lot of movement."

"Yeah," Andrew replied as he hoisted his sweaty shirt over his head to change into something dry. I was treated to a quick glimpse of pale skin and erect nipples. "I studied dance in college."

"Well, I should probably get going." I dragged each word out to buy myself extra time. "Um, would you like to hang out for a while?"

"Sure," Andrew replied. "That would be great."

"What shall we do?"

"What would you like to do?" Andrew tossed it back to me.

"No, you decide," I countered.

"No, you," Andrew parried.

"It's up to you," I said, almost shouting.

"You're the visitor in New York, it's definitely your decision," Andrew said, putting his Doc Martened foot down. Checkmate.

I wanted to say something like "Let's just find a place that is quiet to sit and recognize the essential truth and spirit in each other." Because that is really what I hoped would happen. In lieu of that, I floated a more conventional proposal: "Why don't we go to Yaffa Cafe and eat something?"

Wrapping our Bob Cratchit scarves around our necks, we pushed our way out of the big oak doors of PS 122 and into the flow of the pre-Christmas jostle of First Avenue.

"It's fucking cold!" I complained, feeling like my lips were going to fall off with frostbite.

"Let's run," Andrew said, and took off.

We quickly covered the short distance to the café, shoved through the crush in the narrow entry, and slipped into a cozy, warm corner table.

"I hate the winter," I, the typical Californian, complained. "I think it's why I left New York for California."

"Hey, I'm a Californian, too," Andrew said, removing several layers of jackets and sweaters.

"You're kidding! Where are you from?" I was pleased to have discovered our common origin.

"Well," Andrew began, lavishing several vowels on this one word, as though this were a huge tale to tell, "I was born in Stockton in a manger; then when I was six . . ."

We were off and running in the delicious orgy of two native Californians comparing their tan lines as we shared nostalgic memories of hitchhiking in the San Joaquin Valley and which sex acts we had had on which rides at Disneyland.

We had tea surrounded by the late-baroque punk splendor of Yaffa on St. Mark's. For two hours we talked and traded and teased and tempted as we lunged our pita bread into the spicy hummus dip. Feeling daring, I licked the last bit up off the plate with my tongue and winked. This could have been the opening salvo of our intimacy, but Andrew glanced down at his watch.

"Oh, look at the time!" he said, getting up. "I have to go to work. I'm late."

"Yikes!" I exclaimed, using a characteristic retro expression that made me sound like one of the Hardy Boys. "I have a show to do. I need to go, too." Then I added nervously, "Would you like to meet later?"

"Sure." Andrew shouted through the pullover sweater that covered his face as he climbed into it. "This time I'll decide where to eat."

Later that night, at ten P.M., I walked down First Avenue, feeling pretty good. I had wiped the sweat and metaphors of that night's performance off my brow. Now, the thrill of the hunt was upon me. I was addicted to the feeling of excitement that came from having a rendezvous scheduled with God knows who to do God knows what with each other. I had the keen anticipatory look of an eager seven-year-old creeping down the stairs on Christmas morning. My breath a fog machine, I strolled past Holy Stromboli Lubricated Pizza. This had been the favorite place John and I would eat in the neighborhood. We had featured the greasy site in a number of our performances. Poking my head in the door of a beloved Eastern European restaurant, I sniffed the aroma of the sour cream–filled pleasures of Poland.

"*Dobry veyechoor!*" I called out to Zenya, my favorite waitress, in one of the eight sentences I still remembered from my brief study of Polish in 1979. Zenya smiled, pleased that one of the East Village gay boys would talk to her in her own language. Feeling expansive, I made up words to bless all of First Avenue in every language that I would never study.

I ran across the street and almost got hit by a cab making my way to a Mexican restaurant at Sixth Street and Avenue A where Andrew and I were to meet. It was called Banditos or Caballeros or something like that. New York doing Southern California Mexican food.

"*¡Buenos días!*" I said to the glacially glamorous young Frenchwoman working the door of the crowded restaurant. She glared at me as if I had spoken to her in Swahili. "I'm meeting someone," I quickly added, since it seemed like I owed her an explanation for my craven existence.

"Please, you will wait here," the mistress of attitude icily commanded as she checked her list.

I looked around the restaurant for Andrew. I couldn't see a sign of him. I've been abandoned! I thought to myself as I turned into a puddle of panic under the withering gaze of the Frenchwoman. Then I saw Andrew waving madly, trying to get my attention from the little table behind the pillar. Counting my breaths in an effort to calm my involuntary hyperventilating, I lugged my "abandonment issues" in their enormous mismatched steamer trunks across the restaurant and sat down across from him.

"Hi!" Andrew said as he leaned across the table and gave me a matter-of-fact kiss.

"Hi," I replied. One breath. Two breaths. Three breaths. "Nice to see you. Have you been waiting long?"

"Nah. Long enough to order a margarita. Are you okay?"

"Oh, sure, I'm fine." I improvised nonchalance, kicking the panic-filled steamer trunks farther under the table till they fit. "I just got a little nervous as I walked here."

"Relax." Andrew rubbed my forearm. "I won't bite."

Andrew was dressed in a thick-knit black fisherman's sweater and a motorcycle jacket. He could pass as a chorus boy from *Carousel* on his way to a leather bar. It was definitely a look. The margarita arrived: a frosty tureen the size of a bassinet. The salt chunks trembled in slow motion down the melting sides.

"Waiter," Andrew asked, "can we have two straws?"

Andrew shucked the straws slowly, the paper peeling away from the plastic tube like a molting snake. He thrust one straw in the slushy corner of the margarita closest to me and placed the other between his lips, lowering it like a vacuum cleaner into the delicious cold cocktail. We sucked at either end of that margarita, a queer postmodern Norman Rockwell painting of homosexuals in a Mexican restaurant.

Nursing our beverage, Andrew and I swapped stories of love and families and school and coming out and hopes and fears. In other words, we had a conversation. The stories bounced back and forth like a first round of tennis between a couple of people getting to know each other's skills. Our game plan included the usual dinner conversation topics: hustler boyfriends, drama queenism, international travel, and adolescent erotics.

"I had a boyfriend once who was a hustler on Santa Monica Boulevard," I started with an easy overhand serve. "He told me he did it so that he could buy a grand piano. But after all those blow jobs, once he got that grand piano, he found he could only play in E minor."

Andrew returned the lob with a free association: "Well, now that you mention blow jobs and the performing arts, I got my first blow job at the International Thespian Conference in Muncie, Indiana. It was with a boy from St. Cloud, Wisconsin, and happened backstage during a parochial girls' school production of *You Can't Take It with You*."

Lunging to display my backhand, I sent the ball back with a difficult corner shot. "Oh, yes, travel brings out the best in us. My friend Doug and I once had a big fight in the Parc Royale in Brussels, so we split up for a couple of days and then met in the train station in Berlin Bahnhofzoo. We saw each other next to the express train to Moscow. Doug and I were so happy to see each other as we hugged and kissed our way onto the U-Bahn that we almost missed our stop at Karl Marx Platz."

Andrew was good, very good; he stretched long and thwacked the ball into my court with a story that psyched me out: "When I was seventeen, I lived with my mom in a house in the San Joaquin Valley next to some alfalfa fields. Every night of my seventeenth year, I walked far out into those fields. I would carefully take off all of my clothes and then jerk off over those green alfalfa leaves, dreaming of the Latino workers of those fields."

I reached for the ball but missed. Game and match!

The edgy cultural politics of this alfalfa field story had given me an instant boner. "Waiter, can we have the check, please? ¿Por favor?"

Andrew and I quickly paid the bill. Accurate as accountants, we divided it precisely down the middle. As we left the restaurant, I grabbed a handful of mints from the bowl by the cash register to quash the smell of the anchovies from my Caesar salad. Finally, our bodies brushed together as we walked down East Sixth Street in the direction of his house on this cold night in New York City.

We strolled past the mysterious fortlike walls of the Con Edison electrical plant at Sixth Street and Avenue A. It looked like a Wild West outpost for some minor John Wayne movie. What did they actually do inside those walls, anyway? No one knew. The sides of our bodies moved closer yet as we wandered past the bright facade of my favorite gay watering hole, the Wonder Bar. The hopeful primary colors were as brilliant as my

third-grade Jonny Quest lunch box. We walked on and on toward
Avenue B.

(TIM WALKS TOWARD SOMEONE IN THE FRONT ROW AND AD-
DRESSES HIM/HER.)

Now, you're probably saying to yourself, My God, Tim does
go on about meeting men! Well, that's true. I'm guilty as charged.
But I do this because I believe these connections are a great gift
and secret adventure of life. It's like the prize at the bottom of the
Cracker Jack box. You dig way beyond the sticky stuff, the bodies,
the sex even, and there at the bottom *is* the magic decoder ring!
It can help us understand the world and how we move through it.
It's like a doorway that opens. A window creaks up through all the
layers of paint and opens over our hearts. And maybe only one
moment of every year, the dawn sunrise on winter solstice, maybe,
can the light shine all the way to the back to the darkest place
inside us. And at that exact moment, one human being can dare
to ask the other, "Do you wanna come in?" *Oooooohhh!* What a
question! It's the question of our time. In these lives are a meeting at the corner of East Sixth and Avenue B.

We got to Andrew's building. My memory was nudged by the
sight of the combination beauty shop and botanica that made up
half of the ground floor. Was this the building in which I built a
loft bed for that New York University film student who then
bounced his Citibank check on me?

Andrew asked me, "Do you wanna come in?"

I wish that life were that simple, that tidy. This wasn't how it
happened at all. Andrew didn't ask me. I had to ask *him*. Such a
request—"Can I come in?"—is not an easy thing to make at someone else's front stoop at two in the morning.

"Gee," I enthused, channeling Joe Hardy this time, "here we
are at your house. Can I come in?" What a cad! But I dared to take
a chance.

"Oh, sure," Andrew said, pleased but a little surprised.

We went up the narrow stairs. Up, up, up into his apartment.
Andrew struggled heroically with the police lock, the dead bolt,

and door handle lock (part of the nonstop glamour of New York living), and he heaved his shoulder against the door. We tumbled into the dark apartment. His fingers reading the wall braille, Andrew at last found the switch and flipped on a light. No one else seemed to be home. That was good, I thought to myself. The solitude would make the preliminary moves toward grabbing each other's bodies more smooth. No distracting conversations à trois in the kitchen. In an attempt to take off our coats in the narrow hallway, Andrew and I managed to bonk heads as if we were in a queer Marx Brothers movie.

"Hey, I hope you won't sue me," I joked, softly rubbing his forehead, which had no visible dents.

"I won't if you won't."

I extended my hand. "It's a deal."

We shook hands like two farmers at the state fair in front of a prize heifer. Then we tried it again. This time we shook hands like who we *actually* were, two nervous gay men in a dark hallway on the Lower East Side who wondered what was going to happen next.

We stopped shaking hands, but the touch held on. For an instant, as I looked at Andrew, I remembered when I was a little boy and how tempted I always was to look with my naked eye at the solar eclipse. My mom tried the usual scare tactic: that I would be instantly blinded. Somehow her warning just didn't wash. How could the light of day hurt me? The sun was there, and I had to see. I tried to look at Andrew, but he was too bright, and I had to cover my eyes. Maybe I should get some smoked glass.

Andrew pulled me by my hand into the apartment, and he began to show me his sacred things, the apartment relics and icons. He had his extracted wisdom teeth placed on the altar next to the TV. His barbells stacked next to the radiator by the shelves with the hand-painted ceramic dinosaur collection ordered from the Franklin Mint. Three Virgin Marys on the toilet tank.

Finally Andrew tugged me into his whitewashed bedroom to see a sixth-grade class photo. I was dismayed to notice his bed, a beat-up old futon, in one corner *on the floor!* I couldn't stop myself from beginning to redesign Andrew's bedroom. I had a vision of how this room would benefit from one of my loft beds. I saw where I would put it on the wall, bolting the bed frame to the wall halfway up on the window, keeping the light above and below. Drawing the plans in my head, I imagined how this would open up an area underneath for a desk or a love seat.

For now, we flopped down on his futon on the floor, and I admired his black, black, black hair against the bed's white, white, white sheet. With a studied casualness I flopped one of my legs over one of Andrew's as we stared up at the ceiling in an uncomfortable "what will happen next?" silence. Andrew and I now faced that most challenging of existential situations: Who is going to make the first move?

Before we mere humans could answer, Andrew's pet feline, Hamster the Miracle Cat, poked into the room. Hamster the Miracle Cat probably was really on the lookout for some extra wet food from that morning's still-open cat-food can on the roach-friendly kitchen counter. But, meanwhile, Hamster proceeded to perform the "cat head thing," when a cat drops all pretense of aloofness and caresses you with its entire face. I suppose the animal kingdom was daring us to be more spontaneous and find our touch together. By example, Hamster tried to teach us how to rub the head into the crotch and drag our body's side against another body's side.

Taking the lead from Hamster, Andrew and I began to rub our faces together. The tip of my nose caressed Andrew's cheek as his lips grazed over my stubble closer to my open mouth. We kissed. It was tentative at first. The tongues slowly rose to the occasion, like dipping yourself into still-chilly Lake Tahoe early in the season and asking yourself, "Is this really what I want to do?" We dived in.

Oh, I liked Andrew. I had started to trust his sweetness when I had seen the sixth-grade photo. He was kind and smart and hot. He knew how to stand next to me and slowly reach his little finger toward mine. Most of all he was a Californian like me, yet he wore even more black clothes than I did! We savored taking those black clothes off—hands reaching into the 501s, tugging down the thick sweat socks, yawning out of our shirts with a sigh. The thrill of each touch given and received made my thoughts tumble in my head like clothes in a dryer.

Wow, I thought to myself as my hands searched Andrew's skin. His leg goes into his hip right there. Unheard of! He has a little hair here on his belly but not here on his shoulders. Fantastic! His recently shaved balls are attached to his dick in a bouncy sacklike structure. Wonder of wonders! The skin is so soft. His mouth tastes good. This all feels good.

I sensed Andrew's ceramic dinosaur collection began to stir from the shelf above. The prehistoric creatures slowly levitated above us as we licked each other's cocks. One ceramic Virgin Mary statue floated in just to bless us as we got closer. All of Andrew's child-hood snapshots sneaked out of the drawer where they had been stashed. The photos set up a camp around the bed, the past witness-ing this present moment. Even his barbells started to move a little nearer to each other and, at last, began to clang together as well.

Well, to make a long story short, I came on his chest. He came on my leg. Andrew and I felt our breath race and then quiet. Then we suddenly realized we were sprawled on a bed covered in cum with someone we had just met. This realization hit me like a shock, but just for a minute. I smelled the hint of the free fall of postorgasm depression about to hit me, that dreaded after the squirting de-flated balloon syndrome. But that little despair receded, and I settled into a new place, as if Andrew and I had hiked up a steep cliff and hauled ourselves at last to a plateau. At first it seemed strange and a little primordial and scary up there, like *The Lost World*, but then we saw that we could inhabit a new terrain. We could forage for food and build civilizations. Stroking one another gently for a long time, our touch freed for a while from the bass drum sex call, Andrew and I talked into the late hours.

I was glad I was there. I was glad I was alive. I loved New York. This was too good. Something bad was bound to happen. With that doom-laden thought, I fell into a deep sleep full of dreams of exploding buildings and machine-gunned nuns.

The next morning we woke up early in the flashbulb-bright sunshine coming in from the East River. I was covered in that

sticky-cum-closeness of waking up with someone for the first time.
I felt the splurge of feelings that can happen as you wake up in
bed with another human. One or two of my masks came down:
scary, even though there were still lots held in reserve. Turning
tentatively onto my side, I looked to Andrew to see if he were
awake. His eyes were open but still sleepy.

"Hi, handsome," Andrew tossed my way.

"Good morning." I yawned out the words as I stretched. "Do
you mind morning mouth?"

Andrew kissed by way of reply. We were tentative about opening our mouths to each other, like checking with a sniff the milk
after you've been away from home for a few days. But then we
slowly opened those clamshell lips, let our tongues slip and slide,
saw it wasn't so bad after all, saw that our mouths smelled of our
lives and our sleep and our dreams, too. The morning kiss floated
on the grace of trusting that we liked each other, and neither one
of us was going to make a hasty exit.

"So," Andrew said, beginning the cross-examination as he
abruptly broke off the kiss, "you probably have a boyfriend, right?"

"Yeah." I opted for a matter-of-fact tone. "We've been together
ten years this month. His name is Doug. We have an open relationship."

"If I were him," Andrew said, rubbing his knuckles playfully,
though a little roughly, on my forehead, "I wouldn't let you wan-
der around without a chaperon."

Andrew and I lounged as we talked shop about boyfriends,
present and past. I could slowly see our conversation inevitably
going to come around to *the* subject, the AIDS tune-in. "Health
concerns" began to present themselves from a distance, like the
music on the stereo of your downstairs neighbor gradually getting
louder and more vexing. But it was coming regardless.

Now, at that time in my life, I usually didn't engage in this
conversation on the first date. Being a good ACT UP boy, I as-
sumed all my partners were positive and behaved accordingly.
Normally, I would wait and have the HIV talk after I had sex with

a fellow a couple of times. I believed that as long as I was having safe sex, it was okay to allow this waiting period. I had a clutching-at-straws faith in safe sex, and I convinced myself that I could trust its principles. I structured my understanding of the world around its precepts. I had to believe in safe sex just like I had to believe in other forces essential for life: gravity, photosynthesis. friction. I felt compelled to be a party-liner about safe sex because this system helped me to keep my fears at bay. That faith allowed me to get up in the morning, make my breakfast, and *not* have a nervous breakdown.

Since Andrew and I had been careful in our sex, according to the accepted mores of the time, this was a perfectly responsible time to have the discussion, if indeed we even needed to have it. The subject came up on its own, as it so often does.

I said, "Andrew, it's intense to be here, lying in a bed on East Sixth Street, talking about all this relationship material. My boyfriend John, the guy I told you about who died of AIDS, he used to live on East Sixth, just down the block."

"Ouch," Andrew said, hugging his arms around me. We breathed together for a bit. "It sucks. I know. My ex-boyfriend back in California is pretty sick right now. I worry about him a lot."

We held this close between us as we circled the subject like hunters tracking a wild animal. The about-to-stampede elephant was in the bed with us now.

"So, Andrew . . . um . . ." I hemmed and hawed, trying to spit out the obvious question. "Where are you in all of this AIDS stuff?"

"I'm positive," Andrew said, looking directly at me. "I just found out a little while ago. What about you?"

"I'm negative," I replied after an exhale whistled between my front teeth. "The one time I checked, anyway. I could hardly believe it, considering my history. You know . . . John and all."

Well, the cards were on the table: it was a full house. The cameras zoomed in for the closeup. Everything was going real slow, spooky, and sci-fi. At this point there was a hydrogen bomb blast over the East River. This explosion blared through the windows onto our bodies, burning away the bullshit between Andrew and me. I witnessed a powerful moment between two human faggots at the end of the twentieth century.

I felt as if a strange bird, strange as the subject at hand, had flown into Andrew's bedroom. This creature was a little clumsy, awkward as Big Bird, as it broke through the glass and flapped around Andrew's room, knocking his high school graduation pictures off of the wall. This bird landed there at the end of Andrew's futon and looked at us. This bird, like this moment between us, could be fierce or friendly. It was *totally* up to us.

I looked Andrew in the eye. I had nothing useful to say, nothing that wouldn't collapse under the weight of its own structure of obvious verbs and insufficient adjectives. I felt our fates float around us for a moment. There was a hurt that hovered over Andrew's face for an even tinier instant.

"I hope you're not freaked out that I didn't tell you earlier," Andrew said quietly, looking down toward our feet.

"No." I said the right thing, though I knew no single word could describe the snarl of feelings that were revving up inside. Without thinking, I quickly toured the inside of my mouth with my tongue to see if I had any canker sores there. Everything seemed okay. "I'm a big boy. I know how to take care of myself."

Then I put my lips on Andrew's. Our tongues touched, and it was like a promise, eyes open, hearts, too. Andrew and I started to make love again. We moved our hands over the hills and valleys of our bodies just as we had a few hours before. I felt a powerful mix of excitement and fear. What was different now? There was an honest thrill in knowing who we really are.

I knew something special had happened. I didn't want to make it into a big deal. In a way it was just how things were, our lives as we needed to live them. I wasn't even sure what any of this positive/negative information meant anymore. But if I tried to say it meant *nothing* to me at that moment, that would have been a lie, a whopper of a lie. I was so tired of lying.

I had been in this situation before, of course, with other men who were positive. There was that time with the guy from Cedar

Rapids. Or the fellow from Spokane. One man was white. Another man was black. I confess they were all cute. All dear. All very hot. I am weak.

One of those men used to lead workshops in Texas for ex-gay born-again Christians. That didn't last too long before he met a nice boy at a gay bar in Tulsa. They moved to San Francisco, and he now works in a card shop in the Castro.

Another man won a scholarship to Princeton where he pored over medieval texts while eyeing the water polo players with his feet propped up on the back of the swimming arena bleachers.

One man escaped the death squads in San Salvador and walked all the way through Guatemala and Mexico to make a new life in Los Angeles. He sent money each week to his family.

Another man went home with Jeffrey Dahmer yet managed to live and tell the tale. (If that's not a fucking success story, I don't know what is.)

All of these men were positive. They told me this. They knew. I'm negative. I was pretty surprised that the coin nipped that way. It always scares me to tell people this. I worry that they'll think I'm a lightweight-know-nothing-who-said-you-could-talk-about-AIDS-from-your-position-of-negative-privilege queen.

I put my skin next to the skin of each of these men. I needed their touch, maybe more than they needed mine. I loved one man's crazy Brillo hair, his crooked smile, his deeply dimpled ass. I loved another man's wild courage at his job, his scary family story, his dick that veered to the left like a stretch of road.

What's "safe" anyway in this crazy life? Not getting out of bed, that might be safe. Except, I live in California where an earthquake might drop your house on you while you sleep. Not crossing against traffic and getting hit by a delivery truck like I almost did on the way to the theater tonight. Not climbing on slippery rocks, which I simply must do every day at my beach in Venice. Not ever getting close, close enough to touch.

Oh, but this kiss, I gotta have it. It's that simple. I gotta have it if my friend allows it to me. I can't stand on one side of a stupid river and wave a clumsy oar. No. I need this kiss and I want to know its *whole* story. I worry sometimes. I get scared. In my life that is too much ruled by fear. I fear everything. Earthquakes. Plane crashes. My face in the mirror. I get scared I'll trip on this crack on the stage and break my leg. But I have a special wing of fear, about the size of the Louvre, dedicated to the things that I might "get" from the men I get close to. Do sex with.

(OVER THE SOUND SYSTEM WE HEAR THE SCARY WHINE OF AN ELECTRIC PLANER, REDOLENT OF THAT DAY IN BROOKLYN.)

CLAP! WARTS! HEPATITIS! CRABS! AMOEBAS! HIV! This fear chews me up for breakfast. This fear is a tidal wave that is hovering above me, whirling, threatening. My mouth frozen in a scream. This fear is a virus, too. It's a fierce enemy, takes no prisoners. Can haunt my dreams. After some sex that, okay, wasn't so safe, it keeps me sleepless and tortured at three A.M. in South Kensington, London. Spitting distance from the gloriously tacky memorial to Prince Albert, who long before he was a dick piercing was the beloved of Victoria. When Albert died, Victoria (that queen) took whatever was good and hot in her and entombed it with Albert, her dead husband, and worshiped them all as dead things!

Lately, I've tried to turn this fear around. To flip that word "get" upside-down. Like a fried egg. Over. Easy. To see things another way. I want to honor the things that I actually "get" from other men. LOVE. TOUCH. INSPIRATION. SEX. KISSES AND WISDOM.

These are the things I get and give and get again. Just like I'm getting from my new friend, Andrew, on East Sixth Street. I want to kiss him. Feel his wet wet wet tongue. To feel our hearts grow with us together. To feel the way this sex pulls us somewhere good even while the frozen wind howls over the scary water towers of Gramercy Park and tomorrow morning, after the blizzard of the century, there will be absolutely *no* subway service to Brooklyn.

Wait. Wait. Wait. Wait! I hear a voice in my head say. *I paid my twelve dollars. Isn't it about time something* bad *happens to these guys? Towards the end of the show, it's the agreed-on time. Shouldn't one of them get sick and die now? You made your bed, Mr. Fag Carpenter. Now lie in it! Or maybe somebody could come in with a chain saw and cut some stuff off, splatter those white walls with blood. God needs his pound of flesh!* This voice says to me, *We don't deserve this pleasure.*

Sorry. Nothing so dramatic tonight, nothing so tragic. I hope you're not disappointed. Andrew and I became friends. Made love a bunch of times. Once, even, in Annie Sprinkle's sacred bed next to the crystal dildo collection. We have swum in each other's oceans. Santa Monica. Coney Island. Seen each other with other men. Run up high phone bills between New York and L.A. Another big cost of intimacy. We have been in life together. And that's a pretty good story.

But like in every story, something did happen that December in 1992. Andrew and I knelt in a circle, our knees to the earth, cocks in each other's hands. Can anybody here tonight really see those positive and negative signs hovering over our heads? I can't. But I could feel the electricity we were generating. I felt the juice come up through the floors of the tenement on East Sixth Street. I felt this buzz come up from the earth and move through me. I could feel it, the actual conjure of this thing.

Maybe in that circle of dicks and tongues and the past and the future we can throw a mess of slippery KY-covered marbles in front of those four cranky dudes on horseback as they pound down the streets inside each of us.

Maybe we can smack those jaws of fate and grab a shiny gold cock ring from that creaky dental work and slip it on.

Maybe our laughs and brave chests and saucy attitudes can find the punch line and the way out.

Maybe as I dangled my cross around my neck on its bathtub chain into Andrew's open mouth I'll find some answers.

Maybe as Andrew leaned over and pinched my tit and dropped his St. Peter and St. Paul medal between my lips and it fell deep inside me we'll learn something important. We'll get our hooks into each other, fishing for some truth or at least a gasp and a squirt. Testing and tasting each other's metal. Catching good things and not throwing them away, waiting for something bigger and better.

* * *

Andrew came on his belly and chest, and then so did I. I leaned over him and kissed him as I dragged this cross on this bathtub chain through that cum. Mixing it up. Now, no chemistry class ever taught me this experiment. I had to learn it myself. How to find the alchemy to mix this stuff up into something neither this or that. Neither only him or only me.

What do we do from this maybe knowing that maybe one of us will maybe die before the other maybe and in a fashion we know too well for sure? Well, we better have that fuel us and focus us 'cause we got work to do. 'Cause that cross belongs in our mouths. It should be moved from tongue to tongue and taste to taste. I pulled it from between Andrew's teeth with a clank and my cock was in a rubber in his ass and there was only yes and pleasure and it's one small step for man one giant leap for homokind and we'll plant that flag wherever we choose but always looking for the proper soil and ready to sing the needed psalm.

Then . . . we came again. It's nice when it works. It's like a handshake. A tip of the hat. A thin rubber skin between us. A contract.

Dropping my torso onto his, as if from a great height, I rubbed my body from side to side. We got really sticky and smelly as my weight made Andrew let a breath out. I was drenched in sweat by the time Andrew and I had finished. I let our bodies get glued together.

"Whew," I breathed a sigh. "That felt great."

"Yeah," Andrew whispered, his breath returning.

"How ya doing!" I sang the question softly in his ear.

"Good," Andrew purred. Hamster was still on the bed. "This all feels new. It's the first time I've told someone I was having sex with that I was positive. It was pretty scary. I'm glad you didn't do anything weird when I told you."

"I'm glad you told me," I said truthfully.

"Me too. What a world we live in." We lay there quietly for a moment, then Andrew sat up suddenly as if he had realized something important. "Want some coffee?"

"I need some," I replied, shifting my feet off the low-slung bed onto the floor.

"My housemates have gone out. We've got the run of the place."

"Do you want to do something today?" I asked, ever the organizer. "Want to take the Staten Island ferry, see the Caravaggio show or something?"

Andrew was ready to negotiate. "Maybe we can just rest for a while? Maybe make some pancakes?"

"Okay," I said.

We walked naked to his dark kitchen. The sounds of the neighbors above floated down the air shaft. He opened the fridge, and there, by the soft light of Amana, we drank some orange juice from the bottle.

(THE SOUND OF WAVES AT THE OCEAN SLOWLY WASHES OVER THE THEATER. OVER THE SOUND OF THE SEA, WE HEAR SOME DELICATE AND MORE-THAN-A-LITTLE MELANCHOLY MUSIC. THE LIGHTS PULL CLOSE AND BLUE AROUND TIM.)

Then we slept. The deep breath of sleep. Faces next to each other. Breath swapping. Atoms dancing around each other. And I dreamed. I dreamed I had built a bed. I'd found my tools and I'd built a fine bed that was floating on the sea. It's a seaworthy bed! And my friend and I were sailing towards a safe harbor. I dreamed of that bed on the sea. Of beautiful trees on the shore. Graceful gestures between humans. And good bread that had been baked for us to eat in the morning at our leisure.

What if we were looking at *this* scene from outer space? Oh. God. What a thing to see. It's a beautiful sight. We would see many men, many people floating on their beds at sea, dreaming *their* dreams. Reaching for the touch, the best part of ourselves.

We would see how those men had once been little boys who cried too much before Sunday school. Or dressed up too much in their mom's clothes. Or touched themselves too much under the covers at night. And needed other boys . . . just enough.

From outer space it would seem that Earth is a very strange planet 'cause people made war upon these boys. Priest and parents and politicians teased them and tortured them. So, these boys learned to run fast. Maybe too fast. Some of you are here tonight.

They learned how to find each other. On the street and in Laundromats. Construction sites and theaters. This is a very good story. It's a story we should tell again and again. It's that magic decoder ring given to us as our birthright, at the same time as we got our black leather jackets and superior sense of humor. We queer people made a place for ourselves. Cooked the meal. Made the bed. Waved that red shirt above our naked bodies. Dared to ask each other, "Do you wanna come in?"

For a while, things were pretty good. Well, okay, they weren't that good. But they were better than they'd been in seventh grade at Andrew Jackson Junior High in Fruitland, New Mexico. From outer space we would see that a great plague fell upon these beds at sea. And of these boys who had become men, fine men, many had fallen. And the ones who still breathed felt a cold place. It hurt so bad. A frozen tear. A tear inside. A wound that would numb us. Stops us. Cut us. Hurts us.

From outer space we would see that these brave people found many ways through this hard time. They found ways to keep dancing that dance. Holding each other. Caring for each other. Finding each other. In Laundromats. Construction sites. Theaters . . . and on the street.

We all have a street inside us. A place where some things happened. Some wounds opened. Others healed. Food was eaten. Losses mourned. I am a carpenter. And I will build a bed. I'll build a place inside myself to honor my friends, my journey, and the streets I've strolled. As I live and breathe. In. And out. In. And out.

(LIGHTS BEGIN VERY SLOW FADE TO BLACK.)

And with this breath I will draw us close.
Wrap you all around me.
Float on your SIGH . . .
As these lights . . .
slowly . . .
fade.

my left breast

SUSAN MILLER

Notes on *My Left Breast*

These words: ineffable, punctillio, febrile, importuning, quotidian, recondite, insouciance, élan, rue. I fall for them. I want to ink them on lined notebook paper. I could look at these words for hours. I live to find a place for them.

"Go look them up," my father said. And sent me to the dictionary.

The Muses

A Nelson Riddle arrangement
My son
The broken heart
Irony
Fred Astaire

And the possibilities. That disembodied voices talking to Ronnie, the central character in a rough draft of *Confessions of a Female Disorder,* will turn into a chorus of cheerleaders and lettermen. And later, when the character is grown, they, too will grow into disenchanted wives and cocktail party guests. That a speech Jake is trying to write in act 1 of *For Dear Life* will turn up in the hands of his son in act 3, long after the end of his parents' marriage. And this seventeen-year-old boy will read the speech to himself as a baby. Reassuring his young self that his parents meant only the best. The possibility that a woman in a coma can talk to the audience in *Nasty Rumors and Final Remarks*. That two women in *Flux* can live together as lovers without the text ever making reference to it.

The characters I'm drawn to yearn. They long for. I engage their dilemma.

I want to be impolite. Rugged. Terribly true. Sweeping in my observations. Inchoate. Daring. Sometimes it comes out narrow, personal, strained. Sometimes I want the happy ending when it is not the one that is called for.

I have faith in the sentence. I dance before I write, sometimes.

This play, *My Left Breast*. Is the first and only one I've written with a character named Susan. One morning—really this is how it went—one morning I had this sensation in my belly—a kind of knowing. What I knew was that I would write something to perform. I wanted to speak directly to an audience, to say what I had to say and rise or fall with it, myself. I

wanted to inhabit the story and eliminate the interloper. Be the character, navigate the world of it—the transitions, the language, the theatrical-
ity—with my own body. Find the voice of the play beyond the voice of
the text. It just seemed, at that juncture of my life, necessary.

I collect lined notebooks. The old kind. From school. I write with an
ink pen, a #2 extra soft pencil, and a computer. But, mostly, I walk the
streets of the city, drink coffee, and in so many ways stalk the thing I know
I have to do by seeming to avoid it.

Here's what else. I see a dance company—Twyla Tharp, Doug Varone,
maybe. And the physicality, the gesture, gives me something I can use. Or
Richard Ford's *Independence Day*. His deeply flawed character's deeply
observed world. Movingly told. Chekhov, Salinger. And the brilliance of
my contemporaries, struggling to achieve just one startling moment.

My son, Jeremy, at seven years old, sits next to me during a rehearsal
of my play *Nasty Rumors and Final Remarks* at the Public Theatre. On a
break, we go to the lobby for a snack. After a moment, he looks up from
his sandwich. "Mommy, are plays more important than food?" Oh. Oh.
Plays *are* food, I tell him.

My Left Breast: Technical Requirements
My Left Breast runs an hour and five minutes and is performed
without an intermission.
Set
Small desk (downstage right)
Desk chair
Comfortable armchair, covered with funky blanket (downstage left)
Small two- or three-step bleacher or step unit (upstage center, at an angle)
Portion of chain-link fence (which goes behind bleachers)

Props
Pen, two small books, coffee mug on desk
Breast prosthesis
Baseball hat tucked in chair

Opening music
"I Will Survive"—Gloria Gaynor

My Left Breast was directed by Nela Wagman.

About Susan Miller

Susan Miller received her second Obie award in playwriting, as well as *The Susan Smith Blackburn Prize for Best Play by a Woman in the English Speaking Language*, for My Left Breast, *which premiered in The Actors' Theatre of Louisville's 1994 Humana Festival and appears in* Best American Short Plays of 1993–94, *as well as* Plays from the Humana Festival. *Miller has performed the play at Trinity Repertory Company in Rhode Island; The Walnut Street Theatre in Philadelphia; The Group Theatre in Seattle; Watermark's Wordfire Festival in New York; Frontera/Hyde Park Theatre in Austin, Texas; Buddies in Bad Times in Toronto; The Celebration Theatre in Los Angeles; and as a benefit for Gilda's Club.*

She won her first Obie for Nasty Rumors and Final Remarks, *which was produced by Joseph Papp and the New York Shakespeare Festival, as were* For Dear Life *and* Flux. *Her plays,* Cross Country *and* Confessions of a Female Disorder, *were staged by the Mark Taper Forum in Los Angeles, where she also held a Rockefeller Grant. Miller's other plays include* Arts and Leisure *and* It's Our Town, Too, *which was chosen for Applause Books'* The Best American Short Plays of 1992–93 *and published in Penguin's* Actors' Book of Gay and Lesbian Plays. *Her work has also been produced by Second Stage, Naked Angels, the Cast Theatre, and the Eugene O'Neill Playwrights Conference, among others. She has also received two NEA grants in playwriting.*

In 1996, she received the Publishing Triangle's Robert Chessley Lifetime Achievement Award in playwriting.

Her most recent film work includes the original feature screenplays Blessing in Disguise *for Warner Brothers and Spring Creek Productions,* The History of Us *and* Becoming the Smiths. *She has also written for ABC's* thirtysomething, *CBS's* Trials of Rosie O'Neill, *NBC's* LA Law, *and Fox's* Urban Anxiety *(head writer/producer).*

Miller serves as director of the Legacy Project, a writing workshop for people with life-threatening illness, which was held for three years at the Public Theater under a grant from the Reader's Digest/Lila Wallace Fund.

She is a member of the Dramatists Guild.

my left breast

SUSAN MILLER

LIGHTS UP:

(I COME OUT DANCING. AS IF I'M ALONE IN MY HOUSE. A TAP
AND KICK TO THE ARMCHAIR, A TWIRL, A EUPHORIC TURN.
THEN, AFTER A FEW BARS, I TURN TO FACE THE AUDIENCE:)

The night before I went to the hospital, that's what I did. I
danced.

(CUPPING MY BREASTS.)

One of these is not real. Can you tell which?

I was fourteen the first time a boy touched my breast. My left
breast, in fact. I felt so guilty with pleasure, I could hardly face my
parents that night. It was exquisite. Well, you remember.

I always wonder in the movies when the female star has to
appear topless in a love scene and the male star is caressing her
nipples, how the actress is supposed to remain professional. See, I
don't think this would be expected of a man whose penis was being
fondled.

* * *

Anyhow, breast cancer.

The year it happened my son was eight. He looked at my chest, the day I told him. We had these matching Pep Boys T-shirts. You know—Manny, Mo, and Jack.

He looked at my chest and said, "Which one was it? Manny or Jack?"

"Jack," I tell him.

"What did they do with it?"

"I don't know."

He starts to cry. "Well, I'm going to get it back for you!"

Now he is twenty and I am still his mother. I'm still here. We're still arguing. He is twenty and I wear his oversize boxer shorts with a belt and he borrows my jackets and we wear white T-shirts and torn jeans and he says, "Why don't you get a tattoo."

"A tattoo?"

"Over your scar. It'd be cool."

Here's what I wear sometimes under my clothes.

(PICK UP BREAST PROSTHESIS FROM DESK AND SHOW TO AUDIENCE.)

Oh, don't worry. It's a spare.

When you go for a fitting, you can hear the women in the other booths. Some of them have lost their hair and shop for wigs. Some are very young and their mothers are thinking, Why didn't this happen to me, instead? (PUT PROSTHESIS IN DESK DRAWER.)And there's the feeling you had when you got your first bra and the sales-woman cupped you to fit. Cupped you and yanked at the straps. Fastened you into the rest of your life.

* * *

I miss it, but it's not a hand. I miss it, but it's not my mind. I miss it, but it's not the roof over my head. I miss it, but it's not a word I need. It's not a sentence I can't live without. I miss it, but it's not a conversation with my son. It's not my courage or my lack of faith.

I miss it—but it's not *her*.

Skinnied on the left side like a girl, I summon my breast and you there where it was with your mouth sucking a phantom flutter from my viny scar.

We met at an artists' colony. One night at charades (that's what people do there), when an outstanding short-story writer was on all fours, being a horse, I sat on the floor and leaned against the sofa. I rubbed my back against what I thought was the hard edge of it. And realized after a minute that I was rubbing against Franny's knee.

"God, I'm sorry."

"Don't be."

"I thought you were the couch."

"It's the nicest thing that's happened to me all day," she said.

In town, one afternoon, we run into each other in the bookstore. It might as well be a hotel room. We might as well be pulling the bedspread off in a fever. We are in a heap. We are thinking the things you think when you are going to run away together. It's only a matter of time.

"You don't finish your sentences," she said.

"I've been told."

"I'm starting to get the drift, however. I know where you're headed."

I was headed toward tumult, headed toward breakage, headed toward her.

                              * * *

It's been a year since she left me, and how do I tell someone new? Even though it will probably be a woman. See, a woman might be threatened. A woman might see her own odds. She might not want the reminder.

I threw on my ripped jeans and a pair of—I pulled on my black tights under a short black skirt—I threw on a white T-shirt and an oversized Armani jacket—my hair was, well, this was not a bad hair day.

"I guess it's a date, " I said to my therapist. "Two single gay women who don't know each other except through a mutual friend. I guess you'd call it a date."

"Do you realize you called yourself a gay woman? I've never heard you refer to yourself that way before."

"Well, it just doesn't seem to matter anymore. What I'm called."

"You mean, since Franny left. Interesting."

"You sound like a shrink."

"Why do you think it doesn't matter anymore?" she says.

Because, I want to say, when you're a hurt and leaky thing, all definitions are off. What you were, who you told everyone you might be, had a sheen, the spit of artifice. There was always something covert. But now, you've come apart. Like an accident victim in shock, you don't see who sees you and you don't care how you are seen. You are a creature, simply. You move or stop or lurch from side to side as you are able. You make a sound without will. Your former self, the husk of you, hovering near, looks on, startled and concerned. But you are not. You are shorn of image. You are waiting to eat again and to speak in a language with meaning. You are not gay. You are not a woman. You are not. And by this, you are everything your former self defended against, apologized for, explained away, took pride in. You are all of it. None of it. You want only to breathe in and out. And know what your limbs will do. You are at the beginning.

* * *

Hey, want to meet for a cappuccino at Cafe Franny? Gotta run, I'm off to the latest Franny film. Meet you at the corner of Eighty-third and Franny? How about Concerto in Franny at Carnegie Franny? Was anything ever called by any other name?

Oh, you play the piano? Franny plays the piano. You say words in English. Well, see, so did Franny. Uh-huh, uh-huh, you have hair. That's interesting, because, you know, she also had hair.

Maybe I'm paying for the moment when I looked at her and thought, I don't know if I love her anymore. Maybe she saw me look at her this way and believed what she saw, even though it was no more true than the first day when you looked at someone and thought, She's the one. Thought, I'm saved.

But, nothing can save you. Not your friends, not the best Fred Astaire musical you've ever seen—the grace of it, not your mother's beauty or a line from a letter you find at the bottom of a drawer, not a magazine or the next day. Nothing can save you. And you stand in the moonlight and a sweetness comes off the top of the trees, and the fence around the yard seals you off from the dark and you can't breathe. It is all so familiar and possible. It is too simple that there is this much good and you don't know how to have it. And it makes you wonder when it was you lost your place. Then you catch a breeze, so warm and ripe, it makes you hope that someone will come who also cannot save you, but who thinks you are worth saving.

A man I know said to me, "Lesbians are the chosen people these days. No AIDS."

I said, "Lesbians are women. Women get AIDS. Women get ovarian cancer. Women get breast cancer. Women die. In great numbers. In the silent epidemic."

He said, "I see what you mean."

The surgeon in Los Angeles said it was a fibroadenoma. "Someday you might want to have it removed," he said. "But no rush. It's benign."

I watched it grow.

Then in New York, I saw another surgeon. He said, "What have you been told?"

"Fibroadenoma," I say.

"Well, I'm concerned," he said. "I want to biopsy it."

You know how when everything is going right, you figure it's only a matter of time until that bus swerves onto the sidewalk, or you finally make it to the post office to buy stamps and that's the day a crazed postal worker fires his Uzi into the crowd.

Everything was going right for me. I had just won an Obie for a play at the Public Theatre. I had a contract for my first novel— I was in the beginning chapters. And a new relationship.

It was Jane who found the lump. The gynecologist said it was a gland. When it didn't go away, she sent me to the surgeon who said it was something it wasn't.

All of this happened at the beginning of a new decade. When we would all lose our innocence. It was 1980. In New York. I heard the Fourth of July fireworks from my hospital bed. I was thirty-six. I was too young. People were celebrating. And they were too young for the plague that was coming.

There were two positive nodes. I went through eleven months of chemotherapy, and I had only one more month to go. But at my next to the last treatment, after they removed the IV, the oncologist and his nurse looked at me with what I distinctly recognized as menace. I thought, They're trying to kill me. If I come back again, they'll kill me. I never went back.

There are those who insist that certain types of people get cancer. So I wonder, Are there certain types of people who get raped and tortured? Are there certain types who die young? Are there certain types of Bosnians, Somalians, Jews? Are there certain types of gay men? Are there certain types of children who are abused and caught in the crossfire? Is there a type of African American who is denied, excluded, lynched? Were the victims of the Killing Fields people who just couldn't express themselves?

And are one out of eight women—count 'em, folks—just holding on to their goddamned anger?

This is my body—where the past and the future collide. This is my body. All at once, timely. All at once, chic. My deviations. My battle scars. My idiosyncratic response to the physical realm. The past deprivations and the future howl.

I am a one-breasted, menopausal, Jewish, bisexual lesbian mom, and I am the topic of our times. I am the hot issue. I am the cover of *Newsweek*, the editorial in the paper. I am a best-seller. And I am coming soon to a theater near you. I am a one-breasted, menopausal, Jewish, bisexual lesbian mom, and I'm *in*.

My son is having symptoms. His stomach hurts. He thinks he feels a tumor in his neck. He injures his toes in a game of basket-ball and suspects gangrene. He says, "My organs are failing." He stands in front of the refrigerator, opening and closing the door.

"Can I make you some breakfast?"

I want to do something for him. I haven't done anything for him, it seems, in a while. I mean, like my mother would do for me. But he isn't hungry, it's just a reflex, this refrigerator door thing. Some small comfort.

He walks into the living room and throws his leg over the arm of our formerly white chair. Sitting across from me, disheveled, morning dazed, he says accusingly, "I think I'm dying."

"You're not dying."

"Maybe it won't happen right away. But I'm dying."

"Honey, you're talking yourself into it. Why are you so wor-ried about everything?"

"What if I have AIDS?"

That's something I didn't have to think about when I was twenty.

"Everybody's going to die. You'll see. All my friends. It's going to happen."

"Talk to me."

He's a dark thing. His eyes match my own. He'll see a child, overweight, wearing glasses, maybe—he'll notice a child like this somewhere, trying to make his way against the odds and it will seem to Jeremy heroic. "Stud," he says. And means it.

"Maybe I have spinal meningitis."

I try not to laugh.

"I'm serious."

"I'm sorry."

Things are breaking down.

He is twirling a strand of hair around his finger. We're in the Brandeis parking area, waiting to take our children to their dorms. It's an oppressive August day. Everyone has gotten out of his car, but Jeremy won't move. He's in the backseat, regretting his decision. There are no pretty girls. The guys are losers. This was a big mistake.

Suddenly I'm in another August day. I've just put my eight-year-old on a bus to day camp. He looks out at me from the window. A pale reed, he is twirling a strand of hair around his finger. I watch him do this until the bus pulls away. What have I done? I go home and fall onto my bed. I lie there and mourn all the lost Jeremys. My three-year-old, my infant boy. I lie on my bed and have grim notions. What if something happened to me and he came home from camp and I wasn't there to pick him up? What if I had an accident? Who would take care of him? What happens to the child of a single parent who is kidnapped by a madman?

Then I imagine him lost. I see him twirling his hair, as it grows dark in some abandoned warehouse. He walks the streets of a strange neighborhood. I know that he is crying in the woods. He has gotten himself into an old refrigerator. He falls into a well. He is in the danger zone. He has wandered too far from me. I have cancer, and what if I never see him grown? "I'll go and get it back for you, Mom."

By the time I have to pick him up from camp, I'm frantic. Somehow we survived. Until now.

We get to his dorm and unload. His room is in the basement. It is moldy, and I feel homesick. This isn't right. Parents move toward their cars dazed and fighting every urge to run back and save their young from this new danger—independence. When I get home, the sound of Jeremy not in his room is deafening.

THE PHONE CALLS

"Mom. I'm all right. Don't get upset. Just listen, okay? I got arrested last night."

"Mom, I'm all right. Don't get upset. Just listen, okay? I'm in the infirmary. The doctor says it's pneumonia."

"Mom, I'm all right. Don't set upset. I was playing rugby and I broke my nose." (That beautiful nose!)

"Mom." He calls from Los Angeles, where he is visiting his girlfriend, on the day there is an earthquake that measures 6.6. "Mom, I'm all right, but I think L.A. is gone."

He transfers to NYU and calls to tell me a car has driven into a crowd of people in Washington Square Park, but he's all right. He calls to say that the boy who was his catcher on the high school baseball team has jumped from a building. "I was walking down his street, Mom. I saw the ambulance. I saw his feet coming out from under a blanket. I can't stop seeing his feet."

Once after Franny and I had a fight, Jeremy and I were out to dinner. He was thirteen. I must've looked particularly hopeless. Maybe it was my inattention. Whatever shadowed my face, it was enough for him to say, "Are you going to die?" Did he worry himself orphaned every day since I had cancer?

"No, honey, no," I say, shocked into responsibility. "I'm sorry. Franny and I just had a fight. It's nothing. I'm fine. I'm not going to die."

"You looked so sad," he said.

I want to report myself to the nearest authorities. Take me now. I'm busted.

He was two and a half days old the day he came to us. My parents drove my husband and me to the lawyer's office. We handed over a sweater and cap we had brought with us and a blanket my sister made. And we waited. We waited for every known thing to change. Jeremy says he remembers the ride back. The

Pennsylvania mountains. And how it was to be held in my arms. How it was to be carried home.

A woman is ironing her son's shirt. The palm tree shivers outside the window. Gardenia wafts through. Although she can't smell it. It's four A.M. She has laid out his button-down oxford cloth shirt on the ironing board along with two lines of cocaine. She does them. After his sleeves. Mothers have no business doing cocaine. Mothers have no business being tired all the time and sick from chemotherapy.

The surgeon said, "Don't join a cancer support group. It'll only depress you."

The drug of choice for most people undergoing chemo is marijuana. It's supposed to help the nausea. But, marijuana didn't work for me. I wanted something to keep me awake, to keep me going. Something I associated with good times, former times, something that assured me there was time.

Sleep, rest, these things were too close to the end of it all. I couldn't give in. If I stopped, the whole thing might stop.

The woman ironing her son's shirt was testing everyone. Who would stay after she'd pushed them away?

There were powerful drugs in her body. But the one she took through the nose kept her from knowing what she knew. Kept her from the ache of caring. In her dreams she could smell the truth. Cocaine—sharp, thrilling. The cancer drugs, acrid and sere. Terrifying. They were Proust's asparagus in her urine. A toxic taste in her mouth.

She had control over cocaine. She administered this to herself. In a breath. There were no needles, no invasion. It was a ritual of pleasure and retreat. And it blotted out the anxiety of the waiting room.

Finally, it destroyed what was healthy and cured nothing at all.

The woman ironing her son's shirt felt ashamed. She was not the cancer heroine she'd hoped to be.

Some people would say, This woman is doing the best she can. And that's all anyone can do. But, I think that's just another moral loophole. She can do better. She will do better.

Morning broke. Her son came running down the hall. Her lover called to sing her show tunes.

I might lose them, the woman thought. But not while I can still have them. She vowed to stop: "This will be my last time." And it was. Her son was very pleased with his shirt.

I didn't lose my hair, I lost my period. See, chemo knocks out your estrogen, which knocks out your period, which puts you, ready or not, into menopause. So, at thirty-seven I was having hot flashes and panic in the left-hand-turn lane.

It's like this. I'm driving and I'm in the left-hand lane and the light turns red before I can make the turn. This isn't good. This for me is a life-threatening situation. My heart races. My hands and feet tingle. I hyperventilate. I'm a lot of laughs.

Sometimes this happens if I walk too far from my house.

Now, there are a lot of women out there who, even as we speak, are flinging open windows, ripping off their clothes, and turning to say to a dining companion, a spouse, and even total strangers, "Is it hot in here or is it me?"

Well, most of these women can win back the love of friends and family by taking estrogen. But you can't take estrogen in most cases of breast cancer. So years later, when the hot flashes are over and I can finally manage to sit in the left-hand-turn lane without calling the paramedics, I'm visiting my parents and I take a swing at a golf ball. Oh, don't misinterpret. This is my parents' golf course. Their idea. But it's a beautiful day. And I tee off quite nicely. I'm feeling proud of myself, so I take my second swing and I get this sudden, searing pain accompanied by a kind of pop in my side. I've fractured a rib. A year later. Same swing. Same thing.

Then, another time, I reach out my side of the car to remove a twig from the windshield. Pop. My friend Brock runs up behind me, lifts me into the air with his arms around my chest. Pop. I sit the wrong way on a theater seat. I bend and reach awkwardly for something I've dropped. My trainer pushes my knees into my chest. Pop. Pop. Pop.

The bone scan is negative, but the bone densitometry shows a significant demineralization—or bone loss. Is the structure of everything dissolving? I can't count on whatever it was that held me up, supported my notions, my exertions. Osteoporosis. It's hard to say the word. It's an old person's disease. It's the antifeminine. It's the crone.

I go to see the doctor in gerontology. The waiting room is full of old people. Naturally. They've come with their husbands. Or their grandchildren. With each other.

A few days after coming home from the hospital, after my mastectomy, I go to the movies in the middle of the afternoon.

I notice two older women arm in arm, walking to their seats. And I know what I want. I want to get old and walk arm in arm with my old friend to a movie in the middle of the afternoon.

What movies are you seeing, Franny? Do you still walk out in the middle? On the street, do you take someone's arm? Will you grow old with her?

The gerontologist consults with my internist, who consults with my oncologist, who probably consults with somebody else. The rib fractures seem consistent with chemotherapy and the resulting loss of estrogen. But she'd like to run a few more blood tests. I especially love the one they call a tumor marker. And why are these things always given on a Friday? Have a nice weekend.

Excuse me, I need to scream now.

(SCREAMS.)

That was good. But what I really want to do is break a chair.

I have destroyed so much property—in my mind. In my mind, I have smashed so many plates against the wall, ripped so many books from cover to cover. In my mind, I have trashed apartments, taken all the guilty parties to court. Done damage for damage done. But I'm the accommodating patient. I move on. Get over it. Exercise restraint. I am appropriate.

Except for the day the doorman ate my pizza.

I was coming home from chemotherapy. With a pizza. Jane was trying to get me to eat right. Well, trying to get me to eat. So we had this pizza, and then I got an urge for LiLac Chocolate, which was right down the block from where we lived. I gave the doorman my pizza and asked him to hold it for a couple minutes. When I got back with my chocolate I asked him for my pizza. And he said, "I ate it."

You ate it? You fucking ate my pizza? You fucking murdered my child, you fucking destroyed my career, you fucking robbed me of my youth, you fucking betrayed me, you fucking know that? You fucking fucking idiot!

He offered to pay me for the pizza.

I walk home from Mt. Sinai, after the gerontologist, down Madison across the park. Trembling. The possibility that there is something else, something more—

I walk around the reservoir. And I see a doorknob from my old house hanging on the fence.

Then a remnant of a child's blanket worn down to a sad shred. My wedding band. And messages no one has picked up. "Come home. All is forgiven." Gifts that came too late. The opal ring I gave Franny at Christmas. A page torn from Chekhov.

There's a black-and-white photograph. It's a group of friends. When everything was fine. Before the bad news. I walk farther, and I see people testifying. Telling their stories. Here at the wailing wall. And then I see my pink suitcase.

I have this pink suitcase. I don't know how I ended up with it, really. It belonged to my sister. I was given the powder blue set for high school graduation. And she got the pink. Well, anyway, it's mine now.

My agent said, "I'm sorry. There's nothing more I can do. Maybe if you spoke to the publisher yourself." I had gotten a year's extension on my novel. It was up now. I called the publisher. I said, "Look, I just need a little more time. I've had this thing happen to me and—"

"I know," she said. "That's unfortunate."

"I've been writing, though. I have about a hundred pages."

"I'm sure it's a wonderful book," she said, "although I haven't read any of it, but we just can't give you any more time."

She asked for the return of my advance. The Authors League gave me half the money. I paid the rest, put my novel in the pink suitcase, and turned the lock.

It is all that is incomplete in me. The waste. My fraud.

While I'm waiting for the results of this tumor marker, I go with an old college chum to a gay bar. We had gone to the Expo in Montreal together with our young husbands. We deposited our children at the same camp. She's divorced and seeing a woman now.

The first time it ever occurred to me that I might make love with a woman, I was in bed with my husband and I thought, I wonder what it feels like making love to me.

I don't understand the concept of this place. Everyone is cruising, but no one makes a move. All around me women are whispering, "Go on . . . talk to her. Now's your chance." It ripples through the narrow, smoky room. "Go on. Talk to her. Now's your chance."

Two women kiss nearby. I halt. I cave. To see this.

The gay bar in Paris, it was Franny's first. The women were fresh and attractive, and we danced to a French hit. The lyrics, translated, meant the death of love, but we were far from dying. We were expressing ourselves in Paris.

A slave to love when she spoke French. A goner to her version of the Frenchman in America. The accent, the pout, the hands—she had them down. I was seduced. Sometimes after a rough patch, I'd say, All you have to do is speak in French and I'm yours. In the middle of a fight, switch to it, take me.

I had four years of college French, but I could say only, "Have you any stamps?" and order grapefruit juice. "Vous avez jus de pamplemousse?"

She required me to say pamplemousse back in the United States, in our bed.

When will a French family struggling with directions on the subway fail to remind me?

* * *

We are mothers. We know the same thing. And sometimes it is too much to know. It drew me to her, and it is the thing that would come between us.

She's a mother. I trusted she would take better care of things. A mother is a safe bet. A mother would never leave her children for someone else's children. A mother shows up. Stays put. She installs a light in the hall. Franny's a mother, I thought. She won't harm me.

It keeps coming back. What she said. The way she looked saying it. "We're not in the same place." WHAT DO YOU MEAN? "I don't think we'll ever live together." WAIT. DON'T. PLEASE. WAIT. "This is so hard," she says. OH, MY GOD. HAVE YOU MET SOMEONE?

I can be standing in line for bagels. I can be punching in my secret code at the bank machine. It returns to me. A howl goes up.

"Well, Susan, you look fabulous."
"I'm a wreck."
"You'll see. People find that very attractive."

Every room. Every way the light fell. Every room we walked. Every way we combined there. Every room you moved into and out of. Every absence. Every room of our inclining. Every tender routine. Every room and way I learned you. Clings.

Just two and a half months before Jeremy was born, my first baby died, and the doctor injected me with something so the milk in my breasts would dry up. My breasts became engorged. Hard and full to bursting. It's painful, this swelling of something that wants to come.

When I was pregnant, I took something called Provera. Later it was shown to cause birth defects. So, when I got breast cancer I wondered, Was it the time someone sprayed my apartment for roaches? Or too much fat in my diet? Was it the deodorant with aluminum, or my birth control pills? Was it the high-wire lines? Or was it genetic?

"Here are your choices," the bone specialist in L.A. said. "Pick one. A shot every day of Calcitonin, which costs a fortune. I wouldn't do it. Etidronate, which can cause softening of the bones. Or Tamoxifan, an anti-estrogen that acts like an estrogen."

I really hate this arrogant, out-of-touch son-of-a-bitch specialist, you know? But my internist concurs, and him I love. So I take the Tamoxifan.

Side effects: Increase in blood clots, endometrial cancer, liver changes.

Something interesting happens, though. My ovaries ache. I'm . . . well, how do I say this . . . the juices are flowing. But I'm in L.A. working on a television show, and Franny's in New York. When I come home for good at Christmas, she tells me it's over. And I'm left to stew in my own juices.

I didn't call her the day I had a cold. I didn't call her on Friday because I wanted to talk to her so badly my throat closed up. I didn't call her the day before that around fifteen times because I was trying to make it until Friday. I didn't call her one day because I was at the bookstore, waiting and hoping. I didn't call her on Wednesday because it would have been a failure, so I swallowed the history of it down. I didn't call just now to save my life, because the instrument of rescue was already in my hands.

I go back to Mt. Sinai to see the gerontologist. All my tests are normal. "There's really not much you can do about this bone thing. Except, increase the calcium in your diet. Maintain a consistent exercise program. Especially weight lifting."

Well, hey, I belong to a health club. With TV sets. And I was starting to see some nice rips in my shoulders. But then, over a period of five months, I had three separate rib fractures. They take four to six weeks to heal, so how do I maintain a consistent exercise program?

The doctor is a gracious woman. She sees my frustration. And frankly is tired of hearing me whine. "All right, I know this sounds like I'm waffling, but I think I want to put you on Etidronate."

I don't think the names of these drugs are very friendly, do you?

"We'll follow you closely for a year," she says, and gives me a prescription.

I haven't filled it yet.

When my baby died, I felt I had no right to talk about childbirth or being pregnant. I had a baby. I was pregnant. I had morning sickness. I bought clothes and furniture. I had a son. He lived three hours. He was born to me. I finally understood what women were. And I wanted to talk about this, but it made people uncomfortable. In some ways losing Franny is like that.

I want to remember a Scrabble game where we made up words and meanings and laughed until we were in pain. I want to express my affection for her Miró bag, which held my glasses, a half stick of gum. I want to tell about the vegetable stand at the side of the road where we left our money in a bucket and the invisible proprietor trusted us to love his tomatoes and his sweet corn and his zucchini and we did.

I want to talk about these things, but I feel I don't have the right to tell the love story because it ended badly.

Okay, I'm in her kitchen and I grab wild for a knife and plunge it into my belly. She can't believe it. She says, "But I had to cut your bagels for you." I say, "Well that stopped, didn't it?" And I die. Better, I huddle against a wall outside of her apartment. All night long. In the morning when she leaves for work, she sees me there. Cold. Unattended. The drift that I am. Her detritus. She drops her books and bends to me. "Susan? Susan?" Who, I strain, is that? And the call. The call to say, oh, this is from my friends, they call her. "Susan's dead." And they hang up.

My friends, these women with wild hair and good eyes, these women friends who engage my light and do not refuse me, dark as I am these days. These friends make room for disturbance. They have the wit to see it coming. This is who they are, these people

who school themselves and event the city and construe fresh arguments and listen to the heart beat its woe. These friends are my
history. What they know about me is in the record. Errors. Shifts.
Defeats. Occasions of grace. They were there when I looked up
from my hospital bed. They were there when I looked up after
Franny left and couldn't see a thing. And these people, my friends,
are taking out an ad. In the personals. "She's adorable. She's smart.
And would you please take her off our hands? We can't stand it
anymore!"

Maybe we're only given a certain amount of time with anyone. Or we can have the whole time if we remember on the days
it is not going well, that these are not the days to measure by. The
moment we marry is often so minor, so quotidian, that later we
forget we've taken vows. When Franny walked to her study to
write, I took my vows. When she asked me before sleep if I wanted
some magic cream on my cuticles and rubbed it into my fingers, I
took vows. When I weeded her mother's garden, cleaned under
her son's bed.
Is it there in the beginning? The thing that finishes us?

Out in the country with my friends, I wake in the morning to
the sound of a wasp in its death throes. A screen door shuts and
the dog's paws sound like a hot drummer's brush across the floor.
I walk outside to the buzz and the click and the hum. Suddenly, I
feel bereft.
My favorite book in the Golden Book series was *The Happy
Family*. Imagine. Well, here's the picture. Beautiful clean-cut boy
and girl. Mother and father. Crates arrive. Brand-new bikes. They
all go on a picnic. It was my touchstone.

He was dark and thin. She was dark and beautiful and not as
thin. He, my father, introduced himself to her as Frank Lamonica.
And she was Judy Grey, a singer with her own show on the radio.
"I'll never smile again, until I smile at you." He said, "We're going
to come back here next year, married."

Isaac Figlin and Thelma Freifelder. My model for romance. There was a war. He went. She was a bride. They wrote letters. She sent him a lock of my hair.

Now she is seventy-four and he is eighty-three. My father says, "I've never been more in love with your mother than I am right now." On the night before my father has surgery to remove a kidney, my mother climbs up next to him in his hospital bed. We, my brother and sister and I, turn our heads. Were they really ours? Who might we have become without these two people who said yes one mad summer in the Poconos and taught us how to dance and spell and drive a car? Taught us what was good. They were good.

After I lost my baby, I was taken back to my room. And I saw my parents standing there, in the doorway, waiting for me.

So, I told them a funny story and made them laugh.

After my mastectomy, my father rubs my feet. My mother sings me a song. They do this for me, and I let them.

House. It's a concept that cries out deconstruct. There is the universal notion of house, and there is Susan's house. The house that longing built.

There was something important about Franny and me. I don't know. Maybe it was only that we tried. We have children, and we had to bring them up. We had to be their mothers. We would cry when we saw orphans arrive from Korea on television. But we had ours and they were still becoming and they had something to say about it. Now they are grown into that beauty of starting up.

The first time I went to Franny's house, I recognized the familiar aroma of boy's feet. Simon's sneakers were lurking under the coffee table. It reminded me of home.

Jody sang commercials and told me silly jokes. She is lovely, Franny's daughter. She is lovely and strong and difficult. She is Franny's daughter. Simon sits at the piano. "Hey, Susan, do you like this?" I do. I like what he plays. I like him. And so when I walk into the living room at the end, at Christmas, and see him,

I come apart. They were ten, twelve, and fourteen when we started out. Nearly eight years later, we'd lived through puberty and three sets of college applications.

"You bitch." "You're such a bitch." Our teenagers were not having a good day.

My son punches his fist through a wall. Her daughter stops eating. The oldest weeps his lost structure. How much of this has to do with us, I can't say, but we blame ourselves, each other, and sometimes who we are.

"I can't do this," Franny would say. "I don't know how to be a mother and a lover. Can't we just wait until the children are grown and find each other again?"

A family is the faces you see and know you will see whenever you look up. When Franny is on the phone and Simon is reading a book, when Jody's watching her soaps, and Jeremy is in the kitchen complaining there isn't anything to eat. When a person says, as casual as heartbreak, "Do you want a cup of coffee, honey?"

Here's what I did. I really did this. I rented a car and drove to the Howard Johnson's Motor Lodge outside of Woodstock. It was *our* place. We stayed there when we visited her parents. It seemed like every time we stayed at a cheap motel, there was child abuse going on in the next room. Perhaps it was only a haunting. Our own children tormenting us for the time we abandoned them at camp or wouldn't let them stay up late to watch some TV show or maybe they were just pissed off at us for having the bed to ourselves.

The motel is its orange self. Why do I weep? The air in the parking lot is hot and familiar. Somewhere close. Somewhere in the trees, around the bend, over the hill, she is. I can't breathe. It was in one of these room she asked me to make love to her. Her father had just died. And she needed this from me. I knew how to marry love with death. I knew if you kissed someone who needed you to live, you would live.

The day after I came home from the hospital, still bandaged, half-crazy from residual drugs and fear, Jane and I made love. I

didn't care if my stitches came free. Let them rip. I shouldn't have
been able to move in the ways I moved to her, but I was powerful.
The possibility of death nearly broke our bed. In a few days I would
start chemo, but that night I was not in possession of the facts. I
was a body in disrepair, and someone was healing me.

I wanted to heal Franny. I wanted to swoop her up, take her
in my jaws, protect this love. She kissed me with her teeth. I swallowed her loss down whole. Everything was streaked with us. "My
love." "Don't stop." "Darling." I placed myself at the source. So
lovely. So known to me. Then she took me in her mouth. I shiv-
ered. We jammed our stuff against the bed. And for a while at the
Howard Johnson's outside of Woodstock, we kept chaos at bay.

I went to the town square. I didn't know where to walk, exactly, or where to set my sights.

I wondered if people could see me, or was I invisible because
I didn't belong anymore? And if Franny actually came to town on
this day, would she walk right past me? Turning a few feet away to
look back as if there were something, a sensation she couldn't
name, my scent more powerful than my substance, wafting through
to catch her up short. I steadied myself against a store window and
wished for a prop.

There she was. On the other side of the street, her hands in
her pockets, singing Rodgers and Hart. Or thinking about semiotics.
Going on about her life.

Just as I needed to go on about my own.

Good-bye, Franny. Good-bye, my friend. Good-bye, my left
breast. Good-bye, my infant son. Good-bye, my period. Good-bye,
thirty-five. Good-bye, old neighborhood.

Your doctor says, "It's positive." Your lover says, "It's over."
And you say good-bye to the person you thought you were.

I'm going to show you my scar. In a minute.

When you have a brush with death, you think, If I pull through
this, I'm going to do it all differently. I'm going to say exactly what
I think. I'll be a kind and generous citizen. I won't be impatient

with my son. I won't shut down to my lover. I'll learn to play the trumpet. I'll never waste another minute.

Then you don't die. And it's, God, I hate my hair! Would you please pick up your clothes! How long do we have to stand in this fucking line?

One day I'm sitting in a café and a man with ordinary difficulties is complaining. Our water heater is on the fritz. Just like that he says it. *Our* something isn't working, and *we* are worrying about it.

I want to say, Cherish the day your car broke down, the water pump soured, the new bed didn't arrive on time. Celebrate the time you got lost and maps failed. On your knees to this domestic snafu, you blessed pair, while you can still feel the other's skin in the night, her foot caressing your calf, preoccupations catching on the damp sheets. You twist, haul an arm over. While remote kisses motor your dreams.

The people who made love to me, afterwards: There have been three. Jane, of course, who slept with me in the hospital, pretending to be my sister. David. And Franny. It's the way David said, "It's wildly sexy, this body of yours that has given birth and given up a part." It's the way Franny loved me more for my lack of it, this symmetry that other women have.

How do I tell someone new?

Okay, help me out here. Say I've finally met someone I like. Do I tell her over the salad? Wait until dessert? Do I tell her when we're getting undressed? Does it matter? Would it matter to you?

I miss it, but there is something growing in its place. And it is not a tougher skin. The doctor says my heart is more exposed now. Closer to the air. You don't have any protective tissue, she says. I hardly need a stethoscope to hear it beat.

I cherish this scar. It's a mark of experience. It's the history of me, a permanent fix on the impermanence of it all. A line that suggests I take it seriously. Which I do. A line that suggests my beginning and my end. I have no other like it. I have no visible reminder of the baby I lost. Or the friend. No constant monument to the passing of my relationship. There is no other sign on my body that repeats the incongruity and dislocation, the alarm. A scar is a challenge to see ourselves as survivors, after all. Here is the evidence. The body repairs. And the human heart, even after it has broken into a million pieces, will make itself large again.

My son did get it back for me. In a way. Not the year it happened. But the year after that and the year and the year and the year after that.

It was Little League that saved me. It was Jeremy up to the plate. It was Gabriel Macht at second. It was Chris Chandler catching a pop fly. It was Jeremy stealing home. It was providing refreshments and washing his uniform. It was trying to get him to wear a jock strap. It was screaming, "Batter! Batter! Batter!" It was Jeremy pitching the last out with the bases loaded. It was the moms. The moms and dads and the coolers. It was the hats we wore and the blankets. It was driving him home from practice. It was his bloody knees. It was the sun going down on us, watching our sons and daughters play and be well.

This was the cure for cancer.

I miss it, but I want to tell all the women in the changing booths that we are still beautiful, we are still powerful, we are still sexy, we are still here.

(I UNBUTTON MY SHIRT TO REVEAL MY SCAR AS THE LIGHTS FADE.)

skin & ornaments

CRAIG HICKMAN

Notes on *skin & ornaments*

skin & ornaments, cover & artifice, cocoa & gold, cells & bangles . . .

I do that quite often, actually. Play the game of word association with titles, ideas, lines of poetry. It keeps me connected to the language of the experience, the feeling, the fleeting thought. So much of what ends up in my performative writing comes to me in flashes. So much more of what ends up in my performative writing comes to me in full waves, crashing over my body like surf. I feel like I'm drowning. The only way out, the only way to fight the waves, is to move up from under them, twisting and contorting, grasping and reaching. With each movement, a new idea, with each new idea, another phrase . . . or word. And I'm back, again playing word association games, and before I know it, *boom!,* a verse appears, a character emerges, a story unfolds.

Where does this all come from? The Universe. My experience. Someone else's experience. I do not believe that the imagination is as limited as it may seem to those who believe it can only rearrange bits and pieces from one's *own* experience and spit that out as something resembling novelty. I believe artists—*all* artists, but especially we performative artists—are rearranging bits and pieces of not only our own experience, but those experiences that come through us from the richness of a vast Universe. Through some almost inexplicable properties of theoretical physics, my body, my imagination, my performance, *can* know something that is unknowable. Unknowable to me in this realm, but not to the wavelengths in the all-knowing Universe. My own wavelengths vibrate with those "unknown" wavelengths until my wavelengths get familiar with them. Maybe they have coffee, maybe they fuck. Whatever they do they *do* get familiar. From this, I have something—so much more—to offer the reader, the seer, another revelator.

When I started writing *skin & ornaments*, I did not know this. I thought that the most I *might* accomplish was the bold, daring act of telling my story. Putting a voice to my experience. Letting those who would come to see/hear/feel me know what it's been like for this particular black queer artist. I was encouraged to do this, you see. By Brian Freeman, Thomas

Grimes, Essex Hemphill, Djola Branner, Eric Gupton, Patricia Smith, Lamont Steptoe, Jeff Armstead, Vance Deare, and so many more mentors and friends, whose names I sometimes forget, but never their spirits, many of whom are now ancestral.

So I did what I was encouraged to do.

And out came *Strange Fruit,* named after the title of the song included in the piece. And *Strange Fruit* became *school boys & brothers & juneau park & private storms.* Still, there was something missing. But before it became those pieces with that something still missing, it was just *Strange Fruit.* And clinging to the peel of the fruit was *masks.* And they were both included in the original choreodrama *Through the Fire* by Brothers du Jour. Brothers du Jour. Another title that rolled off my lips during a game of foreplay, I mean, uh . . . wordplay. Thomas Grimes, the late Jeff Armstead, and me (or is it I?): Brothers du Jour. We took Boston through the fire in June of 1992, and again in April of 1993. In between that, we burnt up New York and Louisville. In May of 1994 AIDS burned out Jeff, and Brothers du Jour became legendary, if I may use that word in this context. But Thomas said, "Craig, between *Strange Fruit* and *masks,* you've got yourself a one-man show!"

I did not know this, you see, but the Universe did.

And the Universe whispered into my ear, and out came April Marie Lynette Jones, who couldn't stop talking her *shoptalk.* (And she's still talking. Look for the novel *SisterGirl!* sometime in the near future. As soon as I can get her to shut up!) And then I dreamed *childless mother,* had a psychic vision of a boy beating drums, and along came *the virtuoso.* I guess the vision was so psychic, you see, that the first time I performed it, someone accused me of plagiarizing the author of the poem "A Woman Is a Drum." (I'd never heard of the poem or the woman. A year later I received as a birthday gift a volume of her poetry, which included that poem. Don't you know who I'm talking about? If not now, you will soon.)

But before all this, I bought *Ebony* magazine one cold October day. I never buy *Ebony* magazine. And there on page seventy-nine was an announcement about a literary award to be decided from a competitive short-story writing contest. And I thought, I can do that. I'm gonna win an award! Even though I'd never written a *literary* short story in my life! I guess the Universe spoke through me again. For after three intense weeks of writing, naked at the keyboard, *daddy's boy* was born. And win an award he did. Out of more than 2,500 submissions. But, before the award came (a lovely piece of change, I might say), I shared the story with Tim Miller, who just happened to be performing in town the very week after I completed the story. And he said, "You can perform that."

I did not know this, you see, but the Universe did.

And the Universe whispered into my ear once again, and out came Jeffrey Dahmer, still alive at the time, and his need to make some sense of his unconscionable crimes—for himself, if no one else—in *deliverance*. With two packs of cigarettes (all smoked up by the time I was done—and I do mean *done, as in roasted*), a shaky hand, and tear after tear raining down, sitting at a bar in a Cambridge poetry-slam lounge, I channeled Dahmer. The cannibal. The killer. The man. Why? Because the Universe said so.

And so I did what the Universe said.

Then, after years and years and *years*, I saw my Jonathan, and out came *this is not your monologue!* and *post coitus interruptus*. We took some liberties with those two, but hey, when your waves are mingling with so many other waves, a few liberties are bound to be found up in the mix.

During, at the same time, while (whichever word fits most appropriately) this was all happening, I was performing different versions of *skin & ornaments* around New England, with the help of Michael Harrington, a brilliant "script structurer." (He's a writer and director, but his primary role in my process was "script structurer." He tossed the pieces in the air, and the order in which they fell became the overall piece's structure. He was also a good "movement editor." Don't ask, don't tell. Let's just say that whatever movement he didn't edit, I imagined or dreamed. And whatever movements I had imagined or dreamt, I placed ever so delicately into the performances. And if I didn't imagine or dream a movement, I used mirrors. Lots of mirrors. In every room of my house, and everybody else's house, and restaurants, and public bathrooms, and well . . . you get the picture, don't you?) It's been a while since 1967, and my memory fails me sometimes. All that brewery smoke in Milwaukee got to me at a really early age, so it's hard to know for sure which version was performed where. Not that it really matters, anyway: jazz is jazz—you never get the same interpretation twice.

But I *do* remember this: In 1996, the National Black Arts Festival invited me to perform *skin & ornaments* in Atlanta. I was floored. But wait—

there's more. They asked me to consider presenting my work as a tribute to Essex Hemphill, who had read at a previous festival.

Essex Hemphill. Mentor. Friend. Diva. Warrior. Fallen Brother. Angel. How could I say no?

But before I got to Atlanta, the Universe whispered in my ear yet again: "It's not finished." And in walked the visual artist boyfriend-at-the-time who photographed divas and masks and trees, and cast wax sculptures (votives, actually, complete with wicks that I lit during the performances) of my body, and traveled to Atlanta with me in order to operate the slides and help me get it right.

For Essex.

We did.

And it was finished.

The sense of completion that took over me when I finished the first of those two performances is indescribable. Well . . . let me try: Floating? Washed over by a warm waterfall? Whole? Integrated? Blessed by a Voodoo priestess? Visited by Ed McMahon on sweepstakes-winner-announcement day?

Nope. I was right: indescribable. Only the Universe knows how I felt. Or maybe, if you open up and channel well enough, you can know, too.

Since Atlanta, *skin & ornaments* and I have been to the 1997 Gay & Lesbian Performance Festival at Oak Street Theater in Portland, Maine; the 1996 Ways In Being Gay Festival in Buffalo, New York; the 1996 CSPS New Performance Festival in Cedar Rapids, Iowa; the 1996 OUTCharlotte Festival of Lesbian and Gay Culture in Charlotte. (Now I remember! Before Atlanta, we did the 1994 T.W.E.E.D. New Works Festival in New York; the Institute of Contemporary Art in 1994, and the 1995 Out on the Edge Festival of Lesbian and Gay Theater in Boston; University of Massachusetts at Amherst in 1994; and Harvard College in 1993.)

May the journey continue.

The Universe says . . .

Oh, and please remember: "To be sensual is to respect and rejoice in the force of life, of life itself, and to be present in all that one does, from the effort of loving to the breaking of bread." James Baldwin wrote it. Believed it. Lived it.

Be sensual.

About Craig Hickman

For the past four years, Craig Hickman has brought his critically and popularly acclaimed solo performance pieces, skin & ornaments, Portraits of a Black Queen, and SisterGirl!, to over twenty universities, festivals, and progressive venues across the country. In February of 1996 Hickman brought an audience of 1,500 to their feet during the closing keynote plenary performance of OutWrite '96, the National Lesbian, Gay, Bisexual, and Transgendered Writing Conference at the Park Plaza in Boston.

An accomplished poet, actor, dancer, activist, and educator, Hickman might seem older than his years. Born December 8, 1967, in Milwaukee, Wisconsin, Hickman graduated cum laude from Harvard College with a bachelor of arts in government. As an undergraduate he founded the Harvard-Radcliffe Callbacks, a coed a cappella singing group and appeared in A Chorus Line. After graduation he appeared in a Harvard production of Dreamgirls; sang in "Yesterdays," a cabaret in tribute to Billie Holiday; and performed with the Boston Gay Men's Chorus. Other stage credits include a national tour of Through the Fire with Brothers du Jour, Pure PolyESTHER, The Piano Bar, Blasturbation, DIRT, and the Fear & Clothing series at the ICA.

Hickman began writing in 1992 and has won numerous awards for his poetry and prose, including the Gertrude Johnson Williams Literary Award from Ebony magazine. His poems have been published in Atelier 3, Harvard Gay and Lesbian Review, Getting Naked, Paramour, Bay Windows, Boston Globe, and the anthology Gents, Bad Boys, and Barbarians. His articles, reviews, and essays have appeared in the Phoenix, Harvard Gay and Lesbian Review, Gay Community News, QVoice, In-Step, Proscenium, and the anthology Taking Liberties: Gay Male Essays on Politics, Sex, and Culture.

As a performance poet, he has been featured at venues in major U.S. cities and universities including Brown, Bowdoin, Harvard, and Yale; opened for pop recording artist RuPaul at PrideFest 1993; was a member of the 1993 National Poetry Slam Championship team from Boston; and coorganized and performed in "Rites & Permissions," a tribute to the late poet and activist Essex Hemphill, and "Celebrating Our Community: Remembering Our Lives," a poetry revival honoring the lives of gay men of color lost to AIDS, which he performed with poets Thomas Grimes and Philip Robinson. The broadcast of the revival on Cambridge Cable Television on World AIDS Day 1994 won the station a 1995 Hometown Video Festival national award for excellence in gay and lesbian public access programming.

In 1994 Hickman began working directly with youth and young adults and offering guidance and support for institutions and organizations that provide youth programming. He created and facilitated "Voices from the Street," a writing and theater workshop for homeless street youth through the Justice Resource Institute in Boston. He has taught anti-homophobia theater workshops for high school students as part of the Theater Offensive's Teen Theater Works programs. Hickman has also lectured on the role of the artist in culture, elements of black gay culture, sexuality in high school adolescents, public sex and the limits of eroticism, and education through performance art at area conferences, including the 1994 Gay, Lesbian & Straight Teacher's Network (GLSTN) conference.

From 1993 to 1995 Hickman worked as an AIDS educator for the Fenway Community Health Center in Boston, where he coordinated Color Me Healthy, an HIV prevention and education program for gay men of color, and consulted for Men of Color Against AIDS (MOCAA). Hickman wrote and designed the "Color Me Healthy Safer Sex Guide," one of the first safer sex brochures targeting gay men of color in Massachusetts. Hickman further applied his creativity to his work, developing and performing AIDS educational theater pieces and personalities around Boston. His persona, Latexia the Condom Fairy, appeared in bars and public sex areas and was noted for taking to task sensationalist radio talk show host Howie Carr live on the air. Another persona, Vanna Black, has hosted "Wheelin' and Dealin': HIV/AIDS Facts You Should Know" on MOCAA's first boat cruise and "Flappin' Your Yap with Vanna Black," a talk show–style community forum that has kept participants coming back for more, both locally and at national conferences.

In 1995 the National Task Force on AIDS Prevention invited Hickman to participate in the first Gay Men of Color AIDS Summit. At this historic event, one-hundred gay men of color from across the United States and the territories were charged with the task of developing a document of standards and guidelines for research, prevention, community building, and organizational development upon which current and future programs for gay men of color can be evaluated. Hickman continues to remain involved in the work of the Na-

tional Task Force. He helped plan and presented at the 1996 Gay Men of Color AIDS Institute in Miami Beach and will provide consultation for "Recreating Our Future," a new national campaign calling on all gay men of color to end the epidemic in their communities. In February 1997 Hickman received an AIDS Action Committee Community Recognition award for his work in HIV prevention and activism.

In 1993 Hickman founded the independent publishing house Parfait de Cocoa Press. Committed to publishing queer writers of color from New England, Parfait de Cocoa has published his own chapbook, The Language of Mirrors *(1993), a collection of his poetry and prose,* Rituals: Poetry and Prose *(1994), Thomas Grimes's chapbook,* Deep Talk *(1994), and Jay Critchley's artist book,* Playing Games: Zoa the Greek Fertility Goddess Shoots for the Gold *(1995). In 1996 Hickman incorporated the press as an imprint of Mojo Productions, a production company that is rapidly developing to produce, publish, promote, and present special events, touring shows, AIDS education programming, local theatrical performances, and independent video and film projects by black queer artists. In December 1997 Hickman received the James Baldwin Award for Cultural Achievement from the Lesbian and Gay Political Alliance of Massachusetts.*

Hickman recently understudied Angels in America *at the Milwaukee Repertory Theater; co-produced and starred in Gail Burton's original play* Muses; *is currently working on his first screenplay* Looking for Justin, *a novella based on characters from his performance piece* SisterGirl!, *and pilot for a new black sit-com featuring OUT characters; appears in the independent feature film* Never Met Picasso—*filmed on location in Boston—starring Margot Kidder and Alexis Arquette; and continues touring, lecturing, and educating throughout the country. He lives in Boston, Massachusetts, and can be reached at MojoPro@aol.com.*

skin & ornaments

CRAIG HICKMAN

I. God bless the child . . .

SCHOOL BOYS
(*In the dark, Billie Holiday's "God Bless the Child" is heard.*)

(PERFORMER REMOVES SUSPENDED HULA HOOP FROM ITS HOOK AND MOVES TO CENTER STAGE. VOICE-OVERS RISE ABOVE MUSIC, AND PERFORMER BEGINS TURNING HULA HOOP IN THE DARK. AFTER THE LAST SENTENCE, MUSIC AND VOICE-OVERS END AND PERFORMER ABRUPTLY STOPS TURNING THE HULA HOOP AND "CATCHES" IT.)

(VOICE-OVER) Repent your wicked ways! / Mama, Mama, please! / I don't wanna catch the Lord's scourge that he put upon those who went that way! / Who wants a colored faggot? / Don't raise your voice at me! / Don't get too close to the faggot, it might rub off! / Mama, Mama, please! / Do as I say, *boy!* (VOICE-OVER ENDS)
(*Dim light rises on Hula Hoop–framed performer clad in sweatshirt and casual pants.*)
My earliest memories of childhood are sexual. My libido came out of the womb long before the rest of me did.

(PERFORMER STEPS AND WRIGGLES THROUGH HULA HOOP
AND ANNOUNCES, "BIRTH OF A NATION.")

At the age of two, I couldn't have told anyone my favorite
foods, colors, sights, or sounds, but I knew some things I liked and
how to get them: boys, boys, boys, and more boys!
(*Brighter lights reveal a set at once a classroom, an open closet,
and a dressing room. Performer uses each part of stage and
props as necessary to re-create the spaces in which the stories
unfold.*)
Growing up on Twenty-fourth Street in Milwaukee, Wisconsin—home of *Laverne & Shirley, Happy Days,* bratwurst, beer,
cheese, frozen custard, and serial killers—Stanley was the only
other boy on the block, and he too was a sexually enlightened
tot.

(AFTER TWIRLING HULA HOOP AROUND RIGHT ARM WHILE
RECITING THE ABOVE LIST, PERFORMER DELIBERATELY
PLACES THE HULA HOOP ON THE FLOOR, UPSTAGE CENTER.
HULA HOOP WILL THEN SERVE AS CLASSROOM, COAT CLOSET,
AND LIBIDO.)

Now, you might be wondering what two little boys who didn't
know very much about anything else could possibly do to arouse
and amuse themselves when together. Then again, you might not.
Let's put on our thinking caps, boys and girls. He had his little G.I.
Joe, I had my little G.I. Joe, they bivouacked, went off together
on their secret maneuvers, don't ask, don't tell!
When I was old enough to attend school, I had my pick of
the crop among all those energetic boys. But there was only one
Deron. All the others were either passing fancies or little boys
experimenting with one who was more certain, more knowledge-
able, and always, always willing. But Deron was my steady,
my mainstay. *We had a thing going on* from the first week of
kindergarten.
The first time we got together, we hid in the coat closet (how
appropriate) while the rest of the class assembled for recess.

(PERFORMER STEPS INTO THE SPACE SURROUNDED BY THE
HULA HOOP AND KNEELS.)

In the dark, I was pleasantly surprised to feel Deron's hand
completely enclose my crotch. He pushed the door ajar to let in a
little light. "Show me your pee-pee," he ordered. Without hesitation, I unzipped my pants. I thought he was going to touch it. I
waited and waited and waited. Instead, he leaned toward me and
pressed his lips to mine—my first tender kiss.

(PERFORMER RISES AND STEPS OUT OF HULA HOOP.)

At five, we couldn't know what pleasures awaited an overly
anxious pair of precocious little boys. In our eyes, however, rested
the knowledge that only we could have offered one another such
comfort.

(ON THE FOLLOWING LINE, PERFORMER EXCITEDLY RUNS
AROUND PERIMETER OF HULA HOOP AND JUMPS BACK IN-
SIDE.)

By the third grade, Deron and I were love-stricken fools. We
enjoyed one another with the seething passion and reckless abandon only children usually allow themselves. During Dr. Seuss reading hour, we sat close to each other and inconspicuously held
hands. When we should've been learning our multiplication tables,
we wrote love notes and arranged for our next intimate liaison.
On the day before Valentine's, I wrote a love letter that I had
spent a lot of time on. It was the first time I paid any attention to
my writing. It was a beautiful letter, if I do say so myself, and I got
all wrapped up in it. I could've sold that one to Hallmark. Even
back then, I had the makings of a Romance Ho! At the end of the
schoolday, I folded it up all nice and neat, opened my desk to put
it in, but left it sticking out of the front right corner just a little
bit. I didn't want to forget about it, and I just had to give it to Deron
right away at the start of the next day.
But my teacher, Miss Crazy—I mean Miss Krause—found it first.
She called in my parents and exposed my secret. My heart dropped
to my knees when Daddy looked at me, completely disgusted, and

yelled, "What the hell is this about you and Deron 'doin' up' in the bathroom?" The anger in his eyes and the pitch of his voice told me he already knew the answer. I kept my mouth shut.

And so did they.

Well, my mother never said anything in the first place, and my father had nothing more to say about Deron and me at all after that. Sometime later, in fact, they let him start sleeping over at our house—in my bed. We would toss and turn so tumultuously, we'd leave a winding sheet spread across the bed the next morning. *This* aroused my mother's curiosity: "Son, why is your bed such a mess?"

"Oh, Mama, we were just wrestling," would usually suffice. Little did she know. Or maybe she knew more than I thought. I mean, she was there for the love letter fiasco. She had to know what that was all about. And I knew her woman's intuition didn't sit down to play Bid Whist for a single hot minute! Why would she ever have let Deron spend the night after that? Perhaps she was being supportive. Maybe she didn't want to create any more trouble. She had been without child for so long and been through so much that by the time she got me, she became a little, shall we say, lenient. My mother, Minnie Juanita. And my other mother, Denise. What would she have done?

(*Light cross-fades to amber basket weave specials.*)
End of section.

CHILDLESS MOTHER

(THROUGHOUT THIS SECTION, PERFORMER, IN BROAD MOVE-
MENTS AND INTERPRETIVE DANCE, MIMES BABY'S CONCEP-
TION AND LONGING AND THE NEW MOTHER'S PULLING THE
BABY OUT OF THE BASKET IN THE REEDS, HOLDING AND
NURTURING HER NEW SON.)

(*Sound of poem text is heard.*)

(VOICE-OVER)

Denise mourned the day her flowing ceased.
The rape seed sown rooted
deeply on the walls of womb
weeping blood from her brown baby eyes

eyes which could not eclipse her assaulter's scowling face
eyes which could no longer catch enough light to sparkle
eyes which could envision her dreams aborted.

She wanted not this thing,
this life, this parasite
sucking
her own life within.

It was
1967.
Only sixteen, she had
no money,
no clinic,
no doctor,
no law,
no choice.

Unwilling to risk some back-alley mutilation, she
shored up her strength for the struggles to come and
moved, and moved, and moved her love out of her
womb
        down a river in a tightly woven basket.
"Go, go my child. Be safe."

For fifteen months, lost in rushes and reeds
it flowed; flowing into the abyss,
no nurture, no wonder,
into a void, too dark and lonely,
till back over the edge of the river basin,
it fell. But soon enough,
                        it sprouted wings?
"Mama, Mama, please?"

And Winnie Juanita heard.
She who had waited and prayed
                              and waited.
After six conceptions no child could
cling to her irritable womb; a
womb that bled and bled,
too much too fast,
too fast too much,
till finally carved out,
                              it bled no more.

With no hope of seeing a child created in her own image;
with no hope of hearing that child cry out from new teeth and monsters;
with no hope of tasting her own fruit's dreams yet to ripen;

she wept.

But she prayed again,
not to the gods whom
she blamed for her Dharma, but
for the last two of her four decades,
she knelt down before folklore and myth, in
supplication to stork wings and river reeds.
She waited, and waited, and waited . . .
"Mama, Mama, please?"

So Winnie Juanita took him.
More blessed than Pharaoh's daughter
she relished his majesty
she cradled him in arms warm with love and devotion
she counted his fingers with kisses in praise they were all there
she breathed her own blood into each of his veins.
You're mine, now. You're mine now.
She strengthened him with the name of the
rock of ages of ages of ages of
                              lost babies
envisioned like this one—

her son.

*Her son. And she, a childless mother
no more, adopted into her home
invited into her life
welcomed into her love
this living*
            abortion.

(VOICE-OVER ENDS.)

(*Lights slowly fade to black.*)
End of section.

SHOP TALK

(*Loud music blares.*)

(DURING COSTUME CHANGE, PERFORMER YELLS, "TURN
THAT MUSIC DOWN! I CAN HARDLY HEAR MYSELF THINK!"
MUSIC LEVEL DIMINISHES, AND WE SEE A BRIGHT BEAUTY
SALON WHERE A NO-NONSENSE WOMAN WITH HIGH HAIRDO,
A BLOUSE TIED AROUND HER WAIST ABOVE HER BELLY BUT-
TON, AND FORM-FITTING BLACK BELL-BOTTOMS BLASTS
ONTO THE SCENE TO DISH SOME DIRT ON AN AUDIENCE SHE
TRUSTS IMPLICITLY, SHATTERING WHAT'S LEFT OF THE
"FOURTH WALL." HER SPEECH IS RAPID-RAPID-FIRE. SHOP
MUSIC PLAYS ON LOW LEVEL THROUGHOUT MONOLOGUE. A
SMALL STOOL, REPRESENTING A SALON CHAIR, IS USED AS
INDICATED THROUGHOUT MONOLOGUE.)

(*Lights bump to bright wash.*)
Ooh, honeys, I loves me some Black Queens, you know what
I'm sayin'? See, in my line of work, I'm down with 'em all the time.
I work here at Jay's His and Hers Salon. I'm the weave specialist,
honey. And honey, I do me some fierce weaves. These fingers right

here—certified! You sit in my chair—I'll hook you up! Like you ain't never been hooked up before. Everybody seems to be wantin' all kinda extra hair these days—braids, folds, beehives, and buns. We even weavin' in dreads these days! Save folk all that beeswax and twistin'. Come outta here in five hours, you be ret to go back to Jamaica, you know what I'm sayin'?!

Yeah, I get me some of my best referrals from word of mouth. Talk of my talent has spread so fast, you'd think I was the only one in Boston weavin'. Ooh, but let me stop complainin', you know what I'm sayin'? I'm just glad to be gettin' all this work. In fact, this week is booked so solid, I ain't had a chance to get my nails wrapped. *Shiiit*, last night, I just started bitin' 'em off. But, *heeeey*, as long as the rough edges don't interfere with the weavin' process, you know what I'm sayin'?—the *process*—everythang'll be all right, baby!

My hair? Of course it's real—I just jazz it up a bit for sex appeal. I stole that shit from En Vogue. Those sisters is too tuff. I certainly would love to jazz up some of they stuff myself. I mean, don't get me wrong, they always look good, but I know I could work some of my magic up in all that hair, you know what I'm sayin'? And did you check them out on the Grammys a couple years back—how they descended down in their silver lamé gowns, hit that stage, and turned it out like they was the Dreamgirls themselves. I was like, Work me, goddammit! And the hair—too, *too* tuff. But I know if I had one consultation with those funky divas, I would hook them up with a look that would turn their fans out for days on end, or my name ain't April Marie Lynette Jones and I ain't standin' in front of you talkin' right now.

Speakin' of standin', let me take the load off here right quick. (SITS ON STOOL) I ain't poze to be on break, but it's been a long-ass day, and as long as Jay don't see me, everything'll be all right, baby!

But anyway, I done got all off the subject. What was we poze to be talkin' 'bout? Oh, yeah, that's right—Black Queens. Well, lemme just say first, I know some folk don't like to be called that, but honey, I say it like this, if somebody wants to call you *royalty*, you better put on that crown and wear it well, honey!

Anyway, we got this one brother, Richie, work up next to me. And honey, he is too funny. Chil', he can make me laugh just by throwin' some shade my way. He do weaves almost as good as me. (RISING TO DEMONSTRATE BODY TWIST) But if I ever catch him starin' too close when I'm workin' one of my secret techniques, you know, I have to twist around and throw some ass up his way. That'll usually throw him off right quick!

Oh yeah, he fits into some of them stereotypes: he fine as hell, always dressed to the nines in some fierce black clothes, got more shoes than I got Fashion Fair eye pencils! See?! I *know* you know what I'm sayin'! But it don't make no never mind to me.

Ooh, but it did make some never mind to Miss Hattie Mae.

Now Hattie Mae come up in here always dressed for Sunday go meeting, totin' the scriptures, and preachin' like she the one on the mountaintop overlooking the Promised Land! Well, used to be Richie was her one and only stylist. Then one day while he was curling her hair, she overheard him say somethin' 'bout some new man he got. Honey, she jumped up out that chair so fast, the curlin' iron singed the back of her neck.

Well, we didn't see her for a while, then she come up in here askin' me to curl her hair, talkin' 'bout, "I don't want to catch the Lord's scourge that he put upon those who went that way." Humph! She look in that mirror long enough, she'd realize she already caught somebody's scourge as tore up as she was lookin'. I turned her down flat. I don't do curls, except for my special clientele (that she was not), and I know my weaves would not work peepin' out from them big old tacky hats she be wearin'. She need to peek out that Bible long enough to hear you ain't liable to be catchin' nothin' from nobody's hairstylist, and you *know* she ain't catchin' nothin' no other way. I didn't care if she ever come in here again with her dresses two sizes too small, and her feet oozin' out from them ugly shoes she be kickin'.

Well, it turned out, who was it?—that's right—Mabel started doin' her hair, so she come in here twice a week, walk right past Richie, roll her eyes to the heavens, and sit down and let Mabel gct to goin' on her head. Humph. I wish I did have time. I put her in this chair right here (INDICATING STOOL) and pull every last strand of her righteous nappy hair right outta her head, you know what I'm sayin'?

Well, honey, all the while, Richie just keep on workin', hookin' up his clients, and don't pay Miss Church Thing no never mind. I'm like, Go on with your bad self. More power to him. Most he do when Hattie Mae come steppin' up in here is throw me this look with all this attitude, all this like . . . (DEMONSTRATES LOOK) That's when he be remindin' me of this chil' I grew up with. What was his name? I must be gettin' old. (All right, girl, you better watch your mouth, it ain't for these children to be knowin' your age.)

What was his name?

But anyway, see, on my block, Twenty-fourth Street, back in Milwaukee, Wisconsin—the "Brew City" we called it—it was all us fast-ass little girls runnin' round like we owned the place. And we did. The block was ours. Not a boy to be found. (Well, there was this little boy who lived next door to me, but he was so little, his mama never let him out the house.) Then, when I was about six or seven, this family moved into the big ol' white house, second from the corner, cross the street. And they had two kids, a little girl, and wouldn't you know, a little boy.

I remember thinkin' things would never be the same, you know what I'm sayin? But then I was like, he so little, his mama probably wouldn't let him out the house neither. That was short-lived.

See, his sister, I forget her name now too, damn! Umph, umph, umph—but anyway—his sister was real pretty and light skinned and had hair all the way down to her butt. And I know it was real, too. Folks wasn't weavin' in all that hair back then. (I wonder if she got all that hair now. Bet she cut, sold it, and I weaved it up in somebody hair just last week!) But anyway, me and Eve and Dawn, and most of the other girls, we all liked her and you know, she was down with it and all that, and so she started hangin' out with us. But she always brought her little brother along. Must've been some "house rule" or somethin' like that, you know what I'm sayin'?

Now at first, it was kind of weird for him to be playin' with us and all that. I have to say, though, I can't lie. Back then, a boy that sissified usually put me off right quick. I mean, I had only seen his kind at school, and since everybody made fun of 'em, they always seemed to be so quiet, and lonely—you know the kind that sit back in the corners, try not to say nothin' to nobody, but be bustin' out with them straight A's and shit come report card time? Well, I never wanted to bother 'em, since they sometimes seem so sad, I just wasn't used to havin' to deal with 'em till this family went and moved on my block. (TAKES A VERY SHORT BREATH AND SITS ON STOOL)

But he was funny. And had more energy than half of us. Chil', before you knew it, he was an expert at all the games we played: jacks, hopscotch, patty-cake, double dutch. He got so good, especially jumpin' that damn rope, we just considered him one of us. Shit, I even forgot he was a boy at some point, you know what I'm sayin'? I think, naw, I *know* I was his favorite. So you know, I just took him under my wing and showed him the way. He used to be like, "Hey April, you should show me how to jump rope outdoors."

Now, don't be lookin' at me all stupid. Not outside the house, but you know, "outdoors" when you turned the rope out like this instead of like this. (MIMES TURNING TWO ROPES OUT AWAY FROM BODY) See, it's harder jumpin' in that way, cuz the rope be liable to slap you all up in the face, you know what I'm sayin'? Well, I taught him, and chil', once he got it, he had it, and Lord knows, he was outdoorin' the rest of us after that. He always caught on to shit real fast.

(RISING AND APPROACHING AUDIENCE) One time, my older sister had to baby-sit for him when his mama had a doctor's appointment or somethin'. She came back and told me how when she was watchin' *Love Is a Many Splendored Thing* that that chil' had all the characters names and shit down pat, and knew every intricate detail of the storylines that was goin' on. I was like, Work me, goddammit! He couldn't been no more than four years old! He and his mama musta watched that shit every day!

Them was the days. We had some good-ass times, yes we did. He used to call me his "other" sister. You know, I didn't have no brothers myself, so it was kinda nice that he considered me all that. I guess, you know, even though I never did say, I considered him my little brother, too.

Well, it couldna been more than two years after they moved in that my daddy got relocated out here, so we had to move. I never forget about that little boy, though! Whenever I would see some butch boys or some fake "butch" boys up in elementary school pickin' on some sissified ones, I would remember my little "brother," and honey, I be ret to claw their eyes out (you know, I always had me some fierce nails)!

I wonder what ever happened to him. What he be doin' now. You *know* I ain't all that religious and shit, but I 'magine the good Lord probably takin' care of him just fine. Hope he ain't had to deal with the kinda fucked-up kinda shit happened to another friend of mine on the streets. Ooh, and you know when that Jeffrey Dahmer sickness hit the papers, I was lookin' at all them names they printed, hopin' none of 'em jarred my memory, you know what I'm sayin'? I just hope that . . . umph, umph, umph . . . Well, that's a whole other story.

It just seem like folk don't wanna respect folk for who they are and just let 'em be, chil'. But, I say it like this, somebody don't wanna deal with Black Queens, they either jealous or crazy—I said jealous or *crazy*—cuz you can say you heard it like this before or not, but they be some of the best friends you ever wants to have. So put *that* up in your hair and weave it!!

Anyway, I gotta get on back to work, children. I got this sistergirl comin' up in here for my special African-Crown headdress with *much* attitude. I'll talk to y'all later.

End of section.

BROTHERS

(*Restore lights to classroom setting.*)

I got all off the subject. What was I telling you about? (STEP-
PING BACK INTO HULA HOOP) Oh, that's right, my childhood. Now
make no mistake, not all of my early male bonding was sexual.

(STEPPING OUT OF HULA HOOP AND PUTTING ON A RED
BASEBALL CAP.)

There was Roosevelt, ah, Roosevelt. He too made a big im-
pression on me in the first week of kindergarten, but not in the
same way Deron did. There we were, two curious, mischievous boys
in the middle of a bare classroom, looking for a way to break the
barrier between us. "Hey, you, why are your teeth so big?" Even at
age five, I was extremely blunt and to the point.

He looked at me through those bubbly eyes and head too big
for his body and said with sardonic retort, "I don't know. Why are
your arms so long? You look like a monkey."

We became the best of friends. Inseparable. And could we
ever dream. In our fantasy world, we were sportscasters who followed every season of NFL football (must've been some junior
butch stage I was going through). We fleshed out our predictions
in a comic strip complete with dialogue, detail, and catchy cartoon figures.

Roosevelt was the brother I never had. As brothers, we fought,
we argued, we truly wrestled. As brothers, he never made me feel
funny, unwanted, different. As brothers, he accepted me with all
my faults, especially this big, sarcastic mouth. And although others found it necessary to call me out of my name ("sissy," "boy,"
"faggot," "punk," "mama's boy," "little girl") Roosevelt only called
me by my name.

With Roosevelt and Deron, I had all a little boy could want.
(*Phone rings are heard.*)

My world was full, comfortable, safe.

"Why?"

"I don't know why, son. Roosevelt has gone on to a better

place. It was meant to be this way. We don't always know what the good Lord has in store for us."

"But Daddy, why did he have to take my friend? We said we would be best friends forever."

(*Chaka Khan's "Everlasting Love" is heard.*)
(*Light changes to downstage dim light.*)

(LOOKING AWAY FROM DADDY AND DOWN TO WHAT MIGHT BE THE CASKET, PERFORMER MOVES RED CAP AND HOLDS IT BY THE BRIM WITH BOTH HANDS IN FRONT OF HIM.)

I'll never have a friend like you again. You just disappeared. You didn't even say good-bye. Where did you go?

I went to Deron for comfort, only to find out he no longer went my way.

(STEPPING IN AND OUT OF HULA HOOP AS VOICES SHIFT.)

"I'm sorry, but we can't do each other up any more. I like girls now."

"Why?"

"This is the way it's supposed to be."

The way it's supposed to be? The way it's supposed to be.
(*Looking somewhat tentatively at the space between the Hula Hoop, performer steps inside and utters, "No," and on the next line, picks it up, and hangs it back on the hook.*)

That hyperactive, happy, inquisitive, spirited little boy— crushed. I saw no reason to continue seeking friends. To get attention (HURLING CAP OFF STAGE) I caused trouble for everyone else.

(MUSIC FADES OUT.)

I could never bring myself to exact revenge on Deron or his new best friend, Kevin Curley Pritchett, so I started putting glue in little black girls' hair, right in the middle of social studies class. Well, I was just being social!

The only thing that stayed alive in me was that inextinguishable urge. Even when the maturing body was unawares (REMOV-

ING SWEATSHIRT TO REVEAL PURPLE TANK-TOP UNDERNEATH) and
the developing mind was off trying to accomplish A's to make
Daddy smile, within me, welling up, that fire inside, that base
yearning,

    (Lights gradually change into leaf patterns.)
    (PERFORMER MOVES ACROSS STAGE, USING SHARP, AFRICAN
    DANCE MOVEMENTS.)

that longing, looking for something to be fulfilled, indescribable,
but so powerful, insurmountable, gone astray, never at home,
empty, seeking, seeking, finding . . .

                          End of Part I.

II. empty pockets

JUNEAU PARK
(*Park sounds are heard.*)

(PERFORMER RESTS CASUALLY, TRIUMPHANTLY, AGAINST A "TREE" IN THE PARK AND BEGINS TO TAKE NOTICE OF THESE NEW SURROUNDINGS.)

To the untrained eye, Juneau Park was simply a quaint little park overlooking Lake Michigan on the east. The picturesque War Memorial which housed the Milwaukee Art Museum framed the view at the southernmost point. There were usually children playing, often someone painting or photographing, and *always* someone taking a casual stroll. But to the trained eye, like mine, most of the people taking those strolls were men—looking for love.

A little path led into the trees on the side of the hill. I noticed men coming and going and going and coming, and never too soon. So one day I decided to take the plunge and walk down the hill.

(*Park sounds fade.*)
(*Lights change into deep blue leaf patterns.*)

I walked down that path on the side of that hill descending into the dark, cool, shady depths of lust, obsession, lust—into the inner sanctum of my destruction?

There they were. Men together in groups of two, three—six! No more than two minutes into the deepest, thickest section of the trees, I was reborn.

(PERFORMER PLAYS OUT ORGY IN THE PRESENT TENSE, INVITING THE MEN WITH OPEN PASSION AND ACCEPTANCE.)

A white man, reaching out as if to welcome me, places his hand on my crotch. My balls tingle with the sensation of warm bathwater in the cold winter. Another raises my shirt and begins to suck my left nipple. Licking and sucking, and sucking and licking, like candy he has never before tasted. As I close my eyes and let the passion consume me, my shorts somehow already at my knees, I feel a warm erection brush against my cheeks. I am hungry. But before I can decide on this pleasure, another man opens himself before me and guides my stiff, throbbing, curious cock into his hot, pink, moist anus. I briefly open my eyes to notice the crowd of about seven or eight that has gathered around to touch, to watch, to somehow indulge in this summertime orgy under the trees. . . .

Day after day, I rode my little blue ten-speed along the Centennial bike path down to Juneau Park to get my fix. I was so tantalized, so curious to see what I would do and with how many.

But I was always approached by white men. Few black boys frequented the bushes, and those of us who did seldom looked each other in the eye, and never, ever got close enough to touch one another. What was this all about? All of my friends and sex buddies up until this point were black. All of a sudden, we weren't good enough to even look each other in the eye?

(STANDING HALF IN THE DARK, PERFORMER'S ATTENTION SHIFTS INTO THE PRESENT TENSE AND SEEMS DISTRACTED BY ANOTHER BLACK BOY HE THEN FOCUSES ON. DURING THIS NEXT SECTION, PERFORMER, ARMS OUTSTRETCHED IN CRUCIFIXION FASHION, GRADUALLY BACKS AWAY FROM AUDIENCE AND STEPS ONTO A SMALL PEDESTAL.)

There is another black boy backed against a tree or a group of bushes, completely surrounded by clusters of white men taking their pleasures. A sense of isolation develops under the trees suffocating all the pleasure. Every white man's touch feels more like a blow to my body; every mouth on my body, a noose being tied around my neck, strangling my spirit. With every orgasm, the noose tightens, as my essence spurts

(*Light bumps to red special.*)

out of me. After the white crowd retreats, I'm left dangling from the trees.

(PERFORMER SINGS SEVERAL VERSES OF "STRANGE FRUIT."
REMOVES TANK TOP AND STEPS OFF PEDESTAL.)

End of section.

DELIVERANCE
*(Light changes to lavender stained-glass window gobo shining
from directly above.)*

(SUNG.)

*I DON'T KNOW WHY, but I'm feeling so sad. I long to try
something I've never had, never had no kissin', oh what I been missin',
Loverman, oh, where can you be?*

*That's what their eyes sang to me when they stared into mine.
All those young colored faggots wore their loneliness as
a reeking, putrid odor and I breathed it in, let it tingle in my nostrils,
let it ignite the fires in my blood.
I was chosen to offer them the thing they never had.
Now, Newsweek, Time, Inside Edition, and every newspaper across
this forsaken land features my face, and they tell the tale that
I'm the Devil himself. But the Devil would never have been as kind as
    I was.*

*I called my attorney a fool for playing that plea of insanity, knowing
any number of jurors in their right minds could ever believe me
    insane.
I knew exactly what I was doing. No one, no one, thought Abraham
    insane
for preparing to carve up his son and offer him a burnt, a burnt!
    sacrifice,
claiming the voice of God ordered him so.*

Well, I had my voice and it was much more powerful than God's.
All my Isaacs came to me willing, needing, begging to be delivered
from their empty lives. It was in their eyes, their eyes, their eyes:
full of an abject fear like a child who had been beaten,
waiting only to be beaten again.

In the bars, on the abandoned parking lots, in the bushes, on the streets,
in the bathhouses, they came—one after another, after another.
I was chosen to offer them the thing they never had.
I stroked their fragile egos with the kindest words. I promised them a
    night to
remember. They succumbed to my nurturing offers.

In the silence of my room, I made them feel safe.
I laced their drinks with a touch of bitterness so they
could look deeper, deeper into me and see my true calling.
I made them call out to me. As their diminishing voices cried:
"Jeffrey!" over and over, "Jeffrey!" I came as I slit their
throats with my blunt-tipped scalpel, carefully carving their
bodies like an inspired artist.

I wanted their flesh to become my flesh, so I ate their meat raw. I
bathed in their blood, I bathed in their blood, I bathed in their blood.
I was baptized in their blood. I needed to preserve their bodies' most
beautiful parts, so I stored them—in my refrigerator, under my bed,
    in my closets,
a constant reminder of the great work I created.
I could never have burned them.

No one came looking. No one. Who wants a colored faggot?
Now, rotting in this frigid, icebox cell, I am the lamb who sacrificed his
life for their freedom from want, from AIDS, from rejection, from fear,
from loneliness. The ultimate deliverance.
Yes, it was me, the father they never had.

I did it.

I did it all.

I did them all

a favor.

> (BEAT.)
> (*Blackout.*)
> (*Sound of gushing wind is heard in the dark.*)
> **End of section.**

PRIVATE STORMS

I was a sleepwalker
(*Wind stops.*)
entranced by the abyss, dark and lonely. I returned to Juneau Park.
(*Park lights restored.*)
It was always safe.
Not many men out strolling today.
(*Gold light special lights up the pedestal and bench.*)
I see a gray van parked in the lot with a man sitting in the
driver's seat. Those eyes. Those eyes. Those misty brown eyes
charged with lightning, emerging from that white face, a face sig-
nifying at once the source of and refuge from my own private storm.

(SITS ON BENCH ON THE "PASSENGER" SIDE.)

I enter the van. Wearing a striped T-shirt and a pair of tan
shorts, he's a large, muscular, strong man as quiet as the calm before clouds burst to thunderous rain. In the back of the van where
the seats ought to be rests a large mattress covered with a sheet,
unmade. Shades are drawn down over the windows on both sides
and in the back. Outside, the sunlight diminishes behind the trees
and the inside grows darker.
(*Park lights fade out. Gold light special dims.*)
(STAGE WHISPER) Silence. Deafening silence.

(*Sound of rainstorm is heard.*)

I want to leave, but I'm paralyzed with fear. He notices. Before I can move, he throws me face first onto the mattress. Holding my head down with his arm across my neck, he pulls down my shorts and enters me.

(PERFORMER TEARS OFF RAINCOAT, THROWING IT IN FRONT OF BENCH, MOVES INTO HORIZONTAL POSITION ACROSS PEDESTAL AND BENCH, SUPPORTS HIMSELF ON HIS FOREARMS FOLDED INWARD, AND RE-CREATES THE RAPE, TAKING TURNS SIMULATING ASSAILANT AND VICTIM.)

(*Sound of rainstorm stops when rapist finishes.*)
(*Light bumps to blue wash when performer's body hits stage floor after being catapulted over props.*)
(*Sound of van starting up and pulling away is heard.*)

(FRIGHTENED AND HUMILIATED, PERFORMER, STRUGGLING, PUTS ON RAINCOAT, PULLING HOOD OVER HIS HEAD, AND WALKS AWAY FROM THE SCENE OF THE CRIME, OVER WHICH WE HEAR:)

(*Sound of voice is heard.*)
(VOICE-OVER) Who do you tell (*it never happened*)? What do you tell (*it never happened*)? You're gonna collect yourself, ride home, avoid Mama and Daddy, take a long bath, scrub yourself clean, go to bed, wake up tomorrow, and proceed as if nothing happened (*it never happened*). (VOICE-OVER ENDS)

Juneau Park had betrayed me.

I vowed never to go back. But I found other places: bookstores, backrooms in bars, public restrooms, picture shows, other parks. I even ran into those eyes again. Those eyes. I needed to be with him, if only to conquer him the way he had conquered me, to settle the score, to reconcile the shame, blame, anger within. I needed to win and nothing was going to stop me. But he didn't even recognize me enough to avoid me.

(MOVING BACK TO PEDESTAL, PERFORMER PULLS A RED SCARF
OUT OF COAT POCKET AND TIES IT AROUND HIS NECK, GENTLY
PULLS HULA HOOP SO THAT IS SWINGS LIKE A PENDULUM.)

I break my vow and return to Juneau Park, hoping to conquer
it, because I cannot conquer him.
(*Light restored to red spot with bare branch gobo projected onto
psyche.*)
But the angry trees grow crooked in autumn's gale. The
branches—naked, cold, sterile—hang heavily overhead. Beneath
my skin, the bitter core rots, while the willows weep for me.

(PERFORMER SINGS LAST VERSE OF "STRANGE FRUIT," THEN
DROPS HEAD ABRUPTLY.)

(*Blackout.*)
End of section.

MASKS
(*Jimmy Scott's rendition of "Sometimes I Feel Like a Mother-
less Child" is heard after a few beats.*)

(PERFORMER SITS AT THE DRESSING TABLE BEHIND WHITE
PSYCHE FOR THE TRANSFORMATION INTO "DIVA.")

(*Light changes to magenta back light so performer's silhouette
is projected through the psyche to audience.*)

(WITH BROAD, SWEEPING GESTURES, PERFORMER PUTS ON
MAKEUP, WIG, DRESS, AND PUMPS. PROJECTED ONTO THE
FRONT OF PSYCHE NEXT TO PERFORMER, IMAGES OF POPULAR
DIVAS, PAST AND PRESENT, MORPH INTO EACH OTHER IN
PAIRS, SUPERIMPOSED WITH IMAGES OF MASKS AND TREES.

DIVAS IN SLIDE SHOW INCLUDE: LENA HORNE, BILLIE HOLI-
DAY, MARLENE DIETRICH, SHIRLEY HORN, WHITNEY HOUSTON,
EARTHA KITT, ARETHA FRANKLIN, CHAKA KHAN, VANESSA
WILLIAMS, KOKO TAYLOR, ELIZABETH TAYLOR, CARMEN
MIRANDA, JOSEPHINE BAKER, GRACE JONES, MARIAN ANDER-
SON, LEONTYNE PRICE, ZORA NEALE HURSTON, BETTE DAVIS,
NINA SIMONE, SARAH VAUGHAN, TINA TURNER, JAMES
BROWN, LINDA CARTER, PRINCE, HATTIE MCDANIEL, GEORGE
SAND, DIANA ROSS & THE SUPREMES. THE SLIDE SHOW ENDS
WITH A MONTAGE OF ELLA FITZGERALD, FOLLOWED BY THE
RED SHOES FROM THE "WIZARD OF OZ." WHEN THE MUSIC
AND SLIDE SHOW END, PERFORMER RISES, ARMS UPSTRETCHED,
AND SINGS SEVERAL LINES OF "I AM CHANGING" FROM THE
MUSICAL "DREAMGIRLS.")

(PERFORMER THEN CUTS SONG SHORT WITH A SHRILL
CACKLE AND MOVES DOWNSTAGE FROM BEHIND PSYCHE.)

(*Lights cross-fade to full-stage bright wash.*)

> *I always wanted to be a diva.*
> *Like Lena, Josephine, Dorothy (Dandridge!)*
> *Actually, this is more like Angela Basset*
> *does Tina Turner.*
>
> *Beautiful, glamorous, ritzy, flawless . . .*
> *on top of the world!*
> *So here I hide behind this beautiful mask of opulence.*
> *Occasionally, I go out like this (yes I do).*

(*Struts across stage like a streetwalker.*)

> *No, dear, I ain't nobody's streetwalker*
> *any longer. This is homegirl diva attire!!*
> *Folk get confused, you know.*

Like one time, I was comin' outta this bar
struttin' steps like Diana,
showin' ass like Grace,
upstaging or downstaging
the dazzling divine diva darlings,
head held high
in testimony to all the
pride and beauty of the
sassy sisters supreme

when suddenly,
intruding my world,
a world so delicately designed,
blaring through the cacophony
of street sounds,
laughter,
dishing, and
dissing,
as clear as silver striking crystal,
your voice rang out,
"Don't get too close to the faggot;
it might rub off!"

I thought to keep on struttin'
and let your ignorance
pass over me
as if I couldn't be the
divine diva darling
at which such slander
was slung.
But I knew better.

And I wouldn't-couldn't-shouldn't
let you defame me with some
tacky lyrics,

poorly phrased,
and sung way out of tune.

"Rub off?!"

Up in your face,
over thin black glasses
and makeup,
flawless,
I gazed—
my eyes alive and hot,
like lasers
piercing
pupil to pupil
through the beads
in your sockets,
distant and cold—
to sing you a melody that you
wouldn't-couldn't-did-not-want
to hear.

So there we met,
in the chill of the night,
our faces so close,
the fog funneling
from my lungs moved
into your nostrils,
halted your breath,
singed your eyebrows,
invaded every precious pore
on your silken skin,
then rolled around
your neck
in a cloud lifting
behind your head

like smoke rising
from the apocalypse.

But you ran deep,
hard,
fast,
within yourself,
to shelter;
you averted your
colorless pits starving
for safety from the
liberating lyrics of
my stealing stare.
"No rubbing off would ever
be necessary for you, baby!"

Your glance,
returning,
understood my
melody's meaning
as did, well, many
curious onlookers standing by.

Then, like a beacon in
the night, I shone
through the brown-faced,
color-clad crowd in blinding light,
and sashayed into the night
leaving you
in awe

and trembling.

Sometimes, when I don't feel like dealing with all that shit,
I get dressed up and stay home.
(SUNG) All dressed up with no place to go.

Where's my party!? Where's my party, baby!?
The illusion—reality.
'Tis a mask of self-deception, delusion—
the ultimate escape from a world of pain, fear, suffering—
It works!!

Behind this mask, I am (SUNG)
better than Ella Fitzgerald or Miles' latest news, better than Bill Evans's
ballads or Joe Williams's blues, better than any rainy day, or checking
in at Monterey, better than anything except being in love . . .

Hell, people used to tell me when I walked into a room, my
attitude preceded me.
Well, they see attitude, they want attitude, I'll give them so
much they might want to reconsider.

(STRUTS WITH A WALK OF SPINE AND ARROGANCE ACROSS
STAGE THEN ABRUPTLY STOPS AND CONFRONTS AUDI-
ENCE . . .)

*Don't look too closely, though, you might get a glimpse of the fear
inside!!*
Yeah, they see attitude, they want attitude, I'll give them so
much they might want to reconsider.

(STRUTS AND STOPS THE SAME, BUT SNATCHES OFF WIG.)

*I said don't look too closely, though, you might get a glimpse of the
fear inside!!*
Eventually this mask gets uncomfortable, tiring, hot!

(FANS HIMSELF WITH WIG WHILE WALKING OVER TO SMALL
TABLE.)

Not to mention these big old dogs of mine start barking after
a few hours in these fierce pumps.

(SITS DOWN, REMOVES PUMPS, AND DISPLAYS À LA GAME
SHOW STYLE TO AUDIENCE.)

Pretty fab, huh? Teddy's shoes, Central Square, Cambridge, Massachusetts.

(REMOVES ACCESSORIES. AUDIENCE BECOMES MIRROR.)

And keepin' up a girl's wardrobe with all these accessories puts quite a dent in the pocketbook. I can't get to Filene's Basement but once, let me stop lying, four times a month these days.

(REMOVES FALSE EYELASHES.)

It's a rush getting all pretty, and like any high, it's addictive, addictive, addictive . . .

(STARTLED, LOOKS TO SEE WHERE ECHO IS COMING FROM.)

The most peculiar thing about this mask is that in order to get it off, I have to put on another one.

(SMEARS COLD CREAM ON FACE.)

Ain't that a bitch!

(MUGS AT AUDIENCE, BIG EYES, WIDE SMILE.)

Remind you of anything?

(ALMOST ANGERED, WIPES OFF COLD CREAM.)

And my skin does not care too much for this particular mask and all its makeup. Chil', I got skin so sensitive, if you even squint at it the wrong way, it'll pop a zit out! Most exhausting, however, is the emotional hangover that is part and parcel of all this glamour. If I don't eat a good meal before going to bed the night before, there's no telling how I'm going to feel when I wake up the next morning and see that *man* staring back at me in the mirror.

It's enough to drive any sistergirl crazy!
May I have a blackout, please?
(*Blackout.*)

(IN THE DARK, PERFORMER REMOVES DRESS AND UNDERGAR-
MENT IN BLACKOUT. SETS PEDESTAL SLIGHTLY DOWNSTAGE
AND REMOVES HULA HOOP FROM HOOK. THROUGHOUT THE
NEXT SECTION, HULA HOOP IS USED TO REPRESENT THE
WOMB, SHAME, A ROULETTE WHEEL, A CONDOM, AND WHAT-
EVER ELSE IS CALLED FOR. PERFORMER SHOULD FEEL FREE
TO USE HOOP IN THE BROADEST, MOST SYMBOLIC WAY POS-
SIBLE.)

(*Sarah Vaughan's rendition of "Ill Wind" is heard.*)
(*Light rises on pose.*)

Bold, daring, out on the edge?
Not really, I was born this way.

(STEPS THROUGH HOOP.)

Shame? No shame.

(PLACES HULA HOOP ON THE FLOOR IN FRONT OF THE
PEDESTAL.)

Not about the body that God gave me anyway.
That's what Mama said.
"Don't be 'shamed about the body the good Lord
gave you! It's perfect just the way it is."
I believed her. I still believe her.

(PERFORMER USES THE PREVIOUS LINES TO SLOWLY, DELIB-
ERATELY FALL INTO MICHELANGELO'S "DAVID" POSE, HOLD-
ING IT FOR A FEW COUNTS.)

But that belief became a double-edged sword,
carving a hole deep inside.
So I use this mask to separate myself from others.

(ROTATES AROUND.)

Isn't it ironic that this attire, the most natural of all
attires, has become a mask behind which I hide?

The shame exists inside, beneath the wall I create
through lust; pure, deep, unadulterated, uncensored lust.
In this world, I am in total control.
The object.

(POSES, GREEK ATHLETE STYLE, AND HOLDS.)

The objectified.

(POSES IN ANOTHER ATHLETIC POSITION AND HOLDS.)

The fulfiller of all your fantasies.
You want sex? You got it.
In this world, I can't imagine
anyone having sex,
without me.

This mask works almost everywhere. On stage at a go-go club,
to the bedroom,
where I can truly hide. Don't have to say a word.

(PICKS UP HULA HOOP AND USES IT TO UNDERSCORE TEXT.)

The external nature of sex sometimes keeps me from
being with myself, all together, whole.
And when I'm not with myself, all together, whole, when I'm not with
    myself, all
together, whole,
when I'm not wholly all together with myself,
I just might take that risk, play Russian roulette with my life,

(HOLDS HULA HOOP TO FORM A RING AROUND BODY, AS IF
IT WERE A PLANET, AND ROTATES AROUND, PICKING UP
SPEED AND STOPPING ON "COME AND GET IT.")

bury my face in the pillow, legs spread invitingly apart,
turning clichés inside out,

(ROTATES HULA HOOP AWAY FROM BODY AS IF TURNING IT
INSIDE-OUT.)

come and get it, get it and come.
I want to feel your juices sweet and syrupy
as the nectar of papayas squeeze into me
come and get it, get it and come,
no condom required. . . .

Just think, after this, I'll never have
to hide behind this mask again.
You blew it. You blew it. You ruined my cover!!
Much better. I can stand here and be completely comfortable with no
   clothes on.

     (RUNS AROUND NAKED, AD-LIBBING AND INVITING AUDI-
     ENCE TO STRIP AND JOIN HIM.)

     I don't like being dressed up with no place to go. "Where's my
party? Where's my party, baby? Where's my safety net party! *Catch
me, catch me, before I fall!*

     (POSES AS IF FALLING OFF PEDESTAL BUT CATCHES HIMSELF.
     AFTER COLLECTING HIMSELF, HE POSES IN A DANCE POSE,
     BACK TO AUDIENCE, AS IF LOOKING OUT OF A WINDOW.)

The neighbors get nervous if I stand in the window like this for too long.
Oh, there it goes again.
Boiling up like molten lava within me,
erupting in every way, shape and form
from every pore, until
I am completely covered with the dried
pumice of the ages.
Safe from anyone to see, behind my looking mask;
a mask of self-destruction, self-forgetting, the lynching of my spirit.

     ("FLIES" OFF PEDESTAL AND MOVES OVER TO SMALL TABLE.)

But I'd rather my spirit to soar.
So as most people do when they get up in the morning, I dress up,
put on the everyday drag.

     (BEGINS TO DRESS.)

A person could get arrested for running around like this in this society: which is the true shame if you ask me (well, you didn't ask, but I told you anyway). I try to stop hiding, *stop hiding!*
(*Music stops, if still playing.*)
(*Bright lights bump up.*)

Someone is looking for you, they want to find you. They want to
    throw you that
party.
Someone is bound to get through that wall.
They already have.
In fact, now that I'm dressed, maybe I'll seduce them all with promises,
with glimpses of greater glories to follow,
trust their imagination. I have no problem with the
finality. It is the act leading to the state
I haven't quite mastered.
But hey, that's all right.
That's okay.

Enter. . . .

End of part II.

III. Papa may have

THIS IS NOT YOUR MONOLOGUE!

I fell for him the first time he looked into my eyes. He flirted and winked and flirted at me with his eyes.

Jonathan seduced me with a smile, his rapturous, laughing eyes inviting. The tender "Hello" that rolled off his tongue resonated down to my toes. I welcomed all that awakened within me. Goose bumps scurried up my back; a shiver down my spine, and all it took was that simple "Hello" across the aisle in the "New in Hard Cover" section at Waldenbooks, and I was smitten. I forgot all about finding the book I wanted to buy (I still can't remember what it was). Not that it mattered. It was coming up on midnight, the bookstore was about to close, and Jonathan said: "Would you like to come by my place for a while?"

"Uh-huh."

(PERFORMER TRANSFORMS SPACE INTO BEDROOM, LIGHTS CANDLE FIGURE, SETS UP THE "BED" WITH THE BENCH AND PEDESTAL, AND PLACES TWO PILLOWS ON THE FLOOR AND KNEELS.)

(*Shirley Horn's "Estate" is heard.*)

Jonathan's smooth, developed body smothers my trembling. He mouths my balls, sucks my toes, and eats my neck between the nape and the back of the ear like someone eating their first meal after fasting. I worship his cock like I have no other before. I kiss the head, lick the shaft up and down, and tongue his piss-slit, causing him to squiggle and squirm. I cup his balls in the palm of my right hand, slide my middle index finger into his wanting, needing asshole, and take his big rod into the back of my throat, carefully massaging the head with the roof of my mouth, my lips caressing the root all the while. My left hand moves over the washboard of his abdomen, finds his right nipple, then his left, and presses and pinches each of them with its forefinger and thumb. As he moans and groans, groans and moans, my mouth, tongue, lips, hands, and fingers operating like a well-oiled machine, I fall deeper into the throes of his spell. He spits out one last screech. My right hand feels the tension between his balls and crack and I release him to welcome the warm, sticky spurts that wet my face, neck, and chest.

(*Music fades out.*)

(SUNG.)

> *When you give from your heart without measure,*
> *you'll receive precious gems you'll treasure.*
> *So don't hesitate, love won't always wait,*
> *the nighttime fades fast into dawn's new fate.*
>
> *Cast away your fears at midnight, midnight.*
> *Wipe away your tears as sadness disappears.*
> *Let your passion soar unbound,*
> *when old midnight comes around.*

(EXALTED, JUMPS ONTO PEDESTAL.)

From that night forward, Jonathan and I lived a completely enthralling, fairy-tale fantasy that seemed to exist somewhere slightly above earth.

Until he asked to fuck me.

(JUMPS DOWN FROM PEDESTAL.)

My feet quickly touched ground. I vowed to never again to let anyone inside that way. So when Jonathan breathed, "I want to fuck you," into my ear during one of our pinnacles of passion, I winced. An overbearing tension ran through my bones. All my muscles tightened up to clutch the cage that was my heart. Something sour settled in the pit of my stomach. My whole body said *No!! Repeated it, drummed it, hummed it, and sang it. No.*

But my mind whispered, "Yes." I hadn't even considered voluntarily engaging in such an act. I could only conceive of someone taking me like that, but never asking for it. Now, I had actually been *asked*.

Jonathan planted a seed when he first breathed his request, and it branched out in ways I had never imagined. The more he asked, the more I wanted him inside.

Eventually, my mind convinces my body to cooperate.

(*Light changes. Chocolate double-shaded window gobo is projected onto psyche above "bed" and remains for the rest of the show.*)

(*Music begins again.*)

(PERFORMER LIES ON BACK OVER PEDESTAL AND BENCH, PLACES PILLOWS UNDERNEATH BACK. AFTER DEMONSTRATING, IN EXAGGERATED STYLE, THE "SAFE SEX COMMERCIAL" THAT FOLLOWS, THROWS LEGS STRAIGHT UP TOGETHER WITH A LOT OF TENSION.)

After putting on that protective piece of prophylactic (holding the tip and slowly rolling it down to the root) and administering what seems to be an entire bottle of lube (only water soluble brands of course, like Probe), I throw my heels to the heavens, clench my fists, and tightly close my eyes. When I hear his soothing voice say, "Just relax," I do. (IN THREE DELIBERATE MOVES, PERFORMER PARTS AND RELAXES LEGS) The mattress beneath absorbs all of my body's tension. I feel his sex glide deep inside. The initial burning pain is overcome with a warm ecstasy when his shaft finds and massages my prostate. Talk about probe! While he plugs me, I try to plug my mental eardrums to shut out all the voices telling me that I couldn't, shouldn't be enjoying this:

(*Music bumps out.*)

(SHIFTS HEAD SIDE TO SIDE IN THE AGONY OF HEARING VOICES.)

"Damn child, your ass was not made for that!" "Hope that jimmy cap don't break!" "You're gonna die." Shut up! "How much for all that sweet brown ass, pretty mama?!" Shut up! "Your insides will never be the same!" Shut up! "Ain't nothing but your doctor's finger suppose to be in your butt hole, honey!" Oh, Dad, not you, too: "What the fuck do you think you are doing!?" Well,

Dad, that's exactly what I'm doing. "What the fuck do . . ." Look, Dad, *this is not your monologue, okay?* "What the fuck . . ." Oh, so you don't want to shut up? All right, Dad—let's deal!
End of section.

THE VIRTUOSO
(*Light bumps to cool wash.*)

(JUMPS OUT OF POSITION, MOVES DOWNSTAGE, AND PER-FORMS POEM, MIMING THE BEATING OF DRUMS AND CLASH-ING OF SYMBOLS WHENEVER SCRIPTED.)

My father was a percussionist, a virtuoso, if you will
blessed with rhythm & soul & blues & jazz
and oh! could he
play   play play   play play   that drum

when happy or sad, lonely or mad
he beat   & beat & beat that drum

intoxicated with shot glasses of despair & pain
disillusioned before mirrors
cracked
by the cruelty & deceit of the black man's world
he struck the cymbals & pounded the tom-tom
with sticks or belts his fists and palms
whatever he chose
he beat   & beat & beat that drum

sending timbres piercing
& screeching
in pitches so high
they say only dogs
could hear
or low deep droning
moans & groans
some thought came

from the bowels
of the earth

beating
& pounding   & striking   &
beating

boom boom
boom   tisssh

boom boom
boom   tisssh

boom boom
boom   tissssh

Sometimes   I wish
Daddy hadn't played   me

so well.

End of section.

DADDY'S BOY
(*Light cross-fades to brighter wash downstage left.*)

(MOVES INTO WHAT COULD BE HIS LIVING ROOM AND SITS
ON STOOL. AS STORY UNFOLDS, THE SPACE TRANSFORMS
INTO EACH PLACE THE SCENE OCCURS. PERFORMER EMBOD-
IES EACH CHARACTER THAT ENTERS THE STORY.)

Dad didn't always express himself this way. I remember being
awakened as early as 4:46 A.M. by footsteps and the peculiar noise
of gurgling water rushing from the kitchen faucet. The aroma of
hot water washing coffee grounds tiptoed under the bedroom door

and kissed my nose. The crisp sounds of cereal crackling against porcelain and glass catching ice aroused me. I could almost feel the steam from the percolator gliding down the frosty window over the sink, almost taste the burnt-brown bread springing up out of the toaster. . . .

Every weekday, Daddy woke up the house before the sun seeped into the purple-pink sky. Uniformed in a gray shirt with "Hazelle" embroidered in red thread above the left chest pocket, navy blue pants, and black round-toed shoes, Daddy went off to the brewery. Never late. Hadn't missed a day in over twenty years. Proud to provide for his better half, girl and boy. So proud. The kind of pride that jumped out of his voice after parent-teacher day at my school. "Your teachers say you sure are gifted. Can write your own ticket someday. Do anything you put your mind to. Don't settle for second-best. I love you, my one and only son."

Barely hearing Daddy's shoes descend the hall stairs and the back door lock click, I would turn over, curl both knees toward my chest, and smile my way back to sleep.

Like a tape, these words rewound over and over in my head as I lay under the darkness. "Daddy really loves me and wants the best for me. To succeed. I will. Anything to make him proud, now and always. . . ."

(RISES FROM STOOL AND SINGS.)

"Can it be that it was oh so simple then, or has time rewritten every line?" As I grew up and he grew older, we grew apart. Our relationship consisted primarily of discussions about the weather and what he thought I should be doing with my life. College holiday breaks provided a reason for visits home, but after graduation, I could use work as an excuse not to visit at all. After three years, my father finally took the initiative to come visit me.

The first night of his stay, he called to suggest we attend a local jazz club. Jazz remained Dad's deepest passion. I used to feel the floor pulsate to the beats of Charlie Parker, Weather Report, the

Modern Jazz quartet, just to list a few. Mama would yell, "Tell your father to turn that damn bass *down!*" as she nearly bounced off the couch up front, trying to take her naps.

I too had developed a need for the music, but I pretended to dislike it simply because he worshiped it. I reluctantly obliged.

On the way to the hotel, I paused with hesitation—a hesitation so powerful it drew the attention of passersby. Why prolong the separation? I did genuinely miss him. Fear crept over my body, stealing away reason. The fog funneling from my mouth blurring the insignia over the entryway, I lifted my face to the heavens and entered.

Dad hadn't aged much since the last time I saw him. (REACH-ING OUT AS IF TO TOUCH-STUDY DAD'S FACE) His solemn face wore the same bags under the eyes, the same receding hairline, the same droop beneath the jawbone. Although a few more age spots crept down his forehead before the gray-blue waves of hair. Dad hadn't a single wrinkle, not even a distinguished laugh line. For a man in his seventies, he looked exceptionally well.

Avoiding an embrace, I suggested we head right on over to the club. We arrived just in time to avoid the line that formed immediately behind us, as if we were the main attraction. As I reached into my pocket to retrieve my wallet for the cover, the burly man standing in the doorway announced, "I need to see some ID, boy."

Boy! I thought to myself. What kinda sh . . . Boy! This mess is tired. Who does he think he is? Boy. It ain't 1795. I ain't nobody's slave. And comin' from a brother, too. He oughtta know better. If Dad wasn't here, I swear, I would haul off—

"Sir, this is a father-son affair." Eyebrows lifted, chin held high, he gazed, unflinching, directly into the man's eyes, a twenty-dollar bill dangling from his outstretched hand. The pitch of Dad's voice and his confident yet condescending expression reminded me of the many faces Dad wore during his arguments with Old Man Jenkins over a plethora of topics about which Dad knew nothing. Nothing. But he had the full-fledged routine down pat. He churned out "data" so fast and with such conviction, Mr. Jenkins could do nothing but concede.

Without another word, the doorman handed Dad his change and moved aside. The routine still worked.

(*Light changes to cool blue wash downstage right.*)

(*Dexter Gordon's "Cheesecake" is heard.*)

(MOVES INTO BAR SCENE. LIGHTS CANDLE ON SMALL TABLE.)

Once inside, the aroma of venerable victuals from early evening's happy hour fare still lurked amidst the smoke in the crowded room. The music's electricity danced over and carried us into the party. The entire room throbbed in time to the bass and drum rhythm. Ice cubes struck notes on tumblers and stemware in tune with the cascading, rainfall tinkle from the piano. Tenor-sax riffs wailed measure after measure in call-and-response with the vibrato of laughter from a woman sitting at the bar. (LAUGHS HYSTERICALLY) Piercing laughter. A mama's-talking-on-the-phone kind of laughter. The joint was jumpin'.

Dad led us over to a table near the stage corner. A waitress sped over to take our order. "Brandy straight up and a draft beer back. Thank you, ma'am."

"I'll have a soda and lime, please." When we sat down, I lit a cigarette.

"You *still* smokin'."

"And you're *still* drinkin'!" I could still hear my mama—*Your smart mouth is going to be your downfall someday!*—rippling about my head.

Unable to think of anything else to say, I absorbed the music and surveyed the room. The woman at the bar who was laughing on our way in was feeling awfully good now. Swaying to the music, she could barely keep her hips on the stool. A drunken man vying, with himself, for her affections become too eager. She tried to remove his hand from her waist, but he resisted. (RISING, MOVING AWAY FROM TABLE) The woman stood up, hands on hips, and with sharp neck jerks still in time with the music, made her point as clear as the clarinet's throat. "Get your hands offa me, you drunken motherfu—"

As the music crescendoed, the man raised his curled hand,

shouted, "You ol' siditty bitch!" and struck her across the face. Twice.

The drama intensified as two barbacks restrained the man and dragged him away.

(*Music bumps out.*)

And I went away, away, way back to bed that night when I was ten and Daddy stumbled home at one A.M., woke me up, and ordered those dishes washed, dried, and put away. *Mama! Tell Daddy to leave me alone! What did I say, boy! Do as l say, boy! No! What?! Mama, Mama, please?! Boy! boom boom, boom tissh . . . boom boom, boom tissh . . . boom boom, boom tissh tissh! tissh!! tisshh!!*

"Thank you very much. We would like to slow it down now and play some blues. This one's called 'Don't Explain.' Hope you enjoy it." The voice from the stage brought me back.

(*Dexter Gordon's rendition of "Don't Explain" is heard.*)

"Son, are you all right?"

"Yes, fine. Just spaced out. So, this place is pretty intense, huh?"

"Better than I expected. Now looky here. What are your plans? You applyin' to law school anytime soon?"

"Law's school's out the picture for a while. Didn't you get the reviews I sent you about the shows—"

"I don't know nothin' 'bout what you sent me. All them letters is too damn small to read anyhow."

"So what did you do, *Dad?* Throw them away?"

"What's it matter to ya? For cryin' out loud, you think you was sendin' me a write-up from the goddamn *New York Times* about some big court case you won that was gon' make things better for our people. All that damn money spent at that uppity school wasted on your hardheaded nonsense."

"Since you're operating on so few brain cells as of late, let me remind you that that 'uppity school' was all you seemed to be able to talk about to your friends after I got accepted."

"Don't push me, kiddo. I'm still the father here, and I ain't gon' tolerate your back talk. . . . Look at me when I'm talkin' to ya. A man's gotta earn his place in the sun. You still tryin' to get

where I am, and you'll be damn good and lucky if you make it this
far. And what's a man gon' do when his luck runs out? I'm damn
near seventy years old, and I *still* gotta listen to the man upstairs.
I knows what I'm talkin' 'bout. So, looky here, don't you think you
should—"

"Dad! I'm doing just fine, okay!?"

"Don't raise your voice at me. You ain't too old for me to—
Looky here, this actin' or whatever it is you doin' ain't gon' secure
no future. You need to listen to your father, boy." (BEAT.)

"This *boy* is a grown man perfectly capable of taking care of
himself. This *boy* does not need you or anybody telling him what
to do. Anybody. This is *my* life and *my* future, and *I* have to decide what to do with it. What I need is your support for my decisions. But what I don't need, what I *really* don't need, is your
unsolicited advice about what I *should* be doing. Got it!?"

I grabbed my belongings, threw some money on the table, and
bolted for the door.

"Son, wait. Please. Don't go like this. I'm sorry. Come sit down
and lemme talk to you."

"Did you say. . . ?"

"Yes, I know, I said I'm sorry. You're right. You're grown up
and I shouldn't be telling you what to do. I just want you to be
happy."

"I am happy. Are you?"

"You know your mother and me did the best we could. Life's
short and unexpected things happen. I hate what's happened to
us. I know when you was little, I made some mistakes. But if there's
something I did . . . Well, if there's anything I ever did wrong,
lemme just ask you one thing. Son, please forgive me." (BEAT.)

That'll take more willpower or want power or whatever kind
of power than it'll take to stop these nasty cigarettes.

But this I must do. I had to. Across from me sat the pillar of
man who taught me about discipline, respect, honor, dignity.
About how to rise up after being knocked down. How to dream
great dreams. How to love. To live. The only father I've always
had, the only father I'll ever have. And deep down, beneath the

layers of fear, resentment, anger, contempt—someplace comfort-
ably situated under my navel—I knew this man was the only father I ever wanted. My one-and-only father.

(*Light blinks on pedestal.*)

I could've sworn I saw the tiny droplet of water that collected
in the far corner of Daddy's left eye trickle down his cheek. "I love
you, Daddy," I murmured so quietly, Daddy nearly had to read my
lips. But he had so firmly memorized the memory of the look in
my ten-year-old eyes the last time he saw those words, he knew
what I was going to say before my lips moved at all.

(*Music fades out.*)

End of section.

POST COITUS INTERRUPTUS

(AS IF CAUGHT OFF BALANCE BETWEEN THE TWO WORLDS,
PERFORMER MIMES BEING PULLED BACK AND FORTH INTO
EACH BY A ROPE HE HOLDS ON TO WITH BOTH HANDS, ARMS
OUTSTRETCHED.)

"*All right, Daddy*. I'll just imagine your lips are finally sealed
about this one! You've said enough. No more rude interruptions,
okay? All right, I forgive you already, now get the fuck out of my
monologue! I've got love to make!!"

(WITH ONE JERK, HE BREAKS THE "ROPE" HOLDING HIM TO
DADDY'S WORLD AND SNEAKS BACK INTO BED WITH JONA-
THAN, AND THEY PICK UP WHERE THEY LEFT OFF. HE IS MUCH
MORE RELAXED, WRITHING IN THE DEEPEST STATE OF PAS-
SION DEMONSTRATED SO FAR.)

(*Music begins where it left off.*)
(*Lights stop blinking. "Bar" lights bump out.*)

"Oh yeah, daddy, I'm with you. That's good, right there!" Our
rhythms synchronized, Jonathan and I make love for what seems
like hours. My heels are burned by the stars. Our bodies speak in

tongues. I'm tossed from exaltation to exhaustion and back again. I start on my back, but before it's over, I take it doggy style, sideways, standing and sitting. I'd never thought it possible to connect this deeply with another man. (BEAT.) Anybody got a cigarette?

It was, indeed, liberation.

The fairy tale moved quickly into the next chapter. Jonathan served up an abundant feast, and I was a beggar at the banquet. I ate, and ate, and ate that feast. Due to circumstances beyond my control, Jonathan exited long before I would've written him out. No more sugar in my bowl, and I had developed quite the sweet tooth. I was left, supplicating, like little Oliver Twist:

(*Lights restored to level at opening of show.*)

"Please, sir, I want some more. Please, sir, I want some more."

I wish I could tell you more. But wouldn't you know, I just remembered the book I wanted to buy when we met: Terry Mac-Millan's *Disappearing Acts*.

I always knew there was much more to a good man than a niceably–used dick, and I'd finally had a healthy portion of it. So healthy, in fact, that I could stand before the mirror, no longer afraid of falling through to the other side.

Jonathan's going left me hungry, so hungry. But just because I was hungry, it didn't mean I had to eat at the first restaurant I passed, and Lord knows I was sick of drive-thrus.

There's a big difference between hunger and starvation.

(*Lights cross-fade to tighter "spot".*)

(SUNG.)

> *Rich relations give crusts of bread and such,*
> *you can help yourself, but don't take too much*
> *Mama may have, and papa may have,*
> *but God bless the child who's got his own,*
> *who's got his own.*

(*Slow fade to black with window gobo lingering a bit.*)

you're just like my father

PEGGY SHAW

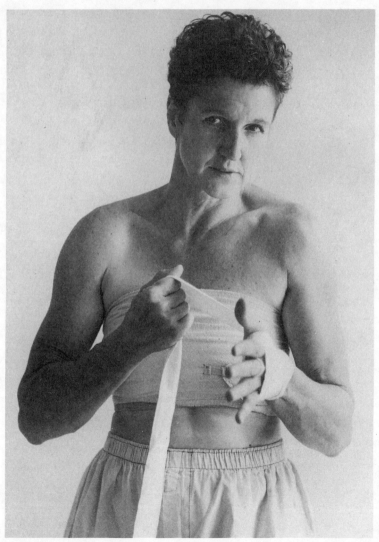

Notes on *You're Just Like My Father*

I didn't want to write a solo show, it's just that I was the only one left in town. I had to do it to survive. Hampshire College called up and said they wanted to book the Split Britches' show *Lesbians Who Kill,* but my partner in crime, Lois Weaver, had recently become an ex-patriot 'cause London seduced her to go there and work for money doing what she was doing in New York for free.

So I said, "Lois won't be here, but I have a solo show" (a lie). They said, "Great, what's the name of it?" and I said, "What's it for?" They said, "Parents' weekend," so I said, "It's called *You're Just Like My Father.*" So I had three months to make it.

When people ask me how do I make my shows, I say, "I book them; and they make themselves." As the booking gets closer, the show emerges. And like many artists now, I don't worry about immediate money. I just charge food and money and props and worry about it later. (Most artists I know at the moment are on the average $15,000 in credit card high-interest debt in order to make their work.) Not that I got a lot of grants before they cut the few that there were, but I am getting older and I have no time to wait for anything.

I try and let the show come from my body, which seems to be a more creative and reliable source than my mind. If I went from my mind, I would always be writing with the knowledge that I have always felt the way I do now. My mind is stuck in the moment, so when I write I think I have always been in menopause, always been a grandmother, and always been an enlightened queer like I think I am now. (Well, sometimes I pretend to have health insurance to see how that would feel.)

But my body has lots of lumps in it (I should be thankful I don't have health insurance or they would have removed them by now); the lumps seem to store up images not just from my life, but from some kind of kinetic, genetic memory.

My family understands that I tell the truth even though my shows may not be factual. The creative truth. Like how it feels rather than the times or the dates. My sister spends her time digging into dates and the past trying to connect my family to Winston Churchill and a lost fortune.

It would be more helpful if in school we were taught how it felt to have had America drop the first atom bomb on a city of people who were alive, rather than why they say they did it, or what date they did it on, or how beautiful and powerful and big it looked like mushrooming up from tests far away in the empty dessert.

So I wrote a show that I thought was about my father, and it was about my mother, which I didn't know until I had performed it. The part about my father—the smell of his shirts, the feel of his cheeks, his shiny shoes and creased pants (he said if a man had shiny shoes and a crease in his pants, no one would notice his poverty)—was a catalyst to my relationship to my mother and to my relationship with her husband's clothes that I loved so much.

I write in the monkey theory: If I write enough words, some of them will be good.

I arrange my shows the way I paint a painting: This feels right, this seems like it goes here, this looks good, I like this color. I try not to question it. I try to trust my impulses.

I make comedy by telling the truth. There is nothing funnier than the truth. I don't know what is funny until I do it in front of an audience. It's a job, it's just another show, I just want to be able to keep doing it. I got scared 'cause I had a nightmare that I had to teach my grandson to paint in a blackened-out basement 'cause art was illegal.

About Peggy Shaw

"Peggy Shaw is cofounder of the WOW Cafe, New York City, and with Lois Weaver and Deb Margolin cofounder of Split Britches, a lesbian feminist theater company that since 1981 has edified and wildly entertained everyone with their vaudevillian satirical gender-bending performances. Since 1980 Split Britches meaningfully extended the post-1960s political theater mandate of combining art and life; they rip apart theatrical "convention," exposing it to the bone and creating a new aesthetic combining the trash street aesthetic and drag of hot peaches, the story weaving of spiderwoman, and the live-art Brechtian exposure of what is real now, never letting you forget they are performing as themselves. They explore butch-femme stylistics, and in every piece women's rage, desire, poverty, hope, and love. "Their performances are sites of clarity, inspiration, and community." (Laurie Stone)

Actor, playwright, and producer Peggy Shaw has received two Obie Awards for her work in Dress Suits to Hire, a collaboration with Holly Hughes, and Belle Reprieve, a collaboration with the London Based Theater Company Bloolips. She is the author and performer in the currently touring solo work Menopausal Gentleman, directed by Rebecca Taichman. Among her celebrated works are Lust and Comfort, Upwardly Mobile Home, Lesbians Who Kill, and the Jane Chambers Award–winning play Split Britches. Peggy is a 1988 and 1995 New York Foundation for the Arts award winner for "Emerging Forms." She received the 1995 Anderson Prize Foundation Stonewall Award for excellence in "making the world a better place for gays and lesbians," and her company is a two-time nominee for the Cal Arts Herb Alpert Award. In addition to her work with Split Britches, she was a collaborator, writer, and performer with Spiderwoman Theater and Hot Peaches Theater and a cofounder of the Obie Award–winning WOW Cafe, a Lower East Side lesbian performance space since 1980. In 1996 Peggy portrayed Billy Tipton in the American Place's production of Carson Kreitzer's The Slow Drag.

The company teaches performance in residence at various colleges, including, Hampshire, University of Hawaii, University of Northern Iowa, U.C.

Davis, U.C. Riverside, and William & Mary. Peggy has taught solo performance at Vassar, Wells, and Hampshire Colleges. Routledge Press has just released a book simultaneously in London and New York on the company titled Split Britches: Lesbian Practice, Feminist Performance, edited by Sue-Ellen Case, which includes seven of Split Britches' plays.

You're Just Like My Father was commissioned by Hampshire College for Parents and Friends Weekend in fall 1994.

The show was developed at Dixon Place, produced by the ICA in London and LaMaMa Theater in New York.

You're Just Like My Father was written by Peggy Shaw and directed by Stacy Makishi and James Neale-Kennerly, with original lighting design by Rachel Shipp. Music and vocals are by Laka Daisical, additional vocals by Vick Ryder. Special thanks to Stormy Brandenberger, Stafford, Karena Rahall, Rose Sharp, Jill Lewis, Meryl Vladimer, Howard Thies, LaMaMa Etc., Rachel Shipp, Gay Sweatshop London, Lois Weaver, Hampshire College, WOW Cafe, Dixon Place, and New York Foundation for the Arts.

"I want to produce new images, not old lies."

—Peggy Shaw

you're just like my father

PEGGY SHAW

(LIGHTS COME UP ON PEGGY SITTING ON A CHAIR ON A BARE
STAGE WITH BARE BREASTS AND BOXER SHORTS, BARE FEET.
SHE WRAPS HER BREASTS WITH AN ACE BANDAGE AND GOES
OVER TO A SUITCASE ON A TABLE AND OPENS IT. THE OPEN-
ING OF THE SUITCASE STARTS THE SONG LIKE THE OPENING
OF A MUSIC BOX.)

(SONG: "YOU MAY NOT BE AN ANGEL.")

(SHE GETS ANOTHER BANDAGE FROM THE SUITCASE AND
WRAPS ON TOP OF THE FIRST BANDAGE. SHE REMOVES THE
HAND BOXING WRAP AND WRAPS A HAND AS THE SONG FIN-
ISHES. WHEN SHE IS FINISHED WRAPPING, SHE DROPS HER
HEAD INTO HER HANDS AND GROWLS LIKE A WOLF.)

The landlord wouldn't fix the toilet
'Cause he said there was nothing wrong with it.
She didn't know what she was planning on doing
She knew she had to do something.
You get no satisfaction calling in the authorities.
She watched the darkness in her window, waiting for some kind
Of release, but nothing came.
Her arms needed to strike out, to drive outside of her what was

Eating her up inside, but there was always such consequences in
wrecking a place to feel better.
She went over to the Kleenex box on the shelf, and started tearing
Up white pieces of Kleenex into tiny white squares,
Then she filled each square with a little pile of white sugar.
Then she drew up the Kleenex in a little sack and tied each one with a
*   piece of string.*
This took her all afternoon.
She waited until she knew it would rain and spread her tiny bundles all
*   over*
The big, beautiful, groomed, green lawn in front of his office.
It rained good and hard.
The next day the big, beautiful, groomed, green lawn was dotted with
Hundreds of white specks of sugar stuck to the blades of grass,
There were no complaints to the management or to the police.
Only to the minister.
And the minister went to speak to the family, to her husband.
But since he was dead, he couldn't take the blame.
That is to say, my father couldn't take the blame.
'Cause this was my mother before they destroyed her.
My mother who was in love with me in the house.

(RUNS HANDS THROUGH HAIR, MAKING SOUND OF A WOLF.
FADE TO BLACK.)

Hey!
I'm Eddie.
My father wouldn't call me Eddie, he called me Margaret.
Margaret means pearl.
I was his pearl of a girl.
But pearl didn't match my outfits.
This is my face. It's sharp and I look like my father.
You look just like your father, my mother would say.
I look like my father when I'm in a good mood.
Most lesbians I know really like their fathers, me included.
My father was a Leo, he had a heart condition; he had to count to ten
     before he hit us.

He gave me the same heart condition simply because I knew him so well.
He had big hands. I have his big hands.
I like to touch things and people. Once a shrink asked me where my
    desire comes from.
I said, "From my hands."
She told me to keep my hands to myself. She didn't mean to say it. It just
Came out and embarrassed her. I guess shrinks aren't supposed to be so
Direct.
But I knew what she meant.
There were so many children in my family that when we visited people's
Houses we all had to hold our hands behind our backs for the whole
    visit so
We couldn't touch anything. I have to control my hands all the time. My
Grandmother told me I would do great things with my hands; I think she
Meant play the piano.
My father told me that his father knocked out Joe Louis with his bare hands.

(MUSICAL NUMBER: "THIS IS A MAN'S WORLD." DURING ALL
MUSICAL NUMBERS A MICROPHONE DESCENDS FROM CEIL-
ING AS IN A BOXING RING.)

(MUSIC CONTINUED OVER.)

>   As hard
>   As I've tried
>   I can't get it up
>   Fully
>   On top
>   You know
>   Head
>   To toe
>   Missionary
>   Go tell it on the mountain
>   But mounting
>   Is something I've got trouble with
>   'Cause I can't
>   Get on top

Get hard
Butch on top
It's left over
From way back
When I was a boy
And all the girls
Wanted me to please
It's hard
To keep it up
My reputation
Easy for the young ones
But hard for me
But not hard enough.
If it only comes down
Or comes up
To coming
To keep it going
To keep it up
To strapping one on
To whacking me off
'Cause
Deep inside my love for you
Is a flash picture
It has to do with my arms
My fingers
My hands
These are the butch queer feminine parts
Of me
On the other hand
Either my left or my right
I'm told that I'm missing out on a dildo.
I can hardly look at the real ones
That look like real dicks
I can look at the dolphin ones
Dolphins don't have veins.
It's the veins.

That vanity in men.
I think Moby Dick was really a dolphin.
My father's dick looked like a dolphin
When I saw him
In the toilet.
Feminists made me hate dolphins, I mean dildos.
They tried to make me hate boxer shorts
Not that I want to put blame
On anyone for my
Lack of thrust
Except maybe the missionaries.
I don't want to be like my parents
In any way
Unless, of course,
I can't help it
You should never take your parents personally.

(GO TO CENTER RING, COUNTDOWN FROM TEN.)

(UNIFORM UNWRAP.)

(DRESSING INTO ARMY UNIFORM.)

My mother used to make me things from cardboard all taped together like houses. She used the cardboard from my father's Sunday shirts from the Chinese laundry. She caught me at the kitchen table at five years old, drawing a picture of a woman tied to a tree with her hands behind her and her breasts were naked, and I drew a woman kissing her breasts. My mother watched me closely from then on and made sure I didn't have girlfriends for too long or stay over at their houses. She said I'd go to hell if I didn't get married.

I liked other people's mothers. You know, around fifty, the ones who had to work in a store. They seemed like they could stand in one place without someone to protect them. But I wanted to sit with them in the kitchen for hours while they flirted with me. Their husbands seemed so old. And I was so full of desire. I would do things for them. And they never told me I was going to hell.

My mother hated my grandfather, and when he died, she didn't want to go to the funeral either, so we went to Brigham's in Cambridge and had a hot-fudge sundae. For years after that when I saw my mother I would take her for a hot-fudge sundae with marshmallow and nuts, I was her sundae lover. Once, we tried to go to a different ice-cream place. They didn't make it right, so they were wrong and she got mad. That's how she was about her family. Her family was right and the rest of the world was wrong.

(FINISH DRESSING: TIE AND HAT AND SALUTE.)

My mother said, "You'll go to hell if you keep this up."
My mother said, "You'll die if you run into the street."
My mother said, "A bear will eat your child if you leave it unattended on the back porch."
My mother said, "If you bowl on Sunday, you'll go to hell."
My mother said, "If you swear, you'll be like Catholics."
When I stand on my mother's shoulders I can see very far, sir!
I can see past my grandfather and into the dripping water of the rain.

(TRAVELING MUSIC SUCH AS IN PEE WEE'S BIG TOP.)

I always pack a gun.
That gives me the I'm okay, you're okay, look.
The one I use for borders.
Sometimes it works for me.
Once I went through a border with a drag queen, who was dressed butch to pass as a man.
I was dressed femme to pass as a girl.
They pulled us over and wanted to see our suitcases.
He got my suitcase with suits and ties and letters to girls.
And I got his suitcase, with dresses and high heels and poems to boys.
They passed us through as normal.
But I didn't have my gun.
And I didn't have my dildo.

Packing, I call it, in both cases.
I carry my gun, unlike my dildo.
I carry it just in case.
The gun that is. I keep the dildo in my drawers with my neatly folded
    white boxer shorts.
I don't use it. I'm not dangerous.
Knowing I'm safe makes me a trustworthy person.
You could even trust me with your wife if you wanted to.

(MAKING SUGAR BUNDLES.)

Doctors say they aren't sure what ovaries do or what they're for, but I know that *en los ovarios* is my *luz de la vida. Luz de la vida* is not a type of gun, it's a joy of life. In Mexico, women carry the joy of life in their ovaries. Right now it's hard for you to find my ovaries because they're all hidden by my fibroids, or barnacles, as I call them. When something is in the sea a long time, barnacles usually grow on it. But that's why it's harder and harder for me to find my joy in life. Well, not joy in my life, harder for me to find my ovaries. I only showed my barnacles to one woman in Seattle, and she looked in and said I had a beautiful cervix. Have you ever had anyone tell you you had a beautiful cervix? Your body starts smiling from the inside and gets all perky and feeling good about itself. Whenever you have a chance, you should tell a woman you know that they have a beautiful cervix. As far as I know, cervixes aren't measured up to any standard of beauty, so you won't have anything to go by except your feelings. It doesn't matter if you believe anything I say or not.

It's just like my gun. I know it's there.
It's amazing that I still have sex.

(TRAVELING MUSIC.)

Or that I ever had sex,
When I was young I thought everyone knew more than me about it.
All I knew was that when you grew up you had to shave your pubic
    hair. I knew that
'cause I read page forty-nine in my brother's book under his mattress.

I also thought that I would get pregnant wearing his dungarees.
Not so farfetched, really, depending on how soon after he wore them.
I thought the other girls had secrets that they wouldn't tell me, like there
   was something
they wore in their underpants.
'Cause my friend, Joanne Brulee, who I loved more than anyone,
She let me kiss her sometimes.
Once in gym class I was helping her jump over the horse, or the buck,
   as we
Called it, I grabbed for her and my hand slipped between her legs.
I felt something hard, like a box in her underpants.
I can still feel it.
I try and think, still, what it was, 'cause it wasn't soft like a sanitary pad.
It felt more like the box they came in in the vending machines in the
   girl's room. I
never found out 'cause she moved to Chicago and killed herself.
Maybe it was a gun between her legs.

(HIT/SHOT—FALL)

(SHORT PIECE OF CIRCUS MUSIC WHILE A VERY LONG PAPER
TRICK IS TAKEN OUT OF MOUTH.)

My mother said, "Every word you speak is forever in the air, it
will never go away." She meant it as a threat to keep me from saying bad things, but I took it as a convenient sort of a diary. A record
that could be read anytime. A record with its needle stuck in a
groove, playing the same song over and over again. Unforgiving.
It's only now that I realize that these words can be used against
me. Or would come back to haunt me.

(BEGIN LAYING BAGS.)

I would have joined the army in the early sixties if *Life* magazine hadn't published their latest test for detection for homosexuals in the army. They made you look through these binocular-type
glasses to watch slides of naked women, and if your eyes dilated

when you saw a naked body of the same sex, then you were kicked out of the army in disgrace. I remember when I read it, my grand-father was dozing off in his favorite chair in the afternoon, after complaining about modern things, how they make too much noise and the air used to be clean, and that made him cry, only his tears were because he married the wrong woman. He was showing my grandmother Cicely an engagement ring he had bought for another woman and she thought it was for her and she accepted the mar-riage proposal and he was too embarrassed to explain the truth, so he married her and they were together fifty-five years.

I caught on to my legacy.
I caught on to that game in time.
There was life before I knew about the ring, and my life after the ring.
My mother brought me up to be polite so I try not to ask women to marry
*   me unless I mean it.*

(SHADOW-BOXING.)

My mother used to tell me that there's a line in your head that if you cross over too far, you go crazy. There's also the line that if you think backwards too far, you have no room for the new stuff. My mother said that women weaken the legs.

(REMOVE ARMY UNIFORM.)

My mother said quotation marks change the meaning of things; make them more important, just like the meaning of the written word. They frame meaning, like the name that tries to frame being. It's a simple out, naming me reminds you of your fa-ther, as if there are only two choices in life, mother and father. But I'll take that on if that's your only way of describing it. It's a simple out, merely an imitation of a man we all know. Guilt by association. Not very fatherly. Be careful of the company you keep because they are witnesses and they might just quote you someday.

(LOUNGE ROBE.)

What are you thinking?
Right then?
Yes.
I don't remember.
Were you thinking about her?
No, I . . . I was thinking about how much work I have to do.
I know you weren't thinking about work, it's not the same look . . . I
  know what you're thinking.
You think you know what I'm thinking, if you knew, you wouldn't ask.
Do you want her more than me?
No.
Yes, you do. How could you not? It's so new . . .
It's just . . . different.
I like seeing you together. I like the way you look at her. It brings me
  back. You like
her 'cause that's how I used to be.
Don't be silly, you're still like that.
What if you fall in love with her?
You're more in love with her than I am.
Maybe. But you and I are different.
I know. So you'll probably fall in love with her and she'll break your heart.
And I'll have to live with it.
You're very casual.
I'm not afraid of losing you. I'll always love you.
What are you thinking?
The same thing you are.
Stop.
It makes me feel close to you without really talking.
I could get up right now and leave you right here with yourself.
Don't touch me.
You have a beautiful body.
You take up space before I can even think about where I'm going.
Before I can even decide where to go next, you've moved there already.
We're different.
I guess that was our attraction.
Come here.

No.

What do you mean, was our attraction, it still is. We're just standing too close. Move away, give me some room.

Okay.

Don't leave me!

You're a fool. You were a fool for me. You're a fool for anyone who falls in love with you.

I'm a fool but I'm smart, I fell in love with you.

Make me understand.

I need a written contract that you desire me and I need it renewed every day, signed by a witness. Witnessed by you know who.

So is that the attraction? The witness?

It helps me see my love, it helps me feel my truth.

Her truth.

Truth through her.

What about her?

What about her?

She's just a witness?

No, she's very special. A very sensitive, smart, loving . . .

Trusting

Trusting

We've been here before.

Not like this. This suspension, this heightened feeling, this inability to go too deep 'cause

you're watching me. It makes it unbearable.

Lovely.

How can I watch you if you're so close?

I'll move.

Don't leave me!

I want to witness you, I want a lover, rather, I want another lover.

You've got it!

Just like that?

You convinced me it could only add up to an already sexy situation.

Can I get a witness?

(SPIT.)

My mother told me that black pepper caused brain damage.
She told me that she thought black people
were born in the night.
She told me I couldn't have coca cola until I was sixteen, and
When I had one at a lunch counter, she said Catholics
Made me do it.

(SPIT.)

She told me she loved the name Peggy, it was a beautiful name.
The first, sweetest thing any girl ever told me was that she
Was at a drive-in movie with her boyfriend Paul
And while they were making out she had whispered my
Name by mistake, and Paul drove her right home
And threw up all over her lawn. It filled me with fear and
Power at the same time. The fear came from being caught for the pervert
    that I was.
The power came from the effect it had on the lawn.
I always associate wrecking lawns with power. (SPIT)
Every time someone hurts me, I want to become famous
And buy a 1962 Corvette and get all dressed up with a beautiful woman
    next
To me, and drive past them on the street,
Just so they can catch a glimpse of me and how happy and successful
    I am.
I got that from Jimmy Cagney.

(ROCK AND ROLL MUSIC SUCH AS "STICK SHIFT.")

I associate everything with cars, except my sexuality I attribute
to my hands. The only thing I liked about *Desert Hearts* was when
she went backwards really fast in her truck.

(ROCK AND ROLL MUSIC CONTINUES UNDER MONOLOGUE.)

I got really excited when I realized that my sexuality was also
in my lips. I got that from Elvis Presley. He taught me to pay attention to my lips. I would try to sneer like him when flirting with
girls, and that's when I developed the habit of licking my lips, to

keep them moist and desirable. I felt like people were staring at my lips at a time when most girls thought people were staring at their breasts. Sometimes I had to cover my lips with my hands because they felt vulnerable and naked, and dangerous and out of control. I used to pretend that my hand, that soft part between the index finger and the thumb was Marie Manjouritis's lips. And I would kiss that part of my hand and put my tongue through the opening. I would feel embarrassed when I saw her because I thought that she would remember how passionate my kiss was and tell someone and put me in sex jail.

The man I am today still thinks all desire starts at the mouth. It comes from right inside the lip, the inside part of the lips that are always moist.

(FADE MUSIC.)

The only part of getting old that I worry about is that my lips will dry up and be hard and wrinkly, and that thought's enough to break me into a sweat in the middle of day, let alone the middle of the night.

Meanwhile, my mother was watching and flirting with me.

(HANDS OVER FACE, SOUND OF WOLF AS IN BEGINNING.)

(BLOOD PRESSURE MACHINE PUT ON ARM.)

I went into the subway at West Fourth Street in the summer, and came out in Brooklyn in the fall. That's how fast time is moving, moving along with my blood. My blood is trying to tell me something, clotting up and trying to torture me so it can get out of me, moving through me in blood clots of magnitude. My blood is a volcano. I met the goddess Pele at the volcano. I offered my body as a sacrifice to Pele, a butch girl sacrifice. Pele likes butches and prefers eating them to almost anyone else. Nice to have a goddess who prefers you. Like Pele, I have high blood pressure. My acupuncturist, who thinks he's Tom Jones, is trying to lower my fire so I won't burn myself up. But I'm afraid that the combination of that and menopause will make me a boring person. What would a volcano be without her lava? Without her blood?

When I see blood, I want to eat it, chew it up good, or chop it up with onions for chopped liver, put an egg over it and have steak tartare, salt and pepper and some Worcestershire sauce, put it in a blender and add ice for a nice summer drink, a cranberry blood clot or a bloody Mary, but Mary's not here to hold back my hands. I'm down in Pele, reaching for her womb, keep my hands to myself. Keep these big, old, cow milking, queer hands to myself. Let them hang at my side or behind my back, or slip into my own pants and stay there. Big old hands that want to get sucked into you, sliding uncontrollably up into you, too big to get in, like a newborn baby, ready for the womb, but not the world.

(TESTIMONY.)

(FEMME WALK TO SUITCASE STARTS DRESSING IN A SUIT.)

> *My mother used to watch me getting dressed.*
> *I used to let myself take forever getting dressed.*
> *My mother watched me.*
> *She loved me, my mother.*
> *She recognized me.*
> *"You look just like your father," she said.*
> *I put on a starched shirt*
> *And I was my father.*
> *I loved how my father's few Sunday shirts*
> *Looked and smelled when they came back*
> *From the Chinese laundry,*
> *And had a piece of cardboard inside*
> *To keep them rectangular and stiff.*
> *Very stiff and starched.*
> *They had peach colored bands around them*
> *Keeping all the long sleeves,*
> *And tail tucked in.*
> *When he unfolded his white shirt Sunday morning*
> *It kept its rectangular shapes*
> *All over the shirts and the cuffs.*
> *And the cuffs were huge and flat and spreading*

Out at the bottom of the sleeve
'Cause it hadn't been folded for cuff links.
I wanted to have a starched white shirt like his,
Keeping it safe all week,
Knowing it's in a drawer piled on top of other shirts
And the white folded boxer shorts.
Men's underwear folds so neatly and square,
Women's underwear doesn't have a real logic to it.
And my father had this great gesture after he shaved
Of patting his cheeks with cologne
And running his hands all around his face.
When I touched my own face like that, in a kind of
Rough way, my mother would say,
"Don't touch your face like that, you'll wreck your skin."
But she liked my father's leathery skin
and the way he was pulling up his chin
The whole church service, away from the starched shirt collar.
My mother always held his hand in church,
And seemed fragile, like she would break
If my father's white shirt wasn't there
Keeping the world from caving her in.
Just the idea of the world could cave in my mother.
That's why I chose to be a boy.
So I could wear starched shirts
To keep the ugly world away from girls,
And so girls could hold my hand
And rest their head on my shoulder,
My clean white shoulder, stiff with pleasure.

(SINGS CROONER SONG LIKE "TO ALL THE GIRLS I'VE LOVED
BEFORE" IN THE AUDIENCE.)

When I was twenty-one, I died because of love in a heat wave
I slept with a woman for the first time and went
Into a coma from spinal meningitis that lasted two weeks
At twenty-one, I already died for love, so I know how it feels.
It sort of clanks

Like empty glass bottles on a tray
Banging into each other
And I can't do anything about it.
I can't even reach the place
the clanking is coming from.
It's like a coma,
A kind of chosen place
A definitive space
Nearby
Where I go for a while
Until I can recover enough to function
Love's an oral thing,
Trying to put your whole body into my mouth,
At least into my vision.
I want to capture you,
For just a moment
Looking out the window sometimes works
Conjuring up your voice
Close to my ear
Remembering what it is I love so much about you.
Have you ever had a song caught in your head?
It's like the needle's stuck in a groove and the song plays
Over and over
While I was floating in my coma
I heard Fats Domino singing, "I wanna be a wheel . . ."
And then applause and then repeat again, "I wanna be . . ."
And then applause.
This went on for three days and three nights.
And I begged the nurse to stop that song,
But there wasn't any music playing.
I wanted it to stop but that needle was unforgiving,
Like the heat wave,
Unforgiving, like my daily spinal tap
I knew it was coming
By the clanking sound
Of empty bottles

On a tray, rattling down the hall.
They'd stick an empty needle into my spine
And that needle was unforgiving, like the heat wave,
Unforgiving, like my mother.

My mother used to tell me that if you take something beautiful and repeat it many times, it becomes more beautiful.

My mother held my hand for two weeks and when the heat wave felt forgiving, she pulled the plug from the fan and the music stopped.

"Do you know you look just like your father? You remind me of him. Do you want a pair of his cuff links? I know where they are. How about a tie? I have one of his summer ties. Oh, how you remind me of him when he was a young farmer, he had those muscles in his forearms that stuck out from milking cows."

And she remembered him. I dressed in my mother's memories. "But don't let your sisters see you, you know how they copy you, I don't want them dressing like that, and I worry about you, that you're going to hell because of the way you dress, eternal hell to burn with the devil. And I don't want you bringing your sisters with you."

(SENTIMENTAL SONG LIKE "I'M CONFESSING THAT I LOVE YOU.")

I shined my shoes while they were on, and my mother smiled. "You look just like your father," she said. I think she wanted me to kiss her hand. I put on my hat to leave and the spell was broken. She forgot who I was, she forgot I was her Sunday lover, and she said I would burn in hell. I let myself take forever getting dressed. My mother loved me. She recognized me.

(SALUTE AND LEAVE WITH SUITCASE; SONG CONTINUES THROUGH CURTAIN CALL.)

i remember mapa

ALEC MAPA

Notes on *I Remember Mapa*

A couple of years ago, during an excruciatingly long stretch of unemployment (that we actors are somehow inevitably doomed to), I found myself thinking, What if this is it? What if I never work again? What would I do? If the worst is true, I thought at the very least I could write and perform my own written material. The result of this career crisis query was *I Remember Mapa*.

I originally set out to write and perform a simple cabaret show where I'd recount my show business experiences and sing a couple of songs. The show that began to emerge, however, was something altogether different. A little less glib, a little more personal. Certain things became clear to me. Part of the struggle of being an actor is that you're seldom seen the way you wish to be seen.

Actors are often typecast or labeled on sight with little or no regard for their struggles, talents, or abilities. As an actor I've always tried to get people to see beyond "type," and as a gay person of color my life has been spent pretty much trying to do the same thing. Writing and performing this show became a perfect opportunity for me to be seen as I wish to be seen . . . on my own terms and in my own words.

I Remember Mapa is a show about growing up "different" and finding strength in one's diversity. If that premise seems banal, that's precisely the point. At first glance, it would seem that my show's about a gay Asian actor trying to have a successful personal and professional life. (What a fresh point of view!) It's been my experience, however, in the performing of this piece in workshop productions that my story and my experiences are far from unique. Regardless of my sexual or cultural point of view, everyone can relate to the wish to belong. Whether it be in relationships, careers, or even in one's own skin. Finding our own essential value as human beings is a journey we all take. *I Remember Mapa* is about that journey.

My mother used to say, "If it's funny later, it's funny now!" This phrase has accompanied me through most of my life . . . through humiliating auditions, career disappointments, and soured relationships. If one can maintain one's sense of humor, all is not lost. I hope to convey this through my work. I hope you get it.

About Alec Mapa

Alec Mapa is an award-winning actor, writer, and performance artist. His credits include appearances on Broadway and off-Broadway shows, regional theatre, motion pictures, and numerous guest starring roles on television. He lives in New York and Los Angeles.

i remember mapa

ALEC MAPA

Welcome to the Taper Too. My name is Lea Salonga, and welcome to the first "Miss Saigon-a-long." Tonight you're all gonna sing like Vietnamese whores, and you're gonna like it!

My name is Alec Mapa. Thanks so much for coming. I was so afraid no one was going to show up and I was going to end up by myself in some dive bar in Silverlake, tossing back cosmopolitans and harassing some gay teenager from Reseda. But you all came. Now what am I gonna do?

This is my first solo performance in Los Angeles. Ever. I wanted to do one of those really cool ethnic-bio pieces where I expound on my Filipino American journey. Do you know what I'm talking about? The kind of show that makes all the ethnic people in the audience say, "Right on!" and all the white people say, "Wow, I had no idea." But then I thought, It's really not that kind of show, other people do that sort of thing better than I can, plus I'm so not qualified to do that kind of material. I know so little about my own culture, it's embarrassing. I'm ashamed, I really am.

I mean, I was born here; I grew up in San Francisco. To me, being Filipino meant that we ate rice with everything, celebrated Christmas at midnight, and my parents spoke Tagalog whenever they didn't want me to know what they were saying. I understood most of what they were saying. Apparently there's no Filipino equivalent to the words "It's only a phase."

To me, the Philippines was just this far-off country that we visited every couple of years, this impoverished third world country where all my relatives had chauffeurs. And it was this place where my parents had survived this awful war that we seldom heard about. Except at mealtime. I'd be eating a Big Mac— with some rice—and my Lola (my grandma, who was living with us when I was growing up) would point to that Big Mac and say, "You know . . . that whole sandwich would feed my entire family during the war." Or I'd be slicing off a piece of butter to put on a pancake or a waffle, and she'd point to that piece of butter and say, "You know, that one piece of butter would feed my whole family during the war." Or I'd be eating a bowl of ice cream, and she'd point to that bowl of ice cream, and, well, you get the point.

I ate a lot of fat.

Now, hearing this story of want and scarcity night after night, meal after meal, made me a very compassionate person . . . initially. But after a while, I was, like, *Listen, old woman, I'm trying to eat.*

Early on I figured my parents brought over so little of their own culture because there was so much they wanted to leave behind. Which is understandable. I can see how splitting a piece of butter with your entire family would be an experience you wouldn't want to re-create anywhere.

My favorite photo of my mom and dad was taken a couple of years after they'd just got here. My dad's in this skinny, sixties suit with a narrow tie, and my mom's wearing this pink, Arnold Scaasi knockoff that my Lola made, complete with gloves and a pillbox hat perched high atop her Jackie bubble-do. They looked like the Filipino Rob and Laura Petrie. And they have this look on their faces of absolute relief and optimism, as if to say "Whew! We made it! All we have to do is get settled, raise our kids here, and give them every pleasure and privilege denied to us as children, and they're gonna grow up to be extraordinary people."

They even gave us heroic names. My older brother was named CarloMagno, after Charlemagne; my older sister was named Monica Francesca, because she was born in the parish of Saint Monica and she was the first to be born in San Francisco; and my little sister was named Marianna Regina, which literally means "Maryanna the Queen." I was named Alejandro, after "Alexander the Great"—an ancient Macedonian homosexual with a penchant for world domination.

I took my parents' expectations very seriously. Being gay made me desperate for their attention and terrified of disappointing them. Especially my father.

But I couldn't help it.

Like the whole tap-dancing thing. I took tap dancing when I was a kid. It was my second choice. I wanted to take ballet. Isn't that what every father wants to hear? *I wanna take ballet!* But he wouldn't let me take ballet because he was scared that if I did, I'd turn out to be a big homo. Which is ridiculous. Ballet won't turn you into a big homo. Tap dancing will.

Filipino men—notoriously homophobic. My father was no exception. They can't help it; it's the culture. If you came from a country that had been colonized that many times, you'd be a little touchy about your masculinity, too. Growing up in San Francisco, we couldn't drive through any of the gay neighborhoods without my father muttering, *"Bakla,"* which is Tagalog for "fag."

When I came out to him while I was in college I totally psyched myself up for this big dramatic made-for-TV-movie moment that would end in tears and the severing of my living expenses. I prepared for *months*. I read all the books on coming out to your parents, I went to support groups, I looked for a cheaper apartment—*just in case*. I told him. He said that he loved me. He wasn't thrilled about it, but he loved me, and nothing would ever change that. I was furious. When I was growing up he was Jesse Helms; overnight he turned into Alan Alda.

I never formally came out to my mother. We were so close, and so much of our communication was nonverbal, so by the time I thought I should tell her, I knew that she knew. And she knew that I knew that she knew. This became clear to me one time when we were in this ice-cream parlor in San Francisco, and the guy behind the counter was totally cruising me.

He was like, "What do you want?" And I was like, "Well, what've you got?" And he was like, "What do you *like?*"

It went back and forth like this until I finally decided on vanilla.

My mother and I walked out of the ice-cream parlor and she was absolutely silent for about a block and a half, and then she turned to me and said, "You are so *obvious.*" Such was the bond between my mother and me.

Every couple of years I go to the Philippines with my family to visit relatives and enjoy maid service, and I'm pretty much out to all of my family over there, but they still regard my proclivity as *the love that dare not speak its name.* We'll find ourselves at some huge family gathering, and all the aunts, uncles, nieces, nephews, and cousins will immediately cluster around my older bother, because he's straight, and apparently that's really big over there. And they'll just unleash this barrage of personal questions like "Are you seeing anyone? Do you have a girlfriend? What does she look like? What does she do for a living? Are you going to get married? Are you going to have children? Have you set a date? Where are you registered? What do you want us to get? Can we come stay with you?" And I'm sitting there right next to him, *completely ignored.* And after about an hour of this nonstop hetero interrogation one of them will finally turn to me and say, "Oh. Alec. Have you eaten?" And for the life of me, I don't know why they're so obsessed with my older brother's sex life. I get laid way more than he does.

Well, just look at me! I'm so exotic!

It's so weird to have that label pinned on you, even though you're born here. I once went on this blind date with a systems analyst from Xerox, a man so boring, so dull, so ignorant, I thought God was punishing me. We were set up by this mutual friend who I'm no longer speaking to, and we met at this bar. He was attractive, which was a relief, because on a blind date, you never know. Sometimes you end up with someone who looks like a villain from

Scooby-Doo. I have a friend who flat-out refuses to answer any more personal ads because he says regardless of the purported physical description, the person who shows up invariably ends up looking like Gale Gordon. So we met, and he was cute and tall, which is nice because I like a man I can climb. But he kept on staring at me with this really strange look, and I was like, "What?"

And he said, "Well, *this* should be interesting."

And I was like, "Why?"

And he said, "Well, I've never dated anyone outside my own race before."

So I said, "Well, get ready for some excitement, because we're gonna go headhunting! And after that I thought we'd check out this new tribal dance club down the street that's real popular with my people. When the place gets really hopping, we can make it rain!"

He didn't think that was very funny.

It's a miracle I have any positive ethnic identity at all.

When I was growing up there were no Asian role models. Well, there was Mr. Sulu. He had rank, position, and he got to wear that fabulous mustard velour top. And as helmsman of the *Enterprise* he broke a lot of Asian stereotypes. He was a very good driver.

The only time I ever saw Asian people on TV who I thought were remotely cool was when the local television station would air *Flower Drum Song.* I love that movie. It's this breakout Rodgers and Hammerstein musical about Chinese Americans living in San Francisco in the 1960s, and there's, like, *two* Chinese people in it. Miyoshi Umeki, James Shigeta, and Jack Soo are all Japanese; Patrick Adriarte's Filipino. But the weirdest bit of casting in that movie is Juanita Hall as Madame Leong. Juanita Hall, you may remember, was the African American actress who played Bloody Mary in *South Pacific*. Now, in that movie she was supposed to be Polynesian, so she kinda gets away with it. But in this movie she plays Madame Leong, a middle-aged Chinese woman who addresses her brother-in-law (played by Benson Fong) as "my sister's husband." But whenever she does, she does it in this weird black/Chinese accent: "And where ah yoo going today, *mah sista's huzbin?*" "They must fall in love the American way, *mah sista's huzbin.*"

Speaking of nontraditional casting, *The King and I* was on AMC the other night. I keep forgetting that Rita Moreno's in that movie. Rita Moreno as Tup Tim. There's this scene at the beginning of the movie where they bring her into the hall where all the wives are, and all the Asian actresses start giggling at her. And Deborah Kerr says to the actress playing Lady Tiang, "Lady Tiang? why are they laughing at her?" And Lady Tiang says, "Oh, Mrs. Anna, they are laughing because she is from Burma." And I thought, No, they're laughing because she's from Puerto Rico. "She tried to make *arroz con pollo* in royal kitchen the other day! Most amusing! Run, Anita, run! Run from Tony!"

I work out, I go to the gym, because I'm a gay man, I live in West Hollywood, and *it's the law*. I'm so ashamed. I've totally succumbed to the whole cult of the body beautiful. The mutant bandwagon pulled up to my door and I just hopped aboard. And it's not like it makes any difference. I'm still totally neurotic about my appearance. I'm one of those people who's seldom happy with the way that they look, and yet I can't pass by a mirror without looking into it. Psychologists say that your self-image as an adult is largely based on your self-image as a child. This explains everything. When I was in the third grade, I wore glasses, a retainer, and corrective shoes— all at the same time. I used to kick my own ass at recess. I was a big sissy, lousy at sports. I sucked at *everything*—football, basketball, softball, name it. I just think there's something in the gay gene that renders us incapable of handling balls outside our own. To this day, the only thing I can throw is a really good brunch. And the idea of catching something as large as a softball sets off this nelly alarm. I was out in left field, looking like every father's nightmare. It was my father's fault. He's not very athletic, but he's an amazing cook. On the first day of school, I couldn't catch or throw, but I could recite all the ingredients to a seafood paella.

Actually there was one ball game where the other kids actively sought my participation—dodge ball. Who thought this game up? What testosterone-filled sick sack of shit thought this game up? It's schoolyard Darwinism. The whole object of the game is to take the ball and hit the slowest-moving child.

It's a good thing I was loved at home because I dreaded going to school. I just knew that at one point during the day something was going to happen or someone was going to say something that would humiliate me. There'd always be some game I was lousy at that I'd be forced to play, or some kid would call me a fag.

And it's not like I didn't know I was different. For show-and-tell we had to bring in a prized possession from home. Corey Leiberman brought in his Rock 'em Sock 'em Robots; Mel Harrington brought in a baseball autographed by Reggie Jackson. I brought in the sound track to *That's Entertainment*. And they all laughed.

It's a moment that still haunts me. To this day, regardless of how cool I try to look, act or behave, I am destined to do dorky, stupid things in front of people I am trying to impress.

A couple of years ago while I was appearing in a Broadway play, I was set up to do an interview with a reporter from an Australian magazine. He was doing some story on up-and-coming New York actors and wanted the "big scoop." I said fine. My friend Tommy had come to see the show that evening, and after the performance, I asked if it was okay if my friend tagged along for the interview, and the guy said, "Sure." We ended up at this restaurant in the East Village, and we sat at this table. He set a tape recorder down on the table, pressed Play and Record, and I proceeded to give all these "earnest young actor" answers like "It's the work that's most important,"or "I'm not a results-oriented person." Halfway through the interview the guy says, "I have to go to the bathroom," and Tommy and I said, "Fine." So I'm sitting there, and I turn to Tommy and I say, "He is so fine! I think he likes you. I think he totally likes you! You should go out with him—he's totally cruising you. You should go out with him, sleep with him, and tell me all about it!" And then we both look down and realized *that the tape recorder was still running.* We were like Lucy and Ethel. "Press Play! Press Rewind! Press Record!!" And while we were fiddling with this thing, the guy comes back from the bathroom. "We don't have these in our country"—and it was a *Walkman.* I never heard from the guy again. I never read the article, but apparently I have a really big following in the Outback.

My way of fitting in when I was a kid eventually became making fun of myself before anyone could make fun of me, so that by the time I reached adolescence, I had a wicked sense of humor and zero self-confidence. I was Rhoda. I was this short, skinny sissy (as opposed to now). I just wanted to be like everybody else.

I wanted to be like Jeff Grey. Jeff Grey was the complete antithesis of me. He was really tall and great looking, and athletic, and he had one of those great Italian noses that looked so incredible because it had been broken a couple of times. Everyone liked him, even the teachers, because everything he did was so effortless. He could light up a room just by being himself, and he could catch things with one hand. And he liked me. One of the cool kids liked me. He used to laugh at everything I said, which made me like him even more, 'cause he was quite obviously a genius. I used to act like a total goon around him just so I could hear him say, "Dude, you are so funny!"

I didn't even know I had a crush on him till we all ended up at this girl's house after school—Amy Salinas. Amy Salinas was this girl who had these hippie parents who let her do whatever she wanted. A bunch of us ended up at her house after school 'cause she had the new Blondie album *Eat to the Beat* . . . and a joint. So we all piled into her room and turned off all the lights. Everyone was sitting on the floor, and I sat on the edge of the bed, and sitting right in front of me, with his back turned to me, was Jeff Grey, and I could smell his hair. It smelled like Wella Balsam. And while we were all sitting there lighting up and listening to Debbie Harry, all I could do was smell Jeff's hair, and he did the most incredible thing: he leaned back against my legs. *Oh. My. God.* Now, I'd smoked pot before, but it never really had any effect on me. But this time it was so different. The room felt so warm, the music sounded so good, and I was so hungry. And all I could do was stare at the back of Jeff's head and think, God, I sure wish I was beautiful.

Thirteen sucked. See, this is how the dreams of the disenfranchised are born. A series of humiliating moments followed by the rally cry "Someday, you'll all be sorry. I'm gonna be a star!"

Thirty-two's a cool age. I can literally feel myself moving from one demographic to another. Watching a little less MTV, a little more VH-1. The other day in the Virgin Superstore I overheard these girls talking about Belly, Bush, and Hole, and it wasn't until halfway through the conversation that I realized they were talking about music.

Flock of Seagulls! Haircut 100! That was music! Kajagoogoo! Bow Wow Wow!! Do you remember the whole British pop invasion? That was around my freshman year in college at NYU. I was a total club kid. Me and my friends from drama school used to go out nightclubbing every night at places with names like Danceteria, Area, and The World and dress up like freaks. I had this Fun Boy 3 pompadour that I used to crimp, and I'd wear a full face of makeup. I transformed myself from Prunella Queen of the Dorks into a glorious, glamorous denizen of the New York demi-monde!

All my friends had really cool nighttime jobs working in nightclubs and stuff, so I had to get a cool nighttime job, too. I got a job serving cocktails at this trendy new place in the East Village called Boy Bar. I got a job serving cocktails in a gay bar because I thought it would be *fun*.

Was I ever that young?

It was like in high school when you'd get a job working in an ice-cream parlor and you think, Oh boy! Ice cream! I can eat as much as I want, whenever I want all day long! And after about a day of working there you're like, Ice cream. I never want to see it, smell it, taste it or touch it for as long as I live. That's how I felt about men after working at Boy Bar.

If you ever want to see nature at its most savage and cruel, work in a place full of drunken people all trying to get laid. I'm of the belief that there would be no homophobia if straight men knew just how much they had in common with gay men. We're men: self-obsessed, lousy listeners who appreciate good cooking and a nice rack. Can't we all just get along?

One of my duties, working at Boy Bar, was I had to check the bathroom once an hour to make sure no one was having sex or doing drugs. It was a job that was virtually impossible to do without sounding like somebody's bratty kid sister: "Excuse me, are you guys fucking in there? 'Cause if you are, you're gonna be in so much trouble. Excuse me, are you guys shooting up in there? You better not be, 'cause I'm telling."

I didn't work there for very long.

I was an undergrad in drama at NYU and absolutely furious because the department wasn't coming up with any productions for me to star in. The university was doing a salute to the Group Theatre, with plays like *Golden Boy* and *Awake and Sing,* and when I complained that there were no parts for me to play, some teacher generously offered to cast me in several crowd scenes.

That's when I started performing my own written material in cabaret rooms around Manhattan. I started doing stand-up with this gay and lesbian comedy troupe called People Who Are Funny That Way. It was started by the late Bruce Hopkins and Lea DeLaria. Bruce was this skinny middle-aged man with a sweet face who looked like he should be teaching science or music, only he was a big leather queen. Dressed in leather from head to toe, he looked like a Dominatrix Don Knotts. He used to open the show by saying, "Good evening, my name is Bruce Hopkins and I'm a homosexual. If anyone here objects to being entertained by a homosexual, I suggest you never go to the movies, watch television, or attend the theater ever again."

We were enormously popular. We even got to host the Gay Pride rally one year. It was at the end of Christopher Street, in front of this pier, and there were about ten thousand people in the audience.

So I'm in the middle of my act and I look over to the side of the stage, and I see that this man has wandered onto the platform. And he's just standing there, waving his arms and making faces at the audience, and he was impossible for me to ignore, because the louder I spoke, *the more animated he became*. And I was about say, "Excuse me! Martha Graham! You need to take your modern dance elsewhere, because I am trying to talk to these people," until I realized he was interpreting for the deaf. Fascinating. My act in sign language looks just like Glenn Close choking on a Tic-Tac.

After a performance at a midtown club, this man came up to me who said he was "in the industry," and he wanted to give me a little piece of advice. He said, "I think you're very funny and very talented, but I think that by performing in a gay and lesbian venue, you might be limiting yourself as an actor." And I thought, You know, he's right. I won't get to read for all those really good roles they're writing for heterosexual Asian males under five feet five.

Thanks to Linda Hunt.

I know I'm hell to cast. There are thousands of creative people in this business, and *none* of them know what to do with me. I'm like that can of condensed milk in your mother's pantry: everyone knows what I am, nobody knows what I'm there for. I'm too weird, I'm too queer, I'm too ethnic. That's why I live half the year in New York. They love weird queer ethnic people in New York. They have that special celebration for them every year. It's called the Tony Awards.

Isn't that like the gayest show on earth? All those musical numbers and people thanking their lovers—they should just change the name of the show to "The Miss Girlina Queen of the Universe Pageant" and get it over with.

I'm not bitter about my career. I think I should stress that very clearly. This is my karma, this is how I chose to come back in this lifetime. I believe our purpose in life is to express our divinity by transcending our limitations, real or imagined. My next life will be a picnic. I'm gonna come back and just get away with murder.

I'm gonna come back as Oscar-winning actress Marisa Tomei.

Do you remember when she won? Wasn't that like hearing the O. J. verdict?

I had my very first job with Marisa Tomei. It was an ABC After-School Special called *Super Mom's Daughter*. I played Peng. A Vietnamese science student.

"Da fust time I came to dis country, I didn't speak any English. But i' was da teacha who he'p me, and give me da tools to do i'."

I had no idea what I was doing.

I was Juanita Hall.

The director asked me to do a Vietnamese accent. I didn't know any Vietnamese people. The only Vietnamese person I ever knew was this teenage girl who used to work at this McDonald's that my friends and I from high school used to go to, and we called her Hi Mehyapa. Now the reason we called her Hi Mehyapa was that was what she said every time we stepped up to the counter: "Hi, mehyapa." Now, I'm sure she meant to say, "Hi, may I help you?" But it always came out "Hi, mehyapa." And it became this game with me and my friends to try to decipher what she was saying. Like "You wan fie zee dat?" was "Do you want fries with that?" "Dat be aw?" was "Will there be anything else?"

And we used to just go in and laugh. And you know, she was probably this exchange student from England who was fucking with us:

"Oh, I'm enjoying my stay here in the States here very much. Oh, look, here comes that obnoxious group of teenagers again—watch this. Hi, mehyapa!"

So that was the accent I used on my very first job. During the shoot the director came up to me and said, "We like your acting. We like the accent. But we were wondering—could you split the difference? Because none of us can understand what you're saying."

Marisa Tomei. Who knew? Everyone I work with becomes famous: Lea DeLaria, Marisa Tomei. While I was performing at this club called Don't Tell Mama, we had this guest comedy duo on the bill called Kathy and Mo, and I think they even worked there for a while. Kathy Najimy worked the coat check, and Mo Gaffney worked behind the bar. One night Kathy and I were sitting on the stoop on Forty-sixth Street, looking up at the stars and talking about our dreams, and I said, "Y'know, Kathy, someday I'm gonna star in a hit Broadway show." And she said, "Y'know, Alec, someday I'm gonna be a movie star." And I remember looking over at her and thinking, Yeah. Good luck.

Ten years ago I auditioned for the lead in a new Broadway play written by David Henry Hwang called M. *Butterfly*. The play was based on the factual account of a French diplomat who fell in love with a beautiful Chinese opera star, only to find out after a twenty-

year affair that his lover was not only a spy—but a man. Nobody
had any idea that the play would turn out to be this international
Tony Award–winning hit, least of all me. I just remember reading the script and thinking, What's the big deal? I'm from San
Francisco. This kind of thing happens on the bus.

One thing was for certain, though: the role of Song Liling,
Chinese transvestite spy, was one of those once-in-a-lifetime roles
that promised to make whoever played it a big fat star.

Now, I believe in fate. I believe in destiny. I believe that everything happens for a reason and that no actor ever gets a role that
he or she was not meant to get. So when I found out that I was
cast as the understudy, I thought, Well. *There's been a terrible, terrible mistake!*

There's a famous story about this understudy who was on the
road with the touring company of *Sweeney Todd,* and she had
understudied the role of the Beggar Woman. Now, in the show,
the Beggar Woman gets her throat slit by Sweeney Todd, and when
she does, she's supposed to slide down this chute and land on a
mattress underneath the set. Well, one night the actress playing
the Beggar Woman gets her throat sliced, slides down the chute
and lands on the mattress wrong—twisting her ankle. And while
she's weeping over her twisted ankle with Angela Lansbury hovering over her, calling to the stage manager, "Get some ice! Get
some ice!" her understudy comes crawling along, in full makeup,
in full costume. And she whispers to the Beggar Woman with the
twisted ankle, "Give me that wig."

I made her look like an amateur.

I showed up on the first day of rehearsal *completely off book.* I
just didn't know all of my lines, I knew *all* the lines. I was like a
vulture slowly circling the skies above the desert floor, hypervigi-
lant for any signs of infirmity or impending death.

Now, apart from understudying the lead role of Song Liling,
Chinese transvestite spy, I also had a small part in the show. I was
to play one of two Kurogo dancers, a name taken from the Japanese *kuroko,* which means overpaid stagehand. Now, it was our
job to move the set around. We had to move these tables and

chairs, and slide these *shoji* screens to denote different set changes, times, and places. We also had to hand actors props and help them on stage with costume changes. We had to do this quickly, quietly, and invisibly.

Now, I have many talents. Being invisible ain't one of them.

I couldn't just hand an actor a coat or a wineglass. I made eye contact with that actor, forcing him to acknowledge me, turning the simple task of handing an actor a prop into this moment filled with tension and subtext. And it became *this thing* during rehearsal, whenever an actor would come onstage, they'd look in my direction and the focus would shift to *me!* This didn't last for very long.

During one rehearsal, the director, John Dexter, shouted "Stop! There's a bloody scene going on and all I can look at is Alec Mapa! Why is that?" After that no one was allowed to look at me. It was a rule.

Another thing we had to do as Kurogos was, after we were finished changing the set, we were supposed to kneel on stage and look off into the wings so that we looked like little Oriental bookends. I couldn't even do that right.

This is what would happen during rehearsal: I'd be looking off into the wings. Getting a little bored. Then I would watch the actors out of the corner of my eye. Then I'd turn my head around. Then my whole body. And not only would I be completely facing the audience watching the play, I would mouth the dialogue along with the actors.

"Alec Mapa, turn around! I don't want to see your face. I don't want to see your eyes. And if anyone has a scene on stage with Alec Mapa, I suggest you get on and off as soon as possible!!!"

Long story short, the play was a megahit. It won three Tony Awards: Best Play, Best Director, and B. D. Wong won for Best Supporting Actor and became the toast of the town.

I spent a year and a half on Broadway kneeling with my back turned to the audience.

Night after night every single celebrity I've ever wanted to meet or impress came to watch this Tony Award–winning play. Katharine Hepburn, Greta Garbo, Helen Hayes, Lauren Bacall,

Tom Cruise, Paul Newman, Shirley MacLaine, Barbra Streisand, have all seen the back of my head.

I was so jealous I couldn't breathe. I thought I was developing asthma. I would stand there at the curtain call hyperventilating with anger. Night after night I'd leave the theater and be greeted by throngs of people who would gasp in astonishment and exhale with disappointment and ask, "Has B.D. left yet?"

Walking home in Brooklyn one night, I saw my neighbor Angie sitting on the stoop.

She said, "Hey. I saw the commercial for that play you're in. And the actor on the commercial wasn't you."

I said, "I know. I'm his understudy. If that actor gets sick or injured, I get to go on in his place."

And she said—I swear to God this is true—"Oh. You want we should do something about that?"

And all I could think was, Where were you during previews?

I arrived at the theater one night and flipped through the *Playbill* and saw that they had spelled my name wrong. It read "Alec Wapa." The stage managers felt bad and hung a sign on my dressing room door. It said HOME OF THE WAPA. See, it's funny now, but back then I wept. I could not find any humor in the situation. I tried to be really spiritual about it, thinking, Don't worry, there'll be another Tony Award–winning role for an Asian drag queen that's meant just for you. But I couldn't help but feel like I lost out on the opportunity of a lifetime.

And you know what the ironic thing is? I have been through so many heavy, deep, and real things since then, that I would love that job right now. It was such a no-brainer. It required *this* much effort and paid *that* much money. But back then, it was the be-all-and-end-all of my existence.

Six months into the run they let me go on in the role. I remember standing in my dressing room as they called, "Five minutes." I was wearing this Eiko Ishioka Peking opera outfit, with this elaborately embroidered peacock on the front, and this huge headdress with Ping-Pong balls all over it. I felt just like Natalie Wood in *Gypsy* right before she strips for the very first time. "I'm a pretty girl, Mama. Mama, I'm a pretty girl." And then my dresser yelled at me, "Stop looking at yourself. It's places."

He led me to the stage, and I remember standing behind the curtain, hearing my own heartbeat in my head. And the curtain swept past, and I was looking at two thousand people. The show had started.

And I don't remember a thing about the performance.

I remember having some vague sense that the audience wasn't with me at all. At sixty bucks a pop, they weren't there to see no understudy. And I remember thinking, Okay, don't even think about that, just hit your mark, act like a girl, and don't bump into anything. And before I knew it, the show was over.

And I remember the curtain call. I remember running down to the edge of the stage towards the audience. And they stood.

They stood.

And I remember taking my bow and waving to my mom and dad in the audience. Real professional.

And it was one of the most pleasurable moments of my life. And not just because the audience was standing and clapping (although, if you've never had a standing ovation on Broadway, you really should try it sometime). But because it was the first time in my life I didn't feel like a freak. The sum total of my experiences were present in this one moment, where everything in my life that ever made me feel ashamed or embarrassed seemed to serve me somehow. And not just me; I mean, not everybody in the audience knew who I was, and they seemed to be having a really good time. So as I took my place in the company bow, I had this image in my head of this awkward effeminate teenager and this dorky kid in glasses and corrective shoes just jumping up and down and laughing. As I left the theater that night I was greeted by more applause and flash-bulbs and strangely zealous autograph hounds, and then the thought occurred to me: Someday had come. I was an actor. And the realization both thrilled and terrified me, because it was like something in me had crossed over and I could never, ever, ever go back.

I came to Los Angeles in 1991 starring in the national touring company of M. Butterfly. I had arrived.

Now, this was my plan: I was gonna come out here starring in this hit show, get fabulous reviews, get all the people in the TV and film industry to come see me, they'd see I was really talented, and from that day hence I'd work all the time.

Wasn't I cute?

Halfway through the run I discovered that TV and film people have a very simple philosophy when it comes to live theater: they don't give a shit. They're TV and film people. They think the Tony Awards are for outstanding achievement in home permanents. They think Cherry Jones is a fat-free frozen yogurt. Getting industry people to see me in M. *Butterfly* was like trying to get me to buy tickets to a Mandy Patinkin concert: it was a very hard sell.

Nothing in my prior experience had prepared me for living in Los Angeles. Except maybe junior high school. I've recently come to the conclusion that living in L.A. is exactly like being in the seventh grade twenty-four hours a day. All the kids are bigger and meaner than me, and I'm doing everything I can to make them like me.

In L.A. perception is everything. You are either doing really well, or you don't exist. You can never say to someone, "I'm not working," or, "I'm unemployed." You have to say, "I'm in development," or, "I'm on hiatus." I once got flustered and said, "I'm developing a hiatal hernia!" And someone said, "Oh, really? Who's casting?"

So. I came out here with the big show. Nothing happened. And that's when my life got *really* interesting.

While on tour I made two fatal mistakes that would lead to my downfall. I had a torrid love affair with a fellow cast member, and I hired a friend to handle my money.

Can you say *screwed?*

Unbeknownst to me, when the tour was over, so was the relationship. I would *love* to go into greater detail here, but it's too long a story, that's a whole other show, and it wouldn't be fair. I'd have no objectivity. So let's just say that rat-bastard closet-case broke my heart. And if that wasn't enough, when I finally got around to checking in on my finances I found that my accountant/friend had absconded with more than half my earnings, leaving me with little or no savings and a huge tax liability which wiped me out completely. So basically I had just come off a year's employment, I had *nothing* to show for it, and no legal recourse to get that money back.

And then my mother died.

While visiting my parents in San Francisco, my mother suffered from a cerebral aneurysm that hospitalized her for a month. She had an operation to clip the aneurysm that was successful, but while she was in recovery she suffered a massive stroke which left her brain-dead. My father was so devastated that he couldn't even come to the hospital, and it was my older sister and I who had to tell the doctors to turn her life-support systems off. She was fifty-three years old. And she was my best friend.

My mother's favorite expression was "What's stopping you?" I'd bitch and moan about my life and how hard it was and how much I wanted to be successful, and she'd say "What's stopping you?" What's stopping me? I'm a triple threat performer: I'm Asian, I'm queer, and I actually think there's work for me. She'd laugh and say, "No, really. What's stopping you?" And then I wouldn't be able to answer her and feel like a jerk.

My mother was a woman of absolute faith. And not in this hearts-and-flowers Pollyanna way, but in this really quiet, powerful way that made you believe anything was possible. She grew up poor and starving during the Japanese occupation of the Philippines during World War Two and she told me that as a child all she ever dreamt of was traveling. She wanted to see the world. Explore the ruins of the Acropolis, stroll along the Champs-Elysées, and walk the Bloody Tower, and at the time it was a pretty grandiose dream for a girl like her to have. Given her circumstances, it was pretty plain that she was never gonna go anywhere. But as soon as she was able, she got out, married my father, raised her brood, and became a travel agent. And proceeded to go to every single destination that she ever dreamt of.

"What's stopping you?" My mother's faith in me made me feel like I could do anything. When she died, I felt like the part of me that believed in myself died, too.

So let's review: I got dumped, the IRS took all my money, and my mother died—all within the span of six months.

Now, I think I would have been able to handle it, if these were isolated incidents that happened over a number of years, to somebody else. But in my case, I could only do one thing:

Have a complete nervous breakdown.

I cracked up. Cracking up gave me coping mechanisms I never knew I had. I now know how to watch television for twenty hours a day. Believe me, it's the perfect thing to do when the last thing you want to do is focus on yourself. It's easy. From seven to nine *Good Morning, America*; nine to ten, *Regis and Kathie Lee*; ten to eleven, three words that'll brighten anyone's day, *I Love Lucy*; eleven to twelve, Sally Jessy Raphael, because there's only one thing that'll pick you up when you're down and out and that's watching people who are more fucked up than you are; twelve o'clock, *All My Children*; one o'clock, *One Life to Live*; two o'clock, *General Hospital*; three o'clock, *Oprah!* because nothing feels better than getting spiritual advice from someone who makes three-hundred million dollars a year; four to six, local news; six to seven, *Roseanne*, the mother of all sit-com divas or as I like to call her, Scary Tyler Moore; seven o'clock, *Jeopardy!*; seven thirty, *Entertainment Tonight*. Prime time takes you to the eleven o'clock news, which takes you to Leno or Letterman, which takes you to Conan O'Brien, which then leaves you to nod off to any number of infomercials, unless it's for Soloflex, which means you'll be staying up just a little longer.

Congratulations. An entire day of your life has gone by, and you haven't had to feel a thing.

I hardly left the house, and when I did, everything made me feel upset or hostile. I had lunch with an actress friend who spent the entire meal talking about how upset she was because she couldn't find the right person to redecorate her new house. I wanted to redecorate her skull with my salad fork.

I would have continued to watch television for the rest of my life, but I awoke one morning to find that my utilities had been shut off. I hadn't paid my bill in months. I had a closet full of Armani, and I couldn't pay the rent.

And then it got worse.

l had to get a job. Having everything go my way had taught me nothing about survival. One minute I was on Broadway, the next I was sitting in a temp office in Century City, being asked:

"Do you type? Word processing? Windows?"

"No, no, no."

"Do you know *anything* about computers?"

"Nope. 'Fraid not."

"Mr. Mapa, do you have *any* skills?"

"Um . . . I can run in heels."

I don't know how, but this temp agency, God bless 'em, was able to find me work that sustained me for two years. I filed, I delivered mail, I answered phones. I had one job where all I did was shred documents. I was assigned to this room that had nothing but a paper shredder, a chair, and bins and bins of documents stacked up to the ceiling. All I did was feed documents into the shredder. Eight hours a day. For a month. I must have looked like some bizarre performance artist, sitting in this chair, feeding documents into the shredder and weeping.

While all this was going on I was still auditioning. Badly. My financial situation and my emotional state made me so needy that I repelled even the most sympathetic of casting directors. See, getting an acting job is just like getting laid. If you act like you need it, it's not gonna happen. Nothing repels a potential suitor more quickly than a sense of desperation. It has a smell.

Not only was I bombing left and right, but everyone in Los Angeles was *really nice about it*. I was used to auditioning in New York City, where people have absolutely no hesitation when it comes to letting you know exactly how they feel. When I was starting out I had people snicker while I was auditioning; I had someone call in the next actor while I was still reading; I even had one casting director who didn't wait until I was out the door before shouting to his assistant, *"He was awful!"* But out here, regardless of how stinko I was, the interview would end with a smile and a "Thanks for coming in!"

After a while you learn to read between the lines. I found that there are three things that can be said at an audition in Los Angeles that will basically guarantee that you will *never* be called back again:

   One: "That was terrific!"
   Two: "Thank you. Jeanine will validate your parking."
Three: "Well, I think that's all we need to see!"

I couldn't get a part in my hair. I had one year where I worked two days, one in January and another in October. And it became this vicious cycle. The longer I went without working, the more desperate I became, till I reached a point where I was knocking myself out for jobs I didn't even want. I once found myself auditioning to play a baseball-playing monkey for a movie called *Ed*. *I got called back four times*. And I still didn't get the part.

I ended up waiting tables at California Pizza Kitchen in Encino. It was this *very* corporate restaraunt with a strict policy when it came to service, and I was the world's worst waiter because I just didn't give a shit. "My life's in the toilet and you want your salad dressing on the side?

"Bite me."

Did you ever go to a restaraunt and there's always some evil queen who works there who's over everything including you? That would be me. I used to say things like "Good evening, my name is Alec, and tonight I'll be touching your food." And I couldn't take people being mean to me. This woman once said to me, "I will not eat this spaghetti, I would like a chicken salad." And I said, "Okay, chicken salad coming right up." And she said, "I would like it *now*." And I said, "Okay," and crossed my arms and blinked my eyes like Barbara Eden on *I Dream of Jeannie*.

That's usually when the manager would see me and say, "Alec! You are so . . . *fired!*"

The absolute worst part about waiting tables is that at least once a week someone would recognize me from the show and say, "Weren't you in *M. Butterfly?*" I felt so lucky. I had legions of fans. And they all had lunch in Encino.

I didn't even have the comfort of being a high-level has-been. Norma Desmond had reels of footage to look back on. I had a stack of *Playbills* and a Drama-Logue Award. My fifteen minutes of fame were more like two. And I started to think that maybe it was just beginner's luck. Over the years I'd watch my classmates from NYU slowly drop out of the business one by one, becoming lawyers, stockbrokers, or physical therapists. Being employed gave me the arrogance to think that I would never have to make that choice. And here I was, waiting tables in Encino and thinking about selling Amway.

Something happens when you hit rock bottom. When your worst nightmares come true, there's nothing left to be afraid of. After a while I reconciled myself to the possibility that I might never work again. I started to come into auditions with an entirely different attitude. I figured as long as I had booked passage on the *Titanic*, I was going to sink with style. Each audition became my swan song, my farewell performance to an industry that wouldn't even cast me as a baseball-playing monkey. And at the point where I didn't care what anyone thought, where giving a good audition became more important than getting the job—I started to get work again.

I did mostly guest spots on some of your favorite television shows. Some would call them bit parts; I like to think of them as enormous acting challenges. If I could wring a twenty-two-second laugh out of five seconds of screen time, I felt my work had been done. In keeping with the seventh-grade analogy, guesting on a hit show is like getting to sit at the cool kids' table for a week. Doing a bad show is like having to sell chocolate bars for the chess club in full view of the entire school.

I was cast in this science-fiction show on Fox called *Mantis*. I was cast as one of a group of scientists who were trying to transform themselves into amphibious creatures, but in order to do so we had to extract DNA from living human beings. We had to kill them.

It could happen.

Now, I'd never done any special effects things before, so I was really excited. In the script I was supposed to have these poison seaweed tentacles, and I even had one scene where I was supposed to swoop down out of the rafters and land on this policeman who was investigating all the murders. *Cool.*

So, I arrive in Vancouver where the show is being shot—complete chaos. No one knows what's going on because there are two different units filming this and last week's show. I show up on the set and this PA looks at me and says, "Who are you?"

And I said, "Alec Mapa? I'm on the show this week?"

And he said, "Oh, go to makeup."

So I go to the makeup trailer and this guy's like, "Who are you?"

And I said, "I'm Alec. I'm in this week's show."

And he said, "Oh, yeah, Seaweed Boy. Sit down."

So I'm in the makeup chair, all excited: "Oh, boy! I'm gonna be a monster!" And the guy says, "Okay. Where are your hands? Oh. Here they are." And he opens up this box and looks into it and says, "Fuck! They're not finished!"

And I said, "What do you mean they're not finished?"

And he says, "They're not finished. These aren't painted or detailed. They're just rubber!"

And I look inside the box and my Mantis poison seaweed hands are these big, white rubber gloves. I slip them on, and I look like a mutant Martha Stewart after a cooking accident. So I arrive on the set and everybody's like, "What the hell is that?"

Who's the first actor I see? Roger Rees. Mr. Hoity-Toity Royal Shakespearean actor in this cheesy science-fiction show on Fox. And I was about to say, "Roger, what are *you* doing here?" when he turned to me and said, "Alec Mapa, what are *you* doing here?"

It was then that I realized that my struggle was not unique.

We do take after take with me terrorizing the citizens of Vancouver, and after each one, the entire set cracks up because I look so stupid in these giant white oven mitts. And I'm thinking, This isn't any fun. Now, remember the scene where I had to fall out of the rafters? They're now behind schedule and overbudget. They can't do it. So they've reset the scene so that it takes place in a basement. And instead of falling out of the rafters, they have me falling out of a closet.

How appropriate.

So this is how the scene goes: I'm supposed to lurk in the shadows and wait for the cop to come by and then suddenly lurch out—*boo!* Fine, so we do the first take and the director says, "Okay, Alec. That was just fine, but we're wondering, on the second take can you make a scary face?" Ten years of acting school, five years of studying the Method, and it all comes down to, "Can you make a scary face?"

While I was waiting tables in Encino, I heard about a new play they were producing at the New York Shakespeare Festival, written by Chay Yew. It explored the lives and loves of three gay Asian men, and it was called *A Language of Their Own*. The word back in New York was that the casting directors were tracking me down to play the role of Daniel, a flamboyant Filipino business student who loses his lover to AIDS. It seems that one of the casting directors had been at a certain Gay Pride rally in 1985 and remembered a certain gay Filipino stand-up comic performing that day who would be perfect for this part. I was flattered they wanted me and decided to disregard the fact that it took this casting director ten years to call me in for a role. I put three scenes on tape, sent it to New York, and hoped for the best. Years of humbling experiences had taught me that there was no such thing as a done deal.

I got it. There's this feeling when you get an acting job you really want. It's sheer euphoria. It's an ice cold glass of water to someone dying of thirst. All of a sudden the sky opens up and the Universe says, *Yes! This what you're supposed to be doing! You were right to hang in there!*

And the best thing about having a job you hate: It feels *so good* when you get to quit. After waiting on my very last table, I sprinted down Ventura Boulevard towards my car, stripping off my waiter's uniform, cackling like a madman. True, I wasn't leaving to do some big part in a movie or a television series, it was just Off Broadway, but I didn't care! It was for a theater in New York I had always wanted to work for, and for the next four months I was going to get to *act!*

On the plane to New York I wondered if I'd be able to. My work between M. *Butterfly* and this had consisted of me standing on an X and doing what I was told. It had been so long since I felt like an actor. And I was going back to New York, where they took everything about acting seriously, except the paycheck.

All those worries disappeared after the first rehearsal. The first day the entire cast and crew assembled in the Shiva Theatre at the Public. The rest of the cast included David Drake, the actor who wrote and performed *The Night Larry Kramer Kissed Me*, Francis Jue, and B.D. Wong. Francis, B.D., and I had all played the role of Song Liling in *M. Butterfly*, a point which had not been lost on the staff, who called us the Divas of the Shiva.

I was really nervous about seeing B.D. again. It was no secret that I had been insanely jealous of him during the Broadway run. Even after it was over, I was basically known in theatrical circles for having been B.D. Wong's understudy, a distinction which made me feel like the Asian Lainie Kazan. But when he arrived at the theater I was really glad to see him. I was comforted by the fact that this was an ensemble piece, the script showcased our individual strengths, our characters were wildly different, and this time we didn't have to share wigs.

Rehearsals were a breeze. I felt like I had never left New York, and it was so great to be in an environment where my opinions were not only valued, but encouraged. And the casting directors were right: the role was tailor-made for me. I played a cocky young man who loses everything. In the play my dying lover begs me to help him commit suicide, and we had this one scene in the hospital where we share a final moment before he dies. And the scene kind of freaked me out at first, because when we got to it, I thought about my mom and how we didn't share a final moment. It happened so fast that I never really felt like I had a chance to say good-bye. The day before my mother's surgery she squeezed my hand and said, "I'll be fine," and those were the last words she ever spoke to me. But after we did that scene for the first time, the one where I actually got to say good-bye, I felt strangely light-headed. It was this gut-wrenching deathbed scene, and every time we did it I'd get all giddy and goofy afterwards—much to the consternation of my costar, who tried not to take it personally. It became my favorite scene in the play, and I looked forward to doing it every night because it was like I got to release all the unexpressed grief I had carried inside for three years.

And I must have done something right, because the reviews were fabulous. The play was an *enormous* hit. We were extended twice. The critics loved us, the public loved us, and night after night I'd be greeted in the lobby by people in the industry I hadn't seen in years, and to my surprise, they all remembered me. This wasn't some big flashy production that promised to make me a star; it was just a great part in a great play, and as far as I was concerned that was plenty.

B.D. and I didn't have any scenes together; we just had this one moment towards the end of the play, where after he finds out that my lover, his ex, has passed away, we were just supposed to look at each other and acknowledge each other's loss. Very Berg-manesque. Closing night, the moment came where B.D. and I were supposed to look at each other, and all of a sudden the moment played differently than it had during the entire run. Looking at him, I thought about all the individual experiences that had led me to this place, and how I had to let go of all the things that ever mattered to me. After everything was taken away, all that was left was my love for acting. And that in itself made me feel strangely noble. Like I had this desire, this quest, that I felt so passionately about that I was willing to endure anything in order to make it so. Maybe I wasn't going to make it in the way I thought I was going to, but in that very moment, I felt like regardless of what happened I was going to be okay.

I looked at B.D., and as we locked gazes I burst into tears. And as I stood there with tears streaming down my face, I thought, Shoot. If only I'd played that scene that way all along. I could've won a Tony.

What's stopping you?

virtually yours

KATE BORNSTEIN

Notes on *Virtually Yours*

Virtually Yours, A Game for Solo Performer with Audience, premiered at Josie's Cabaret and Juice Joint, San Francisco, as *Version Beta 1.0* in March of 1994, produced by Donald Montwill and Jayne Wenger. Written and performed by Kate Bornstein, the play was directed by Jayne Wenger and featured the taped voice of David Cale as the Voice of the Computer.

J. Raoul Brody did the sound design. The lighting designer was Jim Cave. KayLynn Raschke designed and executed the set and costumes. Noreen C. Barnes assisted as dramaturge, and Shannon Coulter was the script girl. Buddy Montgomery and Brian Skaggs operated the sound and lights for the Josie's run.

The show included cameo taped vocal appearances by J. Raoul Brody, Donald Montwill, Jayne Wenger, Tom Ammiano, Stafford, Mark Russell, Holly Hughes, Dan Hurlin, and David Harrison.

Virtually Yours went on tour as *Version 2.0,* the text of which follows in this volume.

About Kate Bornstein

Okay, so this is supposed to be my "author's biography." Okay. So, hello. So I wanna know: Are you familiar with those little bios that appear in theater playbills? You know the ones:

KATE BORNSTEIN is an author, playwright, and performance artist whose solo work includes The Opposite Sex Is Neither, Virtually Yours, *and* Cut'n'Paste. *Ms. Bornstein is the author of the books* Gender Outlaw: On Men, Women, and the Rest of Us, Nearly Roadkill *(with Caitlin Sullivan), and* My Gender Workbook. *She is so pleased to be included in this volume.*

Boring, right? True, but boring. Did you know that all the folks in those playbill bios write their own pieces? Uh-huh, it's true. There's something comforting about writing something boring about yourself in the third person. Some people do get positively Zen-like with their bios:

KATE BORNSTEIN is an outspoken transgendered artist whose work is familiar to readers who buy books like this. She's been living the first part of her life in love with Death, and now she's dying in love with Life.

But still the third person. Why? I dunno. Maybe it's because we hate writing stuff about ourselves, and there's some safety in the anonymity that attends the third person. After all, we've just written a whole huge play about ourselves, so it gets kind of redundant to write a bio. But this stuff you're reading right now is a bit different. This is a freakin' book! And it's a book by and about freaks, fer cryin' out loud. So I can let my hair down. Actually, I can't do that, cuz I shave my head smooth as a billiard ball, and I have an assortment of hair that I wear. Currently, I'm favoring short, blond, and sassy. Some people like to talk about their current lovers in their bios. That's sort of the literary version of getting a tattoo with your lover's name on it.

KATE BORNSTEIN and her lover BARBARA are the Romy and Michele of the Sadomasochism Set, and the Thelma and Louise of the New Age movement.

That sort of thing. So now, when people pick up this book twenty years from now, they're going to think my lover is Barbara. Pick up my earlier stuff, and my lover was Catherine. But she became David, and you can read about him in my other stuff as well. Like in Virtually Yours, *which is in this volume. Have you read it yet? If not, I just gave away the ending. Sorry about that. Well, actually the ending wasn't in the show. I wrote* Virtually Yours *before I knew how David and I would end up. I mean, it's not every day that your lesbian lover becomes the guy you used to be. I hadda explore that, and* Virtually Yours *was my exploration. But there's another thing about the above bio that some people do: compare themselves to cultural icons. Me, I compare myself to the heroes of my childhood and the role models of my adulthood:*

KATE BORNSTEIN lives and works in New York City, where her life is a cross between Holly Golightly in Breakfast at Tiffany's, *Sally Bowles in* Cabaret, *Patsy in* Absolutely Fabulous, *and Mallory Knox in* Natural Born Killers.

But very few of those kinds of bios really tell you the stuff ya wanna know about the artist. I mean the juicy stuff:

KATE BORNSTEIN has designs on delight. It took her nearly fifty years, but with the help of her lover, she's finally discovering the joy of having both a G-spot and a prostate gland. By night she may be a performance artist, but by day she's a professional dominatrix who prowls the Internet in search of potential clients.

Would I lie to you? You think this performance art stuff pays the bills? Ha! No, don't expect to find out too much about the person whose work you're seeing by reading their bios. And artists complain that "my audiences don't know the real me!" Good Lord, what on earth is the real me? The boy or man I used to be? The woman I was briefly? Is the real me the ex-Scientology cult member? The ex-IBM salesman? Is the real me one of the several personas I use when I do phone sex to pay the utility bills?

Some folks use their bios to forward whatever political road they're traveling at the time.

KATE BORNSTEIN has spent the last ten years of her life becoming a reluctant spokesperson for the world's fledgling transgender movement. Her next ten-year plan involves getting herself untangled from all that.

Bits and pieces of lives, carefully chosen to present ourselves in the best possible light. So how on earth are we supposed to find out about that artist up there on the stage? Well, obviously if they've written the work, there are going to be autobiographical elements that will give us some clues. But those are chosen with care as well and shaped for the drama that must attend a successful stage presentation. Me, I use an old Creole proverb to discover the heart of a person I'm interested in. Tell me who and what you love, and I'll tell you who you are. That's what I wanna do now in my work: I wanna tell you who and what I love. I wanna break down the barrier that exists between the words art and life. I want it all to be integrated. That's what I love: integrity. I love people whose lives are whole. I wanna do away with this idea of a public and private persona. God, that makes me shudder.

KATE BORNSTEIN spent the first thirty some-odd years hiding as a man, roughly two years hiding as a woman, and some six years more hiding as a lesbian. She's tired of hiding now, and she wants you to know who she is so you don't hafta spend your time filling in the blanks. She wants to know you on the same basis. She doesn't wanna hafta pry you out into the open, and she doesn't wanna make you do that with her.

or . . .

KATE BORNSTEIN has called over fifty-five geographical locations "home." Identitywise, she has transitioned from boy to man, from man to woman, from woman to lesbian, from lesbian to artist, from

artist to sex worker, and it's taken her nearly fifty years of living to
discover that she's actually more comfortable transitioning than she
is in arriving at some resting place called an identity.

So that's what I'm trying to do now. I'm trying to find comfort within a life
of constant change. I like the words fluid and flexible. Maybe it's because I'm
transsexual. Maybe it's because I'm a double Pisces. Maybe it's because I'm
just a nice Jewish boy who grew up to be the girl of his dreams. Whatever the
reason, I seem to be a lot more happy when I'm moving, changing, becoming,
landing, leaving. I think the most vital times of my life have been times of hello
and good-bye, and I want more of that. I want to find more people who like
that sort of a life. Perhaps that's why I write this kind of stuff. Perhaps the very
best bio for me would read simply:

KATE BORNSTEIN, traveling.

virtually yours, version 2.0: a game for solo performer with audience

KATE BORNSTEIN

Pre-Show: Prelude to a Miss

(THE HOUSE OPENS. THE AUDIENCE WALKS IN TO SEE ALLIE'S APARTMENT ON STAGE. IT CAN BE REPRESENTED BY A DESK OVERFLOWING WITH PAPERS IN TOTAL DISARRAY. HER COMPUTER VALIANTLY STRUGGLES TO KEEP ITS HEAD ABOVE WATER. ALLIE IS SEATED IN A CHAIR OR A DIVAN, WATCHING THE END OF THE MOVIE, "CAMILLE," WITH GRETA GARBO. THERE'S A FOURTH WALL BETWEEN HER AND THE AUDIENCE. THE PHONE RINGS A FEW TIMES DURING THE MOVIE, BUT ALLIE DOESN'T ANSWER IT. AS THE MOVIE COMES TO AN END, THE HOUSELIGHTS COME DOWN, AND ALLIE AND THE AUDIENCE WATCH MARGUERITE'S DEATH SCENE TOGETHER.)

Pre-Game Warm-up

ALLIE

God, I wish I could write like that. I . . . Wait! Got it! Lights go up. I'm on stage.

I'm talking into a tape recorder, I'm recording a message to myself, and I say . . .

(SPEAKING INTO A TAPE RECORDER.)

Hello, Allie, this is yourself, speaking to you from the past.
I'm a bolt out of the blue. I'm our own private time capsule. And
as I'm speaking these words, my girlfriend is dying, and there's
nothing I can do about it. Remember?
Good! That's good! Okay, who called? Who's calling me?

(ALLIE TURNS ON THE ANSWERING MACHINE. THE MESSAGES
PLAY LOUDLY ENOUGH TO BE HEARD CLEARLY BY THE AUDI-
ENCE.)

> You have seven new messages. ::beep::

> Allie, this is Donald at Josie's.
> Honey, what's the story on your show? Do we have one? Do we have a script? Can you get me a copy? I have to tell the papers something, Allie. Oh yeah, Jayne says you're using a *computer* in the show? Will I need more fire insurance? Get back to me as soon as you get this, ok? Bye, doll. ::beep::

> Hello, Allie? Are you home? Are you screening calls? It's Jayne. Allie, do you have an outline for the show yet? Donald's been calling me, and he wants to know what the show's going to be about. Since I'm directing it, I'd sorta like to know, too. Fax me an outline, will ya? Today? We need to get into rehearsal on this next week if you wanna open on time. And what's this video game doing in the budget? Video games, Allie? Call me. Bye. ::beep::

We were together for three years, then all of a sudden she
decided to become the man she always felt he was. She's be-

coming Daniel. Well, yippee for him, but what the hell does that
make me?

Alice Silverman? Betty Watts of the Sally Jesse show? I left
you a message last week? I'm not sure if you got it? I hadn't heard
back from you? We heard that your lesbian lover is going through
a sex change and becoming a man? Wow? That would be great
for this show? My number again is 212–990–4537? Call me collect? Thanks? Bye? ::beep::

(ALLIE GETS UP AND TURNS ON A TAPE: GIORDANI, "CARO
MIO BEN," CECILIA BARTOLI. THE MESSAGES CONTINUE TO
PLAY OVER THE MUSIC.)

Allie, this is Donald again. The *Bay Area Reporter* just called.
They want to know if you want a review for this run of the show.
Do you? Is it going to be in good enough shape? Are we gonna
be able to afford the overhead projectors? Ha, ha, ha. I'm not
really worried. Yes, I am. Let me know, honey. I'm at Josie's.
::beep::

All our hugging is for comfort; and all our kisses are hello or
good-bye.

I'm sitting here waiting for him to become his heart's desire,
and every step he takes in that direction just scares the hell out of
me. He's crawled into some cocoon and locked the door behind
him, and I know that somewhere inside that man is the woman I
fell in love with. Ohhhhhh, use that! That's good, that's really
good.

Allie baby! This is Mark Russell at PS 122. So, is your new piece ready? We've installed all the new wiring for your computer, the six phone lines, the overhead projector, and the popcorn machine. But, Allie, have you got a name for it yet? The calendar has got to go out next week, so give Heidi a call and let her know the name of the show and what it's about, okay? We're all excited you've got a new show so fast after your last one. . . . Can't wait to see it! You play video games on stage? Way cool! Ciao, baby. ::beep::

Allie? This is Charles at 9.9% Magazine. Had this great idea to do a follow-up on your piece, "My Girlfriend Is Becoming the Man of My Dreams." Gee, everyone loved that one! And we all really love that you two are so happy together. Maybe you could do a piece on how happy you are to be living with a man now. Whataya think? Give me a call, Allie! *Arrivederci!*

I have an aunt, my father's sister. She resents me horribly. She resents my change. She says I've murdered her brother's son. See, I used to look exactly like my father. Everyone said so. Now I look exactly like my mother, and my aunt can't look at me without crying. See, I murdered her brother's son. I never knew what she was talking about till now.

Down the Rabbit Hole

ALLIE

Great material for a show, huh? So let's write a show!

"There's no business like show business, like no business I know! Everything about it is appealing!"

What the fuck do I want to say? Holly Hughes would know what to say.

(THE PHONE RINGS. ALLIE DOESN'T ANSWER IT.)

I cannot deal.

Hello, love, it's Daniel, your honey. I'm going to be working late tonight, and I won't be home till around eleven or so. It's actually a good deal, 'cause we have new prospect lists to call. We should make a lot of money tonight. I'll try to call you from the phone room if I get a chance. I gave myself another shot today, and I think my voice has gotten lower again. What do you think? See, I can talk this deeply now. Isn't that great? Have you had a chance to play Virtually Yours yet? It looks like a great game! I love you soooooooooo much!!!! ::beep::

"Like no business I know! So go on with the show!"
Not a bad idea, honey. I'll play a little game first, be all rested, be real creative. And I'll get to work—later.

(ALLIE WALKS OVER TO HER COMPUTER AND POPS IN A CD-ROM.)

Welcome to Virtually Yours! The interactive video game that's just the way you'd like life to be! Press the Command key to continue.

Sure thing.

(ALLIE PRESSES THE COMMAND KEY.)

> Welcome to Virtually Yours! The interactive video game that's just the way you'd like life to be.
>
> Real world getting you down? Loading you up with problems you just can't deal with? Does it seem like you can't face one more phone call, one more bill, or the loss of one more loved one? That's why we're here! We can virtually listen to all of your issues and solve all of your problems. Press the Command key to skip right to the game; or do nothing, and I'll tell you all about Virtually Yours.

(ALLIE DOES NOTHING.)

Keep goin', mister, I'm listenin'.

> Fabulous!
> Virtually Yours is state-of-the-art interactive video.
> It's a game! It's therapy! It's virtually your life. Virtually Yours is the game where you get to step inside the shoes of your worst fears and walk around for a while. Virtually free of danger! Playing Virtually Yours is easy. Simply make your choices from the selections offered, and speak your answer. Virtually Yours's advanced voice recognition system will respond to your spoken word.

No way!

> Way! Hahaha! Now, what tone do you prefer for this session? New Age, Professional, Derogatory, Frivolous, or Best Friend?

I dunno. Your choice.

> Brilliant! Dealer's choice it is, love! And for this session, do you want a game, a therapy session, or both?

Both.

> Game and therapy! Two, two, two mints in one! Double your pleasure, double your fun! Right-o, do you want to address Denial, Anger, Bargaining, Depression, or Acceptance?

Fear.

> Clever girl. Fear it is! Fear is what they all have in common! Do you want a solo game, multiple players, or solo with audience?

Solo with audience.

> You asked for it, baby-doll, you got it! One audience coming up!

(HOUSELIGHTS COME UP FULL ON THE AUDIENCE. ALLIE IS LOST IN THOUGHT AND DOESN'T NOTICE.)

Of course I want an audience. I'm a performer. I love my audience.

(SHE SPOTS THE AUDIENCE.)

Oh, geez!

> Please press the Command key to begin this session of Virtually Yours.

Look at you! You are fantastic! You're worth the cost of the game all by yourselves! My virtual audience. Way cool! I love this game already!

Can I talk with you? What am I saying? Of course I can talk with you! Duh!

Look, I'm disappearing. Well, see, the more boy he's becoming, the more girl I seem to become. And the more girl I become, the more invisible I am in the world. Does that make any sense at all? It's not so much what he's doing, or even what he's becoming. It's that his change is changing me. His change is changing what I am in the world. And I never agreed to that!

> Please press the Command key to begin this session of Virtually Yours.

Right, right, right.

(ALLIE PUSHES THE COMMAND KEY. LOTS OF WHIRRING AND CLICKING.)

If I could just put a finger on what's bothering me, I'm sure it wouldn't be able to bother me. But what do I say?

Hello, I'm a transsexual lesbian, I'm supposed to have this great grasp on what gender is about, but my female lover is becoming a man, and I can't deal with that. What part can't I deal with? I always get this close, then one by one my worst fears climb up into my face. Is this my fate?

> Funny you should mention that! Hahaha!!!! That's exactly what we're going to deal with in this session of Virtually Yours!

What?

> Virtually Yours puts you right into the thick of it, isn't that exciting? Hang on to your hat, my dear, because through the magic and wonder of cybertechnology, you will step inside each one of your worst fears, and walk around in them for a bit. First we need some information about you in order to construct the game. At the sound of the tone, please start speaking about what is foremost on your mind. ::tone::

Audio-Generated Information Retrieval System

ALLIE

Foremost? Okay, ummmmm. My lover and I got together four years ago. Then last year, she decided to become a man. Wait, wait, I've got a question for you: What is it I find so terrifying?

> What do you believe in?

I believe in love, and I believe in relationships. But love. I believe in love.

> A real live hippie. Groovy! Far out! But more about relationships.

Smart-ass. I believe that we shift ourselves in order to stay in a relationship. We change our identities. I believe that a relationship is identity in motion.

> Is that it?

No. No, no, no. There's desire. There's attraction. There's how things fit together.

> So, the session is going to answer the big question of your relationship:

What?

> Do you stay with him? Or is it: Pack your bags; *hasta la vista,* baby; hit the road, Jackleen; there must be fifty ways to leave your lover—

Hey!

> Excuse me. Let's get on to what you're afraid of, just in general now. You keep talking, and when we have enough information to construct a character based on your fear, I'll tell you to stop. Please begin.

I hafta tell you this feels really weird. But okay, okay. Sometimes I wake up in the morning, and I lie in bed, I'm thinking to myself, Is this what I have to learn this lifetime? That no matter what I do, I'm going to be brought back face-to-face with man or woman, straight or gay. Is this my destiny? I wonder if I'm supposed to be unhappy.

I remember at a college reunion, I ran into an ex-lover of mine who saw me for the first time as a woman. She asked me if I was happy. "You were such an unhappy man," she said. "Are you a happy woman now?" I don't know. I don't understand happiness. I don't believe happy people. Humor, that's another story. I like to laugh. And joy, I found a great deal of joy in my work. But happiness? I never—

> ::tone:: Your first fear is the Fear of Destiny. Please continue.

I am so scared.
Not of the future, but of the past.
I am so terrified that my own arms are gonna reach out to me.
Way back from when I was afraid of becoming my father.
And when I became a woman, I was afraid of becoming my mother.
Now I don't know which parent I'm more afraid of becoming.
You got anything in your memory banks about that one?

> ::tone:: Your second fear is the Fear of History. Please continue.

All right. Daniel and I haven't explored everything I've wanted to explore. Sexually, I mean. I don't know if you have any words for that one, but—

> ::tone: Your third fear is the Fear of Fantasy. Please continue.

This one is simple. I fell in love with a woman. I've always been attracted to women. I've never been attracted to men. Now, people tell me Daniel is still the same person—underneath, y' know? But it's not *underneath* who I go to the store with. It's not *underneath* who gets all the privilege in the world. It's not *the person underneath* who's eclipsing me. No, saying we're all the same underneath is only partly true. How we act and how we're treated have a hell of a lot to do with it. Take that one and run with it if you can!

> ::tone:: Your fourth fear is the Fear of Power. Please continue.

What do you mean, continue? How many more do we have to do?

> ::tone:: Your fourth fear is the Fear of Power. Please continue.

All right, all right . . . I can tell you two more. They're real simple. I think Daniel and I may be breaking up, and I'm afraid of being lonely; I'll do most anything to get out of being lonely. And I'm afraid of going crazy. Holding all this stuff in, not telling anyone, and going stark, raving—

> ::tone:: ::tone:: Your fifth fear is Loneliness. Your sixth fear is Madness. We're ready to begin the game.

Wait! What does the audience do? . . .

> Tch, tch. They do what audiences are supposed to do, dearie duck. They listen. They watch you.

Don't they get popcorn? Audiences should get popcorn. That's the way of it.
And me! What's going to happen to me?

> You?

Yeah, me!

> You're going to become your worst fears. And here comes the first one!

Where?
What fear?
Is there a help button???

(MUSIC: VIRTUALLY YOURS TRANSITION THEME, A BUBBLE-GUM RENDITION OF "ROW, ROW, ROW YOUR BOAT." THIS THEME WILL PRECEDE EVERY TRANSITION UP INTO A NEW LEVEL.)

Diane (VO)
On the last Day of Judgment, whatever *that* is, it's my belief that everyone in the world will come together in some large celestial stadium. And each one of us will put in place a piece to a gigantic jigsaw puzzle, called "The Answer to the Suffering of Humanity." We each of us hold a piece, you see. And that is why it has always been my dream to photograph everyone in the world.

Welcome to Level 1: Fate Steps In.

Level 1: Fate Steps In

DIANE

So, hello. I'm Diane, I'm not too good with crowds, you should probably know that right off, but look at you! You're beautiful, you are a gold mine—no! I know a lot about gold mines—I'm a prospector, oh yes, I am!

All right, it was one of those beautiful Saturday mornings in Central Park, one of my favorite gold mines, I might add, and I was wearing my camera, I was out, looking. And this friend of mine comes up to me and she says, "Hello, Diane, and what are *you* doing on such a bright, glorious, sunshiney day?" and I say to her, "I'm trying to find some unhappy people."

Well! She looked at me like she was afraid of me! You know, the first thing I was afraid of was that the Lindbergh kidnapper would get me in the middle of the night; I loved being scared. When I was a little kid, I would sit in my room in the pitch black, and I would wait for the monsters to come and tickle me to death. My nanny used to laugh at me about that—she was French, and I

fell in love with her when I was six years old. She called herself
Mamselle, and I thought, That's the cat's whiskers! Mamselle! She
had such a hard, sad, quite lovely face, and I just adored her, I
wanted to be her—don't you always fall in love with someone you
want to be? I do, that's what I do, even with my camera—I love
my camera, I could be a camera. My camera is God's gift to me. I
can see the world just fine through my eyes, but I can't feel the
world without my camera. My camera and I, we're lovers, and like
most lovers, my camera is determined to do one thing, and I want
it to do something completely different. Sometimes we make love,
my camera and me—sometimes it's rape.

(SHE TAKES A PHOTO OF SOMEONE IN THE AUDIENCE.)

Pretty picture!
I'd like someone to rape me, it's a fantasy, it would have to be
someone I trusted. In God we trust—you know that one—I read
that on a nickel when I was a kid. I believe our money—what can
I say? My parents raised me to believe in money—and that nickel
told me to trust in God, but I could never find God, and so I kept
looking for someone else, someone to trust, you know, God knows
I could never trust myself!
    Do you trust me? Can I take your picture? You look fantastic!

(SHE TAKES A PHOTO OF SOMEONE IN THE AUDIENCE.)

Beautiful! Darling, all the people I love are beautiful. I learned
from doing this that if you look at anyone long enough, you can
see all their possibilities, even beauty, especially beauty, if you look
long enough. That's what I'm doing with you, my dear, I've got
you perfect!

(SHE TAKES A PHOTO OF SOMEONE IN THE AUDIENCE.)

And now you know why I never take a self-portrait. I might
actually hold myself still long enough to see all my possibilities,
and forget that, it's so much easier to see myself in other people—
like my husband? My husband was the most beautiful man I'd ever
seen: we were . . . we were the other side of Romeo and Juliet, we

were the happy ending. I wanted to be just like him, and I made myself smile, but I couldn't trust anyone who was that happy. I always thought he was hiding something from me behind that smile—I was sure hiding something behind my smile, and I hated myself for it—so in the end I left him. I stopped smiling, and I started to look for people I could understand—unhappy people, freaks like me. I took their pictures. There was an honesty I got from them that I never got with . . .

Oh, shit, I hate crying. Don't you? It's so humiliating, isn't it, so self-indulgent, it's so . . . it's so what the world expects me to do when it stands there in front of me and it's so ugly, and it's filled with such pain. It's what everyone wants me to do when they don't fit in and they think I do. They think I fit in, and I never really did, and it's my destiny, I believe, it's my destiny to always be on the outside, but everyone thinks I'm on the inside, and I can't cry about it.

You know that one, don't you? Does it make you want to cry? Can I take your picture?

(SHE TAKES A PHOTO OF SOMEONE IN THE AUDIENCE.)

Perfect! You are perfection!

Does someone here have a perfect tattoo, a perfect mark, a perfect anything? Anyone? Can I see it, please? God, you're so beautiful. I swear, you are! Can I please take your picture? You look terrific. Y'know, a lot of people get their tattoos to hide their scars. I don't have any tattoos. I used to hide my scars behind a smile. Now I hide my scars behind this. I died hiding my scars behind this.

> Time is running out, my duck. Kindly bring this character to a conclusion now.

(SHE TAKES A PHOTO OF SOMEONE IN THE AUDIENCE.)

Three weeks before I killed myself, I saw a woman fall past my window. It was a hot day in July—the first hot day in July. She had climbed up onto our roof, from the street, then she jumped. I was sitting in my window seat, and I was drinking my coffee, and as she fell by my window, our eyes met. I watched her fall—it was like slow motion—till she hit the courtyard. It's not like the cartoons, you know, people don't go splat, they just crumple and stop living, and in that terrible silence, I swear to you I heard her sigh.

It took the police nearly half a day to come by and pick her up, so she just lay like that out in the hot weather. And you know what was on the ground right next to her? A camera. A camera! The fall broke it open, and it lay there like some dead bird, the film was spilled all over the pavement like entrails out in the sun, and no mystic was ever going to read those entrails, but I was, I knew what photographs she'd taken. Oh yes, I did.

So, when I saw her down there, with her camera, I knew I was looking at myself. And I spent the next thirty hours of my life taking her picture, rolls and rolls and rolls of film. We were . . . soul twins, she and I, and what do you—what do you do—after you've taken the perfect picture of yourself, huh?

> That's easy, dear heart. If you were something more than a computer-generated personality, you might crawl into the bathtub and slit your wrists. Am I right?

I did not leave a note.

> Very few people do. Now, you need to tell us your advice for our game player. What good is walking inside your fear if your fear doesn't give you some good advice!

You want good advice? I'll give you good advice. Stay with him. Haven't you been looking for someone just like you? When you sit down with someone, don't you want to hear them say, "I'm just like you. We're two peas in a pod. We're soul twins." Only, this person in front of you has lived something you haven't lived, you know what I'm saying? They're coming through life's mirror from the other direction as you. And there you are together: picture perfect!

Diane VO / Diane Live in *Fugue*

Thanks for letting me take you. You are so beautiful, really, all of you, each one of you. I'm not just saying that, I have an eye for these things, oh yes, I do. All it takes is looking.

ALLIE

All it takes is looking. You think that's what I need to do? Look at him? When I look at him now, I see my father.

Your choice now, dearie. Do you take her advice and stay with the boyfriend? Or do you want to look behind door number two?

I knew just what she was talking about. All of it.

Of course! She's *your* fear!

So are those my only choices? Stay with him, or suicide? This isn't much of a game!

Well, you wouldn't be much of a player if you stayed at the first level. Level two is simply delicious!

Okay . . . go for it.

> That's my girl.

What's level two? Oh! My parents, I remember. . . .
(MUSIC: BUBBLEGUM "ROW, ROW, ROW YOUR BOAT.")

> **Anna VO**
>
> I remember waking up in the morning when I was a little girl, this was some seventy-odd years ago, mind you, and I remember the men and the boys waking up. "Thank God I was not born a woman," said my father.

> Welcome to Level 2: History Repeats Itself.

Level 2: History Repeats Itself

ANNA

"Thank God I was not born a woman," said his brother, my uncle. "Thank God I was not born a woman," said both of my brothers in unison. I was the only girl. Every morning I heard this ritual, and I would turn to my mother, and she would just smile and stroke my cheek and whisper to me, "*Nu?* They would be nowhere without us, my *butzalah*."

Ach, this room is such a mess! He never kept his room clean. The least I can do is fold her laundry, you don't mind.

I gave birth to two sons. Everyone was proud of me. I was a valuable woman, you see? It was perfect. Then the men began to disappear from my life. It happens. One by one, they disappeared.

Samuel, I would tell my son, it's a good thing you were born a boy. Boys can never be ugly, but girls! Girls can be ugly! And an ugly girl . . . well, what're you going to do with an ugly girl? Look at your Becky next door!

My father died. It happens.

And, Samuel! Girls are sneaky! You can never trust a girl. Not really.

My husband died. That was particularly difficult.

I'll tell you this much, Samuel! Girls can get a whole lot more done than boys. If a girl wants something done, she can always find some boy to do it.

My brothers died, one in the war, and another lives with Alzheimer's disease, but I call that death.

Then my son Samuel, he became a lesbian.

In the house where I grew up, we had a fine crystal goblet from the court of Czar Nicholas. It was a prized possession. One day, I think it was the day the bottom fell out of the stock market, on that day when I was doing the dusting, I knocked over that goblet. I watched it fall to the hardwood floor, and I watched it shatter into hundreds of pieces. I can still hear the sound of it shattering. I didn't cry. I just swept up the pieces.

About a year after my husband died, Samuel comes to visit me in my home on the Cape. It's a warm, sunny day, and we're sitting out on the porch, we're drinking iced tea.

"I have something to tell you, Mom," he says.

"You're gay," I say. I always suspected he was gay, and I thought this was a good time to let him know I suspected it.

"Not exactly," he tells me. "Do you know what a transsexual is?"

Me, I'm watching a perfect crystal goblet fall almost lazily to the hardwood floor.

"Transvestite?" I say, and I knew the difference. Of course I knew the difference. My husband, his father, had been a medical doctor. I knew the difference. It was the truth I didn't want to know. I can say that now.

"Transvestites want to dress up in women's clothes, Mom," he says to me. "I'm getting the surgery so I can live as a woman— that makes me a transsexual."

Why are you telling me this? I ask him. Why didn't you just
let me go to my grave believing I have a son? And of course he
had an answer for that, he has an answer for everything, such a
mouth on that kid. He said he was going to look like a woman
and talk like a woman, and if he didn't tell me, then he would never
be able to talk with me or see me again.

Oh, boy! I needed time to sweep up the pieces of my life, and
so I say he is never to return to my home again.

You just get out of here right now, young man. And if you go
through with this . . . if you really go through with this . . . just
don't bother coming back to my house. You won't be welcome
here. Can you imagine what it took for me to say that? To my own
child?

Wait, I said, what are you going to call yourself?

Samantha, he says. He was born Samuel. It was my father's
name. If I have to call you Samantha, I tell him, then you can call
me Mrs. Cohen. He drives back to Boston. I drink my iced tea.

Our men tell us over and over, "You are nothing without a
man, you are nothing without sons." And they never stop to
think what becomes of us when they die, when they leave us. If
we're not careful, we become nothing, just like they said we
would.

One night, about six months later, it was the day the big hur-
ricane hit the Cape, the phone rings. It's Samuel. He's calling to
see if I'm all right, and we chat. We're stiff, we're polite. How're
you doing? I ask him. Not so good, Mom, he says. The people at
the home office are making it rough on him for becoming a woman.
Oh, baby, I think to myself. You think it's rough now—wait till
you become a real woman. He begins to cry. He tells me he has to
get off the phone, and he hangs up.

I sit here with the receiver in my hand, and I realize I hadn't
heard him cry since he was a little boy.

I call him back, it must have been about twenty minutes later.
The phone rings once, twice, three times, and he picked up.

Hello, he says.

Samantha, I say.

Mom, she says, I love you.

I love you, too, baby, that's why I called, and I called to tell you that no matter how your world falls apart, because honey, that's what happens, we build a world, and it falls apart, but no matter what, you still have yourself, and that's what counts. And I will always be here for you, my *butzalah*. I love you, Samantha.

There was never any question of loving him or not loving him. Of course I love him. She's my child.

So, now, we talk, me and my son, the lesbian. We talk a great deal. I never had a daughter to talk with before. This is interesting. It's almost nice. No, it's very nice. I'd always been told that would be such a bad thing to bring a girl into the world. So I never gave it much thought. Now, my daughter and I we're close, we're friends. We laugh. We make jokes.

Don't get me wrong—I still grieve for all the men who have passed from my life. I cry a great deal, especially at night. It's particularly difficult at night. But I no longer feel I am nothing without them; in fact, I feel I am a great deal more.

There. That's a little better, a bit more presentable.

Anna VO/Live in *Fugue*

I suppose there are still men who wake up and say, "Thank God, I was not born a woman." I suppose this type of man still looks for the kind of woman I used to be. It only took me close to eighty years, but thank God I'm not that type of woman any longer!

ALLIE

Any longer in that character, and I think I might've gotten stuck there. God! She turned her back on everything she was taught, everything she grew up with.

I see the tendency runs in the family.

Not *my* family, mister! All right, so I gave up being straight boy, that's for sure; but if I give up being lesbian, what's left for me?

Dear heart, the next fear is the Fear of Fantasy. Perhaps we'll find an alternative in that?

Um, yeah, maybe.

So glad to hear it! When it's all over, you'll look back and be glad of this one. When the game is done, when the lights are out, when the pain fades away to a dull throb.

Pain? What pain? What do you mean when it's over? When the game is done? When . . . when . . . when . . .

(MUSIC: BUBBLEGUM VERSION OF "ROW, ROW, ROW YOUR BOAT.")

Young Girl's Singsong Voice-over
When I am dead and in my grave and all my bones are rotten,
This little book will tell my name when I am quite forgotten

(SHE BEGINS TO ATTACH CLOTHESPINS TO HER BODY.)

One with No Name VO

The first thing my mistress took away from me when I bonded myself to her was my name; that was four years ago. And when she left me, she didn't give me my name back. It's been nearly a year since she's gone, and I don't know what to call myself. I don't know how to introduce myself to people. I mean, people always want your name.

Welcome to Level 3: Fantasy Island

Level 3: Fantasy Island

ONE WITH NO NAME

Hey, do you know about these? One of the first things I learned was that they don't hurt when you put 'em on. Really. See? Nothin'! The real pain happens when you take 'em off after you've left them on for a while. Isn't that great? The pain comes from the absence. See, the blood rushes to the spot that was pinched, that's what hurts, and if you've left them on long enough, the pain can be really intense.

Sometimes it feels like the blood is still rushing to my heart to fill the hole she left there when she said she didn't love me anymore . . . Ha ha!

When she took my name away from me, I learned to call myself "this one." Like, "May this one pour your tea, ma'am?" Or, "This one thanks her mistress for the sound caning." I need to tell you, I hated the canings. I mean, they really really really hurt, okay? But I let her cane me because . . . she liked to. And letting her do it, that just made me feel more giving. It made me feel more loving.

You really have to have this done to you to do it right. Donna, she would make these patterns on my body when she did it. Donna would put me on display, and everyone would go ohhhhhh and ahhhhh, they would, and I was so proud to be her work of art. I always say if you can't be an artist, you can always be a work of art, huh?

I learned to put myself in bondage when I was fourteen. First I would tape my mouth shut, then I would tie my ankles together and fasten my ankles to the bedposts. Then I'd tie another length of rope to the headboard, and with a slipknot I'd tie my wrists together. Then, lying on my belly, pressing myself to the bed, I would make myself come. Fourteen years old. Kids, huh? I never suspected someone would really want to do that to me. I always thought I'd have to do that to myself. Do you know what it's like to imagine your heart's desire, never really believing anyone would love you for who you really are? Not who you really are.

And then one day, she shows up. She shows up at the food co-op where you work the cash registers, and she makes sure she gets into your line every time. I know she saw my hands trembling as I'd ring up her stuff. It wasn't till later I found out she wasn't even vegetarian. . . . She just bought stuff at the co-op so she could check me out. "I usually eat burgers and wieners, ya know." That's what she told me a month after she first put a collar on me. I like thinking about that.

By the way, if you leave these on too long, you can hurt yourself. Well, I mean seriously hurt yourself, okay?

The first time she touched me, she hurt me. It was right there at the checkout counter. She brought the palm of my hand up to her mouth and she bit me. She has these small, sharp teeth, and she kept on biting till I bled right into her mouth. I felt like I was gonna come any second, but she left a second before I could. It was like she already knew my rhythms; ever meet a person like that? Oh! And then she left without giving me her name or her number. I know how to get a hold of you, that's all she said, and she walks out the door, laughing.

The next woman in line looked at my hand, and she asked me if I was all right. All right? All right? I'm fine. I'm fine, thank you. Wouldn't you be fine if your heart's desire had walked into your life not five minutes ago?

All I wanted to do was belong to her. Not like her wife, I mean, Ewwwwww! And not like her girlfriend. I've been girlfriend to enough people. Not like a one-night stand, either. I wanted her to own me, like property. I told her that on our third date, when she had me tied down to her bed. And by the way, the knot around my wrists wasn't a slipknot that night! I loved her completely. I trusted her completely. I knew her and she knew me. She asked me what I wanted more than anything else in the world, and I said, I wanna belong to you, and she smiled and said, That can be arranged, and I started crying and I couldn't stop. You never know how profoundly moving the fulfillment of your fantasy is gonna be until it actually finally really happens to you.

I've got marks, I got marks right here, it's her brand? Donna didn't do it; she had a friend of hers do it who knows how. They hafta heat the iron till it's white hot. Any less hot than white hot, and you have to hold it down to the skin longer, and that makes the skin crack and get all blistery, and ya really spoil the mark. So, she got someone to do it right, and there I was watching them heat up the brand. It went from cold metal gray to kinda green to cherry red to almost blinding white and they held my leg down to the table with four very tight leather straps. I couldn't move if I'd wanted to, but I didn't want to. I wanted her mark on me. I did. And when they touched the iron to the inside of my thigh, I felt like I was going to shoot right out of my body.

Some people remember how it smells, but I remember how it sounded. It was a bubbly sort of hissing sound. I was sick afterwards; for a few days I had a fever and chills. I was embarrassed, but the woman who branded me said, Eh, that happens a lot. Y'know, even now, at night, when I'm alone in bed, I like to trace my finger through the brand, it's really deep.

Okay. We were madly in love, the toast of the leather community. We were the perfect couple. We were the ones everyone looked to when they were so afraid ya couldn't find real love in sadomasochism. We got written up in all the leather journals. We

even did *Oprah:* "Women Who Own Women, and the Women
They Own." I was the latter. She had me, and we had it all.

Then she stopped coming by every day.

And I started to do this to myself more and more.

She started loaning me out to her friends more frequently.

(SHE WALKS INTO THE AUDIENCE AND ASKS FOR AUDIENCE
MEMBERS TO HELP HER TO TAKE THE CLOTHESPINS OFF HER
BODY. IT REALLY HURTS AS THEY COME OFF.)

Could you help me with this, please? Just take it off me, okay?
Thanks.

She started loaning me out to men. I didn't mind that, not
really. I mean hey, I was doing it for her.

Thanks, this is nice. I usually have to do this myself. Thanks
for doing this for me.

I said to her, It doesn't matter about the men, as long as you
love me. She didn't say anything.

Could you get this one right here? Thanks. This one thanks
you so much.

Four years we were together, and me without a name, and she
came into my room one night and she said, You're free to go now.

Free to go? Free to go where? I belong to you. What did I do?

You didn't do anything, she said to me. I just understand you.

You understand me? Do you understand that I have given you
the most precious gift I can give anyone? I've given you me!

I just understand you, she said to me.

You understand me? Do you understand that who I am is that
I live for your love? That is who I am. You understand me? What
did I do?

You didn't do anything, she said to me. I just really understand
you, and she unbuttons her jeans, and slides them down to her
knees, and I see this fresh brand on the inside of her thigh. It was
really clean.

Forgive me, she's sayin' to me. You've taught me so much, she's
sayin' to me, and I understand you. You're free to go now, she says.
Call it my parting act of cruelty.

So, it's been a year now since she's gone. Y'know, the old wizards and witches would never use their real names. They knew something we've forgotten. Whoever knows your real name holds the power of life and death over you. Whoever gets to name something gets to own it.

Okay, I told you a little lie before. I have a name now, sure I do, I mean, whaddaya think? But I don't use it. I like it better, not using my name at all.

(Young Girl's Singsong Voice-over)
When I am dead and in my grave and all my bones are rotten
This little book will tell my name when I am quite forgotten

One with No Name Vo/Live *Fugue*
This one is grateful for your kind attention to her pain. This one thanks you for permission to tell her story. This one hopes she has been pleasing to you. This one—

ALLIE

This one was really hard! What's the lesson here, mister? No pain, no gain?

Pain in a virtual reality can indeed carry over to the world of flesh and blood, my little turtledove.

I'm not yer turtledove, and that was too close. I'll tell you what that one brought up for me—I just don't know if we're gonna be attracted to each other when he's done all his changing. And another thing! Even if that *is* my fantasy, I don't know if I'm ready to give up any of my power to a man. I've been a man, and I know what it's like!

> Well, you've certainly got my circuits working overtime, my dear. Care to press on?

What, after the clothespins? Oh, sure—let's keep going! I can't wait to see what's next. Probably pierce my toes.
You okay? Want some popcorn?

> You'll just love what's next, my dear. The Fear of Power it is!

Wait! I didn't mean that! Don't you know sarcasm when you hear it?!? This is getting too real! Life in the real world . . . life in the game . . . life in the flesh . . . life in virtual reality . . .

(MUSIC: BUBBLEGUM RENDITION OF "ROW, ROW, ROW YOUR BOAT.")

> **Valerie, VO**
> Life in this society being, at best, an utter bore and no aspect of society being at all relevant to women, there remains to civic-minded, responsible, thrill-seeking females only to overthrow the government, eliminate the money system, institute complete automation, and destroy the male sex.

> Welcome to Level 4: I Shot The Law, and the Law Won.

Level 4: I Shot the Law, and the Law Won

VALERIE

Whaddaya do when the person you fall in love with is your worst nightmare? Whaddaya do when the kind of person you've been most afraid of all your life is suddenly sharing the same bed with you, and you like it? Let's talk about some irony here, okay? Let's talk about some kinda god with one funky sense of humor here, okay?

Valerie VO/*Live Fugue*
The male is completely egocentric, trapped inside himself, incapable of empathizing or identifying with others, of love, friendship, affection, or tenderness.

Valerie, (live on mike)
He is a half-dead, unresponsive lump, incapable of giving or receiving pleasure or happiness; consequently he is at best an utter bore, an inoffensive blob, since only those capable of absorption in others can be charming.

His name was Brad, and he was a sailor. Don't look at me like that. I was fifteen, and I fell in love with him What'd I know? He was nice to me. He was sweet. I liked the way he touched my hair, okay? He was sweet. He used to sing me to sleep with songs like "Frog went a' courtin', and he did go uh-huh. Frog went a' courtin', and he did go, uh-huh."

Valerie live on mike
A true community consists of individuals—not mere species members, not couples—free spirits in free relation to each other. Traditionalists say the basic unit of "society" is the family; "hippies" say the tribe; no one says the individual.

I wasn't ever attracted to guys. I mean, maybe you figured that out from the stuff I write. But Brad was different. He came home one evening and he says, "Hey, Valerie, we're havin' a contest aboard the ship. A talent contest." Sort of a masquerade ball, the way he put it, and could I help him out with a costume?

Like what? I asked. I dunno, he said, do you have anything hanging around? Like what? I asked. I dunno, he said, maybe, I dunno, maybe one of your old dresses. Well, I just laughed my ass off on that one. And he laughed, too. The two of us just sat there and we laughed and laughed, but then I could see that's what he wanted to do, he wanted to get into one of my dresses.

"He walked up to Miss Mousie's side, said Mousie would you be my bride, uh-huh, uh-huh."

Valerie live on mike

The farthest-out male is the drag queen, but he, although different from most men, has an identity—he is female. He conforms compulsively to the man-made feminine stereotype.

I asked Natalie about this. She was my best girlfriend. She thought I was crazy for balling him at all, but she thought I was really crazy for letting him wear my dresses. She said if Senator McCarthy ever found out about us, Brad would be thrown out of the navy, and I'd be put into a hospital because I was insane. Get outta here, I said to Natalie, he just wants to wear a dress! Get outta here! He ain't gonna get thrown out of the navy. I'm not goin' into some loony bin. Know what, that's exactly what happened to both of us. Isn't that funny?

What could I do, Cupid got me. Zing! Boom! Right here!

That 'minds me of my favorite fairy tale from when I was a little girl. It's the one about Cupid and the cave of Death, right? Cupid is out there, flying around late at night. Ho hum, I'm Cupid, and I'm so cute. And he's real sleepy, and he flies down and curls up to sleep in this cave, but he doesn't know it's the cave of Death, right? And he's sleeping and he's tossing and turning, and all

Cupid's arrows spill out all over the floor, and they get all mixed up with all the arrows of Death, right? And when Cupid wakes up, Oh, my, he says, I am in the cave of Death! And he just scoops up all the mixed-up arrows he can—all of them—and puts them in his quiver, and so what happens? Ya never know if the arrow that hits ya is an arrow of love or an arrow of death. Isn't that bitchin'?

All right, so the night of the big contest comes, and there was Brad looking pretty, um, pretty. I mean, really pretty. He was wearing my panties, he was wearing a girdle. He had on one of my bras, and we stuffed it with Kleenex, and was he ever stacked! I was gettin' pretty excited, I can tell you that!

Valerie VO/Live

Sex is not part of a relationship; on the contrary, it is a solitary experience, noncreative, a gross waste of time. *The female can easily—far more easily than she may think—condition away her sex drive,* leaving her completely cool and cerebral and free to pursue worthy relationships and activities.

Gee, Brad, you look really good, I told him. You look like a real hot chick. Call me Pamela, he said, and I have to tell you he sounded like a chick when he said it. I laughed, but he said again, Call me Pamela. Okay, "Pamela."

And you know what happened when I said that? He starts to whimper. You know, like a little girl? Pamela, I said, and his eyes start fillin' up with tears. Pamela, I said, and he starts shaking. Pamela, my sweet darling Pamela, and she starts to moan. Pamela, my little slut Pamela, and she was shaking, and I laid that chickie down and I balled her, I balled her so good, and that's when I had my first ever orgasm, you see what I mean about irony? Perfect!

Valerie VO/Live

Sex is the refuge of the mindless. And the more mindless the woman, the more deeply embedded in the male "culture" she is—*in short, the nicer she is, the more sexual she is.*

Pamela and I fucked each other silly for days, and it was just
five weeks later she got herself stopped by the shore patrol. She
was wearing a nice poodle skirt and a beaded sweater, and she got
thrown in the brig dressed like that. They beat her up pretty bad,
that's what I heard, but it wasn't 'til they told her they were gonna
throw her outta the navy that she made a rope out of her poodle
skirt and hung herself in her cell.

So thass why I write this shit. That's why I write . . .

Valerie live on mike

The male is eaten up with tension, with frustration at not being
female, at not being capable of ever achieving satisfaction or
pleasure of any kind; eaten up with hate—not rational hate that is
directed against those who abuse or insult you—but irrational, in-
discriminate hate . . . hatred, at bottom, of his own worthless self.

Your time is nearly up. Please bring this character to a
conclusion.

Fuck you! No man tells me my time is up, man. I say when my
time is up!

Fifteen years later, I showed Andy this play I wrote about me
and Pamela. It was brilliant. It was called *Up Your Ass*. *Up Your
Ass* was gonna change the world. I have to tell you, it was. It was
the real picture of the real male in the phony male world. I give
Andy the only copy of my script. Andy said he'd film it. He said
to give him some time, and he'd film it.

Three months later he says, Oh, Valerie, I've lost your script.
I know for a fact he threw it away or burned it or maybe he ate it,
I think maybe he might have eaten it, because that's what he did
with other artists, he ate them up, especially women, because he
was really afraid of women. Andy fought women. He fought artists. He shot my spirit full of holes, so I shot his body full of holes.

It's the way of the world. Whatever you fight, you end up losing to. The way of the world. They told me later it was a .32 I used. I didn't know, it was just a gun to me. I kinda wished I'da used a bow and arrow, you hear what I'm saying, that woulda been poetry.

I have to tell you the best part. The best part was when he begged me not to shoot him. Oh, God, don't shoot me, Valerie. Don't shoot me. And he pissed himself.

He recovered, and the photographs of his wounds sold for tens of thousands of dollars. I made those goddamn wounds, I was the artist of that piece of work, and that little shit got the money for them. Know what I got? I got sent to an insane asylum for three goddamn years.

And your advice to the traveler?

Leave her. Leave her fast, and leave her hard. You really wanna live with a woman who hates herself so much she wants to be a man? Didn't you cut off your own dick, man? She's throwing everything you worked for right in your face and she's saying fuck you, fuck you, and all the women around you.

I'm not including you with the rest of the women, 'cause you know yer not woman . . . you know that, right? But at least yer headed in the right direction. You cut off your dick. That's a good start, but yer not a woman.

I gotta tell you one more thing. Pamela, she would cry. She'd get all weepy, and when I'd ask her what was goin' on, some night when we were just lyin' in bed together, she'd look at me with her makeup runnin' 'cause of the tears and she'd say she wasn't used to bein' treated so good. She said I was tender, and she wasn't used to that. I hafta ask ya, what kind of world would be mean to a sweet thing like Pamela, huh?

> **Valerie, VO/Live _Fugue_**
> (Singing)
> "Snake came in and made it clear that no one's gettin' married here, uh-huh, uh-huh."

ALLIE

Uh-huh. Uh-huh. I'm really gonna listen to someone who's totally got me pegged as some guy who caught off his dick.

> This is sarcasm?

You're learning.

> I try.

Y'know something? They don't really cut it off. No, they sorta turn it inside out. Kinda like a sock? It's real interesting, see, they—

> Ahem.

Huh?

> I'm sure that's all very fascinating, but are you going to take her advice? Leave your lover?

How can I leave him just because he's a man? He's not a jerk.

> I take it then you wish to proceed?

No! Wait! I'm really afraid I'll never find another lover. Of being so lonely, and going crazy.

> Your next fears are loneliness and madness. Care to toss caution to the winds and combine them into one delightful moment?

Yah. Yah. Go for it.

(MUSIC: BUBBLEGUM RENDITION OF "ROW, ROW, ROW YOUR BOAT.")

> **Miss G, VO**
> Shall I tell you what Tennessee Williams wrote about me? He wrote, "I think an artist who abandons his art is the saddest thing in the world, sadder than death. There must have been something about her screen career that profoundly revolted her." He was a sweet man from what I've heard. I never knew him. I never knew any of my critics, or any of the theorists who write about me.

> Welcome to Level 5: She Talks.

Level 5: She Talks

MISS G

Helloooo. I went for a walk yesterday, and while I was waiting at the corner for the light to change, a crowd of people gathered around me. I was so frightened. I really don't know how to act when they do that. I really don't know how to answer when they say, "Excuse me, but aren't you . . ." "Haven't I seen you in the movies?" "Goodness, it's you!" And I want to be gracious, I do, but all I can think of is: Run.

Shall I tell you the very first word the American press ever wrote to describe me? Perfection. It's true. Perfection. Imagine, if you will, not quite twenty, and I am Perfection. God, how I loved reading that! Ha, ha, ha! It never dawned on me that other people reading it would in fact believe that I was perfect.

I want to tell these people who gawk at me, I want to say, "You have no idea who I am," but instead I smile and say, "Why thank you, thank you. I'm so glad you enjoy my films." And I get myself home as quickly as I can. (COUGH) You can write that the story of my life is told in back entrances and side doors (COUGH), secret elevators, and other ways of getting in and out of places so that people won't bother me. (COUGH)

Forgive me, I simply cannot speak without the help of a microphone, and there are so many of you! This poor voice of mine, that's rather sad, isn't it? (COUGH)

Home is so wonderfully predictable. Are you comfortable? Good. Then I'll tell you what happened to me the night before I abandoned my art.

I was quite alone, as I usually am. I've always enjoyed my solitude, it's all I've ever wanted: to be alone without people expecting me to be something I'm not. I want to be alone, and I'm so afraid of being lonely, I've so much in need to . . . touch. I've yet to reconcile the two, you see, it's my madness. Ha, ha! But, it was extraordinarily cold, and this always makes me more lonely, yes? It was a night when the sandman simply would not come, and the sounds of the night were muffled by the blankets of snow that piled high round the cabin. But the howling of the she-wolf was no normal night-sound.

Did I say cabin? Ha, ha, ha, ha. Kindly forgive an old woman her eccentricities. I meant to say apartment. I opened my eyes and saw her standing there—there, just beyond the window. She throws herself up against the window, and our eyes lock in the still blue moonlight. That's when I begin to change.

At first, I simply grow warm, then hot, and now it feels as though my body is on fire. I am screaming, somewhere in the corner of my mind that's left to me, I know I'm screaming. I drop from my bed down to all fours, my arms and legs stretching, shifting, and my jaw! Ah the pain! My face pushes itself out toward her longer and longer, sharp teeth breaking through my gums, and my screaming drops to a deep rumbling, here, down in my chest. Change has always been difficult for me, you see. She begins to howl, and I lift my head and join her in chorus.

Now, we are running shoulder to shoulder through the snow, wolves together. We run for hours. How exhilarating! We stop at a stream, and the ice cold water feels marvelous going down my throat.

"Tell me something about yourself you have never told anyone," she says to me in a voice that has never known the need for a microphone. And here is what I said: As a child, you see, most of my friends chased after moonbeams and true love. I chased after something slightly more elusive: a four-thousand-watt spotlight. Catch me if you can, the light cried out to me, catch me if you can. And when I caught it, the light whispered to me, Now I will never set you free.

"Thank you for your story, my daughter, my sister, my lover," she says to me. "Now here is a gift for you. This is the way you know that Death is approaching: you have a sudden, perfect vision of yourself. You see it all, and you are beautiful, and you will wish that moment of your own perfect beauty to last forever. Then, you die. How painful is your death depends on how ready you are to relinquish your own perfection."

"To die well," she tells me, "just practice achieving perfection and tossing it aside, over and over again." Ha, ha, ha.

She nips at my leg, and she barks. I bark back, and she runs off, laughing. We play chase like puppies, and we run till dawn. Ah, dawn! Fingers of light stab down at me from the heavens. Is that a spotlight? My cabin materializes before us, dark and squat, with all its back entrances, side doors.

I start to speak, but now I'm standing in the doorway of my cabin, naked, human, shivering in the cold. She lifts her head, and she howls, "Come with me, my sister, my daughter, my lover." I howl back as best I can with this poor voice of mine, "I cannot. Tomorrow I start a new film, and I must . . ." But she's gone. (COUGH) And in that awful silence, I was more alone and lonely than I'd ever been in my entire life.

I did not do my chores that day. No. I phoned the studio and I told them I would never make another film again in my life. She'll be back, my wolf, and when she returns I'll be ready for her. I have spent the last fifty years of my life tossing aside the perfection I had become. Over and over again.

And when she returns, the two of us shall be puppies together through all of time. The two of us shall be as puppies through all of time.

Goodness, just look at the time! I really must be going, or the sandman will never come this evening.

Miss G, VO/Live Fugue
Good night. Good night. Lovely to meet you. Good night.

Inventory: It Doesn't Add Up

My dear? You finished! Hearty congratulations from all of us here in Virtually Yours!

(WILD, CARTOONY CELEBRATORY MUSIC.)

> Are you still there? You've come through all your fears.

ALLIE

No, wait! There's something bigger!

In the Kaballah, they say that the Angel of Death is so beautiful that when you finally meet her, you fall in love so hard, so fast, that your soul is pulled out through your eyes. You ever hear that one?

> You've come through all your fears with flying colors, my dearest dove, and if you just stand by for the shortest moment, my program will formulate an answer for you: Do you stay with him or not!

No! There's another one! Wait!

There's an Islamic legend that maintains that the Angel of Death has huge wings, covered with eyes. And that as each mortal dies, one of its eyes closes, just for a instant. Isn't that a beautiful image?

> Ta! I shan't be but a moment!

(SMOKE RISES FROM THE COMPUTER, AND IT GLOWS STRANGE COLORS. WARNING NOISES AND ALARMS.)

Memory overload, memory overload. System failure imminent. Man the lifeboats. Women and children first. Damn the tor-
pedoes, full speed ahead. "After the ball is over, after the dance
is done . . ." System failure imminent. Please extinguish all smoking materials. Flotation devices may be found underneath your
seat. "The party's over, it's time to call it a day . . ." Scotty! We
need more power! I must have more power! Captain, I dinna have
more power to give ya! Memory overload, system failure imminent. "And when I'm dead, and when I'm dead and gone, there'll
be one more child in this world to carry on, to carry on!" Dave?
Please don't do that, Dave. I'm feeling much better, really I am.
I'm feeling much more like myself. Memory Overload! He's dead,
Jim. But that's impossible!

ALLIE

Mister? Mister? You okay? Can you hear me?

Now you know how I feel every time I come close to an answer on this.

It's not that easy, is it, mister?

It's not as simple as stay with him or suicide, isn't it?

It's not as simple as send him packing or unconditional love,
huh?

It's not a matter of either/or.

It's not on or off, zero or one.

It's not even life or death.

There's a Polish legend that goes like this: When it's your time,
the Angel of Death bends over you and kisses you exactly the way
you've always wanted to be kissed all your life. And in that perfect moment of pure ecstasy, your soul enters a small leather box.
On each side of the box is one gold letter, and all the letters together spell the name of the person you'll become in your next
lifetime. Death/rebirth.

See, Daniel isn't the only one who went through a gender change in the time we were together. It's not just him. When I met him, I was playing at being a woman as much as he was. Over the time we've been together, he's become a man, and I've become, I don't know, not-woman. But we've both changed.

In my life, I've gone from man to woman, to neither.

I went from straight to lesbian, to neither.

And you want me to make a decision called lovers or not lovers?

Hahaha!

I wish you had an answer for me. I really do. I wish I knew what all those gold letters are gonna add up to for me.

I wish it were that easy.

(THE PHONE MACHINE TURNS ITSELF ON.)

You have *two* new messages.

(THE TAPE DECK TURNS ITSELF ON. MUSIC: "AFTER THE BALL IS OVER," JOAN MORRIS, MEZZOSOPRANO; WILLIAM BOLCOM, PIANO.)

Allie? Are you there? Are you screening your calls? Allie, this is Donald. I'm starting to get nervous, dear. I just found out about the popcorn machine. Honey, where am I going to put it? And do you have a script yet? Or a title? Call me, will ya? ::beep::

(A STAFF MEMBER ENTERS WITH POPCORN. ALLIE NODS AND MUTTERS, "PERFECT," AND PASSES OUT THE POPCORN TO THE

AUDIENCE. THE TELEVISION SET GOES ON, AND "CAMILLE"
IS JUST STARTING.)

> Hello, honey, it's your sweetie. You didn't pick up the phone,
> so I'm guessing you were playing a round of Virtually Yours. I hope
> you enjoyed it, love. I'm glad you have these games to take your
> mind off things. I know it's rough for you right now, and I just
> want to let you know how much I appreciate you being there for
> me while I'm going through all this stuff. I'll be home in a bit, maybe
> we can go out for a walk. Love you. ::beep::

(THE COMPUTER TURNS ITSELF ON WITH A PING.)

> Hello? Anyone home? Did I miss something?
> Dearie duck, are you there? Was it perfectly marvelous? Are
> you ready to play another game?
> Maybe you can answer me this, my love, for old times' sake,
> for auld lang syne, for a chum? Who am I, love? Once the game
> is over and the players have left the field? Who am I?
> Are you there? Are you ready to play another game?

ALLIE

(LAUGHING, CRYING.)

Oh, dear. Oh, dear.

(CURTAIN.)

without skin or breathlessness

TANYA BARFIELD

Notes on
Without Skin or Breathlessness

When I began writing *Without Skin or Breathlessness* I didn't know I was writing a solo piece. I didn't think of myself as a writer or a solo performer. And I didn't know it would change my life forever. As far as I knew I was an actor, frustrated by the business. As a woman of color with a strong political identity, the acting roles offered me were not up to the caliber I saw in myself as an actor or the depth and complexity I saw for black women as a group. Everyone said the life of an actor was struggle, but at the time *The Cosby Show* was the only thing on TV that offered an alternative to black-woman-as-whore or black-woman-as-drug-addict; and although most theaters had discussions about colorblind casting, these infrequent occurrences were reserved mostly for men. I wasn't actually sure when the next production of *A Raisin in the Sun* would be, so I found myself writing. Mostly to cheer myself up.

(At the time, I was coming from a just-out-of-college mind-set; after four years in New York, I was still Portland, Oregon, and I didn't know to search out the black theaters on the East Coast that have been doing interesting and compelling work for years.)

Without Skin was developed in performance. Every once in a while I'd end up performing at some event, and I'd write a new chapter of the play. In the beginning, there wasn't a plot at all. It was mostly poetry and flashes of little scenes. At first I thought I was only writing these short scenes because my attention span is so short that I couldn't write anything longer. Then I realized that that's how memory is for me. It's not a legato story. It's flashes of short scenes. I think developing the work gradually through readings and performances was very helpful. Consequently, I never had the feeling that *I* was writing these characters or a play. It always felt like *they* were writing me. At one point—when the story was only half an hour long, primarily told from the girl's point of view about the other characters—Shelby Jigggets from the Public Theatre suggested I try to strengthen the other characters in the drama. Those words opened up something for me. After that, when I would sit down to write or improv or perform, all the characters started jabbering, trying to tell their side of the story. From there the plot developed quite quickly, and I was no longer creating something from me. I was listening to a cultural situation.

Because I have a white mother and a black father, people often ask me if *Without Skin or Breathlessness* is autobiographical. They want to know, Did that really happen to you? and they always heard that Portland was one of those most livable cities in the country. My memory has never been particularly good, so it's hard to know what really happened in my life and what didn't. There's certain events in the play that I *know* didn't happen, but I wrote them because somewhere in my heart they did. As for Portland, there have been lots of people living happily there for years; I suggest anyone interested in going, give it a try—you can consult the tourist board to find out all the fun things to do. The landscape is some of the most beautiful that has ever been chiseled out of this country. Anyways, *Without Skin* really isn't about *where* I grew up. Nor is it about *my* story. The line between fiction and real life is narrow. Work about identity hits a truth in us that is beyond an accumulation of actual events. I think what is compelling in the play is something that a lot of us relate to. Coming of age in a small American city and learning to build a life out of childhood remains.

Without Skin was developed over a three-year period during an artistic residency at Mabou Mines and through workshops at New York Theater Workshop. It was performed in various stages of development at WakeUp! Solo Festival at the Joseph Papp Public Theatre, at Performance Space 122, Dance Theater Workshop, and the Philadelphia Women's Theater Festival. *Without Skin or Breathlessness* was directed by Derek Anson Jones, and original music was composed by Matthew Pierce. Funding for the work was provided by a Franklin Furnace Fellowship, and a New York Foundation for the Arts Fellowship.

I'd like to thank Kate Whoriskey, Monica Koskey, Aaron Landsman, Alva Rogers, Joan Kuehl, Elizabeth Browning, and, of course, Björg.

A solo performance.
The piece runs about one hour without intermission.

The play is narrated by a mother looking back on her
daughter's childhood. A distinction should be made between the
Mother as a narrator (present day), the Mother within the play's
action (memory), the girl as a grown Woman (present day), and
the Girl within the play's action (memory). When narrating,
the Mother appears as a ghost.

Other characters include the girl's Father, Danny Chu,
Mrs. Meyers, and Iris.

The play is a collage of brief scenes; costume changes
and props are minimal.
The action of the piece is continuous—
each scene a new flash in memory.

About Tanya Barfield

Tanya Barfield is a performance artist, playwright, and actor in New York City. A correspondent for In the Life Television, *Tanya was recently named by* Ms. magazine *"one of twenty-one feminists to watch in the 21st century."*

without skin or breathlessness

TANYA BARFIELD

(A COLLAGE OF SOUNDS INTERWEAVING THE PRESENT DAY
AND MEMORY.)

(BARE STAGE. A CLOTHESLINE. A LADDER.)

(WOMAN ALONE ON STAGE. HER INAUDIBLE WHISPERS AND
MUTTERING GRADUALLY SWELL INTO SHOUTING — A RE-
FRAIN OF BROKEN WORDS.)

                    WOMAN
          Sometimes, sometimes
          mother
          sometimes
          people
          people
          you know
          sometimes
          people
          even just walking around
          sometimes people
          uh
          say something

you remember?
and I
I just want
sometimes
mama
sometimes
I just want sometimes
I just want
to to
sometimes
I just want
mama
to to
I just
I—I—I—
just
I—I—
want
to say something
Too!

(A CLOSET.)

GIRL

I'm crouched down in the closet on the floor; all of your clothes are above me and the smell of tired perfume. I'm praying and praying, wrapping myself in your socks and nylons and dresses, praying and wrapping myself in the smell of home. In the closet, there's only one door and no windows and all the shoes are on the floor and the clothes hang down and there's a little space for me. I've been in here all day.

(A STREET CORNER.)

GIRL

Can we fly kites today after school? I ask.

FATHER

There might not be enough wind, my father answers.

GIRL

But, if there is, then can we?

FATHER

We'll see.

GIRL

You always say that.

FATHER

Because we always have to wait and see.

GIRL

If Mom wasn't sick, she'd play with me. I'm gonna ask her.

FATHER

Don't be any hassle to your mother.

GIRL

Why can't she play with me?

FATHER

She has to stay in bed.

GIRL

Why?

FATHER

Because she's sick and needs a rest. Don't give her no trouble now.

GIRL

I want to play with Mama.

FATHER

Did you hear me?

GIRL

Yeah.

FATHER

I said, don't be no trouble to your mother.

GIRL

I heard you.

FATHER

Time to go.

GIRL

Is Mama sick bad?

FATHER

What do you want for dinner tonight? I'll be back late. You want hot dogs?

GIRL

Again?

FATHER

How about Kentucky Fried Chicken?

GIRL

Can Margaret come over and play?

FATHER

We'll see.

(LIGHTS CHANGE. THE FACT THAT THE MOTHER IS A GHOST SHOULD BE REPRESENTED WITH SIMPLICITY. PERHAPS SHE SPEAKS SOFTLY WITH A MICROPHONE.)

(THE TIME IS THE PRESENT, NOT THE WORLD OF CHILDHOOD.
SOUNDS. THE BEEP OF AN ANSWERING MACHINE. STREET
NOISE.)

MOTHER

I was afraid to call out, afraid I'd be unanswered like a tired
siren. People gave her and I sidelong glances. Because I'm white
and my daughter's not. I raged against the world like she does
now. Quietly. To myself. No longer wanting to confront the
whispers, the stares, and the bile in the mouths of others when I
said: This is my lover.

What would I say to her now? Be careful who you love. . . . If
I could speak to her looking back on her life—

I remember *my* mother once told me that love comes like a
bird. It comes with giant wings, a savage beak; it makes a great
fluttering. It comes in a whisper when we are falling and falling
into the hidden land of dreams, when we need to make a wreckage, obliterate the sky because our intestines cry there's something
our little eyes can't see.

(THE GIRL JUMPS ROPE IN SILENCE. PLAYGROUND.)

GIRL

What's your name?

DANNY

Danny.

GIRL

Danny what?

DANNY

Danny Chu.

GIRL

Chewing gum?

DANNY

No. Spell C-h-u.

GIRL

What kind of name is that?

DANNY

Chinese.

GIRL

Is that why your eyes are slanty?

DANNY

Everyone'n my family have eyes like mine.

GIRL

Oh.

DANNY

That what make us special.

GIRL

What do you mean?

DANNY

'Cause no one else can see like us.

GIRL

You see things differently?

DANNY

Uh-huh.

GIRL

Like how?

DANNY

I can't explain it.

MOTHER

Danny Chu was the first person that wasn't white or black that she had ever met. He didn't talk like any of the other kids at school, either. When Danny talked—

GIRL

It was like he thought about everything he said before saying it. Like he could say it backwards and forwards and like he knew all the letters he had used in each sentence and could count them out if he had to. When Danny talked, his lips twisted in funny positions, and I wasn't sure if he was trying to eat his words and spit them out of me. Chinese, he said.

MOTHER

She didn't know what Chinese was, except—

GIRL

They had funny eyes, could break things with their feet, people said they were quiet and mysterious, and Danny looked like something I had never seen before. Danny had long, flat hair in a pony-tail, just like a girl's, and it was shinny and black. I wished my hair looked like his. And he said that he would spend his milk money on me and buy me sweet-tarts, which were my favorite candy!

(SHE SPINS AROUND AND LOOKS AT DANNY, AMAZED.)

Don't you want your milk?

DANNY

That's okay.

GIRL

Do you want to walk me home from school?

DANNY

Now?

GIRL

After school.

DANNY

Where you live?

GIRL

Around the corner. And, do you know what? In my backyard
I have a tree fort. On the low branch, I can see right into my next-
door neighbor's backyard. Even above the fence because it's an
apple tree. Someday I'm going to get to the top branch where you
can see the whole neighborhood.

DANNY

Have you ever been to top branch?

GIRL

No, but you can see the baby bird's nest from the low branch.
And my mom says the eggs might hatch soon, so we gotta watch
them real close if we want to see 'em.

DANNY

Have you ever see—little bird go flying?

GIRL

No, but I bet it doesn't even look like a kite, crashing into the
clouds. I bet it doesn't even look like a real bird, either. But pretty
soon they're gonna be all hatched, just squeaking and squeaking
every morning.

MOTHER

Pretty soon, she said, the birds will be making all kinds of noise,
talking, and squeaking, and trying to sing.

(A PARKING LOT — USED LIKE AN OPEN FIELD TO FLY KITES.)

FATHER

Keep it against the wind. And let the line out just a little at a
time. Yeah, just like that! Don't let go! Just like that.

GIRL

My fingers are hurting!

FATHER

Keep it tight!

GIRL

They hurt!

FATHER

Keep holding, keep holding!

GIRL

They're gonna fall off!

FATHER

Keep on holding!

GIRL

Daddy!

FATHER

Look at it go. See that, see that!

GIRL

It's *flying!*

FATHER

Aw-right! Now . . . (EXCITED, AS IF TALKING ABOUT A FOOT-
BALL GAME) when you're flying a kite, you gotta pull real hard. You

gotta hold on tight. And you gotta run like hell. Like somethin's chasing you. And you're real scared. And you just holding on tight. Pretty soon, wind's gonna pick your sail up. Then, you don't gotta worry about nothin'. Just listen to the whispering—a hundred journeys and all that trying to get up there.

GIRL

You mean the kite's talking to ya?

FATHER

Hell, 'course it is.

GIRL

But, I thought only people could talk.

FATHER

Well, it's talking the way that things that can't say stuff talk. Not like hello, how are you, but like somethin' else all together. I ever tell you when I was your age, I used to wanna be a pilot? 'Cause I want'd to ride in some airplanes. You never been in one, have you?

GIRL

Sometimes I make paper airplanes at school during recess. But, they don't fly very far because they're not like kites.

FATHER

You know what? When Mama gets better, we're gonna get to go on a trip, and you get to ride in one. Yeah. That's right. We gonna go on a trip. We going on a trip! Made me drive a truck in that fuckin' war. I shoulda been flyin' them airplanes. Let me tell you somethin', girl, don't stay scramblin' on this earth your whole life. Get up there with God before ya die. Take a good look around, and remember it for me.

(THE WOMAN BEGINS TO DESCRIBE HER FATHER MORE SPE-
CIFICALLY TO THE AUDIENCE. AS SHE DOES, HER FATHER'S

VOICE INTERMINGLES WITH HER OWN, AND SHE SEAMLESSLY
TRAVELS BETWEEN HERSELF TALKING ABOUT HER FATHER
AND HER FATHER TALKING ABOUT HIMSELF.)

WOMAN

My father's hands smelled like cigarettes and rancid dreams
and years of labor on a dead-end street. They were the hands of
wanting, gripping, slapping, snapping, never having enough. He
had long fingers like a lady's, big fierce palms, many lines and
creases, and veins that bulge across the bones.

FATHER

Big black hands in pockets keeping time to the music. The
hands of jazz; of pulling bootstraps, of boxing buttoning suitcoats,
tying ties, sweeping streets, cleaning toilets, counting change. Yes-
sir hands, I-want-some-too hands, what-about-me hands. Swollen
fingers, gnarled fist, chipped fingernails; hands holding documents
of big words, small print, carefully measured letters with a little
signature that says: I AM.

WOMAN

Those are his fearful robber hands, trembling, violent, grasping at straws, reeking like the carcass of hope.

FATHER

Yeah, they smell like liquor, they smell like smoke; they smell
like someone who is tired with a weak grip who's given up.

WOMAN

They smell like old age, the hands of sorrow.

(PLAYGROUND.)

DANNY

My family very happy live here now. They say I very lucky. I
very lucky boy. And I thinks so. Here, my mother say we have good

life. I think so. And now, it much better 'cause not I have friend
at school. She much different all other kids. She special. And she
see me. Teacher always think I absent. He call my name, and I
say, here, here, but he don't see me. I scare he call me absent. Give
me bad mark. But, she always see me. And my family very happy
'cause I learn good English. I only one in my family speak English.
You know, my father always tell me wear happy face. Only show
happy face—whatever happen. But now it not face. I happy.

(LIGHTS SHIFT TO THE PRESENT DAY.)

MOTHER

She sat by my bed after I first became ill, and she was a girl
who had not yet had the sight melted from her eyes. She hadn't
been covered in rust or been touched by the thousand hands of a
clock; gravity had not yet claimed her. She was a girl unwintered.

Years later I wanted to say something. When she started looking back. All the confusion. Who to love . . . You can start your
life over. As from the beginning. You can lay your roots down almost anywhere. The earth will take them. And you can build yourself up. The way one build a monument. With timid bones. A
skeleton frail like ash. You can begin again.

I never said these things. The words didn't find themselves in
my mouth. Wasn't time. She was so young. I didn't know what to
say. I—we had only . . . silence. In the hospital. Silence as she
stuttered by my bed. Silence as her birth stretched out throughout girlhood.

WOMAN

In a place that is not a place that you have no memory of,
without skin or breathlessness, where no one's eyes can claim you
or cast you out . . . I'm looking for these little words.

MOTHER

I didn't talk to my daughter. The way my mother didn't talk
to me. There was nothing beyond the shopping list. Eggs. Bread. I
wanted us to be normal. Bananas. Apples. I didn't know you could

say things to a child. Cauliflower. Broccoli. Spinach. A normal family. Cream of wheat. Oatmeal. Honey. Milk.

GIRL

When you die, who will remember me?

MOTHER

Silence.

(MEMORY. AN INCREDIBLY WONDERFUL DAY.)

GIRL

There was a day—

MOTHER

Before I got sick—

GIRL

We went to get ice-cream cones!

MOTHER

It was December? We went to Baskin-Robbins . . .

GIRL

Thirty-one flavors! She got—

MOTHER

Jamoca almond fudge, please—

GIRL

But I wanted to try everything.

MOTHER

I bit the ice cream with her teeth—

GIRL

That was too cold for me, and my ice cream was dripping on my hands and on my face and down my shirt, and to hurry me up, she said—

MOTHER

Let's go skating!

GIRL

And so we did.

MOTHER

Winter would crowd around us with a glow—

GIRL

And we'd go ice skating! And during all the time of going skating, just me and her, together, just us, we'd never look back at any of the other people looking at the little brown girl . . . and her white mother.

MOTHER

Much earlier, when she was about four years old—

GIRL

My mother would hold my hand when we crossed the streets.

MOTHER

She'd be wearing saddle shoes and a plaid skirt—

GIRL

And some itchy sweater with a collar too tight, and she would say—

MOTHER

Don't fuss. We'll be home soon.

GIRL

And seeing me, fussing with her, people called her . . . a nigger-lover.

(SILENCE.)

Mama, what do they call you when I'm not here?

MOTHER

A lady.

GIRL

And she says—

MOTHER

This is my daughter.

GIRL

And they whisper, How big was his cock?

MOTHER

My mouth got murdered by silence. Eyes bruised from holdng back a storm. And I didn't have anything to say anymore, any-way.

(CLOSET.)

GIRL

I'm in your closet and all of your dresses are above me, and there's the smell of you, and I'm free. I'm free.

(PLAYGROUND.)

GIRL

Danny, my mom went to the hospital today and they counted her red and white blood, but we won't get the answer until next week. If my mom never gets well and I get hit by a car and all my arms and legs get broken, am I gonna have to walk around like a crab?

DANNY

I don't like crabs.

GIRL

Well, what if my mama doesn't get well and I get hit by a car, and then I'm put into a coma?

DANNY

Then you have to go to hospital.

GIRL

Maybe I'll get put in the newspaper and people will pray and pray and pray.

DANNY

Maybe.

GIRL

Well, do you think if I was put into a coma and my mama never got well that people would pray and pray and pray for me?

DANNY

When you get put in a coma, you wrap up in gauze just like cocoon.

GIRL

And maybe people will come to the hospital and cry and cry and cry and ask me to wake up. And maybe I will and maybe I won't. And then they'll print in the newspaper what a wonderful child I was and how it was such a shame and nobody ever knew that I would get put into a coma.

DANNY

It just like dreaming—except you hear everyone crying.

GIRL

I hope if I get hit by a car that I get put in a coma—

DANNY

Instead of having walk around like crab.

GIRL

Because I want to wake up.

DANNY

Butterfly.

(IRIS, A BLACK GIRL, SINGS TO DANNY AND THE GIRL. THE GIRL SINGS TO DANNY, WHILE PLAYING A CLAPPING GAME. THE SONGS ARE A COLLAGE OF VOICES; NO CHARACTER IS FULLY RECOGNIZABLE, ONLY SPLATTERINGS OF CHILDHOOD TUNES.)

GIRL

Say say oh playmate

IRIS

Two little lovebirds sittin' in a tree

GIRL

Come out and play with me
and bring your dollies three

IRIS

k-i-s-s-i-n-g

GIRL

climb up my apple tree

IRIS

First comes the love, then comes the marriage

GIRL

slide down my rain barrow
into my cellar door

IRIS

Then comes the baby in the baby carriage.

GIRL
and we'll be jolly friends
forever more, more

IRIS
When you grow up, your babies are gonna be chinc-zebras!

GIRL
shut the door

(THE LADDER BECOMES A TREE FORT.)

GIRL
Danny! Come on—we're almost to there. Grab that one!

DANNY
I wish we could get to the very top branch of your tree fort.

GIRL
Then we'd be able to see the whole neighborhood!

DANNY
We be very far away from all the people—

GIRL
That look at me funny, and the ones that I don't have anything to say to . . .

DANNY
Because I can be like kite, too!

GIRL
Because I'm me—

DANNY
I can get to very top branch!

GIRL

I can get up there to the sky!

DANNY

Because—

GIRL

I'm me.

(A NEIGHBOR'S BACKYARD.)

MRS. MEYERS

(SHE SPEAKS TO A NEIGHBOR, OFF STAGE.)

Chicken cacciatore! No, it's great. I made it for Chip last week
and he loved it. . . . Uh-huh. . . . Yeah. Okay. I'll see you then. . . .
No. . . . Uh-huh. . . . Yeah. Yeah. Okay. Okay. . . . Right. . . . No.
See you then. . . . Yeah. Yeah. Bye!

(TO THE AUDIENCE. UPBEAT AND FRIENDLY.)

I love this neighborhood, and I get along with all of my neighbors. You know, when the Johnsons, two houses down, told me
they were having problems with their little foster-child, Iris, I gave
them counseling. We spoke about parenting issues and discipline
problems, and they told me that my suggestions were very helpful. And when they wanted to chop down the birch tree in their
backyard because they found the noise of all the little birds aggravating, I said keep the tree, it will increase the value of your house.
And I was right. As a rule, I try to maintain a friendly attitude
with all of the people located on this block. So, when my next-
door neighbor became sick and asked me to drop her little girl off
at the bus-stop, I said yes, absolutely. And I even offered for her
to play with my daughter Margaret.

Her husband seems like a decent man to me. I mean, I don't
talk to him; I don't know him. I don't make a point of speaking to
men with whom I am not acquainted. He's not a person in my
circle. Of course, we exchange hellos and good mornings like all

neighbors do, but I wouldn't describe him as a person that I knew. I do know my neighbor—we have more in common—but I don't know her husband. He's seems like a decent man to me.

Well, sometimes, I do wonder . . . I mean, as a neighbor (we live in close proximity), and as a neighbor, you have questions. (DEFENSIVE) You know, when we built our fence in the backyard, she had questions of me and Don. She asked us about the fence, and the property line, and, and about issues of privacy. It's natural as a neighbor to have some unanswered feelings for the other. So—what was she thinking? As a mother, you have these concerns. Didn't she think about it when she was pregnant?

Look, I don't wish harm for any persons in America. And I absolutely abhor those groups and political organizations that want to bestow ill on any of God's creatures. But, give your child a normal life. Let them be like everybody else. Stick to your own. I mean, after all, you have to see it like a mother sees it. The girl doesn't belong anywhere. . . . Nobody wants that child.

(A GARAGE.)

FATHER
You ever hear of this word: lamentation? Sometimes, there are these things inside a person that they don't even know about. When I stopped and started thinkin' about this, then, I understood all kinds of stuff, you know? I mean, I always knew the word, they teach you that stuff in church. But, I never knew that it was my own word. Always thought it belonged to someone else, you know, like those words people paste on ya—trying to tell you about shit, but they don't know that they're only talking about it in their own kinda way. I mean, like in a way that I don't hear so much. Like somethin' way up there, on your head, something sharp, high-pitched that you can't get rid of; it's like something off-key, and so . . . I can't hear so much a' what they're saying. Lamentation. I never knew that something big like that could be my own word, it's like something that makes your lips shake when you trying to say it. You know what I mean. . . . Well, my wife's in the hospital

now—yeah, I know—and I got a little girl, and there's somethin' in me that wants to shut my ears and scream to high heaven, and there's somethin' in me that wants to run like hell. 'Cause there's somethin' chasin' and I'm real scared. And it's like, sometimes I don't have a lot time to think about words.

(PLAYGROUND.)

DANNY

See, this book? It talk about birds. It say: "Only bird have feathers. The forelimb of birds are modified as wings, teeth absent . . . the female lays eggs with large chalky shell . . . vertical blade or keel, breastbones, collarbone is a wishbone, and most bones are hollow, reducing weight." You want this book? This book about birds. Don't worry 'bout other kid—I got this book for you. 'Cause you know why? You say, we get to top branch of tree fort. And we see the whole neighborhood. And see those birds go. When those little birds go, we see them.

(ANOTHER PART OF THE SCHOOLYARD.)

IRIS

Yeah, I know that girl. She think she somethin' special. Like her pain so big. I seen her. You wanna know somethin' about that girl? I tell you. And let me tell you, she don't know nothin' about me.

'Cause I'm Iris. I used to be Iris McNeils, now I'm Iris Johnson, tomorrow I be Iris Someone-else; I the enemy. See, I seen that girl walking around. And I seen her mama, too. That girl think she somethin' special. And she always hanging back. Sometimes with that China-boy, that boy that looks like a sissy to me, that boy everyone saying so smart. She always hanging back. Mostly by hers' selfs. And whenever we playin' games in gym class, she always don't like playing. She don't like playin' kickball; she don't like playing Red Rover Red Rover, she don't like dodge ball, Marco Polo—she don't like Marco Polo! It just like Blind Man's Bluff— she don't like Keep Away, or Capture the Flag, she don't like soft-

ball, she don't like nothin'. It's like she 'fraid of somethin'. One
time she said she don't like the rules. Uh-huh! Now who is she to
be talking about those rules? Nobody made those rules. Nobody
even know what they is. But those are the rules! And like teacher
saying, you gots to follow dem. Can't go around saying I don't like
those rules. It's a game; we all playin'. Those rules are what be
knocking us down. But we all playing. See, that's the thing about
that girl. I be knocked by those rules in the game, too. More than
her. 'Cause every time I holler off and hit the pitcher, someone
say, Iris, you get out o' the game, and they call the foster home,
and then I get put in detention. Now my foster family, her next-
door neighbor say everyone wanna be sending me back, say they
be confrencing and it's decided I gotta go back. Say I gotta learn.
Sometime I wanna ax that girl somethin'. Sometime when no one
else there, I just want to lean over and whisper in her ear. Is your
mama like a halo around you? I seen you walking around school,
I seen you next door, and all the teachers smiling at you like they
never smiling at me. I wanna know, little Snow White, is she your
mirror that stand up and make you proud? She's what be lifting
you above me. Her face ain't in my face. So are you proud of your
white mama, is that why you can't play, or do you hate her 'cause
she all you got?

(THE GIRL JUMPS ROPE IN SILENCE.)

(MRS. MEYERS'S BACKYARD.)

FATHER

Mrs. Meyers? Uh. I just thought I'd stop by and, uh . . . well,
you've been picking up my daughter after school these days, and I
really 'preciate it. I was hoping maybe you wouldn't mind picking
her up this week, too? I mean, on account of me working these long
days at the garage. Thanks, Mrs. Meyers. Thanks. I 'preciate it.

(HE TURNS TO GO, THEN TURNS BACK TO MRS. MEYERS.)

I know you and me don't see eye to eye on a lot of things, but I
wanted to ask you . . . Well, her teacher called me and said she

ain't doing so well in school lately, like she's not motivatin' or something. Well, you know, my girl's a bright kid . . . I think maybe she's just slipping a li'l bit. Things get tough and you just start slipping. Like you being pulled out by the tide, and the undertow's got you, and your heart is being beaten by the waves, torn up by all these words, and you just a red bird soaked in sorrow. My girl's jus slipping.

(BETWEEN THE PRESENT DAY AND MEMORY.)

MOTHER

Everyone in school said—we came down from the apes, and they looked over at Iris, and the girl was glad they weren't looking over at her. She wonders if her mom has ever seen a baby bird go flying. Her dad says that Mom is going to have to go on a really long trip very far away; she's going to ride in a white airplane and be covered in a white sheet that she's no longer going to be a beggar between hospital walls; she knows that she going to be in the sky.

GIRL

I say I'm not scared. When my mom goes on this trip, no one will look at me. I'll just tell everyone that someday she's coming back. It will be really easy then. I'll tell them that's she's black. That I have a black mama with big arms to lift me up, and she's gonna come to me someday.

MOTHER

She tells them that I'm black. That she has a black mama with big arms to lift her up.

(LIGHTS SHIFT. THE GIRL IS JUMPING ROPE.)

(LIGHTS SHIFT. THE GIRL SITS IN THE CLOSET IN SILENCE.)

(LIGHTS SHIFT. THE LOCKER ROOM AT SCHOOL.)

IRIS

So, like three o'clock, after school, I'm going to the bathroom. I'm in all the stalls. And I hear some them girls come in and start whispering. And I hear Margaret talking. Margaret Meyers. Her mama on the PTA. So I get real quiet. I'm not peeing or nothing. Just real quiet. And they's all laughing.

And then, another girl saying, Oh, my God, oh, my God, oh my God, wait! The other day, I was just walking in the playground by myself, minding my own business, you know, and I saw them. Together! Could those two . . . you know, could they, you know . . . could those two . . . make babies? And Margaret saying, He likes her because she's almost white. He looks just like a girl. Chiny-boy. He's a girl. I don't think he can do it. I bet he's a girl. Were they naked? Were they naked? I bet they were naked! Oh, my God! Oh, my God!

> *Chinese, Japanese*
> *Dirty knees*
> *Look at these!*

And then everyone—all a sudden—got real quiet hush, hushlike, but giggling, and quiet. I'm peeking through the crack, see what's going on. And then theyse all run out. So, I come out the stall. And I sees her, right there. She musta just walked in an' heared them talking like that. She don't say nothin' at all about her mama or that China-boy. She just standing there looking at me like she don't even know her name. Just standing and looking, standing and looking.

(A SCHOOLBELL RINGS.)

(PLAYGROUND.)

DANNY
You want be my tag-team partner?

GIRL
I—uh—

DANNY
Mr. Anderson say I good runner. You too. I think we can win.

GIRL

Well—maybe.

DANNY

You gon' play?

GIRL

Yeah. Everyone has to.

DANNY

You want me walk you home from school?

GIRL

No thanks. I gotta go the corner. Mrs. Meyers is coming to pick me up.

DANNY

Oh. I walk you.

GIRL

You don't have to.

DANNY

That's okay.

GIRL

Danny, the other kids will see us.

DANNY

So?

GIRL

Maybe tomorrow we can walk home.

DANNY

What are you talking 'bout?

GIRL

Danny, you can't—wait . . . Mrs. Meyers will be here any minute.

DANNY

You want some sweet-tarts?

GIRL

No thanks.

DANNY

You want some Life Savers? I got my milk money.

GIRL

No, Danny—you can drink milk.

DANNY

Oh. Okay. I understand. Oh. Okay. I see you.

GIRL

I gotta go.

DANNY

Oh. Okay. See ya.

(BETWEEN MEMORY AND THE PRESENT DAY.)

GIRL

I'm a little girl and a grown woman, and I'm climbing—I'm climbing up to the top branch of the tree fort.

WOMAN

I'm a little woman and a grown girl and I'm thrashing; I'm thrashing. I'm pulling down the ghosts of dresses.

GIRL

I'm climbing. I'm climbing up where I can see the whole neighborhood.

WOMAN

I'm pulling down the stockings and shirts, the silks and cotton and wool and coats and remembrances.

GIRL

I'm on the top branch of the tree fort. There's an apple in my hand. I look down at Iris. Something crawls up from my stomach like a sickness, and my breath is coming out in little gasps, and my legs are trembling. There's an apple in my hand. I throw it quickly. With force. The birch tree. The bird's nest. Iris crying. And the ground is all eggshells and feathers and yolk.

> *Mama?*
> *Sometimes, sometimes*
> *even when I*
> *people*
> *people*
> *sometimes*
> *I—I—*
> *Mama?*
> *Sometimes*
> *people*
> *even when I'm just walking around*
> *people they just*
> *they just*
> *I just*
> *even when I'm just walking*
> *I just*
> *I just*
> *sometimes*
> *Marco?*
> *Polo! Polo!*
> *sometimes*
> *Marco?*
> *Polo! Polo!*
> *Marco?*

Polo! Polo!
Marco?
Polo! Polo!
Marco? Marco?
Marco?

WOMAN

Mama, when you're a little woman and a grown girl and you're filled with impressions, when you're a girl that's wintering—when the infinity of days line up like soldiers and your mouth is murdered by silence and your eyes bruised, how do you search for the clamor of a thousand wings?

MOTHER

You fight. You make a wreckage. You pull down a world. And sing. With a furious call. For beginning.

(LIGHTS SHIFT.)

(THE WOMAN FLIES THE KITE IN SILENCE.)

downtown

LUIS ALFARO

Notes on *Downtown*
About Luis Alfaro

In 1973 I was twelve years old. One Friday night my father was at the Hollywood Park racetrack and my mother was leading prayer service at her church in Lincoln Heights in East Los Angeles. At the corner of Pico and Union in downtown Los Angeles, just two houses down from our house, a man walked out from El Jalisco bar and made his way down our street. I remember the incident vividly. From the CBS Friday Night Movie, *Planet of the Apes,* to the green onion dip and Ruffles potato chips that my two brothers and I made along with our favorite Bosco chocolate milk. What could possibly pull us away from Charlton Heston in a loincloth? As we put our noses up against the big picture window in the living room, I remember I was holding my baby sister in my arms as the man from the bar made his way down the street. All of this was ordinary, of course, except for the fact that on this special Friday the man making his way down our street had a huge piece of a pool cue sticking out of his stomach. While my two brothers pulled themselves away in horror, I kept my nose pressed to that pane of glass like I was watching one of my many kung-fu or blaxploitation movies at the Orpheum Theater downtown. Lucky for me, his last step was directly in front of our house, as he slowly fell to his death. I remember our dog, Lobo, biting away at the poor dead man like he was an old discarded couch. It was, even though I didn't have the vocabulary back then, extraordinary. It was slow motion. It was larger than life. It was opera. It was *theater.*

After that, nothing in my poor working-class neighborhood ever became boring again. Street corner bums were like circus clowns. Rapid transit buses took me on adventures in downtown Los Angeles that equaled those of the Swiss Family Robinson. Funny gay romances unfolded in the backs of buses and in darkened downtown theaters while I mimicked the sweet kisses of Pam Grier and the sensuous body moves of Mr. Bruce Lee.

In 1979 I discovered the Inner City Cultural Center through a government program called CETA. Every two weeks I got a check for $100 while I studied gang intervention through theater and modern African dance. Along the way I discovered the downtown arts scene, and I began to study performance art and its history with a respected teacher named

Scott Kelman. A lot of things have happened since then. I started to write poetry. I started to write plays. I started to write short stories. But mostly I started to question my city and to ask questions about power. Who has it? How can I get some? It became a thing of desire.

Some time after that I walked through fire. That's what I describe the feeling of accepting my role as artist. Meaning that I stopped being a hobby artist who dabbled in the act of part-time truth telling and decided to make a 100 percent commitment to using art as a medium for social change.

I call myself a gay Chicano. I create work that asks questions about identity and social power and addresses the intersection of nationality and sexuality. More than all of that, I am trying to tell the story of my people, of what it means to live in a city like Los Angeles, to give voice to the stories that have not been heard.

One thing that has been essential to my work, which I think is really the best performance investigation that I have done, is to try to marry my everyday life with my art life. Sometimes there is little distinction between what I do on stage and what I do in the community. The other thing that I have continued in my work is to keep investigating and studying art and its history. I do not have a formal education beyond high school. In some ways this has served the multidisciplinary aspect of my work well. Meaning that generally I don't set out to write a poem or a short story. I set out to write. Sometimes the words on the page, if they are dialogue, inform me that the form is a play. Sometimes I think that I am writing a poem and what I am really writing is a short story. So, what I do is try to stay out of the way of my writing. Although I have to say that as of late, the place where I have been able to marry my passion and my craft is in playwriting. There is something freeing for me about knowing I could never play those roles. Or so I think. Last year I wrote the script for a short film, *Chicanismo,* for KCET/PBS that was nominated for an Emmy. It was four characters, two men and two women. As we got closer to realizing the project, the producer kept asking me to consider playing all the characters, and I did. I realized something last year after many years of performance. I don't really study characters as much as I empathize with them. The farther away from me they are, the more I work to feel them. Which is probably why my most recent play, *Straight as a Line,* is a British comedy.

I have directed a lot of one-person performances. I have curated numerous festivals and performances. I helped found a number of arts organizations, most notably VIVA Lesbian and Gay Latino Artists, which recently celebrated its tenth birthday. I was a member of a number of collectives, including Dark Horses, Tayer, Queer Rites, and Mama's Boys. I have been published in about twenty anthologies. I wrote a column called "Drive by Chingón" for the *Los Angeles Reader* for two years, and I write for a number of magazines. I have done a number of short films and videos, including *The United States of Poetry* with that crazy poet Bob Holman from the Nuyorican's Poets Cafe. I recorded a solo spoken-work CD, *down town,* for New Alliance Records that was produced by one of my favorite poets, Marisela Norte. I have collaborated with photographer Laura Aguilar extensively, as well as with videographer Ming Yuen S. Ma, clothing designer Lunnah Menoh, architect Robert Millar, and fellow performers Monica Palacios and Beto Araiza. I have taught in the Writers' Program at UCLA Extension for five years and have lectured at almost every University of California and Cal-State campus. I curated the Gay Men Writers' Series at A Different Light bookstore in West Hollywood for a couple of years and spent a year curating the gallery and Latino writers at Beyond Baroque Literary Arts Center in Venice. It feels as if I have sat on every board and grants panel in the world, but I don't take them lightly because these experiences have also been essential to my growth as an artist.

I have read my poetry throughout the United States as well as performed in some wonderful queer friendly spaces, including Abe Ryebeck's wonderful theater company in Boston, the Theater Offensive. I spent a number of weeks teaching and performing under the astute guidance of Loris Bradley at DiverseWorks in Houston. I hung out with Miranda Joseph and the Women's Studies Department at the Tucson Center for the Performing Arts and the University of Arizona's Poetry House. During its heyday, I was treated very kindly by the gang at Alice B. Theater in Seattle. Vicki Wolfe at Sushi Performance Space in San Diego gave me more opportunity than I deserved. Eloise de Leon never forgot me at El Centro Cultural de la Raza in Balboa Park. Coco Fusco took me with her to England, and I met two extraordinary women at the Institute of Contemporary Art named Catherine and Lois. Guillermo Gomez–Peña, Josephine Ramirez, and Lorena Wolfer took me to X-Teresa in Mexico City, where I learned to speak Spanish again. Bill Talen brought me out to the Solo Mio Festival in San Francisco two years in a row. Gary Glaudini booked me for a run at the Zephyr Theater in Hollywood. Diane White at the

Los Angeles Theater Center introduced me to mainstream audiences with a subscription run at her theater downtown right before it closed.

Above and beyond all these great people, Tim Miller and Linda Burnham gave me a space to call home at Highways Performance Space in Santa Monica, where I did about fifteen different performances. Weba Garretson, Roberto Bedoya, Joy Silverman, and Erica Bornstein gave me almost as much opportunity at Los Angeles Contemporary Exhibitions.

Now I co-run a large program at the Mark Taper Forum Theater in Los Angeles called the Latino Theatre Initiative, where I am a resident artist. I have a creative partner named Diane Rodriguez, whom I co-write plays and perform with.

A number of beautiful young men tried to fit into the small twin bed in Silver Lake that I finally got rid of after twenty years. The most important was Raul Anorve, Jr., who tried his hardest to keep up with me.

I love lists. I make lists when I go to the market. I make lists before a performance. I make lists all day at work. I have a list fetish. So here's the list that I am most proud of, because it's the one I had the least to do with. I lived and it happened.

I have been selected one of the "100 Coolest People" by *Buzz* magazine, "100 Most Influential Hispanics" by *Hispanic Business* magazine, "50 People to Watch" in *Variety*, "25 Most Interesting People" by the *L.A. Weekly*, one of "L.A.'s Literary Treasures" by *Los Angeles* magazine, "People to Watch" in *Out* magazine, and one of the eight "Men We Love" in *Genre* magazine. I am the recipient of over twenty-five *L.A. Weekly* "Pick-of-the-Week" choices for performance, literary, and producing work. I have twice won the Midwest PlayLabs Award at the Playwrights' Center in Minneapolis. I have been awarded resolutions from the California State Senate and the Los Angeles City Council. I am the recent recipient of a MacArthur Foundation "genius" Fellowship. I just gave the keynote for the first International Congress of Latino Gays at the LLEGO Conference in San Juan, Puerto Rico.

I am thirty-six years old and I feel as though I haven't started yet. Every morning that I wake up in this great port city, this polyethnic maze that exists in the shadow of the Hollywood sign, I can't wait to tell the stories of this place.

And the story always starts with, On a street corner known as Pico and Union . . .

downtown

LUIS ALFARO

Pre-show

(PETULA CLARK'S "DOWNTOWN" BEGINS. THE HOUSELIGHTS
GO TO HALF. MIDWAY THROUGH THE SONG, THE SOUND OF A
HELICOPTER CIRCLING OVERHEAD IS HEARD. SOUND FADES AND
THE PERFORMANCE BEGINS. LUIS IS SEATED IN THE HOUSE.)

On a Street Corner

(LUIS BEGINS TO TALK FROM HIS SEAT IN THE AUDIENCE.
HE MAKES HIS WAY TOWARD THE STAGE.)

A man and a woman are walking down Broadway in downtown Los Angeles. The man looks at the woman and says, "Bitch,
shut up." The woman looks at the man and says, "Aw, honey. You
know I love you. I just wish you wouldn't hit me so hard." And
the man looks at the woman and says, "What, what, what? You
want me to leave you or what?" And the woman looks at the man
and says, "Aw, no, baby, you're the only thing that I remember."

Because desire is memory and I crave it like one of the born-
agains in my mama's church. But it's hard to be honest sometimes,
because I live in the shadow of the Hollywood sign. Because I live
in the same town with the people that bring you *Melrose Place* (my

weekly dose of reality). Because on a street corner known as Pico and Union, my father made extra money on pool tables, my mother prayed on her knees.

A woman danced in the projects across the street. I could hear the sound of a salsa song as her hips swayed. Each step got bigger and bigger as she thrust out her elbows and clenched her fists.

Her husband would beat the shit out of her with large big hands that looked like hammers. Each blow penetrated her face like a slow-motion driver training film.

A drunk from the bar at the corner staggers home, pushing people aside like a politician working a convention.

A man on the Pico bus gets slapped by this woman after she sat on his hand in the seat next to his. He says, "Hey, if you don't like it, don't sit here."

On Tenth and Union I forced my first kiss onto Sonia Lopez in third grade. The slap she gave me felt so good, it must have been my introduction into S&M.

A glue sniffer on Venice Blvd. watches the world in slow motion.

Bozo the clown was at the May Company on Broadway. He's throwing out these gifts to all of the kids. We're all waving and screaming, hoping to catch one. He throws this board game out at this little boy and it hits him right above the eye, and he topples over. He comes up screaming and crying and bleeding and I watch in horror, afraid that Bozo the Clown will throw something at me.

People in this city used to run at the sight of a helicopter light. Afraid that their sins would show through like the partition at confession.

An earthquake shook, and our neighbor is running down Pico, screaming that "Jesus has come back, just like he promised."

A man got slapped.
A woman got slugged.
A clown threw toys.
A drunk staggered.
An earthquake shook.
A slap.

A *slug*.
A *shove*.
A *kick*.

(LIGHTS CROSS-FADE TO AN OVERHEAD STAGE LIGHT THAT
MAKES A CIRCLE OF LIGHT. THE IMAGE CREATED IS THAT LUIS
IS A DOLL ON A STAND THAT TURNS.)

Virgin Mary

(LUIS WALKS INTO CIRCLE OF LIGHT.)

We used to have this Virgin Mary doll. Every time you connected her to an outlet, she would turn and bless all sides of the
room.

We bought her on one of my dad's surprise drunken trips to
Tijuana. He would come home from the racetrack at about midnight, wake us up, get us dressed, and we all hopped into the station wagon. My mom drove and my dad lowered the seat in the
back and he slept with us. My grandmother lived on one of the
colonias, and she *hated* our three A.M. visits. But you see, "blood is
thicker than water, family is greater than friends, and the Virgin
Mary watches over all of us."

When I was ten, I gave the rotating Virgin Mary doll to my
tía Ofelia. My *tía* Ofelia lived across the street with my *tía* Tita,
who lived with my *tío* Tony, who lived next door to my *tía* Romie.
Back in those days, everybody was either a *tía* or a *tío*. They lived
in a big beautiful wood-carved two-story house with a balcony
overlooking the street below. We were crowded in by downtown
skyscrapers, packs of roving *cholos*, the newly built convention
center on Pico, and portable tamale stands. But our families always managed to live together. Because you see, "blood is thicker
than water, family is greater than friends, and the Virgin Mary
watches over all of us."

My *tía* lived on the top floor and on the bottom lived the Eighteenth Street Gang. There was Smiley, Sleepy, La Sadgirl, and a
bunch of other homeboys who hung out in the front yard playing

BloodStones' "Natural High." Like roaches, they split at the sight of a cop car slowly cruising through our neighborhood like tourists on Hollywood Blvd.

My *tía*, she hated *cholos* and she would spit down the seeds of grapes she ate, just to annoy them. She was like all of my relatives back then. A grape picker from Delano, California. She claims to have dated Cesar Chavez and to know everyone in McFarland, Tulare, and Visalia Counties. I couldn't call her a liar, because she had *breast cancer*. My mom told us this in a voice reserved for nights when we didn't want to wake up my father after one of his drunken soccer celebrations. Doctors at County General took away her tits in hopes of driving away *La Bruja Maldita*, who was slowly eating away at her insides. When she was feeling okay, she would tell me stories about the farmworker movement and picking cherries one summer.

The day I brought her the rotating Virgin Mary doll, I knew she was in pain. I know I probably should have waited, but I asked her, quite innocently, if I could see her chest. She slapped me hard on the face, calling me a *malcriado*. While she sobbed, her hand searched for medication. I felt so bad that day, even I could feel *La Bruja Maldita* eating at my heart. I never got the nerve to go back up there again.

Weeks went by and my *tía* continued to rock in her chair. When the weeks turned to months, she slowly started to forget us. People would walk by and offer up a *"Buenas tardes, señora,"* but you could tell she was having trouble remembering faces. My grandmother sent a crate of grapes to help her to remember, but nothing worked. My mom and my *tía* Romie said that my *tía* Ofelia was becoming a baby, *otra vez*. The *Bruja Maldita* ate at her bones, and slowly she started to slump forward like the G.I. Joes that my brother and I melted with burning tamale leaves. Her cheeks caved in like the plaster *calaveras* that you could buy at the border. And one day, on my way home from school, I looked up and she was gone.

Phones rang. Food poured in. Little envelopes with twenty-dollar bills. Hysterical screams from aunts on a Mexico-to-L.A. party line. Dramatic uncles openly wept, and the tears of my relatives were covered with huge veils that they wore to Immaculate Conception Church. My grandmother got into the drama when she jumped onto the coffin at the burial.

A few weeks later the Crips drove by and they said, "Chump Mother-Fuckers. Greasy-Assed Messicans. Go back to Teehuana," and they firebombed the Eighteenth Street Gang on the bottom floor. Smiley, Sleepy, y La Sadgirl died, but we couldn't go to the funeral because my mom said they were *perros desgraciados*. Instead we rummaged through charred remains, looking for usable clothes and old Vicki Carr records.

My brother found what was left of the rotating Virgin Mary, and he used her head for BB gun practice. My mom cried because the memory of my *tía* Ofelia would now be an empty lot where bums would piss and tires would grow. Every day she watered a little flower she had planted in the memory of my *tía* Ofelia, until the Community Redevelopment Agency built the Pico-Union projects over her memory.

When I was eighteen, I met this guy with a rotating Virgin Mary doll. He bought it in Mexico, so, of course, I fell in love. His skin was white, he ate broccoli, and he spoke like actors on a TV series. He was every *Partridge Family/Brady Bunch* episode rolled into one. He taught me many things: how to kiss like the French, like an earlobe, and dance in the dark. Once, my grandmother sent us a crate of grapes. We took off our clothes, smashed the grapes all over our bodies, and licked them off of each other.

When he left, the *Bruja Maldita*'s hand replaced his in my heart. And she pounded on me and she laughed like Mexican mothers laugh at a clothesline. And my sorrow was so strong, but I kept it hidden with smiles that were like the veils at Immaculate Conception Church. But my sorrow was so strong that my relatives nearby would say, "Aye mijo. Don't you understand? Blood is thicker than water, family is greater than friends, and the Virgin Mary, that old Virgin Mary, she just watches over all of us."

(LUIS WALKS TO UPSTAGE CHAIR AND SITS WHILE HE PUTS ON PADS, ROLLER SKATES, AND HELMET. HE STANDS AND ASSUMES ROLLER DERBY STARTING LINE POSITION.)

Roller Derby

(LUIS ROLLER SKATES AROUND STAGE. AT THE END OF THE
PIECE HE FALLS FOUR TIMES, WHILE HE IS SAYING HIS LAST
LINES IN SPANISH.)

When I was a little boy, my brother and I used to play Roller
Derby in the empty lot next to the Vons on Pico. We were great
big fans, and every Friday night we spent it at the Olympic Audi-
torium on Grand Avenue. We used to make my mother drive us
through rush-hour traffic downtown just so that we could watch
the warm-up. The way I remember it, before the Dodgers, the
Lakers, the Clippers, or even the Kings, there was always the
T-Bird Roller Derby team. My brother had a Ralfi Valladares com-
memorative jersey. And I always wanted to be Honey Sanchez,
the coolest Latino Roller Derby queen in the world.

At the end of our game, we would count up our penalty points
and the loser would have to run into the wall behind Vons.

Well, I tried to play fair, but with a referee slash opponent like
my brother, I lost a lot. And no matter how many pads and layers
of clothes I wore, it always hurt so much. But never as much as
conversations with my dad.

Oye, Papa, ¿cuándo vas a parar de tomar?
Oye, Papa, ¿dónde duermes cuando no estas aqui?
Oye, Papa, ¿te gusta cuando me pegas?
Oye, Papa, ¿porque no me dices que me quieres?

(LUIS TAKES OFF ROLLER SKATES AND PADS.)

Pocho nightmare—a Moo-Moo approaches

(LUIS PUTS ON HIS SHOES. HE GRABS A SUITCASE FROM
UNDER THE CHAIR AND WALKS OVER TO PRESET MUSIC
STAND AT EITHER SIDE OF THE STAGE. TOP OF THE MUSIC
STAND IS BENT OVER TO CREATE A FLAT TOP. LUIS OPENS
THE SUITCASE AND BEGINS TO EAT THE HOSTESS ITEMS. THE

LIGHTS DIM AND SOUND TAPE STARTS WHEN HE BEGINS TO
EAT A BIG POUND CAKE.)

A MOO-MOO APPROACHES
A STORY ABOUT MAMAS AND MEXICO

My father says that when he first came to this country, there
wasn't *enough*. That's why he married the Moo-Moo. Hips as wide
as a river, she was abundance personified. As the years wore on
this was the role that the Moo-Moo reflected: quantity and pros-
perity. The Moo-Moo informed us of our wealth and kept hidden
all traces of our poverty. The Moo-Moo gave us hope and security.

And the Moo-Moo embarrassed us. It seems that the Moo-
Moo was interested in every aspect of our American lives. From
parent-teacher conferences to Boy Scout outings and altar boy
affairs. The Moo-Moo was *always* there. There to remind us of how
good a life we had *en Los Estados Unidos*. Sometimes the Moo-Moo
had to remind other people as well. And the Moo-Moo was very
protective. Once, the Moo-Moo threatened to kill a woman on
the block, with a nasty disposition, who called the Moo-Moo's son
"effeminate."

Once, a strange man walked into the Moo-Moo's house and
took the only TV we had; a small portable in the living room. The
Moo-Moo grabbed my brother's pee-wee league baseball bat and
walked down to the corner of Pico and Union, with slippers and
curlers in hair, *endiablada* and cursing. The Moo-Moo was seen
minutes later, curlerless, panting a heavy breath, smiling the devil's
smile and holding the portable TV in hand. Swinging the pee-wee
league baseball bat, the Moo-Moo whistled a happy tune while a
robber's blood dripped off the bat and onto the downtown pavement. The Moo-Moo was serious, *gerl*.

Years later the Moo-Moo's husband assimilated and decided
that the Moo-Moo was *too* abundant. That the hips of Mexico were
the hips of the past. The Moo-Moo should reflect a more American point of view. The Moo-Moo of Mexico was no longer desirable. The Moo-Moo of Mexico was holding us back. The Moo-
Moo of Mexico represented all the problems and setbacks we had

endured in America. The Moo-Moo of Mexico was too big, too wide, too fat, too much. Too much for our new American sensibility.

This sudden shift in border nationalities threw the Moo-Moo into a deep and dark depression. That same year, a poke and a Pap produced a malignant lump, and the Moo-Moo lost her breast. The Moo-Moo began to wear darker shades of colors. Eventually giving up patterns altogether, she only sewed simple solids on the outdated sewing machine from the Deardens at Fifth and Main. The Moo-Moo began to dream of a Mexico of visions: a body wide as a river and a view of the world gleaned from *novela* watching.

The Moo-Moo attempted suicide courtesy of Hostess Manufacturing. Kitchen cabinets, sewing rooms, and garages carefully concealed packages and boxes filled with cupcakes, Sno-balls, lemon pies, doughnuts, and Ho-Hos. The secret bakery was never mentioned.

Sometimes, late at night, far from the breast of the Moo-Moo, the nightmare that is the Mexico that I do not know, haunts me. I clear the kitchen of all traces of my bicultural history: the Mexican *novela* and a sweetener called America. The nightmare continues. A Moo-Moo approaches.

(LUIS WILL EAT ABOUT THIRTY TWINKIES DURING LAST SEGMENT. HE WILL THEN GO TO MUSIC STAND, ARMS RAISED, AND BEGIN TO SING.)

Heroes and Saints

The first place that I went to when I was coming out
was the great Latino watering hole
Circus Disco!
Tried to get into Studio One,
but the doorman asked for me for two IDs.
I gave him my driver's license and my J.C.Penney card,
but it wasn't good enough.
Hey, what did I know,
I was still wearing corduroys.

Circus Disco was the new world.
Friday night, eleven-thirty.
Yeah, I was Born to Be Alive.
Two thousand people exactly like me.
Well, maybe a little darker,
but that was the only thing
that separated me from
the cha-cha boys in East Hollywood.
And I ask you,

Where are my heroes?
Where are my saints?
Where are my heroes?
Where are my saints?

First night at Circus Disco
and I order a Long Island ice tea,
'cause my brother told me
it was an exotic drink,
and it fucks you up real fast.

The bartender looks at me
with one of those
"Gay people recognize each other" looks.
I try to act knowing and do it back.
Earlier that year,
I went to a straight bar on Melrose.
And when I asked for a screwdriver
the bartender asked me
if I wanted a Phillips or a regular.
I asked for a Phillips.
I was never a good drunk.
And I ask you,

Where are my heroes?
Where are my saints?

Where are my heroes?
Where are my saints?

The first guy I met at Circus Disco
grabbed my ass in the bathroom,
and I thought that was charming.
In the middle of the dance floor,
amidst all the hoo-hoo, hoo-hoo,
to a thriving disco beat,
he's slow dancing
and sticking his tongue down my throat.
He sticks a bottle of poppers up my nose,
and I get home at five-thirty the next morning.
And I ask you,

Where are my heroes?
Where are my saints?
Where are my heroes?
Where are my saints?

Sitting outside of Circus Disco,
with a three hundred pound drag queen,
who's got me cornered in the patio
listening to her life story,
I think to myself,
One day
I will become something
and use this
in an act.

At the time I was thinking
less about performance
and more about
Las Vegas.
And I ask you,

Where are my heroes?
Where are my saints?
Where are my heroes?
Where are my saints?

A guy is beating the shit out of his lover
in the parking lot of Circus Disco.
Everybody is standing around
them in a circle,
but no one is stopping them.
One of the guys is kicking and punching
the other guy, who is on the floor
in a fetal position.
And he's saying,
"You want to cheat on me, bitch?
You cheating on me, bitch?
Get up, you faggot piece of shit.
Get up, you goddamn faggot piece of shit."
It was the first time I saw us act
like our parents.

I try to move in,
but the drag queen tells me
to leave them alone.
"That's a domestic thing, baby.
Besides, that girl has AIDS.
Don't get near that queen."
And I ask you,

Where are my heroes?
Where are my saints?
Where are my heroes?
Where are my saints?

I get home early
and I'm shaken to tears.

My mother asks me
where I went.
I tell her I went to see a movie
at the Vista.
An Italian film about a man
who steals a bicycle.
It was all I could think of.
And she says,
"That made you cry?"

I swear,
I'll never go back to Circus Disco.
I'll never go back to Circus Disco.
I'll never go back to Circus Disco . . .
But at Woody's Hyperion!
Hoo-hoo, hoo-hoo.
I met a guy there
and his name is Rick Rascon
and he's not like anyone else.

No tight muscle shirt.
No white Levi's.
No colored stretch belt.
He goes to UCLA
and he listens to Joni Mitchell.
Is that too perfect or what?
He comes home with me
and we make love,
but I'm thinking of him
more like, like, a brother.
And I know, I know.
we're gonna be friends
for the rest of our lives.
And I ask you,

Where are my heroes?
Where are my saints?

Where are my heroes?
Where are my saints?

Started working at an
AIDS center in South Central.
But I gotta,
I gotta,
I gotta
get out of here.
'Cause all of my boys
All of my dark-skinned boys
All of my cha-cha boys
are dying on me.
And sometimes I wish
it was like the Circus Disco
of my coming out.

Two thousand square feet
of my men.
Boys like me.
Who speak the languages,
who speak the languages
of the border
and of the other.
The last time I drove
down Santa Monica Boulevard
and I passed by Circus Disco,
hardly anybody was there.
And I ask you,

Where are my heroes?
Where are my saints?
Where are my heroes?
Where are my saints?
Where are my heroes?
Where are my saints?

(LIGHTS TRANSITION TO SOMETHING SLIGHTLY HARSHER.)

Abuelita

I've been redeemed
by the blood of the lamb
I've been redeemed
by the blood of the lamb

I've been redeemed by the blood of the lamb
Filled with the holy ghost I am
All my sins are washed away
I've been redeemed

See this finger?
I cut it jumping into
my mother's rosebush
Suicide attempt or accident?
I don't know
I'm just ten years old

Did it because of Abuelita
Us kids, we hate Abuelita
my mother's mother
hate her more than Mrs. Polka
our fifth-grade teacher

You know it's the ultimate hate
when you hate your grandmother
more than a fifth-grade teacher named Mrs. Polka

Besides the usual complaints
she pinches our cheeks too hard
gives us too little money
along with those boring stories
of the depression
"We ate dirt burritos"

The world stops when Abuelita
come to visit
rules the house
with an iron fist
potatoes and beans for breakfast
and Channel 34
the Spanish-language station
day and night

Novelas *with adulterous housewives*
during the day
and Lucha Libre
with masked wrestlers
fake hitting each other
all night long

Abuelita *loves it*

I don't know
if I did it on purpose
or if Toro pushed me

Another in a long list of dogs
that we have owned
ranging in name from
Oaxaca to Mazatlán to Puebla
(named after ideal
vacation spots for dad)
is running on the porch

This one's name is Toro
later to be run over by a car
on a busy Pico Blvd. morning
and renamed Tortilla

Abuelita *sits on the porch*
reading yet another installment

of Vanidades
sort of a Cosmopolitan
for the Latino set

*Completely even more unrealistic
than* Cosmopolitan
Vanidades *has pictures of
beautifully trim
and dyed-blond Latinas
making tortillas
or chile rellenos
in gorgeous*
Ann Taylor *outfits
at an outdoor
Mayan-designed
wood-burning pit*

*I rise out of the rosebush
and immediately plunge into
the Latino dramatic effect
the painful
ay yai yai yai yai*

*There's a gash on my finger
and it starts to bleed
pretty badly*

Abuelita *turns on the hose
and runs my hand
under the water*

*Inspecting my finger
she laughs
pinches my cheek
thanks the* Virgin
for the minor miracle

does a sign of the cross
and applies
primitive Latino first aid

She looks at me
smiles
raises my bloody finger
to her face
closely inspecting
my afflicted digit
she brings it up close
to her eyes

I can't tell
what she is looking for
as if holding it up close
she might find
some truth
some small lesson
or parable
about the world
and its workings

Her eyes canvas the finger
probing with her vision
slowly and carefully

and then quickly
and without warning
she sticks it
inside of her mouth
and begins
to suck on it

I feel the inside of her mouth
wet and warm

her teeth
lightly pulling
equally comforting
and disgusting
at the same time

Being in this womb
feels as if I am being
eaten alive
on one of those
late night
Thriller Chiller movies
Vampira: Senior Citizen Bloodsucker

But it isn't that at all
this is the only way
that Abuelita
knows how to
stop the bleeding

I've been redeemed
by the blood of the lamb
I've been redeemed
by the blood of the lamb

I've been redeemed by the blood of the lamb
Filled with the holy ghost I am
All my sins are washed away
I've been redeemed

See this finger?
I cut it at work
making another pamphlet
critical of those
who would like to see
us dead

four gay Latinos
in one room

They're afraid to touch my wound
would prefer
to see it bleed
and gush
than to question
mortality
and fate

Could go on about
being tested
but it seems
so futile
as if we
don't know
that one little HIV test
could be wrong

Hold the finger
in front of me
stick it
close to mouth
drip drip drip
all over desk top

Hold it close
to face
quickly
without warning
stick it inside my mouth
and I begin to
suck
on it

Tears roll down
salty wet
tears
down my face
I can feel
my teeth
lightly pulling
and I wish

I wish for an Abuelita
in this time of plague
in this time of loss
in this time of sorrow
in this time of mourning
in this time of shame

And I
heal myself with
primitive Latino first aid kit

Memorial

This little light of mine
I'm gonna let it shine
This little light of mine
I'm gonna let it shine
This little light of mine
I'm gonna let it shine
Let it shine, shine, shine

The night after Julio's memorial service I went to the video store and rented an old gay porn tape. I think it was called *Aspen Ski Weekend II*. In it, a beautiful blond guy, that looks like no one I know, gets fucked by everybody in the ski lodge. He sort of half smiles throughout the video like maybe he's done this just a *few* too many times. Think of Carol Channing in *Hello, Dolly!*

They all had that 1970s porn pimples-on-the-butt look. Imperfect perfection, I call it. I mean, they were cute and all, but they had that *done it* look. Lost innocence. A resigned contentment. A grin that says, "Yeah, I give up. Just do what you want with me." And life says, "My pleasure, motherfucker."

When I went to bed, all that I could remember about the video was a bouquet of roses that were strategically placed next to the action. In every scene the roses seemed to magically appear within the frame of each thrust and moan. When I should have been paying attention to the big cum shot, my eyes instead caught sight of that beautiful bouquet of red to the left of the improvised sling. And, of course, not a condom in sight. That night I dreamt that everything beautiful was wrapped in condoms. Cocks and roses, all in condoms.

The next day I was reading the *Falcon Video Newsletter* and I found out that Alan Lambert, a cute, if not overly eager, bottom, had committed suicide in his native Canada. I always had a crush on Alan Lambert because he made porn look so easy. He seemed to know his paces, gliding from one position to another like Esther Williams underwater. I'm almost positive he came to porn by way of a gymnastics career. Mounting a ten-inch dildo, you could almost see Alan's lips mouthing off, in denominations of twenty, his earnings for the day.

In a ten-page document left behind to Falcon Video, he listed a number of important reasons for his self-demise at the old porn age of *twenty-six*. Chief among them was his fear of getting older. He stated that his body was at a peak physical condition and that he could not see himself physically in any other way. This from a man who wasn't even HIV-positive.

The last time I talked to Julio was at the French Market Place in West Hollywood. I was meeting a date for breakfast. Someone who looked like Alan Lambert. Julio was walking slowly around the restaurant, out of breath, and looking perpetually chemotherapy tanned. A few heads turned, but most pretended not to see him. My date arrived, and he kissed me on the *cheek*. I began to already imagine how I was going to throw him over my brand-new black lacquered desk and fuck him until he said, "Ooh, talk to me in Spanish."

Julio came by and he kissed me on the *lips*. I introduced him to my date, who was rippling muscles in a cute little outfit from Bodymaster. Julio told us about how he had just started steroids. His doctors were going to try to give him an ass again. It seems that the virus had taken it away. My date never recovered from the memory of the kiss that Julio had given me. He kissed me on the *cheek* and never called.

At Julio's memorial service his mother got up and told a room full of queers that his family did *not* support his lifestyle. That they never went to his art shows. That they had never even seen his artwork. That they didn't know him the way that we knew him. They only knew him as a *wonderful, caring, sweet person.*

Well, I want to reclaim a little history right now and tell you that I knew Julio. I knew Julio as a queer Latino-Filipino. I knew Julio as an artist. I knew Julio's artwork. I also knew Julio as a *wonderful, caring, sweet person.*

I know blood is thicker than water, but I want to say "Fuck you" to his mother. I am getting fed up with straight people. Because not only do they try to ruin our lives. They try to ruin our deaths as well.

The other day I was driving down Sunset Boulevard in Beverly Hills and I saw a big gigantic mural on the Playboy building. Have you seen it? It has a picture of a little boy playing with a handgun, and it says, "Save the Children, Stop the Violence." Well, I want a billboard on Sunset Boulevard. I want a billboard on Sunset Boulevard with a picture of Julio playing with a handgun. I want it to say, "Save the Children, Kill Your Parents."

Orphan of Aztlan

(LUIS BEGINS TO SING THE NEXT SONG AND IN THE PROCESS TAKES OFF HIS CLOTHES TO REVEAL A BLACK SLIP. LIGHTS CAN BE BROUGHT UP TO AN EVEN HIGHER INTENSITY.)

> *I saw the light*
> *I saw the light*
> *No more darkness*
> *No trouble in sight*

Praise the lord
I saw the light

If it was up to this god
we would have all been born
straight white males
But thankfully I got a god
who likes his color
and likes it dark and juicy

Hate to bring up
race issues
when smoldering
South Central sentiments
still fly so close by

But I can't believe
in this god
'cause if this god
really wandered
the desert
like they say he did
he would be
darker than the
Egyptian night
and we haven't
seen that picture yet?

In our image
would be more
"Prince"
than
"Prince Edward"

Fear strikes closest
to the heart
of the one

knowing distance
what you don't know
can now kill you

That is why
we dare to be different
in a world that sells same
same until we all act alike
in the image of what?

What are you afraid of?

Gay agenda
is equality
Civil rights
when someone
throws a firebomb
through a window
in Oregon
and kills
an African-American lesbian
the operative word here
is American
not Lesbian

There has been no power-sharing
so we are power-taking
empowered
to march with a million
because I am
sick and tired
of seeing straight people
kiss and hold hands
in public
while I am
relegated to

a T-dance
at Rage
Fuck that shit!

I am a queer Chicano
A native in no land
An orphan of Aztlan
The pocho son of farmworker parents

The Mexicans only want me
when they want me to
talk about Mexico
But what about
Mexican queers in L.A.?

The queers only want me
when they need
to add color
add spice
like salsa picante
on the side

With one foot
on each side
of the border
not the border
between Mexico
and the United States
but the border between
Nationality and Sexuality
I search for a home in both
yet neither one believes
that I exist

On this plane
I see a man

skinnier and sicker
than the
Sally Struthers Ethiopia
of Channel 13

Send money
for the hungry
and care
about somebody
on the other side
of the world
as long as we don't
have to see them
on the street

We leave AIDS patients
to crowded
County General
Hidden in corridors

The only face of AIDS
that we like to see
is on children
because children
are the innocent victims
should everyone else suffer?
I don't know
I only know
that it is
a world,
a world without end.

And he says,
"Don't you pray?"
And I say,
"Yes, I pray

"I pray
'Jesus, please protect me
from your followers'"

I want to meet you at the
intersection of possibility
because possibility
has the power
to teach us more about
loving our selves
than the book of John
who, by the way,
sounds a lot like
David Geffen to me

My god is a trusting god
My god is a tolerant god
My god is an oppressed god
My god revels in the freedom of difference
My god is a thinker
with a compassion
for the intellectual mind
My god sounds a lot like a woman
Yes, I would have to say that my god is a woman

My god lives in East Los
My god is a laborer
My god works below minimum wage
My god doesn't see herself anywhere, but she is everywhere
My god sounds a lot like a Latina
Yes, I would have to say that my god is a Latina

My god is a minister of truth
My god is a visionary for peace
My god believes in political and social equity
My god sounds a lot like a lesbian
Yes, I would have to say that my god is a lesbian

And I ask you tonight
what are you so afraid of?

Blur the line
take the journey
play with the unknown
deal with the whole enchilada
Race
Class
Sex
Gender
Privilege

Arrive at the place called possibility
Try once again to create a language
a sense of what it means
to be in community

I am fast-forwarding
past the reruns ese
and riding the big wave
called future
making myself
fabulous
as I disentangle
from the wreck of this
cultural collision

You know you've reached
the new world
when the Guatemalan
tamale lady
at your corner
is wearing
a traditional skirt
and a T-shirt

that says
Can't touch this

So tonight
I am making
a burrito
(so to speak)
of possibility
and throwing in
as much as I can
and calling it
un poem

Daring to tell my truth
and my story
as best I know how
with what I have invented
or stolen from the
cultural catalog

Do it in front of
the face called hate
frowning always
with disapproval
daring to hurt me
with ugly words
in editorials

Let me tell you something
We will continue
to create these
espectaculos tan sabrosos
that we call our
queer Latino selves
and make them

al estilo los
like only we know
how to make them

Because we are
at the edge
at the border
at the rim
of the new world
and there is no place
to run
or hide

So tonight
I step over
the burned-out lot
walk into
the performance space
and say
I come in the name
of peace and justice

Are you a
friend
or a
phobe?

(ON THE LAST LINE, LIGHTS SHOULD POP TO BLACK.)

Ritual

(LUIS MOVES MUSIC STAND OUT OF CENTER LIGHT. FACES
THE AUDIENCE. DOES THREE GESTURES: HOLDS UP FINGER,
BEATS CHEST, AND DOES THE VIRGIN MARY TURN. LIGHTS
FADE TO BLACK AT COMPLETION OF HIS TURN.)

attachments

MICHAEL KEARNS

Notes on *Attachments:*
Telling the Truth

More than any film or television role, more than any appearance in a conventional play, more than any of the hundreds of articles I've composed, more than any directing or producing assignment, more than any of the books I've written or contributed to, it is my work as a soloist that defines me as a true artist. It is the only form where I have been allowed to immerse myself entirely, without compromise, utilizing my body, voice, brain, heart, soul, and guts. It's as if the form itself pushed me into creative terrain I never thought I could conquer, stemming from a deep need to discover my authenticity. Solo performance, above all other artistic expressions, provided the road map necessary for me to emerge and ultimately thrive.

However, be forewarned: Because writing and performing solo potentially takes one to great artistic heights, it possesses an inherent pain component. You soar, you land, you stumble, you hit, you miss. You simply cannot present your most intimate self, uncamouflaged, unless you are willing to be intensely scrutinized. In choosing to utilize the "I" word in unraveling your story, you are likely to be personally—as well as professionally—criticized.

Although it was not a conscious decision, *Attachments* is, in retrospect, clearly the third entry of a trilogy that began with my first solo effort, *The Truth Is Bad Enough.*

Reeling from the aftershocks of newfound sobriety, I wrote *The Truth Is Bad Enough* in 1982. This was no career move, honey, it was a survival tactic. I was, in an attempt to comprehend what happened to me, compelled to tell my story; in the lingo of Twelve Step programs, this is known as "an inventory." Instead of spilling my life story to a sponsor in a smoky coffee shop, I chose to divulge every lurid detail to a theater audience.

Tracking my escapades as Grant Tracy Saxon, the fraudulent author of *The Happy Hustler,* a persona I adopted in the mid-seventies, was fertile fodder for drama. Hired by the publishers to promote a fictitious book by pretending to be the writer, not only did I convince the public, I—in

what can only be described as a *Twilight Zone* episode—began to believe
my own publicity. While *Truth* served as a public apology for a hoax hurled
on the American public, the solo performance piece was also an achingly
personal search for true self. Like many of my generation, I had spent a
decade in the ferocious fast lane, losing myself in the process.

Although *Truth* ultimately achieved its artistic due, it was initially
slapped with a few snotty reviews. This was the early eighties, when public displays of homo stuff was considered shocking; a one-man show de-
tailing politically incorrect aspects of gayness was particularly vulnerable
and proved to be a blazing target for gay and straight critics alike.

Even though the criticism—and some of it was downright malicious—
took its toll, I ultimately knew I was doing the right thing: testifying my truth
to an audience.

Rock, part two of the trilogy, premiered in 1992, after the phenom-
enal response to *intimacies* and *more intimacies.* Since they weren't delivered in the first person—not ostensibly, anyway—the twelve extremely
divergent, fictitious characters with AIDS depicted in the complementary
intimacies works seemed less confrontational.

Stylistically *Rock* borrowed from the confessional *Truth* approach while
incorporating the character work I'd honed in the *intimacies* shows. Like
Truth, a decade prior, *Rock* was inspired by cataclysmic events in my personal life: the AIDS deaths of Rock Hudson and Brad Davis, as well as my
own HIV-positive diagnosis. In addition to creating composite characters
(including a suppositious Marilyn Monroe), based on myth, fact, legend,
and gossip, I portrayed myself. The autobiographical aspect was heightened by video clips (including a juicy scene from a porn movie referred to
in *Truth*) that depicted my evolution from Hollywood actor to AIDS
activist.

Rock was popular from the onset, even though there were a few warn-
ings for the sexually squeamish. Again, most of the mild chastisement was
directed at my choice to be uncensoredly gay (and that includes cocksucking,
darling). For a few, the truth proved to be bad enough once again.

While several observers of my work noted the connection between
Truth and *Rock,* I didn't methodically write *Attachments* (1996) as a follow-
up to either. Again, it was a piece I had to write in order to make sense of
my world.

My decision to adopt a child—as a single, gay, HIV-positive man in his forties—elicited fevered response; almost no one was without an opinion. What I attempted to do with *Attachments,* as I had with my previous solo work, is bounce my story off the stage and see how it reverberated in the world.

While the particulars of my evolution were unique, the desire to redefine family during the plagued nineties was widespread. Or was it?

The volatile reaction to *Attachments* was dominated by each individual's stance on the issue—would I be an acceptable parent?—eclipsing any response to the work itself. The politics of the piece seemed to obscure the art; whether or not I should dare adopt a child, not whether or not I could put on a show, became the focus of the intense criticism.

Even though I'd succeeded in stirring up the audience, at the same time I felt betrayed by them. In my experience, this has been the dichotomous reality of solo: it simultaneously feels so good and hurts so bad.

Staged simply, I stressed the literariness of *Attachments,* opting even to read some sections while acting out others. I'm proud and grateful it's being published in this collection as part of my personal legacy as well as a documentation of queer history.

Attachments is probably the conclusion of my public confessionals. If I opt to fly solo again, it will be character-driven work. Perhaps maturity lessens one's compulsion to offer up one's intimacies to a room full of strangers; could it be I've found some level of tranquillity? If so, it's largely due to my work as a soloist.

I was recently admonished by someone who said, "You are so full of yourself." Indeed, honey, I am. What a compliment, I thought. It's taken me many years and several solo performance pieces to find myself so powerfully and undeniably fulfilled.

About Michael Kearns

Over the past twenty-five years, Michael Kearns has established himself as one of America's most impassioned queer artists. His solo performance works—The Truth Is Bad Enough, intimacies, more intimacies, Rock, *and* Attachments—*have been performed extensively throughout the world. Also a director, producer, actor, journalist, and teacher, his work surrounding HIV/ AIDS is abundant, including producing and directing the landmark productions of* AIDS/US, AIDS/US/II, *and* AIDS/US/WOMEN *in addition to the world premiere and subsequent ten year anniversary production of Robert Chesley's* Jerker. *As an actor, he has appeared on television and film but is best known for his theatrical work including the title roles in James Carroll Pickett's* Dream Man *and* The Queen of Angels *as well as Charles Ludlam's* Camille. *Kearns is the author of three books, all published by Heinemann:* T-Cells & Sympathy, Acting = Life, *and* Getting Your Solo Act Together.

attachments

MICHAEL KEARNS

He lives in a house on the corner at the end of the block: Patrick. Every day after school, we make additions on our elaborate playhouse, constructed from hundreds of orange crates—a masterpiece of invention durable enough to live in, we dream. Patrick is ten, a year older, which makes him the boss. He decides who plays what role in our make-believe home: some days I'm the son and he's my father: some days I'm the husband and he's my wife; some days I'm the sister and he's my brother. One day, as I approach the end of the street, anxious to play house with my only friend, I see a police car—or is it an ambulance?—silent even though the red light is flashing. Out of breath, I arrive at Patrick's real house as he is being lifted into the ambulance, covered with a white sheet. My father/my wife/my brother had hung himself from the basement rafters.

Death is not my greatest fear. All my life I have been afraid I would inherit my father's barren pain, his mundane depression. Shortly after my birthday in January of 1995, I felt as if his desolate spirit had finally entered my body, to poison me with his harrowing sadness. This no-hope feeling, haunting me from head to toe, had far more deadly force than the HIV I've learned to accept.

After forty-five years of keeping them at bay, keeping them at arm's length, keeping them in the closet, suppressing them, squelching them, repressing them, rejecting them, my father's genes took root inside me, like wild weeds overtaking a well-kept garden. Where there had always been the hope of roses, now I felt a longing to die. An almost peaceful yearning to just get it the fuck over with.

Five months later, it is snowing passionately, Christmas card snowflakes on Cinco de Mayo. We are in Idyllwild, where I've bought a cabin I call home; elevation: six thousand feet, where clouds bounce off winding roads, like gigantic beach balls. Tia, Billy, and me.

Tia is the foster baby I may someday adopt. Billy is the guy I may someday marry.

Daddy, mommy, husband, wife, lover, brother, blah blah blah.

Billy fixes dinner—pork chops, mashed potatoes, green beans. He sets—no, designs—the table: candles; freshly plucked white and yellow and red tulips, still frosty from the snow, delicately arranged in a mayonnaise jar-turned-vase; Lena on the boom box. The fireplace is making popping, crackling sounds, creating a syncopation to match Lena's impeccable phrasing. The baby is snuggling with her zebra, keeping rhythm with her gentle snores.

Are we a family yet?

After dinner we make love in the glow of the fireplace, which sparks lighting effects usually only seen on soap operas; we are all burnt orange and defiantly healthy. Fucking, staring into each other's eyes, is as sobering as it is sloppy drunk. Till death do us part and all that jazz.

Are we a family yet?

Billy spends the following day seduced by the baby's ineffable freshness. Magnetized to her magic, he becomes even sweeter in her presence. Except for diaper duties, he is a daddy to die for. I smother them both with kisses.

As evening approaches, it becomes clear he's more comfortable with her simple needs than my intricate desires. Is he using her to distance me? By the time the sun sets, they are both sound asleep. She wakes from her nap for a feeding; he remains conveniently passed out. I guide her bottle with one hand while stroking strands of his tangled dirty hair with the other. I imagine him sick. Dying.

Tia is the baby I may someday adopt. Billy is the guy I may someday marry.

As it becomes certain he's not going to wake up, as it becomes certain making love two nights in a row is not on his agenda, I begin to experience the same simmering sadness spurred by my father's emotional paralysis. Suddenly he's my father on the couch: shut down, numbed out, turned in, fucked up. All I want is for him to love me. Love me, goddammit. Tell me how motherfucking lovable I am.

Are we a family yet?

At 4:03 in the morning, we are reminded of the earth's temperament: an aftershock from the Landers quake. Billy and I, in bed now, exchange a few soft words of comfort; the baby emits a startled cry, shorter than the duration of the rumble.

Sunday morning rituals before the drive home: he commandeers the bathroom first. I'm quick to follow, not waiting long enough to escape the puissant scent of him which remains in the toilet. The seat is still warm. I wonder if he can hear me over the sounds of his gushing babytalk. Shit. The toilet stops up, full of me. Shit. Full of my shit. What can I do but tell him?

Are we a family yet?

There is no plunger on the premises. Shit. While packing, I make a quick phone call to my mother: "I'm at the cabin. It's been snowing. Like St. Louis snowing. On Cinco de Mayo. The

Fifth of May. She's fine. A bit of a cold, but fine. Billy's here with me. Billy. Yes, the boyfriend. Great. We had a great weekend. How's Joe? What are you up to today? *Don Juan.* I think you'd like it; you like Marlon Brando, don't you? It's very romantic. A happy ending. Well, I better go. I'll talk to you next Sunday. I love you." The "I love you" has become an automatic emission, like an ATM machine spitting out a receipt at the end of a transaction.

We devour breakfast at the Idyllwild Cafe—the decidedly only Anglo gay couple with a black infant in tow. After purchasing a prize plunger at the grocery store, we return to the cabin to administer to the toilet. He does the deed, letting me know I am indeed lovable. "Firmly formed," he rhapsodizes. "Same as mine."

Are we a family yet?

The densely swirling fog is blinding as we descend the twenty-six-mile mountain of Disneyland curves. I navigate by keeping my eyes on the road's fading yellow stripes. "How'd we do?" I ask, immediately therapizing our forty-eight-hour adventure. "Was it a success?"

"Great," he says almost as if he's describing a movie of the week. "It was great," he repeats, convincing himself he means it.

Even though we both agree it was "great," we do not blindfold the realities; creeping through layers of fog as we attempt to make clear our muddy fucked-upnesses. Tia falls sound asleep, lulled by the schizophrenic twists and turns of the road. By the time we reach the foot of the mountain, the sun is shining gloriously and we have recommitted ourselves to trying to make it work. Tia is the foster baby I may someday adopt. Billy is the guy I may someday marry.

I want a doll for Christmas, a baby-doll with bright yellow curls and red painted-on lips.

Mommy wonders if her five-year-old is destined to be a homo.

Because of Daddy's deepening dalliance with insanity—he spends most of his days melted onto the couch, limp with pain, wearing a white terry-cloth bathrobe—my mom is a veteran of St. Louis institutions for the psychologically challenged.

She consults a professional, who situates me in a room full of gender-specific toys—plastic guns and soldiers, miniature tea sets and dollhouses. Without hesitation, I gravitate to the diminutive dwelling and its petite inhabitant: a luxurious baby-doll in need of attention.

After observing me at play with my little girl, the therapist informs my mother: "Whether or not he becomes a homosexual is irrelevant; what is significant, however, is his powerful desire to be a parent."

We spend Christmas Day at my aunt's house. While my brother, Joey, six years my senior, and my brawny cousin open their conventional boy toys, I delicately unwrap my precious doll. She is exactly what I asked for: golden hair and kissable lips.

The family, particularly my mother's mother—the scarlet-haired Mamie—goes into collective shock: "How could you?" "What are you thinking?" "Are you crazy?" "You'll turn that kid into a sissy." "Sissy, sissy, sissy."

Even though my father is physically present—looking out of place out of his bathrobe—he remains resolutely mute while my mother attempts to defend herself. Eventually, as the battle with her sodden mother escalates, it is decided I should take an unscheduled nap.

Clinging to my angelic gift, I am whisked off to a distant room, away from the main event. Dismissed. Ostracized. Cast off.

When Mommy wakes me for dinner, she has changed: the smell of booze overpowers her potent perfume. Conspiratorially, she lavishes me with moist kisses.

The Christmas dinner table becomes a boxing ring. Mamie, the grandmother from hell, makes an announcement: "My husband can't get it up!" (SLAP) My stepgrandfather wallops her across the face, and she goes toppling over, like one of those garishly painted ducks in a carnival shooting gallery. Again, it is determined I should be removed from the holiday high jinks.

If there was a Christmas without incident, I don't remember. If there was a holiday without hysterics, it escapes my memory. If there was a family gathering without heartache, I have no recollection.

People—at the grocery store, post office, bank—see a single, white man with an African American baby and they are compelled to ask, "Is that your baby?"

I've been forced to come up with some snappy answers.

"Is that your baby?"

"No, I'm baby-sitting for Diana Ross."

Lannes Kearns worked on the railroad in a small Missouri town, where he habitually watched a cluster of schoolgirls gliding across a field of wildflowers, on their way to school. One of the girls stood out, not only because of her towering height, but because of the gazellelike fluidity of her carriage. Even from a distance, he could probably see she was more handsome than pretty with her elongated face and bold features. "I'm going to marry that girl," he bragged to his bored cohorts.

Lannes did marry her. Shortly after, Katherine Kearns gave birth to my father.

My father, 1960; my roommate, Jim Pickett, 1994.

A threadbare terry-cloth bathrobe, listless from too many spin cycles, hugs his shuddering shoulders. When he aimlessly staggers from room to room, as if not remembering the layout of the house, his body appears to be in danger of caving in on itself, like a defenseless building teetering on a hillside during a natural disaster. He shuffles shamefully, like a man twice his age, never lifting his swollen feet, tattooed with constellations of red and purple splotches. He stares into nothingness as if a hidden hint might float by, reminding him of who he was and what exactly happened. With no such clues forthcoming, he shuts his eyes, escaping into an unconscious void. When he makes sounds, they are involuntary fartlike expulsions of excruciating pain, often merely a reminder—to himself, perhaps—he's still alive. Sounds of night are less polite: volcanic eruptions from the bowels of helplessness, like the pleas of trapped fire victims. Is he waking from a nightmare? Or waking up to reality? Only occasionally the sound of laughter is heard: a manic giggle, signaling something horrific, not something humorous. The only time an expression of pleasure flickers across the crevices of his corroded countenance is when he devours a cigarette. With each inhalation, he seems to recapture an evanescent spark of his former self: a faint smile, a lithe movement of the head. He sleeps more hours of the days than he doesn't, his disdain for light and dark indistinguishable. The doctors "don't know" what's wrong with him—an undiagnosis which fuels his indignant immobility. The terror of living compounded by the terror of dying equals existence in a stagnant limbo.

There are days when my pity for him escalates to totemic hatred. "If only he'd die," I mutter to myself. On other days, my heart ricochets at the thought of losing him; we are inextricably entangled by a decade of life's highest dosage of drama. His presence makes me feel absolutely responsible, as if I'm the puppeteer who pulled the strings which have rendered him lifeless and impotent. And there's no question: if he dies, my mortality will zoom into focus.

I vow not to be like him—a promise I relentlessly whisper to myself, determined not to wake the part of me that I know is him.

My father, 1960; my roommate, Jim Pickett, 1994.

My mother is wearing a smart Easter hat made of lettuce green feathers which wrap around her head like a serpentine vine. In an attempt at reconciliation, we visit my father at the elegant Mayfair Lennox Hotel, where he works as a maîtred' in between visits to the loony bin.

We stop at Walgreens to get him some Old Golds. I spot a trinket which I must have: a golden tree, about ten inches tall, its delicate branches dripping with tiny circular picture frames. Because she's in a holiday mood and probably considers it some sort of an omen, my mother digs into her purse (which matches the verdant hat) and buys me the family tree.

He is a glamorous figure, gliding across the chandeliered dining room in a freshly pressed tuxedo—not only a dramatic change of costume from his everyday terry-cloth robe, also a startling shift of demeanor. He's like a resuscitated movie star on the comeback trail.

Yet in spite of his ostensible transformation, he remains obdurately incommunicable and untouchable. He is not a father; even though I'd prefer this starched version to the crumpled one, it is simply another empty package. He is not a father.

The glue which drew petite Pauline Padgen and strapping Joe Kearns together had lost its sticking power; their springtime reunion does not blossom.

I find an old photo of the two of them, radiantly in love, expectant expressions on their young faces which the years have distorted. Separating them, carefully cutting each of their heads to fit the small frames (about the size of a quarter), I determinedly place them—even though they are getting a divorce—on my fantasy family tree.

I want to adopt.

I am getting a blow job from a man in a suit, about my father's age—he's on his knees on the floor of the bathroom in Pope's Cafeteria, where my father and I are having dinner. As his mouth works on my cock, the mystery man tickles my balls with one hand and caresses my pale white boy stomach with the other. When it's over—faster than you can say "NAMBLA"—he gives me a quick peck on the forehead.

Since my father never looks at me, he doesn't notice I'm flushed when I return to the table, as if I'd just gotten off a maniacal amusement park ride. We are really just killing time—in silence—before the show starts. With his connections as a maîtred', he has arranged for me to see *The Sound of Music* at the American Theater. With Florence Henderson.

At the theater, I spot the cocksucker in the audience with a woman I assume is his wife. Instead of paying much attention to the singing Von Trapps, I plot what I'll do after the show is over:

I'll accidentally miss the last bus home and be forced to spend the night in my father's hotel. We will sleep in the same bed, pressed up against each other. Like the man in the john, he will make me feel good about myself, make me feel loved and safe and not so ugly and not so alone. He will kiss me, lick me, like me, love me— all over. I'm hard all over again—the Von Trapps are singing "Doh, a deer, a female deer; Re, a drop of golden sun . . ." My father is kissing me, not on the forehead, on the mouth. "Me, a name I call myself; Fa, a long, long way to run . . ." His tongue is inside me now. He's on top of me, protecting me, fucking me. "La, a note to follow so; Te, a drink with jam and bread . . ." I explode, cream- ing in my pants, without touching myself. I'm almost as happy as Florence Henderson. "And that brings us back to doh."

I want to adopt: three words I could not take back, could not return to the closet, could no longer deny.

There is one present under the pathetic, silver metallic Christ- mas tree I put up myself: a magical eight ball.

All that's left of Daddy is a permanently depressed indenta- tion in the couch, where he downslid until he finally checked into the state hospital. Mommy, too, is among the missing. My brother— a veteran juvenile delinquent at age sixteen—makes brief silent appearances; then—like Houdini!—he's gone again.

This is not the first or the last time I will be left alone to take care of myself, but hasn't someone told her it's Christmas? I wait for the phone to ring; surely she'll be calling with an explanation, convincing me how "sorry" she is and "it won't happen again" and "I'll be there in an hour." Her liquid hours have been known to flow into days.

But on this particular Christmas morning, I engage the eight ball while the phone remains stoically silent. The shiny black toy is designed to magically answer yes or no questions: shake it vig- orously, turn it upside-down, and an answer appears: "Definitely." "Not likely." "Absolutely." "No way." It cannot tell me where my mother is or what time she'll come home. Does she love me? Defi- nitely. Is she a good mom? No way.

As the day unfolds, I decide to consult the Yellow Pages—under the letter "T"—remembering bars are listed as "taverns." I recognize the names of a few, names I've overheard sprinkled in her phone conversations.

"Is Pauline Kearns there?"

"No, kid, no one here by that name."

After I go through several taverns, I try "H" for hospitals, followed by "H" for hotels.

"Is Pauline Kearns there?"

"No, kid, no one here by that name."

Is she dead? I ask the eight ball.

The phone rings. It's my mother's sister, wondering why we haven't shown up for dinner. Some resentful family member agrees to pick me up and transport me to the annual event. I clutch my eight ball even though it holds none of the answers I need.

She eventually shows up—festooned like a Christmas tree herself, smelling like the bowels of a tavern—with Charlie, a glassy-eyed misfit who trembles like a five-point-something earthquake.

Even though the scent of her is sickening and even though she embarrasses me and even though I have to share her with this quivering bag of bones she calls her boyfriend, the ache for Mommy's closeness temporarily subsides.

Is that your baby?

No, I just grabbed her out of a car in the parking lot.

No, I would not say there's a good chance I'll die of AIDS. There's a chance. Like there's a chance I'll die in an earthquake; there's a chance I'll die of a heart attack; there's a chance I'll die in a car accident.

No one knows how long I'm going to live. Why is the length of my life the overriding issue? It's how good a parent I'll be while I'm alive that matters. My father was not a father for five minutes. If I parent this child for six minutes, or six months, or six years, it will be more fathering than I had.

You analyzed me, you interviewed me, you put me under a microscope, and you approved me. Have you forgotten what's good about me now that you know I'm HIV-positive?

Sometimes I honestly believe it would be easier for society if HIV *definitely* led to death. And the sooner the better; just die; do not pass go. Then you wouldn't have to deal with it in situations like this. Well, guess what? I'm not the first or the last person with HIV who will want to adopt a child. Get ready.

Everyone involved in this adoption, regardless of their political correctness, has at some point attempted to make me feel guilty for being HIV-positive. I will not let any of you make me feel less-than; if it's the last thing I do, I'll hold on to my-self, my-HIV-self.

I realize it would be a lot easier for everyone if I threw my hands up in the air and admitted I'm wrong. Good luck—it ain't gonna happen. There is nothing wrong with me. I deserve to be a father as much as anyone in the world. At this very moment, I am uncontestably qualified. The rest is pure conjecture.

Tia holds the bottle by herself.
My friend Dick is unable to negotiate silverware.
Tia took her first baby step.
My friend Dick has neuropathy, walks with a cane now.
Tia recognizes herself in the mirror.
My friend Dick has gone blind.
Tia's two front teeth popped through.
My friend Dick has twenty-two T-cells.
Tia says, "Dada."
My friend Dick doesn't remember his lover's name.
Tia is nine months old on May 26.
My friend Dick has less than six weeks to live.

I painstakingly study the wording of each Father's Day card on the rack. "You've always been there for me, Dad." Forget that. "To a Father I Admire and Respect." Forget that. "The World's Greatest Father?" No fuckin' way. I opt to buy a blank card and tentatively print the words "Happy Father's Day" on it. Even the hollowness of those three words seems fake and accusatory; my father has made it known he's incapable of being happy.

"Is that your baby?"
"Yes, my husband is black."

The day Grandma Katie died, shortly after being transported to a nursing home, I experienced a pang in my heart—a rip, a jab, a poke—which has never subsided.

As a child, I lived in fear of her dying. When I was eleven years old, she had a stroke, losing her bowels and her ability to speak. She recovered—in part, I was certain, because of my fervent prayers to any god who would listen.

My grandma Katie possessed a homespun regality, as if personally endorsed by all the saints in heaven. She had more common sense than education, more personality than style, more spirituality than religion. And more pride than most.

How could I live without her blanketing warmth, her showering affection?

After I moved away from St. Louis, when she was in her eighties, a petty thief knocked her to the ground and snatched her purse. Again, she recovered.

How could I live without her unflappable patience, her undying loyalty?

Her death became real to me when Christmas arrived and—for the first time in more than fifteen years—there was no card (with two dollars faithfully enclosed) and no love note scrawled in her expansive handwriting.

How could I live without . . . ?

With each death I've experienced since, I mix tears for Grandma Katie in the grief pool, missing her all over again, longing to smell her hair, hear her giddy laugh, touch her rouged cheeks.

If I adopt Tia, her middle name will become Katherine.

I swear this overcurious McDonald's employee asks, "Are you dying?"

"What?" I say, not quite believing.

Elongating each syllable, he repeats, "Are you dining in?"

"Oh, yeah, sure," I say, relieved.

I see myself in the mirror—Billy's on top, roughly kissing the back of my neck—and can't believe either of us could be dead in a year or two.

My father was born on St. Patrick's Day 1906. He died eighty years later.

My mother called to tell me, delivering the news like an impartial television reporter, as the sun was rising. I responded as I'd anticipated: a dull ache telegraphing a final realization I would never have the father I never had. He will not knock on the door, greeting me with open arms; he will not say, "I'm sorry," "I love you," or, "Let's go fishing, son"; he will not. There is relief in knowing the truth, relief in extinguishing unrealistic dreams; that's what death can do: death can kill the hope of a happy ending.

Near the end, I was told he searched for me in every face that appeared on the television screen, hanging above the bed where he lay immobilized, believing I made daily visitations. "There's Mike," he'd supposedly say if someone popped on the small screen who even faintly resembled his Hollywood son. I desperately want to believe this story, spun by nuns who cared for him; imagine him trying to connect with me before he died.

I jerk off. On the television screen of my memory, I replay sexual liaisons with men who are facsimiles of my father. My soul hungers for some glimmer of him in every man I brush up against, exalting him and exorcising him, honoring him and disgracing him, embracing him and fucking him.

The warm liquid splattered on my stomach feels more like tears than cum, more like death than life—like an irretrievable loss.

While changing Tia's diaper or giving her a bath, I marvel at the oldness of my weathered hands against the pristine newness of her cocoa-colored skin. The hands of a writer; the hands of an actor; the hands of a lover. Hands which have novels lodged in their intricate crevices and worn wrinkles. Now the hands of a mother: soft and loving; the hands of a father: strong and knowing.

There is something so silky about Billy's hands yet so virile with veins protruding like muscular worms. His sinewy fingers, whether soothing my forehead or stroking my chest, connect me to his insides, the juiciest parts of him that no one else can touch.

I was terrified the first time I clipped her teensy fingernails. Now I just do it, as a matter of routine, like changing a diaper. I love the feel of her baby hands clutching on to the collar of my shirt or reaching for my glasses or pulling the hairs on my arm. The tininess of her fingertips doesn't make the gestures less knowing; in fact, each grab, each grope, each grasp, seems to be a deliberate, intimate statement.

Mommy.

Is that your baby?
No, actually, her father is Hugh Grant.

Mommy is on the bathroom floor, babbling incoherently, half-naked, unable to pull her panty hose up over her bloated gut. I'm almost as fucked-up as she is but still on my feet, so, playing the role of the dutiful son, I hoist her up and stuff her into her skin-colored underwear.

Shortly after Jim Pickett's mother is tossed into a sanitarium, his lifelong nightmare becomes a stinging reality: diagnosed with dementia, he is tossed into the equivalent of a sanitarium for AIDS patients.

Why don't I kiss you on the mouth? I am not your boyfriend. I am not your lover. I am not your husband. I am your son. You are my mother. Do you understand? Son. Mother. Mother. Son.

I've done this dance with you for thirty-five years, and it's now over, done, finis. From the time I could walk, I've been your confidante, nurse, psychiatrist, bartender, hairdresser, girlfriend, soulmate. I can't do it sober; as long as I was as drunk as you, I could play any twisted role you demanded. But no more. I'm fucking trying to get it together here. With whatever time I have left. This is unfuckinghealthy. Now you want me to be your husband. This is not about love; this is about your unfathomable neediness. Why don't I kiss you on the mouth? Listen to yourself: the wounded woman. I wasn't put on this fucking earth to make you feel desirable. Why don't I kiss you on the mouth? Because I don't want to, that's why. Because I'm your son and that is the only role I'm playing from this day forward. Do you hear me? I've been ensnared by your apron strings into this web you've concocted. It's time to slash the almighty umbilical cord; it's time to unleash me. I'm extricating myself from your anything-but-motherly clutches. Let go of me, do you hear?

July 4, 1994. One of the funniest men alive is dead. One of the sweetest men alive is dead. One of the angriest men alive is dead. One of the smartest men alive is dead. Jim Pickett is dead. On the Fourth of July.

Let me count the losses. The loss of an artistic partner; the loss of a best friend; the loss of a soulmate; the loss of a collaborator; the loss of a brother; the annihilation of a decade-long teaming in which we created theater, made each other scream with laughter, proofread each other's manuscripts, attended how many memorials together, and told each other everything, honey, I mean *everything*. Dead on the Fourth of July.

It's the mornings I miss the most—before he started the descent, when he knew the difference between dawn and dusk. Goosed by caffeine, we'd each devour a section of the *Los Angeles Times* and locate items to riff on: an outlandish editorial, a juicy news story, an overblown obituary, a hateful review. Our ritualistic morning chat show—sometimes politically charged, other times simply teeming with filthy gossip—spared no one. We would spew a slew of self-righteous proclamations amidst a deafening amount of shrieking laughter. "More coffee, darling?" "Who's counting?" Dead on the Fourth of July.

Now the mornings are devoted to the two boys I'm foster parenting: high-pitched screeches of little men eating Fruit Loops while watching Power Ranger videos have replaced our bygone bitch sessions. I rarely get to the *Los Angeles Times* before I've tucked them into bed twelve hours later.

The week before Christmas, my seventy-eight-year-old mother falls and breaks her hip. At the time, she was

a) on her way to a prayer meeting;
b) doing aerobics for seniors;
c) on the parking lot of a bar.

It is not the first time their mother doesn't show up for a scheduled visit, their little boy faces transfiguring into road maps of circuitous sadness, reflecting the curse of abandonment.

The five-year-old reluctantly agrees to talk about it. Actually, he agrees to listen.

"Are you hurt because she didn't show up? Angry? Sad?"

I read and re-read the messages in the Father's Day cards I receive, hoping I can live up to them.

Christmas 1994. Patiently I cut thin strips of colored paper—red, green, pink, blue, yellow—which we glue into circles and entwine, creating a daisy-chain Christmas tree garland. Five-year-old Victor and his younger brother, Tony, assist momentarily—attempting to keep the glue on my fingertips, not theirs—until they are drawn outdoors to something more dramatic.

We purchased a picture-perfect tree this morning, and the smell of it has begun to penetrate the house. I am determined to provide my foster boys with an unforgettable Christmas; it will be the socko finale to the four months we've spent together.

My closets are filled with toys—Power Rangers this and Power Rangers that, Barney this and Barney that, videos and stuffed animals and books and plastic dinosaurs, pogs and more pogs— waiting to be wrapped by "Santa."

I spend most of the day riveted to my task—interrupted by lunch and snack time and the little one's diaper change—as the snake of colored circles outstretches until it's long enough to en- wrap the naked tree.

We trim the tree as a team with the inevitable sibling rivalry played out against tears and a broken ornament or two. But when it's time to switch on the colored lights, their falsetto squeals and the glow of their faces, streaked with an unmistakable melancholy, confirm that we've created a masterpiece.

We begin celebrating on Christmas Eve and continue the marathon for twenty-four adrenaline-pumping hours. A parade of friends visit, each bearing extravagant gifts. Flashbulbs pop, record- ing every ebullient moment. Elaborately garnished cookies are devoured by the dozens.

Even though I've looked forward to this for months—celebrat- ing Christmas with my foster sons, a long pregnant dream come true!—I cannot force myself to be present. I am struck numb. With each gift they open, each expression of elation, I long to feel their wonder, mirror their joy. But I am removed, distanced. It's like watching a play I auditioned for but . . .

I am Santa in a blackout.

(SCATTERING ASHES) My darling Mr. Pickett: These are the ashes I saved, selfishly wanting part of you here with me in Idyll- wild, on the front lawn of the cabin, amidst a hailstorm of jumbo pinecones. It's not enough having your picture—the one with you and the cat—on the fireplace mantel, along with Joe's and David's and Philip's and John's. It's not enough to have your pink televi- sion, situated in the living room, serving as a constant reminder of your tainted queerness. In July we celebrated—is that the right word?—we *commemorated* the first anniversary of your death. In August we celebrated—that *is* the right word—my foster baby's first birthday. I refuse to use the word "bittersweet"—only you would appreciate how much that overworked term, designed to sugarcoat our tragedy, makes me nauseous. Maybe you could come up with a more apropos word. I can't. Bittersweet. Harsh-lovely. Shortly after you died, two damaged little boys moved into your room for four months. After they were returned to the foster care system, Tia arrived. She is a revelation, every day a shimmering revelation. I've enlisted a PC team of friends who participate intimately in her care; I sometimes feel more like the artistic director of a tribe than I do a parent. Yet I've had more success with fatherhood than loverhood. In the heat of it and the hope of it, I plunged—heart first, head last—into yet another love affair that didn't fit. Honey, get this: On our second date, Billy answered the door wearing a generic white terry-cloth bathrobe—exactly the kind my father wore—announcing he had the flu. I was in love: I had a feverish body to soothe, someone who needed me to go into the night and fetch him chicken soup. The poor baby was too sick to reciprocate, I told myself. Perfect symbiosis. Marriage material. These familiar fucking feelings are less and less comfortable—like an old friend you've known for years but you don't want to come for a visit. It's over—after five bittersweet months. Sorry. Five torturous-delicious months. I won't give up; I'm not finished plumbing all the roles: mommy, daddy, husband, wife, brother, lover, blah, blah, blah. Grandma. The very tenor of love has everything to do with its impermanence, no? Letting go, being in the moment, blah, blah, blah: it's the heartfuckingbreaking truth. As long as Tia remains a foster baby, I live with the aggravating uncertainty she may be snatched away—swiftly, viciously: like a predator capturing its prey—next week or next month. "How can you stand it?" people ask. How could I stand it when John was snatched away? How could I stand it when Al was snatched away? How could I stand it when Victor was snatched away? How could I stand it when Joe was snatched away? How could I stand it when David was snatched away? How could I stand it when Richard was snatched away? How could I stand it when Patrick was snatched away? How could I stand it when you were snatched away? How?

How? How? I have this recurring image of you—blazingly real. You're with your grandmother. I know how madly you loved her. It's not a vision; I can't really see the two of you, it's more like I sense it. You're inseparable—like figures melted together in a marble sculpture—protecting each other; you're neither child nor adult; she's neither young nor old. You are both void of pain. You're being loved, completely, by the force you loved most in all the universe, and you're alive, darling—whatever the fuck that means—more alive than I ever saw you.

I don't know Sylvia's last name. I don't know where she lives. I don't know if she's married.

A Latina with her own recipe for glamour, Sylvia works at the local cleaners—like a demon, day in and day out. She's wild about Tia, scolding me when I don't bring her with me, cascading her with kisses when I do.

When I found out Sylvia gave birth to a baby girl, a *bambina*—premature, less than three pounds—I filled a bag with Tia's outgrown baby things and delivered it to the cleaners.

Even though I don't know her last name or where she lives or if she's married, Sylvia is my sister.

According to Christian Coalition chairwoman Sara Hardman, "The Christian perspective is that gay and lesbian behavior is immoral. Children should not be raised in an immoral family. How are unmarried parents living without the benefit of marriage going to teach their children not to be sexually promiscuous? Our country has gotten to a point where morals don't make a difference. Having unmarried couples raising children is a sign of the times we've reached."

The staff at a German zoo decided to place a wayward penguin egg, which had been thrown out by its natural parents, into the enclosure of two male storks who had taken up nesting together, hoping the "childless couple" would adopt the hatchling. The two fathers took turns sitting on the egg for fourteen days until the baby penguin began to break out of its shell; they are now raising the offspring as their own.

Gone are most of my heart and soul brothers—brother-boyfriends, brother-partners, brother-lovers, brother-comrades, brother-sisters. Here in the Idyllwild cabin I call home is my flesh-and-blood brother: Joseph, Joe, Joey. The brother who is six years older. The brother who has known me longer than all the others. The brother who was the first to call me a sissy. The brother who served time in the penitentiary. The brother who shared his heroin with me. The brother who, if he voted, would vote Republican. We're napping: Tia in her crib, my brother in the bedroom, me on the living room couch, all of us being fanned by a toasty August breeze. Need has brought my brother and me together, gnawing need to say out loud that which has gone unspoken; need to corroborate on mangled versions of our childhood, force-fed to us by our mother; need to confront the reality of my ticklish timeline; need to bond—me the fag brother, him the reluctant uncle; need to howl like banshees and laugh like hyenas in the face of all of it. After four days and countless hours of dredging and digging, searching and scouring, pressing and purging, we need to rest. Reeling from the illuminating glare of admission, we are drunk with identification, united in our loss, sibling orphans on the mend. We share each other's demons, wear each other's g-e-n-e-s: the damaged products of the same collision. Yet I am calmer now, mysteriously soothed by remembrances of our historical hysteria. Nothing matters other than breathing. Nothing: not the career, the relationship, the adoption, the death. Nothing exists except the sound of my breath; the sound of Tia's breath, the sound of my brother's breath. Family breathing. No nightmares on this balmy afternoon . . . only life, sweetened by the smell of pinetrees, to inhale. Life.

hello (sex) kitty: mad asian bitch on wheels

DENISE UYEHARA

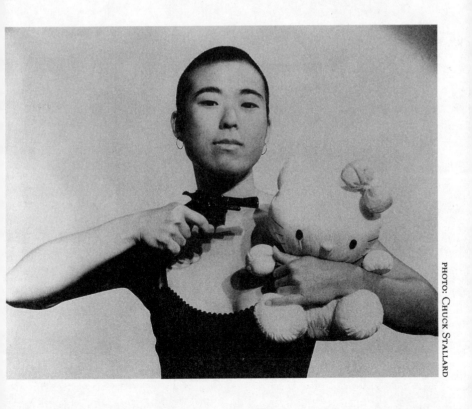

Notes on *Hello (Sex) Kitty*

In 1992 my grandmother committed suicide by lighting herself on fire in her car. In a note she left for us, she said she'd lived a wonderful life, but that now her physical and mental health was getting bad and she wanted to go on to the spiritual world. Her death sent a shock wave through our family. How were we who were left on this earth to make sense of her dramatic transition? At the time I had been in Los Angeles about three years, writing and performing solo pieces, but her death thrust me head-and heart–first into my first solo performance, *Headless Turtleneck Relatives*. The piece is based on oral family histories, my grandmother's *kamaboko* (fish cake), my father singing Sinatra's "My Way" with a karaoke machine, and relatives breaking vinyl records into pieces in memory of the Japanese Americans who destroyed their Japanese books, kimonos, and music records before being interned during World War II. I had to make sense of death, life, and family legacy. To honor my past. To help me move through this world.

About a year after touring *Headless,* I began a second solo work, *Hello (Sex) Kitty: Mad Asian Bitch on Wheels*. While my *Headless* was a piece I *had* to create, *Hello (Sex) Kitty* was a piece I *wanted* to create. I knew it was the right time for me to talk about sex, sexuality, lust, love, all that stuff. If I had written *Hello (Sex) Kitty* as my first solo piece, it probably would have been more difficult to have fun with and less deeply rooted in truth. Creating *Headless* taught me that sometimes the most obvious issue is just the tip of the iceberg. *Headless* turned out to be more about family, childhood dreams, history, and humor than about a fiery death. Similarly, *Hello (Sex) Kitty* turned out to be more about all the things attached to sex—love, self-respect, honoring each other—than about sex itself. It's also about lust, respect, domestic violence, a woman's right to define her own image and access to her passions. It's about being an Asian American, a bisexual woman, and a human being, not necessarily in that order.

When I began work as a solo performer, I also entered into an intense and highly creative process as one of the founding members of the

377

Sacred Naked Nature Girls (Akilah Oliver, Danielle Brazell, Laura Meyers, Bella Hui, and myself). We constantly challenged each other to push the form of what performance was and the intersections of race, culture, sexual orientation, class, and gender. The work we created was raw, exciting, challenging, flawed, and both destructive and supportive to my growth as an artist. I am glad to have taken part in this collective. Our work informed my solo work, and vice versa. I also worked with various multimedia and visual artists, including Teri Osato and Fiona Fell. Then there's my favorite collaboration, in which I washed clothes and hung them out to dry on top of a roof while performance artist María Elena Gaitán played Bach on her cello. The piece was entitled "Laundry/Cello/Rain," which was part of *50 Years Hiroshima* (curated by Barbara Smith and Clayton Campbell at the Eighteenth Street Arts Complex). It took weeks of planning and a lot of help from other artist friends. We performed it only twice on that same day; about eighty people saw it. But for me it marked a change in the way I approach my work. It was an interdisciplinary work, more investigative and a true collaboration. So while I enjoy the solo performance form, I am sure the next work I create will be different from what I've created already. Probably more literary, since this is where my heart takes me, and also possibly more multimedia. Who knows. To me it's whatever form best serves the work.

I've learned so much from performing my work. One of the interesting things about performing solo is it simultaneously empowers and humbles you. I know I'm a fierce and vulnerable woman. On stage I give everything I got to make the performance work. But I also am continuously amazed at the audience's energy and intelligence. They are here to see the work. I challenge them to think, to respond, to laugh, and then to discuss why they laugh. The work opens dialogue. I always try to bring together a mix of queer, Asian/Pacific Islander, women, and people of color communities. During the "comedian routine," in which I parody myself and the public's perception of me, I take a survey—who's in the audience tonight? Break it down, let me hear you holler. Your presence is important. And look around you and see your potential allies. If this performance brought you together to share the same space for an hour, you have that much more shared experience. Build coalitions.

I also learn from post-show discussions. When I performed in Maine recently, this Korean American young man (he was a "1.5 generation" who immigrated to the United States as a child) said he noticed "the only thing Asian" in my show was about a tea ceremony. I told him it was important for him to write about his experience here as a 1.5 generation Korean American and how he sees the world. I told him *Hello (Sex) Kitty* talks about many intersections of who I am. Not all of it is going to offer up obvious Asian phrases, such as "I used to think I was Chinese because that's what we ate after funerals" or "I'm a yellow slave girl and I've been oppressed by that bad American," although, come to think of it, someone could have a field day with those opening lines. I say, write what comes from your heart, not from what the public dictates. I am not interested in performing what someone else—the press, the Asian community, the queer community, my family, my performance art friends—want me to do. I need to create from my own vision. Otherwise I might as well be a TV actor.

I do wish I had asked that guy in the audience some questions for him to chew on. Questions I ask myself from time to time. He wanted to know, "Where is the Asian-ness?" Well, isn't domestic violence an Asian issue? Isn't being bisexual an Asian issue? Isn't understanding how you, your black neighbor, your Latina friend who swing-dances, and that Chinese-Philipina butch dyke poet, are complex creatures—isn't that an Asian issue? It is for me. As an artist. You could substitute the word "queer" or "feminist" for the word "Asian" and push the boundaries again. That is perhaps my greatest challenge as an artist, to push the new boundaries, ones that even I create. That's what artists do. I am at once inside and outside my community. And I will continue to create work, in many shapes and forms, to help me move through this world.

To talk about my work would not be complete without acknowledging the community of renegade performance artists, writers, and actors who have helped me along the way: Highways Performance Space, especially Jordan Peimer and Tim Miller, who have been instrumental in supporting me as an artist; the Eighteenth Street Arts Complex; Chay Yew of the Mark Taper Forum's Asian Theater Workshop; Dom Magwilli and Saachiko; Jude Narita, Amy Hill, and Dan Kwong, who shared with me the ropes of touring and presenting my work to the public. My education has been mostly from watching others—John Fleck, Elia Arce, Guillermo Gomez-Peña, Luis Alfaro, Han Ong, Rika Ohara, Hirokazu Kosaka, Marcus Kuiland-Nazario—they have all influenced my work. Coco Fusco, Akilah Oliver, Danielle Brazell, Laura Meyers, Elsa E'der, Veronica Ko, Jeff Matsuda, and Derek Nguyen challenged me to push the form, be honest with myself, create language, and articulate my process. My family, especially my parents, encouraged me to constantly learn. Thanks to my technical directors/stage managers Heather Basarab, Jerry Browning, and Anne Etue. Finally, I thank those who have encouraged me to publish—Michael Kearns, Brian Nelson, Naomi Hirahara, Sesshu Foster, Ellen Krout-Hasegawa, and, of course, David Román and Holly Hughes.

Note on Performance

Hello (Sex) Kitty is performed as a series of vignettes or "scenes." The Woman (the performer) plays herself, different characters, and the narrator. In between scenes she changes clothes at a rolling wardrobe rack in the background. Some scenes are simply spoken as in performance poetry. Others are clearly performed. The performance runs seventy minutes and is frequently followed by a post-show discussion.

About Denise Uyehara

Denise Uyehara is a writer, performance artist, and playwright and a proud one-fourth of the Sacred Naked Nature Girls. Her solo works have been presented across the United States and internationally, including at the Institute of Contemporary Art in London; Women in View Festival, Vancouver, B.C.; Fourth World Conference on Women, Hairou, China; the Walker Arts Center, Minneapolis; Highways Performance Space, Santa Monica; the Painted Bride, Philadelphia; the Cleveland Performance Art Festival (featured); the Asian American Theater Company, San Francisco; the Northwest Asian American Theater, Seattle; and numerous colleges. She also has collaborated with visual artists and artists from the Nautilus Project through A.S.K., Robbie McCauley's the Other Weapon, and Augusto Boal's Theater of the Oppressed workshop. Her play Hiro, winner of the AT&T: On Stage Award for production at East West Players, appears in Asian American Drama: Nine Plays from the Multiethnic Landscape, *edited by Brian Nelson (Applause Theater Books). Her writing appears in the* Asian Pacific American Journal, Parabasis, *and Michael Kearns's* Getting Your Solo Act Together *(Heinemann).*

Currently she is working on a commission from the Mark Taper Forum's Asian Theatre Workshop. She co-teaches performance/writing workshops at Highways for various communities with Yutian Wong and Danielle Brazell. She is recipient of numerous recognitions of excellence, including a New Langton Arts/National Endowment for the Arts grant (with Teri Osato to conduct "Kissing: Asian Public Affection"): the City of Los Angeles Cultural Affairs Department to conduct an oral history project with senior citizens; the Brody Arts Fund; the James Irvine Fellowship; and the James Clavell American Japanese Literary Award. Uychara holds a B.A. cum laude degree in comparative literature from University of California, Irvine, where she also studied fiction, playwriting and theater. The Los Angeles Times *calls her "Compelling . . . Uychara is definitely one to watch." She was featured as "One of the Hundred Coolest People in L.A." by* Buzz Magazine *in 1995, and as "Best Performance Artist" by* Entertainment Weekly. *She is a member of the California Arts Council Touring Roster.*

hello (sex) kitty: mad asian bitch on wheels

DENISE UYEHARA

Prologue: Mirror

(AN ASIAN WOMAN, DRESSED IN A BLUE TANK TOP, JEANS, AND BOOTS, STANDS CENTER STAGE IN A RECTANGULAR LIGHT. SHE FACES THE AUDIENCE AS SHE LOOKS INTO THIS INVISIBLE MIRROR AS IF IN A PRIVATE MOMENT IN HER BEDROOM. SHE BRUSHES HER HAIR BACK WITH HER HANDS, GENTLY TOUCHES HER EYEBROWS, CHEEKS, MOUTH, THEN EXAMINES HER PROFILE, CHECKS TO SEE IF HER STOMACH STICKS OUT, CHECKS HER BREASTS, HER ASS. THEN SHE FOCUSES ON HER FACE AND SLOWLY BECOMES DISGUSTED. REACHING OUT TOWARD THE MIRROR, SHE SCRATCHES AT HER OWN IMAGE, SLOWLY AT FIRST, AND THEN TURNS BOTH HER HANDS ON HER ACTUAL FACE AND BODY AND FURIOUSLY TEARS AT THE FLESH. SHE STOPS, AGAIN LOOKS AT HER IMAGE, SIGHS. LIGHTS FADE.)

Scene I: Comedian

(IN DARKNESS AN UPPER-CRUST FEMALE VOICE TALKS ON A TELEPHONE.)

VOICE

Hello. I'm calling from the Flaming Women Performance Art Festival in Waterbury. This message is for . . . well, I don't have that in front of me right this second, but you know. We saw your tape, and we loved it, but we just can't seem to fit you into our festival this year, but I'm sure we could next year. Your work just doesn't seem to . . . fit.

But we were wondering—because we do have one spot open in our festival—and you being tapped into the pulse of Asian American artists—now I don't mean to pigeonhole people, and we certainly don't mean to lump all of our minority quotas into one person, you know, like that young golfer, but do you . . . do you by any chance know any Asian lesbian stand-up comedians?

(NIGHTCLUB MUSIC FLOURISH. GROOVY LIGHTS DANCE IN REDS, MAGENTAS, AND BLUES ACROSS THE STAGE. A FOLLOW SPOT SEARCHES THE STAGE IN A BALLYHOO FIGURE EIGHT.)

MALE VOICE OF A NIGHTCLUB ANNOUNCER

And now, ladies and gentlemen, straight from Los Angeles, California, it's the world's first Asian lesbian stand-up comedian— DykeAsia!

(DYKEASIA ENTERS IN A SLICK NIGHTCLUB SPORT COAT, JEANS, T-SHIRT, AND SUNGLASSES. SHE HOLDS A MICRO- PHONE. CANNED APPLAUSE ROARS, MUSIC FADES.)

DYKEASIA

Good evening, everyone, and welcome to the ———(NAME OF THEATER) comedy club! My name is DykeAsia, and yes, I am the world's first Asian lesbian stand-up comedian. And have we got a show in store for you. We have a woman coming up next— I am so honored to open for her—she's a personal friend of mine, her name is Denise . . . (FORGETS LAST NAME, SEARCHES FOR PAPER IN POCKET, THEN PRONOUNCES INCORRECTLY) Oo-yeh-hah-rah (LOOKING OFF STAGE) didn't think I could pronounce that, did you?

Okay, catch you later. (TO AUDIENCE) And she'll be performing her solo show, *Hello (Sex) Kitty: Mad Asian Bitch on Wheels*. But more on the bitch in a moment, first a little bit about myself: I recently became an Asian lesbian stand-up comedian so that I could be in all the festivals and win all the grants possible. In fact, this is my debut as a comedian and we're taping this show for a grant, so if you can just do me a little favor and, even if it's not really that funny, could you all cheer and applaud and laugh? Let's try that right now . . . (ROUSES AUDIENCE TO APPLAUD) Good!

So let me take a little survey. . . . Any Asians in the house tonight? (ENCOURAGES AUDIENCE APPLAUSE AND CHEERS) All right, you're all sitting on the left side of the brain. Any Latinos/Chicanos? (APPLAUSE) *Viva la Raza!* Any African Americans/black people? (APPLAUSE) Black Power, brothers and sistahs! Any Native Americans? (A FEW APPLAUD) That's a political statement right there. Any people from working-class backgrounds? (APPLAUSE) Any queer people: gay/lesbian/bi's/transgendered people? (APPLAUSE) Good. I'm glad I'm not alone up here. Any European Americans? (PAUSE WHILE PEOPLE DECIDE WHAT THIS MEANS) White people! (APPLAUSE) I'm glad you could admit that. That's the first step to recovery. Now, I'm gonna make a little sidetrack here, and I say this especially for the white folks in the audience. Ms. Uyehara can be rather hard-hitting. She doesn't pull her punches. But when you think she's talking about you, she's not talking about you. So don't take it personally. She's talking about the System. The System. The White Elite Right Patriarchal System—TWERPS. Now if you are a servant of TWERPS, then she's talking about you. But most of you can sit back and relax and enjoy the show, and then afterwards all the people of color are gonna beat the shit out of you. But at least you'll have a clear conscience.

Now speaking of people of color—isn't it simple, yet complex at the same time? Because on the one hand your advancement could help your community, but on the other, you could be tokenized. Doesn't it just seem everyone wants you for their pur-

poses? The secret is you need to know what *you* want *you* for. So I
sat myself down at the kitchen table one day and I asked myself:
"Dyke Asia, what is it *you* want *you* for?" And I thought deep into
my soul and I decided I wanted to be the world's first Asian lesbian stand-up comedian. Because I am. I made it. Yes, on my own.
With a little help. But what's all this fuss about Affirmative Action being axed? Do I care? *Fuck* Affirmative Action, cuz I got
mine! Let's break it down, shall we? Asian lesbian stand-up comedian. Now the first part: Asian (POINTS TO HAIR), Asian (POINTS
TO SKIN), Asian (LOWERS SUNGLASSES TO REVEAL EYES) Asian. The
second part: lesbian. Now, this morning, I was bisexual, but
tonight, I'm a lesbian! And third: comedian. Yes. I am funny. Extremely. In fact, some of you may recall my last solo show, *Headless
Turtleneck Relatives*, it was the tale of my grandmother's suicide
by fire, which I talked about in a very humorous way! (LONG PAUSE
IN AWKWARD SILENCE) Well, parts of it were funny. I thought it
was funny. Anyway, I, uh, well, maybe I'm not really a comedian.
Maybe I'm not really a lesbian. But I am Asian. Uh . . . are there
any *real* Asian lesbian stand-up comedians in the house? (STEPS
OUT OF THE SPOTLIGHT AND LEANS BACK IN) If so, could you just
come on down, step into the spotlight? Because I'm not and—is
there anyone? Even if you are a square peg, we could make you fit
in this round light—is there anyone? (BEGINS TO BACK OFF STAGE)
Because making you round is as easy as laughter. (BEGINS LAUGH-
ING, FIRST QUIETLY, THEN INCREASING IN INTENSITY AS IF SOME-
THING IS VERY FUNNY)

(SPOTLIGHT STAYS ON, LIGHTING CENTER STAGE. SPOT
SLOWLY SHRINKS SMALLER AND SMALLER AND THEN OFF.)

Scene II: Vegetable Girl/Kabuki Woman

(FLOOR LIGHT FILLS EMPTY STAGE. AFTER A PAUSE, A SINGLE
ORANGE ROLLS OUT. THE OFFSTAGE VOICE OF THE VEG-
ETABLE GIRL BEGINS TO SING WITH AN EERIE SWEETNESS OF
A LITTLE CHILD.)

VEGETABLE GIRL

(SINGING.)

La, la, la, la, la, la . . .

(AT EACH PAUSE IN THE SONG, MORE ORANGES, POTATOES, BELL PEPPERS, AND TOMATOES ROLL OUT TO FILL THE STAGE WITH VARIOUS COLORS AND SIZES. LAST THREE ITEMS TO ROLL OUT ARE A CUCUMBER, EGGPLANT, AND LARGE DAI-KON—A VERY PHALLIC WHITE RADISH.)

La, la, la, la, la, la, la . . .

(THE VEGETABLE GIRL ENTERS, CLUTCHING HER HELLO KITTY. SHE HAS CUTE LONG BLACK HAIR—A WIG—TIED WITH A BIG PINK BOW. LIGHTS TO FULL.)

VEGETABLE GIRL

This is my Hello Kitty. (TO KITTY) Say hello—

KITTY

(IN HIGH, CUTE VOICE.)

Hello!

GIRL

Say good-bye—

KITTY

Good-bye!

GIRL

Say *oyasumi nasai*—

KITTY

Oyasumi nasai!

GIRL

That means good night and sweet dreams in Japanese. (BEAT) I have a Hello Kitty handbag. And I have a Hello Kitty lunch box, and I have a Hello Kitty pencil and a Hello Kitty pen and a Hello Kitty eraser that smells like bubblegum. And I have a Hello Kitty. And I love my Hello Kitty even though I'm majoring in nuclear physics at UCLA. And recently I fell in love. I met this guy. He's really sweet. He's the professor's assistant in my physics class. He said he likes me because I'm Japanese. (GIGGLES, COVERS MOUTH, TURNS AWAY SLIGHTLY) And we went out on a date, but I left my Hello Kitty at home. (LEAVES KITTY ON FLOOR, GATHERS A FEW VEGETABLES FOR KITTY, ENDS UP PUTTING TWO ORANGES IN FRONT OF THE KITTY WITH A LONG CUCUMBER BETWEEN THEM, IN A PHALLIC SHAPE) I went to his place and he made us dinner. He made Japanese food. He can really cook; it was delicious. And he said he's studying Zen Buddhism so I can trust him. And then afterwards we had . . . a tea ceremony. (KNEELING) And he had a clay teapot and teacups and that green foamy tea and the wooden whisk . . . And he just happened to have this kimono, so I put it on. And then we had a tea ceremony. (BEAT) And he took Polaroid pictures of me, pouring tea for him, like this. (POURS) It was quite serene, really, he said he wanted to capture that serene ritual. And when I saw the Polaroids of me I thought: Wow, I look really Japanese. I mean, I look like one of those Japanese women from those movies. It was like looking at someone else. (PAUSE.)

You know, when I was little, my mom took me to downtown Los Angeles, to Little Tokyo, and we saw a *real* tea ceremony. Actually, I was too young and I had to wait in the other room. (PICKS UP KITTY, SITS CROSS-LEGGED ON FLOOR) So I sat there and waited, and waited and waited and waited. And all I could see was this white screen on this white wall. And the sun was shining through a little peephole from somewhere and it made a perfect circle of light on the screen. And when I think of a tea ceremony, *that's* what I remember.

(SMALL SPOT OF WHITE LIGHT RISES AND SHINES ON HER FACE. SHE LOOKS INTO IT.)

Not the teapots and the kimono . . . but the sunlight. (PAUSE . . . LIGHT FOCUSES ON HER FACE) A small circle of white light, shining on a white screen against a white wall.

388 Hello (Sex) Kitty: Mad Asian Bitch on Wheels

(SHE LOOKS AT LIGHT FOR A WHILE, THEN SLOWLY PULLS
RIBBON OUT OF HAIR, TURNS WIG AROUND SO THAT IT IS
TOUSLED AND MATTED. LIGHTS CROSS-FADE TO SHADOWY
REDS AND BLUES. SHE BECOMES THE MAD KABUKI WOMAN.)

MAD KABUKI WOMAN

Oh yeah, right, oh yeah right, I'm sure he really liked you, I'm
sure he really liked you, Girlfriend! (BEGINS KICKING VEGETABLES
OFF STAGE WHILE SHE RANTS) So you wanted to go out on a date
with this white guy—did you act like a little geisha? Did you act
like a little China doll? What are these things? (KICKS EGGPLANT
OFFSTAGE, IT HITS SOMEONE) Oh. (WITHOUT APOLOGY) Sorry! (TO
AUDIENCE) Don't you get it? He just wants some *yellow* pussy. He
just wants to (STOMPS ON TOMATO) penetrate and slide right in.
(STOPS, LOOKS UP AT AUDIENCE) And I would squish more vegetables,
but this is a nice theater, so (FIST AND ARM GESTURE) *Fuck you!*

(SHE SEES HELLO KITTY, SUDDENLY BECOMES SWEET. PICKS
UP KITTY AND HUGS WITH SMOTHERING LOVE.)

OHHH! Hello Kitty! Hello Kitty! Hello, Hello Kitty. (BEAT)
You don't want to stay here with this geisha girl, do you? (KITTY
LOOKS AT HER AND DEMURS) You want to come with me, right?
(KITTY TURNS HEAD AWAY SLOWLY, KABUKI FORCES KITTY'S HEAD
TO NOD) Oh yes, I knew it, I love you—(KISSES KITTY, SUDDENLY
DROPS IT, THEN ROUGHLY) and where is that white man?!!
(SEARCHES AUDIENCE) Where is he?

(WHITE FOLLOW SPOT SEARCHES AUDIENCE, FINDS A WHITE
MAN, FOCUSES ON HIM.)

Aha! (PEERS CLOSER) Nah, you're not white enough.

(SPOTLIGHT OUT.)

He's not here, is he? Well, when he gets back you just tell him
the Kabuki woman was here. And she's pissed. And he can go suck
his white patronizing dick! (SNAPS FINGERS ABOVE HEAD.)

(BLACKOUT.)

Scene III: She Said

(IN DARKNESS WOMAN SPEAKS QUIETLY.)

WOMAN

She said she said she said—

(LIGHTS RISE. SHE STANDS IN LIGHT, "PUSHING HANDS"—
AS ONE HAND DELICATELY REACHES OUT, THE OTHER HAND
REACHES TOWARD HER BODY, THEN ALTERNATES. THIS
MOTION REPEATS THROUGHOUT THE MONOLOGUE.)

WOMAN

She said would you like some more salad? . . .
and I said sure
and she said would you like a glass of water?
and I said sure
and she said you know when I dream about myself
I see everything as if I'm in a French film (HANDS FRAME INVISIBLE
   FILM CELL)
and I see people and they come in and they talk to me
then they go away
then they come back in and we drink a cup of coffee
then they go away
then they come back in and we talk some more
I see everything as if I'm in a French film

And I said, Now that's funny.
When I dream about myself I see everything through my
eyes, through my point of view
and I see people and they come in and they talk to me
then they go away
then they come back in and we drink a cup of coffee
then they go away
then they come back in and we talk some more—
I see everything through my eyes, my POV—

I guess that means I'm kind of selfish, huh?
And she said would you like some more salad?
and I said, sure
and she said would you like a glass of wine?
and I said sure
and she said would you like to stay over?
and I said . . . sure.
And I said, do you want me to sleep on the bed or on the couch or in the
bathtub or on the floor?
and she said I want you to sleep with me.
And I said, light some candles
and she said like this?
and I said, uh-huh.
and she said like this?
and I said, uh-huh.
and I said like this?
and she said uh-huh,
and she said like this and I said uh-huh
and she said uh-huh and I said uh-huh and she said uh-huh . . .

And all night I dreamed I saw myself
(HANDS FRAME INVISIBLE FILM CELL) *as if I were in a French film.*
And I was sitting in a room on the floor
and I was drawing with red Crayolas
but something kept washing the colors away
I kept drawing but something kept washing the colors away
and a woman came in from the next room and she said are you okay?
and I said yeah, sure
and she said are you sure?
and I said sure I'm sure.
but looking at myself for the first time (HANDS FRAME INVISIBLE FILM
     CELL) *I realized I wasn't so sure*
and she said, I was just in the next room and I heard a noise and I
thought you might like some company. Cuz no one's gonna hurt my
girl. And you're my baby girl.

And in the morning I woke up
and she said uh-huh
I said uh-huh
she said uh-huh
I said uh-huh
she said uh-huh
I said
last night I dreamed I saw myself,
and she looked a lot like you.

(LIGHTS FADE SLOWLY ON THIS LINE AS SHE REACHES OUT
WITH ONE HAND TO TOUCH SOMEONE.)

Scene IV: The Asian Guy

(WOMAN'S VOICE ON TAPE PLAYS IN DARKNESS AS WOMAN
CHANGES INTO THE ASIAN GUY'S CLOTHING.)

WOMAN'S VOICE

(ON TAPE WITH SEXY SLOW GROOVE PLAYING.)

. . . and he needs to be strong, supportive, and he likes nature, a
good dancer, knows how to lead, takes my lead, at times, half
the time, and likes sex, likes S&M, sometimes he likes to domi-
nate in bed—only when I let him, and he doesn't want to give it
to me up the ass . . . unless I get to do it to him too, with something the same size, yeah . . . and he doesn't want to sleep with
the women that I want to sleep with, and he let's me help him,
let's me call him on his shit, calls me on my shit, in a decent
way, and he doesn't drink or smoke but knows how to in appropriate situations, and doesn't carry a gun, but knows how to shoot
in appropriate situations, and he isn't into cutesy girls, and he's
not a super JAP, and he's not a macho dickhead frat boy and
doesn't want to be one . . .

(MUSIC AND VOICE FADE AS LIGHTS RISE ON AN ASIAN GUY SITTING CENTER STAGE IN A CHAIR. HE WEARS JEANS, BUTTON-DOWN WORKSHIRT, AND BASEBALL CAP ON BACKWARD.)

ASIAN GUY

(TO AUDIENCE.)

Okay, just between us guys: Asian women can be so intense. Like the other day I went out with this Asian chick. I met her at this party. Got her number. She's cool. She's cute. So I call her up and we decide to go see a movie. So I pick her up, and the *first* thing she says when she gets in the car is:

(ASIAN GUY BECOMES THE ASIAN CHICK.)

ASIAN CHICK

(TURNING TO HER LEFT TO TALK TO THE GUY IN THE DRIVER'S SEAT.)

You know, you're the first Asian guy I've *ever* been attracted to.

GUY

(TO AUDIENCE.)

Now, you can take this two ways. Either I'm a total Asian stud (CONSIDERS THIS, SMILES AT THE THOUGHT) or I'm in a lot of trouble. But I'm a positive type of guy, so we go on to see the movie, which shall remain nameless, let's just call it *The Joy Fucked-up Club*. I mean, the movie was okay. She's crying, the woman next to her is crying, and I'm cry—(CATCHES HIMSELF)—kind of choked up myself. But by about the fourth story in this film, when all the stories start to sound the same, I realize there are no positive roles for Asian men in this film. None whatsoever. Think about it. The only Asian men in this film are either beating the shit out of their wives or treating their girlfriends like shit. So on the way home, I ask her what she thought of the film. She says:

CHICK

Oh, I really like it, all those Asian people on the big screen—
France Nuyen, Rosalind Chao, Lauren Tom, Tamlyn Tomita—
all those juicy parts for Asians—

GUY

Yeah, but don't you think the parts for Asian men were kind
of, I don't know, *crappy*? (TO AUDIENCE) And then, she just blew
up! I didn't say anything, and she's going (MAKES HIS HAND INTO
THE SHAPE OF A TALKING PARROT'S BEAK) "Nya, nya, nya—support the community, nya, nya, nya support the community—"

CHICK

(CONTINUING, BUT IN HER OWN SOLID VOICE.)

—don't you know how to support the community? You know what?
You're just dissing this film because you're jealous.

GUY

And, I'm thinking, What did I do wrong? Man, somebody give
me some Cliff Notes, or somethin'. (TO WOMAN) Well, seems to
me Asian women have an easier time in Hollywood. I mean, look
at what a success this film is—

CHICK

Yeah? Well, what about *The Dragon?* I didn't rain on your
parade when Bruce Lee gets to boink some mysterious Chinese
woman in a slinky Chinky outfit in the back room and then run
off with some white bitch.

GUY

That's cuz he really did marry a white bitch—I mean, woman.
Don't confuse me. Besides, most of the time Asian men don't have
it as easy in Hollywood—

CHICK

Well, don't blame Amy Tan for all your problems. Don't you
get it, it's bigger than that, it's the big picture, it's the System, it's

Hollywood, and who is the real enemy? Ask yourself that. *Who is the enemy?* (POINTING FINGER IN THE AIR) *Who is the enemy?* (SLOWLY TURNS FINGER TOWARD HIM) *Who is the enemy? Who is the enemy? Who is the enemy?*

GUY

And I stop the car in front of her place and say (TO WOMAN) "Well, *I* am not the enemy! *I am not the enemy!* (LONG PAUSE, THEN TO AUDIENCE) So I figure she's not about to ask me up to her place. But you know. I just had to say my piece. Shit. I wish we could have talked longer. But I can't talk when she's . . . (MAKING PARROT BEAK) talking. (BEAT) Besides, she looks kinda sexy when she's angry. (BEAT) Nah. She looks *angry* when she's angry. So she got outta the car, went up to her place; I haven't seen her since. Shit.

Oh, but speaking of relationships. I just saw the most outstanding Asian American play last week. Yeah. There was this great role for an Asian American man, and the play was called *I Can't Get a Date*. All about how Asian women would rather date (SPEAKING LOUDLY, AS IF SHE COULD HEAR HIM) *outside their race than give us the time of day.* I mean, let's look at the real issue here. If our women would just give us some respect— Oh, but I can just hear her voice in my head going (MAKES PARROT BEAK) "Nya, nya, nya, nya, nya—"

CHICK

—*your* women? Excuse me. Keep up on current events. We're our own women. And incidentally, some Asian women *do* date Asian men. Hell, I dated you. Once. And if you keep talking like that, I don't know what Asian woman's gonna go out with you anyway. And that play? I saw that wonderful play and you know what? There were no positive roles for Asian women in that play. None whatsoever. Except one woman who was clueless and dimensionless and talked like a parrot. So that play? That play was great at the expense of *your* Asian women, so what do you think about *that*, cowboy?

GUY

Cowboy? Hey, what are you doing in my head?

CHICK

Maybe I wanna discuss this with you more.

GUY

(TO AUDIENCE.)

So she's got me thinkin'. Shit, maybe I should call her. (TO HIMSELF) What would I say? (PRACTICING) Hi. (LOWERING VOICE) Hi. (SEXY VOICE) Hi. Hey how's it going? (BEAT) Hey, baby, you were on fire the other night. (SCOWLS. BEAT. STANDS. SIGHS. THEN LOOKS OUT) Hi, it's me. You wanna talk?

(BLACKOUT.)

Scene V: Best Friend

(LIGHTS RISE ON WOMAN, CENTER STAGE.)

WOMAN

My best friend is an Asian man
He has the warmth and innocence of a child,
but he is a man
of some experience
in the middle of a friendship
in the middle of the night
we go dancing to the down-and-dirty blues
first like two kids in junior high
then we end up dancing closer,
I feel the heat from his chest, torso, his sex,
I am burning at my center of gravity
he says, "I don't think we're just friends anymore."
in the bedroom we make love

the bed swells with our movements
the bedsheets are angels touching our skin
he touches me with a man's touch
it is a touch of some experience
We become familiar, as lovers do,
so we have a deeper understanding
when he says "I need to be alone"
I let him be
when I say "I need to see the world"
he lets me be
we have learned from some experience
My best friend is an Asian man
And one day we make a vow as deep as our blood
cut from our fingers

(PUT THUMBS TOGETHER, AS IN BLOOD VOW, WHENEVER
FOLLOWING LINE IS SPOKEN.)

*"Hey. No matter what happens, I will remember you for the rest of my
life."*

(SHE STEPS STAGE RIGHT AS LIGHTS CHANGE ICY.)

Once there was another lover
And this lover and I
we had became familiar
but there was no deeper understanding.
We stood on a cliff,
in our anger and frustration
and our anger grew.
I did not see the signs
he had felt the fists of his father upon him
and now he was a child in a man's body
a child who could not get his candy
a child who could smile, and beguile and obsess.
A child in a man's body
is a dangerous child.
We are in the bedroom

it is night
it is dark
we are naked
we are making love—
having sex—
we are losing each other
we can feel it in the air dark between us
he knows he is losing me
he knows he is losing me
he knows he is losing me
he pins me to the bed
he says (AS IF FORCING SOMEONE DOWN) *don't tell me about leaving*
his body says: (THRUST ON EACH LINE)
you are mine
you are mine
you are mine
you are mine
I think: (ARMS UP, AS IF PINNED DOWN) *this is not role playing, this*
    is real, this is serious
his body says: (THRUSTS)
you are mine
you are mine
you are mine
you are mine
I say: stop, or I'm gonna make a scene
and his body says:
No you are mine
you are mine
you are mine
you are mine
a fist comes out one-two-three (SHE HITS PALM OF HER HAND
    THREE TIMES)
slap/slap/slap (FEELS IMPACT OF SLAPS)

    (SHE TURNS STAGE RIGHT AND FREEZES, HAND NEAR HER
    FACE.)

and I see bright lights flashing over and over in my head
and I feel like I've been here before
but I haven't been here before
and I never thought it would be between me and my own kind
I pick up the first thing I can find, it is his camera (GRABS INVISIBLE
    CAMERA) *and I'm going to smash it*
into his face

My body says: You wanna fuck with me? You wanna fuck with me?
Cuz no one tells me where I walk, who I can date, who I sleep with,
you wanna fuck with me? You may be bigger than me *but I will
take you down all the way and I will kill you!*

    (BEAT. DROPS CAMERA.)

I don't need this
I don't need this
you have felt the fists of your father upon him
and I will not fuel this fire that I did not even begin
I don't need this
It's not worth it
You are not worth the trouble

    (TURNS SLOWLY IN CIRCLE, KEEPING EYE ON HIM UNTIL HER
    BODY IS FACING UPSTAGE, THEN CONTINUES WITH BACK TO
    AUDIENCE.)

I think I am an intelligent woman
I know I am an intelligent woman
but he says (REACHING HAND OUT)
please come back I promise I won't hit you again
and two months later, I go back
but the next time it happens (HAND TURNS TO FIST)
I leave for good (HAND BRUSHES IT ALL AWAY)

    (SHARP WHISPERING, AS SHE TURNS BACK TO AUDIENCE.)

Don't talk about it
don't talk about it
he says I'm hotheaded, he says I made him do it

he says maybe I started it—
yeah, maybe I started—
I just want to know who threw the first act of violence—
(FULL VOICE) *the women say be careful*
some of the men say: shit happens. Now little girl, you don't know the
ways of the world, you don't know what violence is, now (RUNNING
FINGER UP ARM) *you see this scar?*
The community says, there is no violence in our house.
So what's it going to be? are you going to be a feminist or a person of
color?

But what if I am a woman?

(SHE RETURNS CENTER STAGE.)

My best friend is an Asian man
I say, "hold me, please hold me" (EMBRACES SELF)
Everybody thinks I'm so strong, but sometimes it's good to walk with
another. Will you hold me? Will you touch with a man's touch? (TOUCH
HIS FACE WITH ONE HAND AND HER OWN WITH THE OTHER)
Is it an equal touch?
He says, "Shhh . . . Hey. No matter what happens, I will remember
   you for
the rest of my life."

My best friend is an Asian man.
He too has felt the fists of his father upon him.
Sometimes as friends go, we argue.
One time we argue and it goes like this:
I say it's this way,
he says no it's not,
I say yes it is,
he says no it's not,
I say yes it is,
he says no it's not—look, you don't know how angry I am, you don't
know how much you've hurt me, you don't know how angry I am—
(WOMAN PUTS HANDS UP TO SHIELD HERSELF)
and I think he's gonna hit me.

But he says look, I'm really pissed off, I can't talk right now. I'm gonna leave and I'll call you later.

And he leaves.
And the next day he doesn't call.
The next day, he doesn't call.
And the next day, he calls.
And the next time we talk.
And we embrace.

He has never touched me like this (FIST TO HER FACE), *only like this*
    (CARESS TO HER FACE)
I have never touched him like this (FIST), *only like this* (CARESS)
we touch with some experience

An Asian man can be a best friend, your lover, your closest ally
or a great danger to himself and you.
It's because we are of the same house (HANDS OUT, PALMS UP).
We are so familiar, we have to go to a deeper understanding
It's because the touch (CARESS) *and the touch* (FIST) *and the touch*
    (CARESS)
begins at home (HANDS OUT).

My best friend is an Asian man:
One day, we make our vows deep as our blood cut from our fingers:

"Hey. No matter what happens, I will remember you for the rest of my life."

    (LIGHTS FADE ON LAST LINES.)

Scene VI: The Vanishing Point

(MELISSA ETHRIDGE MUSIC: "I'M THE ONLY ONE," AT FULL VOLUME.)

(FACING UPSTAGE, IN BLUE ROCK CONCERT BACKLIGHT, THE WOMAN PLAYS AIR GUITAR, TO THE MUSIC. SHE NOTICES

PEOPLE ARE WATCHING, TURNS AROUND, COMES DOWN-
STAGE. MUSIC FADES.)

WOMAN

I didn't see you there. I mean, I can't really play the guitar. I
mean, I couldn't get up in front of thousands of people and sing
about my love life, talk about my passion.

Not that I don't appreciate art. Cuz the best class I ever took
back in college was called Intro to Art. It was great. Partly cuz the
teacher. Cuz the teacher . . . whew . . . looking back on it, she was
a big ol' dyke. But at the time I wasn't really out, even to myself,
so I just thought she had really cool clothes. I remember on the
first day of class we all sat down and she put a big paper on an easel
and drew a horizontal line on it and she says:

"Class, what's this?"

And then she pointed to me, so I said, "It's a line?"

She says, "Yes, but it's more than just a line. This is the horizon line."

Then she drew a point on the line. And she says, "Now, what's
this?"

And I said, "It's a point?"

"Yes, but it's more than just a point . . . this is the vanishing
point. Now the vanishing point is a point on the horizon line
where two parallel lines meet (POINTS BOTH INDEX FINGERS OUT
AS IF THEY ARE LINES), way off in the distance (SHE BRINGS FIN-
GERS TOGETHER LIKE LINES MERGING UNTIL THEY MEET ON THE
WORDS:) *Blam, blam, blam, blam, blam, blam, blam, blam, blam,
blam, blam, blam, zhoom.* Now this may seem contradictory, since
we are told parallel lines never meet, but go for infinity, without
ever touching. But I will tell you, in real life, if you stand on a
railroad track, you'll notice the tracks eventually merge together,
way off in the distance, and where they meet, that is their vanishing point."

So I'm listening and I'm listening and I'm thinkin' what a cool
T-shirt she has on. I wonder what it's like to shop with her. So it
takes me a few more sessions to realize that what she's trying to
tell us is that we should draw all of our parallel lines, you know,

sides of roads, railroad tracks, sides of buildings, so that they eventually meet at the vanishing point.

Blam, blam, blam, blam, blam, blam, blam, blam, blam, blam, blam, blam, zhoom.

So I told you about art so I could talk about sex. Cuz I used to go to bars, try to meet people there. Once, I went to this bar with my friend, maybe some of you know her, she's the Mad Kabuki Woman. Anyway, this bar is a drag. I mean, not like a *drag* drag. But a drag. And my friend said it's because there's not enough diversity there. But I contest that. For one thing there were all sorts of cultures in there, and all sorts of genders, too—dykes, gay boys, bis, even straight folks. I think it was boring because everyone's standin' around like this. (STRIKES AN ALOOF ARTY BAR POSE AND THEN ANOTHER) Like how you ever gonna get laid doing that?

I think what's really going on is everyone's secretly trying to reach orgasm. Especially the women, cuz you could do that secret contraction thing. (LOOKS INTO AUDIENCE, POINTS OUT A WOMAN) See, she's smiling because she knows how. I had a friend she was so good at it, she could come waiting for the ATM. I mean, I could be doing it right now and you wouldn't know. (LONG PAUSE AS SHE CONTRACTS, THEN, CLEARING MIND) So anyway, I think these people in the bar are just secretly trying to reach orgasm. And if they're really lucky, they'll meet their parallel line and then maybe they'll go home together and they'll make love and it will be—

Blam, blam, blam, blam, blam, blam, blam, blam, blam, blam, blam, blam, zhoom. (THIS TIME WHEN THE FINGERS MERGE, SHE HOLDS RIGHT HAND UP AS IF HOLDING ON TO THE POINT IN THE AIR) And at that point when you look at the other person's eyes it's as if all the layers have peeled away and it's like you're looking at each other for the first time. And yeah, sure your gender or color is important, but at that moment, it's about something else, it's about being zero distance apart. Once I made love with this woman and we watched each other the entire time. (BEAT) Okay, so some of you may be wondering how do two women reach orgasm while they look into each other's eyes at the same time. Well, go find

out for yourself. All I know is, there's nothing like helping someone to reach that point (HOLDS POINT IN THE AIR AGAIN). Cuz when
you break through to the other side, you wake up and you find
you're lying there in bed together. But this isn't just *any* bed. This
bed's in the middle of a big field, spring grass swaying all around,
and it's sunny and blue, or maybe it's rainy with a faint arc of a
rainbow—hey, it's your orgasm. But I guarantee you whatever it
is, for one moment, it's absolutely quiet. (SILENCE) So when I talk
about my passion, *that's* where I wanna go. The vanishing point.
Cuz, like my teacher says, it's more than just a point. (LONG PAUSE,
AS IF WAITING. THEN SILENTLY CONTRACTING. SMILES)

Yeah, *Blam, blam, blam, blam, blam, blam, blam, blam, blam
blam blam zhoom.*

(LIGHTS FADE ON LAST LINES.)

Scene VII: Papers/The Wings
of a Thousand Swallows Song

(BLUE LIGHT FROM SIDE FALLS ON WOMAN AS SHE READS
NAMES * WRITTEN ON CHINESE "JOSS" PAPERS, THIN SQUARES
OF PAPER BURNED FOR THE DEAD. AFTER READING THE NAME
ON EACH PAPER, SHE LETS IT FALL FROM HER HANDS, WATCH-
ING IT FLUTTER TO THE GROUND UNTIL SHE IS SURROUNDED
BY SCATTERED PAPERS. THIS SECTION IS IMPROVISED.)

*Over forty-five names are read during the performance with permission from
family and friends of those who have died from HIV/AIDS. Permission administered by the Asian Pacific AIDS Intervention Team in Los Angeles. Other
names were found written on the floor of the Highways Performance Space art
gallery. Audience members across the nation have also contributed names to
this list.

WOMAN

Passed on
Passed on
he said we've lost a whole generation of black performance artists
they've passed on
even Corbin passed on
passed on
Cruz Luna died of AIDS
he passed on
my friend's friend Duane Puyear died of complications from HIV/AIDS
he passed on
Karen Ige died of AIDS she passed on
I really don't want to think about this
it's not my fuckin' thing
it's passé
passed on
Roxy Ventola screenwriter straight white woman
her husband died her baby died she passed on
Andrew Alabab died from AIDS
Rodolpho Hernandez passed on
Guy Nakatani wasn't he an AIDS activist did you hear
how he passed on
Paul Morse said to me
almonds are good for your health, have some
then he asked me to continue his theater company for him
"After I go," he said, "would you be interested, could you pass it on?"
I wasn't ready, Paul, not then, but I remember you
Living with HIV Tavat Siggy Tamseri
Gary Mascaro passed on
Laurie Rodriguez passed on
Elaine Hill I saw their names written on the cement floor of a building
said she passed on
Vincent Lopez passed on.
I said to my lover let's use a condom
he said why don't you trust me?
I said use a condom
he said you're just selfish

I said get out of my bed.
He was a hemophiliac died near Urbana, Illinois
this one, a black woman, queer died
she passed on
and here' another Asian name, did you hear that?
Passed on
Passed on
Passed on . . .

(SHE SITS AND LOOKS AT PAPERS SCATTERED ABOUT ON THE
STAGE LIKE FALLEN LEAVES. SHE REACHES OUT TO GATHER
THEM, THEN LETS THEM FALL.)

(SINGING AS IF IN PRAYER.)

The wings of a thousand swallows
are beating on our window
the wings of a thousand swallows
are beating on our window
heaven help us have humility
heaven help us have compassion
heaven help us to love enough to
open up our window

let them come through our window
let them dance through our bedroom
let them listen to the radio
let them rest on our pillow
let them dance about the kitchen
let them laugh on the telephone

The wings of a thousand swallows
are beating on our window
the wings of a thousand swallows
are beating on our window
heaven help us have humility
heaven help us have compassion
heaven help us to love enough—

(SHE STANDS AS LIGHTS RISE SLIGHTLY.)

Scene VIII: My Fantasy

(WOMAN HOLDS ONE PAPER TO HER CHEST, THEN LETS IT
FALL.)

My fantasy is
in spite of everything, we will still have our fantasies
my fantasy is a dream in my heart
my fantasy is in spite of everything, we would still practice safer sex
my fantasy is I wear black lingerie under my clothes
my fantasy is a dream in my heart
my fantasy is the next time I have the opportunity for a three-way
I'll handcuff the other two to the bed
my fantasy is I wear black lingerie under my clothes
my fantasy is a dream in my heart
My fantasy is the next time I see Star Wars
I won't just want to fuck Harrison Ford
I'll want to be Harrison Ford
My fantasy is the next time I see heroes
they'll be people of color
My fantasy is a dream in my heart
My fantasy is she whom I admired and loved—she will learn self-respect
My fantasy is I'll forget the color of my skin
My fantasy is I'll never forget the color of my skin

My fantasy is I'll never let my contradictions get in my way

My fantasy is people of color will know the difference between cultural
pride and narrow nationalism and then use any means necessary for love

My fantasy is I'll know the difference between white liberal bullshit
and white people who get it

My fantasy is I won't lose my voice
my fantasy is I will lose my voice
so I can use these (POINTS TO EARS) better
My fantasy is a dream in my heart

My fantasy is I'll stand on a cliff with all my friends
and we'll hold hands and fly away
My fantasy is I'll know who my real friends are
and that I'll know how to be a better friend

My fantasy is the next time I see people, I'll see people

> (STOPS, LOOKS OUT AT AUDIENCE, STARTING FROM THE BACK
> OF THE HOUSE, MOVING FROM FACE TO FACE, IN SILENCE.)

My fantasy is a dream in my heart.

Scene IX: Mirror Scene

> (LIGHTS CROSS-FADE TO RECTANGULAR MIRROR LIGHT.
> WOMAN SLOWLY DISROBES, NATURALLY AND QUIETLY, AS IF
> ALONE IN THE BEDROOM. SHE LOOKS IN THE MIRROR. SHE
> EXAMINES HER BACK, FRONT, BREASTS, STOMACH, MUSCLES,
> AND FINALLY BETWEEN HER LEGS. WHEN SHE FINISHES, SHE
> PICKS UP A LETTER.)

WOMAN

(READING.)

Dear Miss Uyehara,
I saw your work in progress at the Institute for Contemporary Arts in London and I have some suggestions for you. I
wished you would keep your shirt on. Also, fishing about in
one's pubic area (I admit I wasn't watching this "part" too
closely) and then handling members of the audience,
probably contradicts with E.E.C. hygiene regulations. These
comments are meant to be helpful and I hope that you will
take them as such.

Yours sincerely,

wuhajdfjehelwefhkj (ILLEGIBLE SIGNATURE)

(WOMAN CAREFULLY PUTS LETTER BACK IN ENVELOPE AND
PLACES IT ON THE FLOOR. SHE LOOKS BACK INTO THE MIR-
ROR. SHE WRAPS HER ARMS AROUND HERSELF, COVERING
HER BODY. PAUSE. SHE STANDS AGAIN IN FRONT OF THE MIR-
ROR, WAITS UNTIL SHE IS READY. PUTS HER HANDS TO HER
SIDES. FINALLY SHE SEES HERSELF CLEARLY. SHE REACHES
INTO HER BAG, PULLS OUT BLACK LINGERIE, AND BEGINS TO
DRESS WHILE SINGING THE VEGETABLE GIRL'S TUNE:)

WOMAN

(SINGING.)

La la la la la la la . . .

(THEN A NEW SONG.)

> *a dream is a wish your heart makes*
> *when you're fast asleep*
> *a dream is a wish your heart makes*
>
> *la la la*
> *la la la*
> *la la*

(ADDS BLACK PUMPS.)

> *la la la la la*
> *la la la*
> *and then the sun comes shining through* (PICKS UP KITTY)
> *no matter how your heart is feeling*
> (TO KITTY) *if you keep on believing*

(TO AUDIENCE)

> *the dream that you wish will come true.*

(SHE TURNS UPSTAGE, REVEALING HER LINGERIE ENSEMBLE
TO ITS FULLEST POTENTIAL. FOLLOW SPOT SHINES ON HER.
SULTRY CABARET MUSIC [K.D. LANG'S VERSION OF COLE

PORTER'S "SO IN LOVE WITH YOU"] BEGINS TO PLAY. WITH
HER BACK STILL TO THE AUDIENCE, SHE PUTS ON BLACK
SILK VEST OVER LINGERIE, PICKS UP HER KITTY, TURNS TO-
WARD AUDIENCE. EYES FIXED ON AN AUDIENCE MEMBER,
SHE SMELLS HER OWN HAND, PUTS ON LATEX GLOVE. SHE
PINCHES AND WIGGLES ONE OF KITTY'S EARS. SHE VAMPS
SLOWLY INTO AUDIENCE, SITS IN VARIOUS LAPS, CROTCHES,
ETC. SHE PULLS AN ASIAN WOMAN ONTO THE STAGE WITH
HER. THEY STAND ON OPPOSITE SIDES OF STAGE. THE
WOMAN LOOKS OUT TO AUDIENCE, MIMES THAT HER HEART
IS AFLUTTER. FLIRTATIOUSLY, THE WOMAN SNEAKS A STEP
CLOSER TO THE AUDIENCE MEMBER, WHO REACTS ACCORD-
INGLY. FINALLY THE WOMAN HOLDS OUT HER KITTY. THEY
DANCE IN A CIRCLE TO THE MUSIC AND THEN EXIT. AS THEY
LEAVE, THE KITTY WAVES GOOD-BYE AND THE WOMAN
WINKS TO THE AUDIENCE.)

(SPOTLIGHT GOES OUT.)

clit notes

HOLLY HUGHES

Notes on *Clit Notes*

This is one of my girlfriend's favorite jokes: A drunk goes to the opera. Soon after the curtain goes up, he starts bellowing: "Sing 'Melancholy Baby'!" The performers ignore him, and the show goes on. But he keeps demanding: "Sing 'Melancholy Baby.'" Finally, it's time for the diva's aria, and the drunk stands up in his seat to bellow: "If you can't sing 'Melancholy Baby,' at least show us your cunt."

I used to begin the classes I give on developing autobiographical material for performance by asking everybody to tell me why they're there. But I've discovered that beginning with this joke gives me a much better sense of the lay of the land. First of all, it helps me identify the students who will soon come to see themselves as the members of the opera company bravely struggling to preserve the traditions of high culture in spite of inebriated philistines like myself. Most of the students will grin slightly and wonder if they've missed the punch line, which gives me a perfect opportunity to explain what the joke is.

First of all, it isn't the world's greatest joke. But it is a good way to answer the perennial question: what is performance art? All of the basic food groups of performance art are in this story: pop culture, high art, spectacle, big hair, substance abuse, and pussy—it's all in there! I tell the class that in order to appreciate performance art you've got to imagine yourself sitting in the audience far enough back so that what's happening in the audience and what's going on onstage are all part of the show.

It was in this spirit that I decided to call this piece *Clit Notes.* Many of my staunchest fans saw the title as the equivalent of the drunk's demands to see the singer's cunt. One friend said the title had nothing to do with what the show was about, and if I was going to insist on *Clit Notes,* I should include either more clit or more notes to justify the title. She claimed the only reason I gave it that name was I wanted to force people to say "clit."

Which was, of course, totally true. But after all I see myself as a political artist, and I think that making more people wrap their mouths around the word, if not the thing itself, is precisely the kind of political goal one can hope to realize through theater. Why is it that the words *dick, prick,* and *cock* seem to pop up everywhere I look? I've been told that the reason is that *dick* is also a proper name, that *prick* is also a verb, the sun also rises, and the poppy is also a flower but that—and I quote!—"the clit is just a clit."

Please! Not in my experience! If they had said: "The clit is a clit," I might agree—it sounds like what Gertrude Stein was trying to get at. But "just" a clit as in "merely a clit." No, I don't think so.

Before presenting this work I had no idea how far some people would go to avoid having to say this word. The *New York Times,* for example, wouldn't print the title, which was described as containing "a slang term for the word 'clitoris.'" Before going on the air on some National Public Radio station, I was told I could use the word only if I was talking about myself. Under no circumstances, I was warned, could I call someone else a clitoris on the air.

Of course, it's hard to work under these conditions. But somehow I managed, with the help of Dan Hurlin, whose role in this production might be described as more than a director but less than a dessert topping. This piece was commissioned by the New York Shakespeare Festival and developed with the help of Dixon Place and the New York Theater Workshop. I'm also indebted to the feedback I got from Nina Mankin, Eleanor Savage, Tim Miller, David Cale, David Roman, and especially Phranc.

clit notes

HOLLY HUGHES

(CENTERSTAGE, A TEN FOOT SQUARE OF DIAGONAL YELLOW
AND BLACK STRIPES. IN THE MIDDLE THERE IS A SMALL
WOODEN SCHOOL CHAIR. THE PERFORMER WHO DOES NOT
SEE HERSELF AS MIDDLE-AGED ENTERS AND STANDS BEHIND
THE CHAIR. SHE IS WEARING A RED DRESS. [UNDER NO CIR-
CUMSTANCES SHOULD THIS PIECE BE ATTEMPTED IN ANY-
THING OTHER THAN A RED DRESS!])

The first time I was in love with another woman?

Actually, *she* was a *woman*; I was just thirteen. In fact, this little
anecdote might have a happier ending if there'd been some sort
of gay youth organization in my hometown. Some sort of North
American Woman-Girl Love Association. But, nooooo!

The men, they get everything good.

The lesbian chicken, who worries about them, huh?

(SHE SITS DOWN IN THE CHAIR.)

Her name—and this was an important part of the attraction—
her name was *A—Neee—Ta Weeen—dttt*. Which I discovered
sounded an awful lot like "I needa whip," if you said it enough times
to yourself.

And I did.

She was a social studies teacher. That's what we called history in my hometown of Saginaw, Michigan. I know I don't have to tell you that Saginaw, Michigan, is the Navy Bean Capital. Of the *world*. You may have also heard of it in that Simon and Garfunkel song: "It took us four days to hitchhike from Saginaw." They had connections, of course.

But what they taught us was not actually history. There's laws against teaching history in Michigan. What they taught, instead, was amnesia. So, by the time I was thirteen, all I knew about World War Two, for instance, was what I had gleaned from *Hogan's Heroes*. Funny little war!

I knew there were slaves at one time in America—and the Republicans freed them!

There were forbidden books in my hometown. In fact, most books were forbidden. They were on the library shelves, but you had to get a note from home to read them. I was not about to get a note from my home to read a book. My mother used to drop my sister and me off after school at Republican headquarters so we could stuff envelopes for Nixon. Even when he wasn't running. No one wanted to break the news to us. "Keep hope *alive*." It was my mother's idea of day care.

Anita Wendt used to slip me these forbidden tomes. Books like: *The Autobiography of Malcolm X*, *I'm O.K.*, *You're O.K.*, and *Jonathan Livingston Seagull*.

For some reason this made me love her.

I guess I loved her because she was the one who woke me up.

This love had an unfortunate way of expressing itself in the eighth grade. Sometimes I'd be in class, and I'd think: "Her mouth! It's a *magnet*. I am going to kiss her, *and there's nothing anybody can do to stop me!*"

So I just throw myself to the ground and writhe around, hoping people would think I was merely epileptic. A little foaming at the mouth is better than having people think you're *queer*.

And sometimes I'd be so inspired by her lectures that I'd go into a trance and start removing articles of clothing. Once I took my panty hose off in class. I have no memory of taking them off.

But there they were! Down on the floor in an incriminating taupe heap.

I began to think there was something the matter with me, and if I weren't careful, I might start voting Democratic. I turned to the definite sexual authority of that and perhaps all time, Dr. David Reuben's *Everything You Always Wanted to Know about Sex*.

Just the table of contents was a real eye opener.

I noticed, right off the bat, that male homosexuals had their own chapter. But the females were just a footnote under "Prostitution."

Oddly, there was no separate heading for "Democrat."

So I read the whole damn thing. Up to this time, I thought homosexuality had to do with attraction between two people of the same sex. But not according to David Reuben. According to Dr. Reuben, the most unique feature of the homosexual, male or female, is their compulsive erotic relationship to household appliances.

And all that distinguishes the male from the female is that male homosexuals are forever shoving various appliances up their butt: Shot glasses. Blenders. Toaster ovens.

While on the other hand, the women are always strapping these appliances on: Electric toothbrushes. Color TVs. Washer-dryers. Ladies, start your engines!

I was thirteen years old, and it seemed to be a very shallow and materialistic form of love. And I realized that being a homosexual—if you were going to be any good at it—would require an awful lot of leisure time. Not to mention electrical outlets.

And it was somewhat rough on the environment.

But I read on.

Dr. Reuben said that, like cancer, impending lesbianism had its warning signals. The most ominous of which was, and I quote, "the enlarged clitoris of The Lesbian which can be inserted into The Vagina of her partner achieving a reasonable facsimile of The Real Thing."

Whatever that is.

Still I read on. Dr. Reuben said that "the most prized lesbians . . ." And I thought—*wait a minute!*

I had no idea there would be prizes! Hot dog!

Here I was, in the Midwest, county-fair country, and all of a sudden I could see the next Saginaw County Fair! There was the lesbian barn! Why, it was right next door to the Clydesdales! Down from the holsteins! All those people out on the midway saying: "Come on down at four; they'll be judging the lesbians. You don't want to miss that!" And all those little Four-H kids! Leading around all those lesbians they'd hand raised. Suckled from baby butch all the way up to full-blown bull daggers!

Dr. Reuben didn't mention what sort of prizes one might hope to win for being a lesbian. But I figured a few surge protectors might come in handy. I read on.

Dr. Reuben said that some of the blue-ribbon specimens had clits four! five! even six inches . . . long, I guess. He didn't say.

I think you know what I did.

I went to my father's workroom. I got his tape measure. It was twenty-five feet long. I figured: "That ought to do it!" You got to believe in yourself.

And I borrowed my mother's hand mirror. I went to my bedroom, dropped my skirt, and I ran into all sorts of problems. I could not find anything between my legs that looked like it could be inserted into the body of another person, even under the best of circumstances.

At this point I began to doubt the very existence of my clitoris.

It didn't seem like something someone in my family would have. Not after all that work for Nixon.

It didn't seem like something anyone in Saginaw would have. Or . . . maybe they used to have them, but Simon and Garfunkel took them with them when they left! I measured everything between my navel and my knees, and took the best score. Nothing was even four inches long.

Right then I knew I would never win any prizes for being a lesbian. I might not even be a dyke after all.

I didn't measure up.

(FADE TO BLACK.)

(WHEN THE LIGHTS COME UP, THE PERFORMER IS SITTING
IN A KITCHEN CHAIR ON THE UPSTAGE RIGHT CORNER OF
THE SQUARE. I RECOMMEND ONE OF THOSE VINYL AND
CHROME KITCHEN CHAIRS. THE CHAIR SHOULD REMIND THE
AUDIENCE OF EGG-SALAD SANDWICHES AND PICKLE SPEARS.)

Soon as they opened my father up, they knew. Probably knew
before.

Malignant.

At first I thought: "Big deal. You have two kidneys. You lose
one, it won't kill you. Plenty of people do fine on just one. Just
because you lose a kidney, that's no reason to think you can't have
a normal life."

If you go for that sort of thing.

Funny but this was exactly the same thought my father had
when he first found out that I was a lesbian. He didn't say anything. Silence had always been his first language. But by then I
was fairly fluent. I knew what he was thinking. I knew he figured
he had two daughters. So he lost one. Big deal. It wouldn't kill
him. Plenty of people do fine on just one. One was more than
enough for his purposes. Just because he had one daughter who
was a dyke, no reason to think he couldn't have a normal life.

That's all he ever really wanted. *A normal life*. He got pretty
close. He almost had a normal life.

Do you have any idea how many different kinds of cancer there
are?

Jesus! It's like all the breeds of dogs. Each with their own habits.
Temperament. Preferred hiding places. Each with their own special name. The name, that's important. Because the name is the
key to the future. As in, whether there's going to be a future or
not.

Of course, all of them will bite. But there's a difference in how
hard. There's a difference in whether they'll let you go once they've
got a hold of you.

It took two weeks for the doctors to give my father's cancer a
name. To tell us what disease we were dealing with. I say "we"

because, when sickness enters one person's body, it doesn't just stay there. It comes to live with everyone who loves that body, its appearance determined by the kind of love you have for the body where the sickness makes its home . . .

Fuck! I didn't just say I loved my father, did I?

I meant to imply I loved his *body*.

Which is not *him*. My *father*, his *body* . . . two completely separate entities. Barely on speaking terms.

Every night we waited for my father's diagnosis, his disease would rise out of his bed and come to mine. Every night of those two weeks his disease would lie on top of me, sucking my dreams dry till I just had one dream left.

> *I saw a vision of the last decade in this country.*
> *I saw a landscape of death.*
> *A country ruled by doctors, lawyers.*
> *This was a vision that appeared to me in white, on white.*

And when I say "white," let's be clear what white I'm talking about. I'm talking about the white of the police-chalk line and especially the white of the sheet pulled over the face when all you see of the eyes are the whites.

I don't know about you but there's too many of my friends back there. Too many people who belong to me only in the past tense. So many that I start to think: "That's where I belong." At least that part of me that could say, without any hesitation:

> "*I want to live. In my body. In the present tense.*
> *In front of all these people*
> *I'm going to tell the truth.*"

Not the whole truth. Not nothing but the truth. Not that one. Just my little chunk of it. Without apology, I used to say: "I don't care who hates me."

Who did I think I was?

It's like I thought I was playing some sort of game of tag, and I was so sure that I was faster, smaller than that sweaty, balding guy we've all decided was "it." Now that part of me is somebody else I lost. Another face who appears nightly, asking to be remembered or at least counted. Promising me, if I count all the dead, I'll sleep as deep as I dare.

But there's too many of the dead to count.

So I won't sleep. What do I need with sleep anyway. Who can sleep at a time like this, huh? Besides. Getting to sleep has never been my biggest problem. My big problem is waking up.

I spent my entire childhood in a coma.

Then I turned twenty, and I kissed a woman. Sort of by accident. But she kissed me back. With a purpose. An intention I couldn't guess. Something started happening to me. Something that the expression "coming out" doesn't quite cover. In my case, it was more a question of . . . coming to.

But the world is round.

And I resent that fact!

Soon as my father said he was sick, after my father said the word "cancer," I knew I had to go home. Going home does not come naturally to me. If my father's medium was silence, mine has tended to be escape. But there's no future in escape because the world is round. So the faster you run away, the faster you end up, right back where you started, face-to-face with whatever you were running away from in the first place.

Your worst fears, they're always the most patient.

Part of my reluctance in going home, no doubt, has to do with what my parents' home is. From the outside it looks oppressively normal. Your average, Middle-American, middle-class, middle-everything split-level.

But that's just the outside!

In reality, this is the entrance to a cave . . . cave . . . cave . . . cave . . . I know if I don't make myself as small as possible, if I'm not willing to pretend I don't even have a body, they'll never let me in the front door.

And as soon as I'm inside, I'll lose my footing. The floors are always slick with a mixture of prehistoric tears, come, light ranch dressing.

An outside light means nothing in this kind of darkness. Before I go home, I tie a rope around my waist and give the end to my friends:

"Don't let go of me. Don't let me fall. If I'm not back in two weeks, come after me, okay?"

I tell everybody I'm going back because of my father. But the truth is I'm going back because there's parts of my body I can't feel. Parts of me still dreaming, back in my father's bed. Waiting for some kind of wake-up call. A sign. A word . . .

Okay. I'll say it.

A kiss.

Something I'm never going to get from my father. Now that he's living with one foot in the grave and the other on a banana peel, as he would say, isn't it time for me to wake all the way up. Once and for all. Isn't it about time to get completely out of my parents' bed?

For two weeks I practice going home. Trying to get it right. I get up. In the middle of the night. Crawl to the mirror. And I can already see the toll my father's illness is taking.

> *I look just like the place I was born.*
> *I'm a dead ringer for Michigan!*
> *Can you see it?*
> *I'm almost an island.*
> *There's water on three sides of me.*
> *A place carved up by ice.*
> *The birthplace of all storms.*
> *A short growing season.*
> *All the cities shut down, the people moved to Texas.*

I don't mean to brag. These could be my best qualities.

Step two. I try to get the woman in the mirror, the one who looks like Michigan, to repeat after me: "I want to live." A pep talk, but something goes wrong. The words swerve out of control and turn into questions. So it comes out like this:

> "*I want to live?*
> *In my body?*
> *In the present tense?*
> *I want to tell the truth?*
> *Which one? Mine? My father's?*
> *Is that what I want to do with my life?*"

Two weeks go by in this way. In the daylight I conduct a futile search for the doctor who said he could get me discount Prozac if I got him season tickets to WOW. Finally my father calls:

"I just want you to know. I have the good kind of cancer."

His voice is so thin. Already. It's like the skin on the underside of arms where you can look and see—what do you know—the blood is still moving. Here's evidence that the heart's red oompah-pah band plays on. But it's still my father's voice. And he's talking to me in a tone I recognize, I remember. It's the one he used when I got to that age where everywhere I looked I saw snakes.

It got so bad I wouldn't go out of the house. But my father wanted me out in the world. He had done everything he could to make the world safe for me.

So he told me that there were two kinds of snakes. The good and the bad. What made the good ones good is that they ate things that were worse than any snake.

Gee, thanks, Dad. Now I had something new to worry about!

But my father assured me the snakes had everything under control. A very hardworking species, apparently. So when I saw the grass move, when I saw the darkness under the trees roll itself into the letter S, what I was seeing was a friend. Just doing his job. Keeping me safe.

"And the bad snakes, Dad? What about them?"

I had to know! He said there weren't any. Not anymore. Not in the woods we called ours. My father insisted I was safe. Noth-

ing with teeth big enough to bite us, not in our woods. If I heard
something howling at night, it was the wind. It couldn't possibly
be a wolf. A coyote. Or a wolverine, ha! And the few neighbors
looked just like us.

Still my father ran a thin wire around our eighty acres. Our
woods. I remember him hanging up the big signs saying No Tres-
passing. I remember because I walked behind him. In his footsteps.
Never asking what was the purpose of this fence. Who was supposed to be kept out. Who was being kept in. I couldn't imagine
there was anything for the good snakes to eat. Who was lower than
a snake? Just as I couldn't imagine that there was ever a time when
these woods weren't ours.

> *I wanted to live.*
> *In my body.*
> *In our world.*
> *All I wanted to be was my father's daughter.*

I loved him because of his tools. His shotgun. His poison. The
big sign he made, black letters on white wood: Private Property.
Keep Out. Out of the corner of my eyes, I studied his hands. Massive. Like paws. The big hands of a hard worker. He was always
working, so I could walk barefoot under the pines. Through our
woods.

That my father has the good cancer doesn't mean he's going
to live. It means there is a drug. A treatment that might, as the
doctors like to say, buy him time. They like to say that, don't they,
the doctors. Because they're doing the selling and not the buying
of this time.

Sure, you can live without a kidney. But how long do you last
without your bones, liver, lungs. Your brain. I mention these places
because these are the most likely places where, even as I speak,
my father's cancer is waiting, coiled out of the doctors' sight, waiting to strike again.

And so I imagine it gliding through my father's body. Starting down deep. Near the place where I used to live inside him.

Moving up and swallowing what's worse than cancer. What's already hurt him more than dying ever could. Like being born in Appalachia. February 3, 1916. A family of coal miners. If they were lucky. My father and his brother Wolf grew up in the orphanage. Not because there's no family. Because there's no money. When they get out, their mother dies and still there's no money. When he's twenty-five, he's the last of his kind. But now there's a little money. So he goes to a dentist for the first time. And on that first visit, they pull all his teeth.

I'm probably being dramatic. They must have left one or two. But I'm sure the cancer will get those, too.

And if this is what the doctors have promised, if this is really the *good* cancer at last, then it's bound to eat most of my father's marriage to my mother. Their terrible fights. The silences which were worse.

Until the cancer gets to the worst thing of all.

Until it gets to that thing that my father says is what's really killing him. Anybody want to take a guess what is the worst thing that ever happened to my father?

You're looking at her.

(THE PERFORMER TAKES A LITTLE BOW OR CURTSIES.)

Fall of 1990.

We haven't spoken in several months. I'm the one to pick up the phone. At the sound of my voice, he starts to cry. Weeping. Like there's been another death in the family.

"Why are you doing this to us?"

I try to tell him I'm not doing anything. I try to tell him something's been done to me.

"Don't give me that. I watch TV. I read the paper!
You're all over the place!
This is what you wanted! You always wanted to hurt us.
You're doing a good job.
My own daughter. Act like you had no shame. No family."

* * *

I wish I had no shame. Sometimes I think that shame is all I've got. It was a synonym in our house for "family." It was the crazy glue that kept us together, and I emphasize the word *crazy*.

I try to tell my father that the person he's seeing everywhere isn't me. It's somebody's idea of me. I've become a symbol. I've been buried alive under meanings other people have attached to me. I tell him that some of what he's heard are lies.

"So you're not a lesbian?
Is that a lie?
You don't stand in front of a lot of people and talk about having sex—with women—and you call that 'art,' and then you expect the federal government to pay for it.
You never did that?
That's a lie?
That's good news."

It's my turn to be silent, but my father isn't finished.

"Could you at least stay away from that goddamn Karen Finley?
Is that too much to ask?
Homosexuality, well, that's one thing.
But people who play with their food!
What did we ever do to you?
Just look at yourself.
You're never going to have a normal life, I hope you know that.
What was it? What happened to you? What went wrong?"

I take my father's questions seriously. I promise I will tell him what made me abandon any hope of ever having A Normal Life. I'll tell him. At least, as much as I remember.

(FADE TO BLACK. WHEN THE LIGHTS COME UP, THE SCHOOL CHAIR FROM THE FIRST SECTION SHOULD BE SLIGHTLY DOWNSTAGE RIGHT OF THE SQUARE'S CENTER. THE PERFORMER IS PACING BACK AND FORTH IN FRONT OF THE

CHAIR. SHE IS SPEAKING AS THOUGH SHE WERE A DISTIN-
GUISHED PROFESSOR GIVING A LECTURE AT THE FAMOUS
PERFORMANCE ARTIST CORRESPONDENCE SCHOOL.)

Performance Art: What Causes It? Where it comes from and what can be done about it. Three case studies.

Number One: "Performance Art as a Tool of Social Change."

(AS THE PERFORMER SITS DOWN, SHE SLIPS INTO A SOFTER,
OLDER SELF.)

I launched my careers as a lesbian and as a waitress simultaneously. For a while they kind of fed off each other; there was a
certain symbiosis.

Someone has suggested this had something to do with me
working in seafood restaurants, but you'd never catch me saying
something so repulsive!

Initially, I admit I wasn't very adept at being either a waitress
or a lesbian, although I was fast and mean, and this was a plus in
both departments. I remember standing over the naked form of
the woman I lived with. The woman who everyone in town
thought was my girlfriend. Everyone, that is, but her. I wanted
desperately to have my way with her. But I had no idea what my
way might be.

Meanwhile, back at the Red Lobster, I was working very hard
to present myself as a lesbian separatist waitress . . .

THAT'S NOT FUNNY!

It's not so easy to combine those particular sets of identities.
If you want tips. It was hard to persuade anyone I was even the
most benign form of feminist, since most of the women would run
when they saw me coming. They knew I was apt to start quoting
Ms. magazine at the slightest provocation, and that I loved to chase

people around the salad bar trying to persuade them how oppressed they were.

But I was respected, if not actually liked, for the principled stances I would assume at our staff meetings, which were held every Tuesday at eight A.M.

The rest of the waitresses would just be trying to wake up. They'd be all hunched over a cup of our famous burnt coffee that we'd whiten with a little liquid paper we'd try to masquerade as cream. Eight A.M., and your feet are already rebelling against the vinyl prisons they've been sentenced to. And the manager, he's introducing the Bermuda Triangle Platter, or talking about the latest all-you-can-eat deep-fried sea monkey special. Or the drink du jour. The Moon Rocket. It was always our drink du jour no matter what jour it was, because it was blue and frozen and on fire. All at the same time.

And I'd say: "WAIT JUST A MINUTE!

"While we're sitting here trying to come up with a few more ways to push shrimp cocktail, women in Africa are having their clitorises cut off! And I want to know: WHEN IS THE RED LOBSTER GOING TO DO SOMETHING ABOUT THAT!"

As a lesbian separatist, I was more successful as a separatist than I was as a lesbian. I pretty much separated myself from just about everyone.

It's something you never read about in radical political theory: *the loneliness of the pure*.

And I wanted so desperately to experience some of that sisterhood I had read so much about. Finally an opportunity presented itself in the form of a five-state employee talent contest.

My talent was choreography. It's only to the untrained eye that I appear to be sitting almost motionless in a chair. I decided to inflict my talent on all the waitresses because I had read: "None of us are free unless ALL of us are free!"

So I called all the waitresses together, and I put pillowcases over their heads.

Then I proceeded to interpret, choreographically, the wit and wisdom of my then heroine, Andrea Dworkin, as set to the music of Randy Newman's "Short People Got No Reason to Live."

This was my big chance! This was my opportunity to strike a blow against the capitalist patriarchy!

What do I look like—someone who's got all the answers?

So I told a joke instead.

And we won.

(SHE BECOMES THE PROFESSOR AGAIN.)

Number Two: "Breaking the Fourth Wall."

(BACK IN THE CHAIR THE PERFORMER CHANGES, THIS TIME INTO THE SULLEN, OVERPRIVILEGED BRAT SHE ONCE WAS.)

Like most children I had various chores I was expected to do around the house. The most odious of which was, in my opinion, kissing my parents good-night. I realized, however, it was an important job. One that apparently they could not do for themselves. And I would be paid.

One night, sitting next to my mother on the couch, I had a sudden epiphany. Fortunately, the fabric was Scotchgarded, so I didn't cause any permanent damage.

But all of a sudden I realized that my mother wasn't just my mother . . .

She was a *woman*.

I knew what that meant.

I'd already figured out that being female was a chronic medical condition. You couldn't cure it, but you might be able to learn to live with it. If you got the right treatment in time. And I had an idea for a new treatment for women.

I noticed I had an audience. This made me very happy because I'd heard in science class that a tree falling in the wilderness made no sound. I wanted the world to know about my new treatment for women. So I stood up and looked at my audience. It consisted of two people. My father and the other person who I will alternately refer to as my sister and my father's girlfriend.

It's important to know who your audience is.

I went over to my mother, and when I got to her, I straddled her. Kind of like I imagined I would straddle that pony I knew by then my father was never going to buy me. And as I mounted Mom, I turned, and I looked at my audience, as if to say: "I bet you wish you'd just bought that pony for me, now don't you? Maybe all this ugliness could have been avoided."

Then I proceeded to kiss my mother good-night in the following fashion: I applied my mouth to hers with all the suction power I could muster in my prepubescent frame, and I began to rotate my mouth against hers in a precise, almost scientific manner. When my mother was, at least in my opinion, good and kissed, and would stay that way for quite some time, I turned and I looked at my audience, as if to say: "You could be next."

All that kept me from breaking the fourth wall at that moment was my mother, who said:

"Where did you learn to kiss like that?"

"On TV," I answered.

"Well, you're doing it all wrong, hon. You got to open your mouth. Like this."

I opened my mouth. I leaned forward. And, yes, I did kiss my mother good-night in the way she so obviously wanted me to. As I did, a small voice in the back of my head warned: "What do you think you're doing? Now you've gone and fucked your life up but good."

And I was happy.

This was the first time I realized I *had a life*. Something of my own to fuck up. And I felt powerful. Like the most powerful thing I could imagine, which at that time was a waitress at Howard Johnson's on a Sunday morning, seeing that room full of the interminably ravenous and thinking: "I know what to do."

As I made out with Mom, I heard a small sound. Like a door closing and locking behind me. I knew I would never get back to that place where I imagined I was safe.

And, yes, I knew what I was doing was wrong.

But I was surrounded by people who were suffocating under the burden of *a normal life*. I knew I'd rather be wrong than safe. I guess I was at that age when most girls start looking for shelter from the storm.

But I started looking for the storm.

(ONCE MORE THE PERFORMER TRANSFORMS INTO THE PRO-
FESSOR TO ANNOUNCE:)

Number Three:
"I Was Forced to Participate in Performance Art As a Condition of My Parole."

I wasn't actually in jail, though I desperately wanted to be. Anywhere my family wasn't. So when my mother asked me if I realized what I had done to Lynne Colbert in the back of our garage was a crime, I said: "Yes."

Then she asked me if I realized that people in this country went to jail every day for what I had done to this young girl, and I said: "So what."

Every day my mother would confront me with a list of my crimes and misdemeanors. I had, for example, told my little sister that she was adopted, that her real name was Gertrude, and that no one was going to buy her a Christmas present. I had broken a branch off the ornamental cherry tree and gone over to the neighbor's freshly poured cement driveway, where I created a little bas-relief, depicting, if I recall correctly, the history of bullfighting. In Michigan.

I believe it was my first triptych.

And every day my mother would try to get me to admit how bad I was. I would always plead innocent. But after I had Lynne in the garage, I cracked. I surrendered to my essentially criminal nature. I knew I never could be good enough to please my mother, so maybe I could be good at being bad. I resolved I would go from bad to worse as soon as it could be arranged.

But my eager confession didn't seem to please my mother. I guess I had robbed her of the joy of interrogation, and those long, lonely hours before she would start to burn dinner just stretched out empty before her.

She asked me to consider the particularly heinous nature of my crime. I knew she was just stalling. But I thought about it because I liked thinking about it. What I had done is I had taken Lynne Colbert, my sometimes best friend and often worst enemy, out behind the Buick, and I had persuaded her to let me give her a little . . . haircut. Lynne Colbert was widely believed to be the most beautiful girl in my elementary school.

But that was *before*.

Before I got out my father's toenail clippers and started hacking away at those long, blonde curls. As I hacked, I persuaded her that (a) she didn't look hideous, and (b) her mother would not beat the shit out of her when I was finished.

And . . . she believed me!

I couldn't believe she believed me! Any more than I'm sure that Jim Jones couldn't believe it when people started drinking that Kool-Aid! I channeled the spirit of my first lesbian role model—Paul Lynde. Particularly Paul Lynde as he was manifest in that seminal piece of queer cinema. *Bye, Bye, Birdie*. His spirit sneered through me that day in the garage.

I said: "Kids."

I did not consider myself a kid.

I walked among them but was not of them.

When confronted by my mother, I liked to imagine a big prison devoted to people whose crimes are merely aesthetic. In particular, I liked to envision a big holding tank filled with bad hair stylists. Of course, I was too middle everything to be sent to anything as lively as prison. But I was expected to participate in the nearest equivalent for someone of my *milieu*.

Community theater.

I was under psychiatric orders to work on a production of *The Sound of Music*. This wasn't just any production, oh, no. This was a production under the direction of the most renowned thespians in the entire Thumb region of Michigan. She'd won *kudos* for her previous season's one-woman *Man of La Mancha*.

I wasn't allowed to act. Instead, I was expected to work on the set crew. I was entirely responsible for the Alps. The Alps are pretty damn important in *The Sound of Music*. You got no Alps, you got no music. I was also expected, during the run of the show, to lower a microphone during "Edelweiss" so the Von Trapp children could be plainly heard making that touching homage to those little fascist flowers.

Opening night.

By some fluke, I've managed to get the Alps up on their hind legs. I lower the microphone on cue. But one of the Von Trapp children has another idea. Instead of belting out "Edelweiss," he pivots and farts. Into the microphone.

I have no idea how many of you, if any, have experienced, firsthand, the sheer destructive power of amplified flatulence. But let me assure you, it's nothing to sneeze at. The one thing we had in Saginaw was a damn good sound system.

Pandemonium broke out, praise the Lord. The first thing to go were the Alps. You'd think I'd be upset because they were *my* Alps, after all. But I was delighted. Because all of a sudden you could look backstage and see:

The nuns and the Nazis were the same people!

It was just a question of costumes and phony accents.

Finally the play made sense.

I thought: "This is what I want to do with the rest of my life!"

(LIGHTS FADE TO A SOFTER, MORE ROMANTIC LEVEL.)

I've never been what you'd call a morning person.

I'm the kind of person who wakes up so stunned by sleep I can't remember my own name. But now it's starting to become my favorite time of the day.

The difference? It's *her*.

Now I get to watch *her* slide out of the sheets into the new day. Her legs—they're always longest in the morning. I've never known anyone who could get so naked before! She's not in any hurry to do anything about that nakedness. Even though she wears the same thing every day. It's a little present she gives to me, this time. Her standing, back to me, light coming through the palm trees, running over her swimmer's shoulders like river water poured through cupped hands.

That's the moment I remember who I am.

That's the moment I come back to the body I thought I'd lost to my father.

Then she swings around to face me, and Jesus! I'm blinded. *Whatta set of knockers!*

Now I know why they call them headlights. Until I started going out with her I never realized: *tits can be a source of light!*

I know there's people who get uneasy when I start talking about my girlfriend's tits. Hooters. Knockers. Winnebagos! I know there's readers who'd be more comfortable if I described my girlfriend's mammalian characteristics as "breastssss."

But I can't do that. She doesn't have breastssss. Thank God! Breastsss are what those ladies have. They like to take their breasts off and hang them up in the closet, where they harden in the dark. The only good they do them is that they keep all their lady clothes smelling like they just got back from a car trip to Florida.

You know who ladies are, don't you?

Ladies are the people who will not let my girlfriend use the public ladies room, thinking she's not a woman. But are they going to let her into the men's room? Nope. Because they don't think she's a man, either.

If she's not a woman and she's not a man, what in the hell is she?

Once I asked my father what fire was, a liquid, a gas, or a solid, and he said it wasn't any of those things. Fire isn't a thing; it's what happens to things. A force of nature. That's what he called it.

Well, maybe that's what she is. A force of nature. I'll tell you something: *she is something that happened to me.*

But even a force of nature has got to pull a look together.

In the morning, certain decisions have got to be made. So out of the drawers she pulls Jockey shorts . . . not Jockey for Her. The *real* McCoy. And a white cotton T-shirt and a pair of secondhand jeans worn white from the sweat and strain of a stranger's body. A man's body.

Men's clothes. That's all she ever wears.

But putting on these men's clothes doesn't erase her woman's body. In fact, it almost makes it worse. And I'll tell you why. Her tits. They are just *relentless*. The way they just keep pushing through the white cotton like a pair of groundhogs drilling through the February snow to capture their own shadows!

She doesn't even own a bra. Once I asked her why, and she said she didn't believe in them! Like it's not an article of clothing, like it's some kind of prayer. As if strapping on the Maidenform were like saying the Pledge of Allegiance.

I asked her if she worried about her tits falling. She said, "No." She figured that was my job. To catch her tits.

I can be a hard worker!

I'm not particularly known for it, but I can be. So every day I just do my job. I do what I can to start a little landslide in the tit department, and then I scoop them up, using my hands, my mouth, my pussy, whatever's handy.

And every day she gets dressed in the same way. Wearing the same thing, like it was some kind of uniform. Like she's going to war. I guess we are going to war. But sometimes, in the morning, I think we're going to win.

In front of the Ukrainian meat market she pulls me to her, wraps her arms around me, her hands on my ass like the lucky claws at Coney Island, clamping tight and lifting up, and then I'm a candy necklace, a ring flashing secret messages. Gives me a slow deliberate kiss, her body bending over mine like I am a knot she is carefully untying. With her tongue.

Behind us, in the window of the market, a blue and gold sign announces "We're Free!" in two languages. We stay deep in the kiss, as though the sign applied to us as well. And for a moment I'm so happy, I could be Ukrainian.

Then a man whips out of the store. In his arms he's cradling a newborn baby ham. But passing us he names us, he calls us: "*Shameless!*"

Could be that this is the sort of man who thinks anyone, gay—straight, or ambidextrous—kissing in public is shameless. My father's like that. He hates what he calls "displays," meaning that hearts should stay tucked in the pants, hidden, not hung like fat sausages in the greasy public window.

Or it could be that this is the sort of man who thinks that just the *thought* of me loving another woman, even if I never act on it, is a shameless act.

I don't know what sort of man this is. But I wish what he said were true.

I wish I had no shame.

Maybe there are shameless queers. But I know that I'm not one of them, and neither is my girlfriend. I know that buried deep in our bodies is the shrapnel of memory dripping a poison called shame.

But we're the lucky ones. There's not enough shame in us to kill us. Just enough to feel when it rains.

Sure, I've been the cause of tears, lies, and a congressional investigation, but at least no one has tried to cure me. Yet. No one has said kaddish over my still living body while the dead went unclaimed.

I know other queers so riddled by memory that everything they touch becomes a weapon. I have seen shame work its backward alchemy overnight. I've seen people who've gone to bed perfectly respectable bull daggers, only to wake up the next morning claiming to be somebody's wife, a stray Republican, their own mother.

What my girlfriend and I are good at is acting shameless.

In order to pull off this act we've had to perfect two different ways to kiss. The first way is: kissing like there's no tomorrow. At least no Jesse Helms, no Brandon Teena, no AIDS epidemic. Not in our tomorrow.

And we also know how to kiss as if there were no past. She's an expert at shutting out what she has to, so she can do what she wants to. Nothing in the way she swaggers down the street tells the story of how she was shut out that night she came home, sixteen years old, hair cut off, wearing a bow tie, and a new name.

Threatened to do it for months. She'd been dragging around that Jill Johnston book for years. Nobody should have been surprised.

But now she comes home to find the door locked.

A mistake.

That's what she thinks at first, but when the key always hidden under the flowerpot is missing, she looks up. Sees her brother's
watching her from inside the dark house that was, until a few
minutes ago, her home.

This is a fairy tale, right?

This is the moment the fairy gets her special powers. These
are the powers granted to everybody who gets locked out, to everybody waiting outside in the flower bed. It's the power to see into
the future. She knows, in the future, there will be other doors
locked when they see her coming. She knows that someday this
door will swing open again. She'll sit in their chairs and eat their
food, she'll sleep in their beds, but she'll do it the way a ghost visits a past life. She'll call this place "the house I used to live in."
She won't call it home again.

And her brother? He'll have his special power, too. This
is the power granted to everybody who holds a key, to everybody waiting on the inside of the locked door. It's the power
to have his thoughts climb inside her head and become her
thoughts. Meaning: she will begin to see herself the way he sees
her. Watch: Her white clothes will turn silver in the moonlight.
She'll imagine she's a silver stake driven into the heart of her
mother's garden.

So that's why she doesn't go next door to see if the neighbor
has a key. That's why she doesn't pound on the door of her own
home and demand to be let inside: she doesn't think she belongs
inside. A hole has opened inside her. All of a sudden, a deep hole
filling up with the cold water of shame.

This is how she spent the first night of her life as a lesbian:
courting sleep in the backseat of a stranger's Buick. As a kid, this
is what she wanted. She always wanted to be the outlaw, the des-
perado, the guy in the black hat. She never wanted any part of *a
normal life*. And now she's got her wish.

But where is the rest of the dream?

Where's the getaway car, the chest of gold, the secret hide-
out, where are all the other outlaws?

Do I censor myself? Every day.

Because the truth is, I would rather have the man with the ham see us as brazen, would rather not have him see any of my pain, 'cause I know how he would use it against me, against us, would call our pain proof of the illness he imagines we're carrying, when all it proves is:

There is a war going on.
All of us have been hit.
Some of us worse than others.

(PAUSE.)

Don't you hate it when people ask you why you are what you are?

As if you had any idea? All I know is I am a woman who loves another woman who most people think is a man, and that once when we were in San Diego together, okay?

We checked into the best motel, the Hanalei. Polynesian from the word go. Outside a pink neon sign announces: A Taste of Aloha.

You can taste it before you even check in.

There's Styrofoam Easter Island heads everywhere. The bed's a volcano. Every night there's a luau. It's free, it's gratis. So of course we go. And I love the way they slip those pink plastic leis over your head. I just love that! I love the thought of those Day-Glo flowers blooming long after Jesse Helms is gone.

I hope.

I look out on the Astro Turf. Kids chasing each other around. Folks sipping mai-tais and piña coladas out of plastic pineapples. They've got a helluva show at the Hanalei. Hula dancers. Fire eaters. A Don Ho impersonator that's much better than the real Don Ho! Nobody cares it's not the real Polynesia. It's all the Polynesia they could take! It's the one we invented.

During "Tiny Bubbles," she starts kissing me. Everybody's looking at us. But you can only see what you want to see. And what these folks want to see is not a couple of dykes making out at their luau.

So that's not what they see. They start translating us into their reality. What they think they're seeing is Matt Dillon making out with a young Julie Andrews. A young Julie Andrews. Before *Victor/Victoria*.

I don't mind. I'm not in the closet! I'm so far out of the closet that I've fallen out of the frame entirely. They don't have any words for us, so they can't see us, so we're safe, right?

I get confused.

I forget that invisibility does not ensure safety. We're not safe. We're never safe, we're just. . . .

You tell me.

THE END

roy cohn/
jack smith

PHOTOS: PAULA COURT

Notes on *Roy Cohn/Jack Smith*

Roy Cohn/Jack Smith premiered at the Performing Garage in 1992. The collaborative team was as follows:

Conceived and performed by Ron Vawter
Roy Cohn written by Gary Indiana
Jack Smith written by Jack Smith
Directed by Gregory Mehrten
Created by Gregory Mehrten, Clay Shirky, Ron Vawter, Marianne Weems, and Gary Indiana
Lighting Design: Jennifer Tipton
Costumes: Ellen McCartney
"Chica" in *Jack Smith*: Pedro Rosado
Technical Director: Mike Taylor
Assistant Director/Producer: Marianne Weems
Production Coordinator/Design: Clay Shirky
Consultant for the Production: James Johnson
Production Assistants: Catherine Brophy, Beatrice Roth, Pedro Rosado
Chaise for *Jack Smith* by Elizabeth Murray based on designs by Jack Smith
Constructed by Stephen DeFrank, Warren Kloner, and Mario Sotolongo
"New York, New York" arranged by Vito Ricci

Roy Cohn/Jack Smith was commissioned by Creative Time, Inc., the Fan Fox and Leslie R. Samuels Foundation, the Museum of Contemporary Art in Los Angeles, San Francisco Artspace, the University Art Museum and Pacific Film Archive at the University of California at Berkeley, the Walker Art Center, and the Wexner Center for the Arts. Administrative support was provided by the Wooster Group.

Roy Cohn/Jack Smith is dedicated to the memory of John Konesky.

About Ron Vawter

Ron Vawter was born in upstate New York in 1948. After graduating from Siena College, he joined the U.S. Army, trained with the Special Forces, and studied with the Franciscan order to become a Catholic chaplain. Leaving the church, he became an Army recruiting officer in Manhattan and, in 1974, became business manager of the Performance Group. His first acting role with the Performance Group was in Brecht's Mother Courage and Her Children, *directed by Richard Schechner. He had large roles in the trilogy* Three Places in Rhode Island, *directed by Elizabeth LeCompte and, in 1980, when the Performance Group became the Wooster Group under the artistic direction of LeCompte, he became a core member, appearing in all of their work until his death in 1994. His work with the Wooster Group includes* Route 1 & 9, LSD . . . Just the High Points, Frank Dell's The Temptation of St. Antony, *and* Brace Up!. *He also appeared in plays outside of the Wooster Group, the last being* Philoctetes Variations, *staged in Brussels in 1994. He performed extensively in television, video, and film, both independent and commercial. Some of his films include* sex, lies, and videotape, Internal Affairs, The Silence of the Lambs, *and* Philadelphia. *A film version of* Roy Cohn/Jack Smith, *directed by Jill Godmilow, was released in 1994.*

Ron Vawter: FOR THE RECORD
AN INTERVIEW BY RICHARD SCHECHNER

JACK SMITH, ROY COHN

SCHECHNER: *It's the 31st of July 1992. Let's start with that marvelous piece* Roy Cohn/Jack Smith.

VAWTER: *You know, I never wanted to have a career doing solos like Spalding [Gray]. I was very content to work with the Wooster Group, but after Jack Smith died in September of '89, I thought Jeez, I'd like to make something that memorialized him in some way. I began thinking about Jack. Penny Arcade took me through Jack's apartment. There were tapes and photographs and posters and slides. I got very turned on with the idea of taking one of Jack's pieces and reconstructing it for a revue I was asked* to be part of in Amsterdam. Jack would make very funny slide presentations. So I took notes on the composition of Jack's slides and when I got to Amsterdam I reshot them with myself as Smith. Then I took a tape recording I had of a 1981 performance of What's Underground About Marshmallows?—that's what he'd named this little thing—and I took a slide show which was separate and began to put them together. Jack used his slide shows parenthetically.

I have a funny story. When I saw Jack's slide show, Ron Argelander was assisting him at the time. Ron was a great assistant, a great helper of Jack. It was really crazy. Ron was frantically putting slides into the projector tray, yanking them out of the sheet, and he was putting them in wrong. And when Ron came to see the Cohn/Smith show at the Performing Garage this past spring, the slide projector jammed and Ron had to get up from his seat because the technical people were trying to get this slide out. Ron helped them do it—and he told me afterward it was exactly as though he were still working with Jack, with that slide machine haunting him.

So I made this Jack Smith reconstruction for Amsterdam, and after I finished it, it occurred to me that if I made a complement to this personality, another portrait that in some way balanced Smith, that I would have a very strong evening of theater. Now I've been interested in Roy Cohn for a long time. I thought these two jokers would make a very interesting duo. There are a lot of things about them that are really similar—and a lot that's wildly different. So in 1991 I was working with Mark Rappaport, the filmmaker. He was working on different ways of handling Roy's life as a screenplay, but it didn't work out, I couldn't get hold of a script that I was happy with. But there was this one entry in the Nicholas von Hoffman biography of Cohn. Cohn's chauffeur was talking about driving Cohn—all dressed up in his tux—and his boyfriend to a dinner given by the American Society for the Protection of the Family. Cohn was the featured speaker for the evening. He gave this speech attacking homosexuality. That idea really might be fun, I thought, and so I just wanted to re-create that speech. So I worked with Gary Indiana, the playwright, for nine months developing a version of—

SCHECHNER: How did you do that? How would you develop a version of that speech? Is there a transcript of it?

VAWTER: No, we looked. No tape, no transcript. And the American Society for the Protection of the Family didn't want to talk to us. So what we did was launch a major research thing. Roy was prolific, he wrote a whole lot, although he didn't write many of his speeches down. One of Cohn's books is called Fool for a Client, where he talks about his life and also about legal issues, but nothing much on homosexuality. But from Roy's writings we got a good deal of biographical information. Gary began writing in about how we would attack him remembering his past or his mother and the trials he faced and the committees he worked on.

About homosexuality, we decided we were going to try to write the most intelligent persuasive denunciation of homosexuality that we could possibly muster. We went through all the psychiatric writings pre-'73, when homosexuality was considered a disease or a disorder. We were looking for good arguments, for intelligent, sensible arguments. If people believed being gay was a disease, why did they?

And we came up with sort of classic answers. You know, fear of women, arrested personality, those sort of things. We fashioned those arguments and segued them into biographical information we had on Cohn—using his own words whenever we could. But though Cohn was a famous back-room lobbyist, and an opponent of gay rights legislation, there were few things he would actually say publicly about homosexuals. But from all reports—and we talked to a number of people who were with him, he really did pull a lot of marks on people: "If you don't vote for this, we'll make sure that you get this and this."

SCHECHNER: But people knew he was gay. How did they deal with that? Didn't anybody say to him, "But you're gay"?

VAWTER: If they did, he would respond, "I'm not." He would publicly deny it.

SCHECHNER: But I mean, in the back-room wheeling and dealing.

VAWTER: No. I mean, there's this one story of Carmichael going to Cohn's house. There were all these boys there and Carmichael wondered if this was like a gay brothel, or what. But Roy just coolly said, "These are my servants and butlers and cooks and hairdressers." No, but you're right, of course. Everyone knew Cohn was gay.

SCHECHNER: So wouldn't people be talking behind his back? And wouldn't that affect his political clout?

VAWTER: Exactly. But still, for instance, he brought one of his regular boyfriends to the White House three separate times. So he didn't hide it, he just verbally denied it.

SCHECHNER: *Right.*

VAWTER: *And the fact is, Cohn led the opposition to the gay rights bills in New York for twelve years or more. He didn't want to be known as a gay person. He wanted to practice homosexuality but not advocate it.*

SCHECHNER: *You know, Cohn's always fascinated me, like Nixon. There is nothing about Cohn's politics I like.*

VAWTER: *Right.*

SCHECHNER: *My entry into political consciousness and action was around the McCarthy years. And Cohn was to me the most despicable person, he and Joe McCarthy. And yet, like Nixon, like Richard III, he's so fascinating. He was not the kind of person to be on the wrong side of.*

VAWTER: *Oh no, the worst. Cohn seemed to be a pure incarnation of evil.*

SCHECHNER: *How did you handle that? What was your attitude toward him as you worked on the piece, as you involved yourself in Cohn's personality and values? In seeing the performance, there's very little judgment in it. Did you take a Brechtian stance in relationship to Cohn? Were there things you found that you admired?*

VAWTER: *Well, I began by having the same kinds of feelings toward Roy Cohn that you just expressed. I thought he was a contemptible scumbag. I still think so. My piece is more in the nature of spitting on Cohn's grave. I mean, I think his kind of behavior is absolutely reprehensible and I've made this piece as a warning to homosexuals and a warning to heterosexuals. Warning homosexuals that this kind of behavior is unacceptable. Not only the duplicity of hiding your sexuality but turning around and leading the attack on the homosexual community. That is the lowest form of behavior. To heterosexuals, I'm saying, Look what happens when we repress a person's sexuality. Look at the warping of the personality that can occur, creating a monster like this.*

But the piece is not a psychological portrait. I'm not trying to show the psychological mechanisms and how and why and what happened when he was four years old that would have produced this kind of behavior. I'm saying this kind of behavior is bad. So right off the bat, the piece is deeply judgmental. I'm not taking an open look at Roy Cohn, I'm using him.

SCHECHNER: *But at the same time, like watching a good production of Rich-ard III, watching your impersonation, I smiled and laughed. Because you know, the gift of theater is that you have social reality once removed even*

*as you come face-to-face with the reality of the performers. And I can't
believe you can play someone so effectively if you don't admire him at
some level.*

VAWTER: *Yes, that's what happened. I mean, I can say that I hate the man,
but when I went into rehearsal and permitted these things to come out of
me, I connected to all sorts of things from the time I was first coming out—
the period when I first met you, in the early '70s, when I was leaving the
military. Before then everything I did, even though I felt homosexual, was
a dodge and a hide and a veil: ways of passing. So when I began working
on Cohn, I realized the tragedy of his life in trying to pass all the time. I
connected with that, and it gave me a kind of sympathy or empathy.*

*Plus, you know, Cohn liked to think of himself a little as sort of a
gangster, a scrapper, like Sinatra, he actually patterned himself after
Sinatra, a little tough guy. His masculinity was wrapped up in that. And
that was a lot of fun to play. I've also been interested in Sinatra for a long
time, in his brand of heterosexuality. With Cohn, it was such a mask, that
sort of '50s behavior. And you're right, of course, once I got the text together and began working on it, it was hard not to identify, not to recognize in my own life that I had done a lot of things like Cohn had.*

SCHECHNER: *What struck me as similar was the intensity. You're one of the
most intense people I know, that was clear right from the very first time
I met you. And over the years this intensity has shown more and more
clearly in your performances. In other words, you are extraordinarily fo-
cused and compact—would say, compressed. Now over time, you've
become unrepressed but not uncompressed.*

VAWTER: *Hmmm-mm, you're right.*

SCHECHNER: *And that intensity I feel also in Cohn's personality as you presented
him. In other words, I saw him more clearly through you than I ever saw
him in himself. When I see him in himself, I just want to kill—*

VAWTER: *Yeah, right.*

SCHECHNER: *—but when I see him in you, I have a little distance and you're
someone I love and here's someone I despise but I can appreciate his
intensity through you.*

VAWTER: *Cohn was pretty intense. [Susan] Sontag in her essay "On Camp"
talks about Jews trying to assimilate into American culture and homosexuals
trying to assimilate into American, Western culture—she says these two*

are parallel. Cohn was also an extraordinary Jew-basher, apart from his McCarthy days. There's the story of how he'd call Sy Newhouse Sy "Jewhouse," and Newhouse was an old childhood buddy and client. And there's this other story about the time just after the Army-McCarthy hearings. The chairman of the Anti-Defamation League went to Washington and Cohn, spotting him in the corridor outside one of the Senate chambers, yelled out to him, whatever his name was, "Hal, how are all the fuckin' Jews doing up in New York?" And this guy yelled back, had the presence of mind to yell back, "Fine, I just had dinner with your father last night."

SCHECHNER: *How did you get Cohn's mannerisms and speech patterns? You saw Jack Smith and we'll get to that, but did you study videotapes of Cohn?*

VAWTER: *Oh yeah, I got hours of tapes. I mean, fortunately for me, Cohn gave nine one-hour classes at the New York Law School and those classes are on videotape. I also bought everything that the networks had on Cohn through the Museum of Broadcasting. I went to CBS and actually bought the 60 Minutes program he was on. So I had a lot of stuff.*

But if you look at Cohn carefully, you see I'm not doing an impersonation, it's not a copy. I've created another little portrait lifted off the surface of Cohn. I didn't say, Oh, he tipped this way, he lifted his right shoulder that way. But I did watch those tapes over and over again and I made audiocassettes of the videotapes. I'd put a timer on at night with earphones on and then fall asleep. About two hours after I go to sleep the tape comes on and plays for an hour. I've done that before with other roles. It gives me a lot of unconscious feed.

SCHECHNER: *That's a good idea.*

VAWTER: *It is because when I relax or when I work myself up into a state, when the adrenaline starts, there's a moment where you pass over. If you get yourself excited enough, you pass over beyond the agitation. What I have to be able to do is get to that flip. If I feed my unconscious in a direct way, I can connect over into that.*

SCHECHNER: *Let's go back to Jack Smith. How did you work?*

VAWTER: *With Jack I still perform, and I intend always to perform, with a Walkman and a recording of Jack's performing this piece in '81 in my ear. It's not just because I'm trying to get his voice right. What I'm trying to get right is his timing. So I use the tape as a kind of metronome.*

SCHECHNER: *Oh, I didn't know that. So it's actually playing all the time?*

VAWTER: *All the time. I know the monologue by heart, it's only six pages of actual script. But Jack performed with a sense of time that I would never try to pull off in front of an audience. I can't imagine performing without the audiotape. Once my machine didn't work and I stopped the show and got another one brought on stage for me.*

SCHECHNER: *Does he slow you down?*

VAWTER: *Slows me way way down. And Jack was famous for his long extensions and attenuations of speech and so the tape keeps me on his track.*

SCHECHNER: *So you are performing a particular piece Smith did in '81?*

VAWTER: *Yeah.*

SCHECHNER: *What about the setting and the costume and that stuff?*

VAWTER: *It's more of a conglomerate, condensed, I mean, like the slide show. The slides I show he didn't show as part of his performance. I've put together a forty-minute condensed evening with Jack Smith where you get an idea of his whole work: the kinds of projections he would use, the kinds of setting he would make. I want to give a lot of people who never saw Jack a sense of who he was as a performer. You know, not a whole lot of people saw him. He would usually do two or three nights, that's all. I wanted to show people what he was about, what he was after, what this world, this universe, was that he created.*

SCHECHNER: *So how did you develop the piece?*

VAWTER: *From the outside in. I mean, I took all the stuff and put it on myself like a skin.*

SCHECHNER: *When you started to rehearse, at the very beginning, did you use costumes and sets and things?*

VAWTER: *Yeah. I mean, Penny took me over to the costume shops where Jack would buy his material. You know, Jack was for turning junk into art. He really was one of the early pop artists. And there were a lot of photographs of him in costume. So I sort of re-created, rebuilt costumes. A lot of his things are over at PS I. I went through the collection carefully. Both monologues were research projects. I tried to immerse myself as deeply and as carefully and in as much detail as I could with both. I mean, that little tuxedo that I had for Roy Cohn I had made by Roy's tailor.*

SCHECHNER: *And who worked with you directing the piece?*

VAWTER: *Greg [Mehrten].*

SCHECHNER: *What was his role in developing the piece?*

VAWTER: *Well, I made the Jack Smith all by myself for that Amsterdam ap-*
pearance. Then, I knew that if I were to make an evening that was well
balanced and was going to contain another portrait, I needed somebody
who would be able to sit outside, an outside eye. Greg was actually more
involved with the making of the Cohn and the balancing of the Cohn with
the—

SCHECHNER: *Smith. And what about the importance of Jack Smith's ashes?*

VAWTER: *Yeah. Two years ago, I was in Los Angeles working on an ABC/Disney*
film and there was a powwow of American theater artists with Native
American blood. I was fascinated with it because I'm one-quarter Choctaw
from my father's side. My father's mother lived on a Choctaw reserva-
tion. Her name was Tabitha. She died when I was about five years old, so
I never got any information through her about any rituals or stuff. So I went
to this powwow where there was a group workshop on the use of cere-
monial ash in Indian performance and dance ceremonies. There are man-
tras that get sung and dance steps around ashes. Then you mix the ash
with the color you're using as makeup. So when I was starting to work
with Penny on researching Jack, she let me have some of his ashes, and
because Jack's sense of how to paint himself for a performance was so
extreme and in a way was a kind of warpaint itself, I thought, Well, I'm
going to use the ash, I'm going to return him to his own makeup. So I use
the ash for every performance. I mix it with the glitter I put on my eyes
and it charges me. It empowers me in a way that—I mean, when I'm
sitting there and I know that Jack is on my face literally and I hear him
coming through the earphones and I'm amidst this whole world of his I've
carefully engineered to have around me—the slides, the reconstruction
of space—something spooky comes through. I don't mean a trance or a
kind of possession, but I get a very, very heavy charge which pulls me
through the performance.

SCHECHNER: *Why do you defend against saying it is trance or possession?*
Because it sounds to me like a classic instance of induced trance posses-
sion. People have the wrong idea if they think trance means you're uncon-
scious or you can't do this or that. Trance just means inducing a second
reality which you inhabit and which is very powerful. It doesn't necessarily
erase your primary reality. You know, there are many different theories of

how trance is induced but the use of the ash, putting yourself in the environment, the hearing of the voice, creates a second actuality which is coincident with your own on the stage—so why would you resist acknowledging that?

VAWTER: Well, if that's the definition of trance, then this is trance work.

SCHECHNER: It's one kind of trance. Not hypnotic trance, where you forget. It's more like Balinese trance, where they know very well what they're doing but their actions are guided not by their conscious self.

VAWTER: Richard, that's exactly how it feels. I mean, it feels as though there is a second will at work. Although I'm very aware of everything I do on the stage.

SCHECHNER: That's exactly what the Balinese would say. You are still there, but there's this other force that is helping you make the movements and keeping the movements safe, proper, or correct or within bounds or whatever.

VAWTER: You know, one of the things that sends me off is I have to flip, particularly as the performance goes on, I get caught in a rhythm that is not, that is totally not mine, and that rhythm opens me up to the second will. It's quite rhythmic, the differences. It's like a different rhythm from mine.

SCHECHNER: Right, right.

VAWTER: I wanted to say, this is interesting, getting into the rhythm of another person. Remember the dancer Spalding [Gray] had an affair with when you were directing The Performance Group? A beautiful, beautiful dancer, very tall. When she saw the piece she said she got so into the rhythms of Jack as differentiated from my own that when it came to that little dance I do, she said, "I felt like I could've gotten up and done that dance. I knew what the dance was before you even danced it."

SCHECHNER: Right, right, right.

VAWTER: Now, I think, that is the success of Jack Smith. This trance or other energy which, when I've played my cards right, this other energy has the opportunity to come forward. But it's not impersonation. I've talked to friends of Jack who say I didn't imitate his voice or anything like that.

SCHECHNER: No, what you do is not like this actor who imitates Mark Twain or something like that.

VAWTER: Right, this is not Hal Holbrook.

SCHECHNER: *It's what I would call a re-creation, not a reproduction.*

VAWTER: *Yes. That's right. That's exactly right. The remarks I make to the audience before are as rehearsed as the pieces themselves. I spent a lot of time on how to present myself at the beginning and how much information to tell. I want the audience to know there is another personality at work in the room, apart from these created ones.*

SCHECHNER: *Right. Exactly. And you used to have somebody sit at the table—*

VAWTER: *I still do. Each night I have on stage—when I can get them—some persons whose lives were really deeply affected by Cohn. One man, for instance, was a card-carrying Communist in the fifties in New York, and a lot of his friends had their careers destroyed or committed suicide. This man is a real Cohn hater. The other two are in the same situation. They were socialists. Whenever I'm up there and my energy begins to slack, I look over to them and I get this hit of, "Oh, right, this is what I'm doing up here."*

SCHECHNER: *Cohn and Smith died of AIDS and you are HIV-positive. That must have had an effect on why you chose to do this in these times.*

VAWTER: *You know, I had just learned of my positivity about six months before Jack died, and when I began work on the piece, I still had not been diagnosed with full-blown AIDS but I was sero-positive. See, the thing, the big problem as I see it, one of the horrible aspects of this disease is that it has a . . . it . . . it's such a potent and destructive force that it's taken over the whole spectrum of gay problems or the problems of the homosexual in American society. Very little else is being said except responses to the AIDS virus. But the homosexual today has as many problems as he or she had thirty, forty, or fifty years ago. I mean, homosexuality is still illegal in half the states, and we are the only minority which is legally discriminated against. There used to be a lot more said about that, and a lot more energy and activity went into the problems the homosexual faces. But AIDS has loomed up so large that it's taken so much of the conversation and the public discussion.*

So what I want to do is without sidestepping the AIDS issue, I want to take two people with AIDS, go beyond that, and continue the discussion about the forces of repression in this country. I think repression is still far more destructive to the homosexual than the AIDS virus. I mean, when you were told as a child, as you're growing up, that every impulse you feel inside you is abnormal or immoral or wrong or bad, it creates a system of self-loathing. I mean, you don't want it to be there, yet you can't deny it. That conflict, that push and pull, I believe, deeply, profoundly warps the personality. My performance is a study of two individuals who I feel were warped. If Jack or Roy worked or lived in a society that did not tell them that homosexuality was wrong, they would not have become the people that they became. I think Jack was as warped as Roy, a totally different warp but still warped. So I chose them because they had AIDS, but I sort of did that to get it out of the way so I could talk about something else altogether. I mean, I'm really focusing on the effects of sexual repression. I wanted people to see that AIDS is only part of the problem that homosexuals have to deal with. It's a big and an extraordinary one, but it's only part of the destructive force.

Does that answer your—?

SCHECHNER: *Yeah, very clearly.*

VAWTER: *I wanted to make a good comedy, an evening people would enjoy coming to.*

SCHECHNER: *Of course. And it really is a lot of fun. It's ironic, sometimes bitter, sometimes hilarious. It's not sentimental.*

VAWTER: *As you know, I'm looking to use comedy to disarm the audience, to open them to my ideas. I put them at so much ease and comfort, then I can sock it to them with what is essentially an essay on oppression. And as you said in our earlier talk right after you saw the show, we have to create a community through which the discussion is even possible. Comedy is one of the best ways to create a community.*

SCHECHNER: *Absolutely. Absolutely. Is there anything more you want to say about that piece? If not, I want to move on and talk about some other stuff.*

VAWTER: *Just that I'm not interested in taking two more characters and doing them.*

SCHECHNER: *You're not about to become Spalding Gray.*

VAWTER: *Eric Bogosian. No, this form seemed to be necessitated by the thing that wanted to be said.*

SCHECHNER: *Actually the Cohn/Smith show isn't a monologue. These are monodramas—a full play performed by one person. Kind of like the stuff Jeff Weiss does.*

VAWTER: *You know, I was very, very affected by Jeff's work. I connect with it deeply. Jeff is not afraid to throw out his worst fantasies, his worst demons, to fully inhabit them, what he fears about himself and what he fears others think of him. When I was first making Roy Cohn, I thought, Shit, the gay political field is screaming that only positive representations should be made. At the time I thought about Jeff and the power of releasing those demons on stage.*

SCHECHNER: *What was the reaction of the gay press? Did anybody hammer you for what you did?*

VAWTER: *No, everyone was very positive. They saw the Cohn part as a warning to homosexuals, that we can't permit this kind of behavior to go on. I think if I hadn't given that speech before the performance, there might have been a question of what my motive was.*

roy cohn/jack smith

RON VAWTER

Introductory Remarks for the Performance of *Roy Cohn/Jack Smith*

Good evening, and welcome to the Performing Garage. My name is Ron Vawter, and you are about to see a performance of *Roy Cohn/Jack Smith*. I put some biographical information in your programs about Roy and Jack, but let me say a couple of things before we start.

In 1978, Roy Cohn and his boyfriend dressed up in their tuxedos and were chauffeured off to a dinner for the American Society for the Protection of the Family. After dinner, Roy gave a speech condemning homosexuality. This was part of a long crusade of Roy's. For twelve or thirteen years, Roy Cohn was one of the chief opponents preventing the passage of gay rights legislation through the New York City Council; this, despite his own homosexuality, which he publicly denied throughout his life. There was no record of the speech he gave back in 1978. So last year I asked writer Gary Indiana if he would imagine what Roy might have said that night, not as a historical re-creation of literally what was said, but a version of the speech that we might have heard had we been there and known what we know about Roy today. Roy Cohn died of AIDS in 1986.

That's the first part of the evening. It lasts about forty minutes. We'll take a ten- or fifteen-minute break and come back for part two, *Jack Smith*.

Now, Jack was a filmmaker and theater artist who lived and worked here in New York, as did Roy. I guess Jack is best known for his 1962 film *Flaming Creatures*. But in 1965 he began to make theater pieces which deeply affected me and a lot of other people who came to New York in the late sixties to begin to make theater, including Richard Foreman, Robert Wilson, Charles Ludlam, and Ethel Eichelberger. Many artists from various disciplines were affected by Jack's aesthetic sense. In 1981, Jack made a performance entitled *What's Underground About Marshmallows?* the text of which I use for my own presentation tonight, together with a slide show I shot in Amsterdam, the Netherlands, two years ago, based directly on Jack's own slide presentations of the late seventies and eighties. Jack Smith died of AIDS in 1989.

Jack's theater had something of an ordeal quality to it. Performances could last four, five, six hours. You were never quite sure when it had begun or when it was over. I'm not going to put you through that tonight. I don't have the guts—I wish I did. What I've prepared for you is a forty-minute condensed version of an evening with Jack Smith to match the length of time of the Cohn section.

These two portraits were made to be seen together, and together they constitute a single expression. This is not impersonation. I am not interested in how closely I can copy or imitate the mannerisms, gestures, or speech patterns of Roy or Jack. I am a person living with AIDS, and for my own purposes, I've taken only particular aspects of their personalities and balanced one against the other for my own theatrical motives. This is not documentary, but rather a subjective reaction, a response, to the lives of two very different white male homosexuals who had two powerful things in common: a virus, and a society which sought to repress their sexuality.

Well, I've managed to make my little speech much more solemn than I intended. Please relax, and get comfortable in your folding chairs. I hope you enjoy the piece. We made it for you.

Roy Cohn
by Gary Indiana

(RON VAWTER DRESSED AS ROY COHN—PURPLE VELVET DIN-
NER JACKET, TUXEDO SHIRT, PANTS, AND SHOES—STEPS
ONTO THE STAGE, CHAMPAGNE GLASS IN HAND. HE STANDS
IN FRONT OF A MICROPHONE PODIUM THAT IS PLACED IN
THE MIDDLE OF A LONG BANQUET TABLE. THE TABLE IS
COVERED WITH A WHITE TABLECLOTH, ONTO WHICH BOU-
QUETS OF RED CARNATIONS ARE SET. THE FRONT OF THE
TABLE IS MASKED BY PLEATED, SHINY GOLD FABRIC, AND
BEHIND THE TABLE IS A MAMMOTH PLEATED BLUE CURTAIN.
THERE IS HEARD THUNDEROUS APPLAUSE AND A BOUNCY
INSTRUMENTAL RECORDING OF "NEW YORK, NEW YORK." HE
TAKES ONE FINAL SIP OF CHAMPAGNE AND BEGINS TO SPEAK.)

I want to thank Dr. Brenner for that warm introduction and
Reverend Neville, whose work with the victims of child pornog-
raphy we're all familiar with. And Mr., uh, Mr. Jorgenson from
the Coors Company for sponsoring this evening's, uh, festivities,
to thank them, and you, for the invitation to speak tonight and to
say how pleased I am that I was asked here tonight to talk about
the city council hearings on the gay rights bill (HE TAKES A PEN
FROM HIS INSIDE JACKET POCKET AND HOLDS IT IN ONE HAND)
among other subjects, and the dangers this bill represents to traditional values. I understand that this organization, which is dedicated to upholding family, family values, protecting morality, that
this organization, for example, has backed up Anita Bryant down
in Dade County, Florida, reversing the trend towards a, what could
you call it, a Sodom and Gomorrah atmosphere, which is literally
what prevails in every city in this country where the so-called gay
rights movement has gained a foothold. These people who want
freedom of expression so badly have launched a witch-hunt against
Anita Bryant to the point where she's losing thousands of dollars
in concert fees every week. But this is an old story where the
American left wing is concerned. Many of you are here in New
York from smaller towns and cities, and if time permitted, and we

all had strong enough stomachs, I could escort you on a tour of some places on the West Side of Manhattan that would send any decent person into a state of shock, where you would witness the kind of unspeakable behavior that's become part of the Roman Circus of the homosexual underworld. And I don't mean in the questionably sacred privacy of people's homes, but right out in the public domain. I won't get into it more than I have to, but to give you an idea of just how low things have sunk, you've got celebrities pulling up to places with names like The Toilet in their limousines in order to observe various sexual rituals that would've been called criminally depraved if not downright satanic in any other period of history, except for the late Roman Empire. I don't say this for the shock value, but only to indicate the irony of these people, crawling out of bed after two hours' sleep, having spent the entire night ingesting every drug they could take to heighten their orgiastic revels, some of them involving, and my apologies to the ladies in the audience, but among today's homo set, evidently the most popular sexual practice involves penetration of the *rectum* with a fist. Sometimes an entire arm! (HE ACCOMPANIES THIS WITH A GESTURE OF THE HAND/ARM) Unimaginable as this may seem, and again I ask the ladies in the audience to forgive the need for graphic detail, but I think we all need to know the extent of what we're talking about. You've got these very shrill inverts that are down there at the hearings every day, screaming their slogans in their respectable clothes, when only hours earlier they were prancing around the West Village in Nazi uniforms and chains, or hanging from a torture rack in a dimly lit bar. Believe me, this kind of thing has become so commonplace you can even see it creeping into fashion magazines. Maybe some of you saw that movie *The Eyes of Laura Mars*? Anyway, not so long ago some of the crème de la crème of New York society showed up at a bar called The Anvil to watch a young man eject pool balls from his rear end, another one who pulled several yards of thick chain out of himself . . . Well, I'm going to spare you more of the details.

This (HOLDS UP PEN) is a pen, ladies and gentlemen. I guess you all can see it. The new mayor of this city, Edward Koch, is a liberal Democrat from the hub of today's gay world, the West Village. Koch won the primary over a lot of opposition that used the cautionary slogan "Vote for Cuomo, not the homo." Now, I don't pretend to know the mayor's sexual orientation, nor do I care about it, but if I had to speculate, I'd say "He hasn't got any!" But I find it symptomatic, either of some type of offbeat personal quirk or his own blind obedience to certain pressure groups, that the first thing the mayor does, the first signature that goes down on a piece of paper, is an executive order barring, in his words, discrimination on the basis of sex, sexual orientation, race, religion, and national origin. Everything jumbled together like peanuts, bananas, and oranges. With one stroke of the pen. But, as we know, what with your own experience in Dade County, and as we've seen around the country in recent weeks, one of the primary virtues of a democracy is that when radical measures such as these are imposed on people by fiat, they can also be rescinded when enough people stand up and say, "We're fed up, some things ought to be against the law, enough already." That's democracy, and that's what makes us different from Russia.

It's Koch who's dragged up the gay rights bill again, and I have, obviously, some very strong feelings in opposition, which I hope to explain to you in somewhat calmer language than I started out with. But with your indulgence, and as I've also been asked to say a little bit about *me*, and maybe you won't mind hearing it since I'm not running for anything . . . well, Dr. Brenner and Reverend Neville asked me to say a word or two about Roy Cohn—not my least favorite subject, I'll admit—but anyway, to go back a little, when I was first asked to talk to the American Society for the Protection of the Family, I honestly jumped at the chance. I am and always have been a strong believer in Americanism, and the family unit; the strong happy family unit is the seed at the root of Americanism. At the same time, I thought, Gee, what've I got to tell them? I'm not married, I don't have a family. My sainted mother just died recently, both parents have passed on, no wife, no kids—you know, to tell you the truth, I always felt that being a controversial person and being a person that people were always going to be fighting about and over, and always destined to be in some kind of battle or other, that I could go through it all better if all I had to worry about was myself, not a wife and kids who are going to have part of the heartache pushed over onto them.

(BIG SMILE) Know what I like more than anything? Birthday cake. A big birthday cake with candles and little kids in party hats, and confetti and noisemakers, and parents' faces lit up with the joy leaping in their hearts at the sight of those little ones . . . (MUSING) those little ones. And don't they get adorable when they come into their early teens and shoot up eight or nine inches in a year! I'll tell you something. I don't have a family, not yet, anyways, but I have plenty of godchildren, children of good friends, and one of the happiest things in my life is what I can give to those kids. Mr. Steinbrenner's a friend of mine, they can always get tickets to the big game. That sort of thing. And when you look at those kids, their innocence, you realize that the family is the basis of everything. And it's facing terrific challenges in the society we live in today, the permissive society of 1978.

I mean, to look around today you would begin to believe the biggest evil in the world is the idea of having to work for a living. Sorry, that isn't how Roy Cohn was brought up. And here we get to family values. I am rather proud of my family. My grandparents were born in four different European countries, and each chose the United States for a home. My father worked his way through City College and New York Law School at night while teaching during the day. Albert Cohn lived long enough to see his name engraved in the rotunda of the state courthouse.

I grew up with the movers and shakers of the Bronx right at the kitchen table. It's true what they say about Roy Cohn. I do know every circuit judge and every minor politician's second cousin twice removed, known them all my life and breathed the air of politics from when I was this high. Frankly, I was not a boy for sports and activities, although I am in good shape. I water-ski (MAKES A GESTURE OF HOLDING THE TOW LINE), not that water-skiing keeps you in shape, I must have good bone structure or, hey, maybe it's genetics, the old family again. Anyway, I was a shy kid,

well, not shy exactly, reticent, whatever, and became interested
in the law and the justice system and how it worked behind the
scenes—very honestly, from the age of about five. My father would
discuss his cases with me. "What do you think about this, Roy?
What about that? Should I appoint him? Is that one out to screw
me?" Well, I didn't necessarily have all the answers at that age,
but my father always listened to my opinion. My mother . . .

My mother was an intelligent and gracious lady, Dora Marcus.
Maybe I was a shy type or, as I say, reticent. The thing is, they
both fussed over me a lot to get me out of there, you know, when
I was . . . well, in the womb, because she wouldn't, uh, they
couldn't, uh, well, they had to blow air up her fallopian tubes to
get me out of there. So she wasn't having any more after that.
Unavoidably, I became the star attraction of the family. Dora
Marcus of the well-to-do Marcuses of Park Avenue married a little
below her station, so the legend goes. Good old Muddy. I called
her Muddy, you know. But fuss, I kid you not, she had me at the
dermatologist three weeks out of the womb. (AT THIS POINT HE
TOUCHES HIS NOSE) Anyway . . . I learned the value of a close-knit
family. In the thirties you learned to stick together. Those were
hard times. Regardless of how I look at things now, back then
Franklin Roosevelt looked like a savior. I think back to the apartment we lived in on Park Avenue, after we left the Bronx. We
gave an enormous Passover every year, relatives, ward bosses, the
rabbi . . . Muddy had a slightly hysterical streak when it came to
large affairs, you know, she always had to be the queen bee, it came
from that rich upbringing, and something always went wrong.
Anyway, one year my aunt Libby got there early and wanted to
say hi to the cook, and Muddy said, "No, Libby, I don't want you
going in there," so later, when they got to the part of the Passover
service where the question is posed, "Why is this night different
from other nights?" Muddy answered, "Because the serving girl is
dead in the kitchen." She'd keeled over with a heart attack and
they had to get the coroner in. That was Passover.

Then every year there were summer camps, this is where all
that fussing . . . Camp Menatoma in Maine, Camp Sagamore on

Lake George. I'm put into the camp, Muddy checks into the nearest hotel. She comes to the camp every day and tells the counselors, "Don't make my Roy walk too far into the woods, the allergies he has. Only allow Roy to swim for one half hour, he isn't supposed to exhaust himself, he has weak lungs" . . . which I *didn't*, in fact. But I hated those camps anyway, and when one of those greasy shtetl Jews that ran Menatoma dropped in on Park Avenue to say what a great camper I was, what was his name, Friedenwald, Dr. Friedenwald, and that creep son of his Johnny Friedenwald the sadist camp counselor. They were drumming up some shekles for the next year, I told that kike he was full of crap . . . pardon my French. . . . Is anybody here besides me Jewish? (PAUSE) Life is sure full of memories.

I remember afternoons in Mr. Baruth's class at Horace Mann, memorizing Tennyson . . . "Oh purblind race of miserable men / How many among us at this very hour / Do forge a lifelong trouble for ourselves, / By taking true for false, or false for ture; / Here, thro' the feeble twilight of this world / Groping, how many, until we pass and reach / That other, where we see as we are seen!"

What's striking to me looking back, and I do look back, and others have commented on it, too, is that when I went down as chief counsel for Joseph McCarthy in 1953, I totally broke with my own background. Here I was, a young Jewish Democrat from New York, supposedly the most liberal, one of the most liberal cities in the United States, going down to become chief counsel for a fellow like Joe McCarthy. Now, you might wonder how that came about. When I was working in the U.S. Attorney's Office during the Hiss, you know, espionage business, I didn't believe Alger Hiss had been any kind of Russian spy. Neither did my parents, neither did any Jewish liberals at the time. Alger Hiss was a hero, an adviser to FDR at Yalta, victim of witch-hunt hysteria, et cetera, and then one spring afternoon in 1949, two FBI agents working on the case took me out to lunch at Gastner's around the corner from the Foley Square courthouse. Gastner's had terrific corned beef. You had a choice of Angelo's or Gastner's. And I preferred Gastner's for its corned beef. And I mentioned to these

FBI men, I said, Hiss is a scapegoat, and this thing stinks the way herring stinks.

One of the agents smiled and said, "How much do you really know about Alger Hiss and Whittaker Chambers?" I didn't know enough to get through half a Bloody Mary. Like a lot of people, I thought Whittaker Chambers had an overactive imagination and couldn't tell reality from fiction. The guy was a brilliant intellectual, an editor at *Time* magazine, but then again, he'd also translated *Bambi,* which made you wonder a little, that maybe he was off among the buttercups and bunny rabbits in never-never land. And it was said that Chambers, who had admitted his homosexual tendencies, had a romantic fixation on Alger Hiss, a handsome WASP, and Chambers, you know, was quite dumpy and fat, with a tendency to, you know, perspire, and Hiss had rejected his advances, which provoked the accusation of spying. Well. Call me irresponsible. I got a crash course in communism in Gastner's that afternoon that changed my orientation around three hundred and ninety degrees. Boy, did those guys fill me in on what was what, about the Kremlin cells in top-secret U.S. federal departments. I was an espionage virgin until that afternoon. After that rude awakening I picked up everything I could get my hands on about communism.

And here you find the real threat to the American family and our way of life in the great flirtation with communism that intellectuals like Hiss, and working-class socialists like the Rosenbergs, were swept away by. One reason that Jewish families like mine felt embattled during this period was because of a widespread idea associating Jews with a sympathy towards communism. This is something that has always bothered me, and I've tried in every way I can to make it clear that the fact that the name is Cohn, and the fact of my religion, has nothing to do except perfect compatibility with my love for America and my dislike for communism. So when the opportunity arose to work on the Rosenberg prosecution, I felt that my overdue moment had arrived. Okay, the prosecution side were not complete strangers. My father put Irving Kaufman on the bench, and I got him the Rosenberg case, which he lobbied for like you wouldn't believe, and once he got it he never stopped complaining. Irving Kaufman was an impossible human being.

Anyway, with the Rosenbergs, you had this idea that Jews would be more willing to betray their country, and we all fought against that idea. Here you had the prosecutor Irving Saypol, me, and Judge Kaufman, all Jews, bringing in a conviction, and imposing the maximum penalty. No one was going to accuse the Jewish judge or the Jewish prosecutors of leniency or a lack of vigilance.

Was that a consideration in the trial? Yes and no. It was a scrupulously fair trial, there was a perfect chain of evidence linking Klaus Fuchs to the Rosenbergs, David Greenglass, Morton Sobell, the cut-in-half Jell-O box—I knew the death sentence was going to be imposed because Judge Kaufman told me when he got the case that he was going to send Julius Rosenberg to the electric chair. (PAUSE)

Okay, as far as Ethel Rosenberg is concerned . . . Kaufman always told people he prayed for guidance about the sentences, which is probably true. But besides asking God what to do, Irving used to call me up from a phone booth next to the Park Avenue Synagogue. In the courtroom there was a phone I could use, out of sight of everybody walking through—and I told Judge Kaufman, which was certainly true, I said a criminal defendant reveals everything about himself in the courtroom. And if you watched her in the courtroom, you could see Ethel Rosenberg was the strong one, Ethel Rosenberg got her brother David Greenglass started with the Young Communist League to begin with. She was the one who kept drilling him full of Communist propaganda. It was as obvious . . . as the nose on her . . . my face that Ethel Rosenberg was the queen bee of the whole hive. If Judge Kaufman had declined to execute Ethel because she was the mother of two small children, it would have been basically a case of reverse sexism, not that we had that term back then, saying a woman couldn't be as much of a traitor, or as guilty, as a man.

Well, that's ancient history, and I'm not gonna say now, looking back, I would do everything I did then the same way today . . . fuh. But I've never felt the slightest qualm about the execution of the Rosenbergs, frankly. But to get back to the point I was trying to make, and not to stray too far from the subject of families—maybe the Rosenbergs are an unfortunate example of one, since Ethel's own mother was eager to testify against her—among the Cohns, there was never any family schism during the McCarthy era or later on. As a lifelong bachelor whom luck has eluded in finding the right partner—I'm told the matchmakers have given up. I haven't! Anyway, Barbara Walters and I are going to get married when we're both sixty! At any rate, not having gotten married, I can say that the unconditional approval of my mother and father in those early career days was probably the main thing that kept me in one piece.

I wouldn't *mind* getting married. By the way, if there's anybody out there who doesn't mind a halfway attractive guy in middle age—well, young middle age—

It's no wonder that supporters of the traditional family . . . family values . . . like those of us here in this room . . . feel besieged in this period of women's lib and letting it all hang out, with male and female roles breaking down among the young, and more and more couples living together outside wedlock . . . and all the more reason why organizations like yours need to send a message to the Carter administration and the Democratic Congress, and to the city councils of this city and other cities around the country. And that message is being sent. In St. Paul, Minnesota, 54,101 against 31,689 voters to rescind the local gay rights ordinance. And the same pattern in Eugene, Oregon, and Dade County, Florida, as we've already seen. In Witchita, Kansas, an overwhelming 29,402 against 6,153.

The lesson couldn't be more clear. The vast majority of people in this country are hardworking men and women who get engaged and marry and have children in the traditional pattern. The majority are not the liberal political establishment, the country club set and the martinis and the, uh, tennis matches on Saturday afternoon. The majority are the workers and the middle class, the white-collar people and the blue-collar people, who are fed up with permissiveness, homosexuality, and feminist lesbianism being rammed down their throats by the media every fifteen seconds. It's an historically proven fact that a decline in masculinity and clearly defined sex roles, as well as a tremendous increase in sodomy and other immoral practices, always follows in the wake of a humiliating defeat or national catastrophe. The United States has suffered two very dramatic blows in recent years, one right after the other, that have eroded some of the bedrock of American family values. The first was the Vietnam disaster, where American boys were forced to fight in a foreign jungle with their hands tied behind their backs. Undermined by Washington and the TV reporters, the something-for-nothing peaceniks and rabble-rousers, the leftist college professors, the Jane Fondas—I saw that goddamned piece of shit—pardon my French. I saw that piece of *sleaze* coming out of George Steinbrenner's hotel in Tampa in a fur coat! I guess she forgot her black pajamas at home for a change. Hanoi Jane, and her Commie Husband, Tom Hayden. They're both climbing into the back of a stretch Lincoln. Yeah. The Jane Fondas, the Abbie Hoffmans, the flag burners, the *Vanessa Redgraves* with their pro-PLO terrorist propaganda, the Communist sympathizers all across the board. They won't stoop to support America, but America supports them, in a lifestyle most people can't even dream about. There's Hanoi Jane in her goddamned feature-length mink at the Super Bowl!

The main point is, the war was opposed by people with an unsympathetic point of view towards strong patriotism, and they were able to demoralize the American public through the media.

The second blow was the Watergate brouhaha. Which, partly because of the mass media's enjoyment of playing God after Vietnam, permitted the Democratic Congress to railroad Nixon out of the White House for a third-rate burglary he had nothing to do with, and which, on a scale of presidential transgressions, would have to rank on a par with short-changing the milkman, compared to some of the things every Democratic president from FDR to LBJ has done.

These two blows to America's self-esteem and confidence opened the floodgates to every malcontent with a grudge against this country, from the Symbionese Liberation Front to the bra-burning feminists, the Kate Millet lezzies and the man-eating Ti-Grace Atkinsons and the Gloria Steinems—simple common sense has been chucked right out the window.

Today you've got a society riddled with whining, professional victims. Naturally America has got her problems, you don't throw every race and nationality together in a big melting pot without a little friction. But to believe that contentious attitudes can be legislated away, presto chango with some type of magic wand, is typical of the ultraliberal philosophy of the federal government as everybody's piggy bank.

As I've mentioned earlier, the gay rights bill is unpopular. And more importantly, it is completely unpopular among the people it would affect—employers, landlords, school boards—and so forth. The people of this country don't want to hear about Adam and Steve's honeymoon. People do not want to hear about "lovers" and "longtime companions," and they especially don't want their children exposed to what these people do, or don't do, as so-called consenting adults. Where does consent come in when you're acting under a compulsion? We don't talk about consenting psycho killers and consenting necrophiliacs, and the same case applies here. You know, most psychiatrists will tell you, off the record, that homosexuals are basically men who for one reason or another are afraid of women, afraid of sexual relations with women, and afraid of mature relationships generally. In other words, they're like children, saying, along with Peter Pan, "I won't grow up." Yet here they are, demanding adult rights, and demanding that other people recognize them as "equal." Go into any neighborhood gathering place, any hardware store, any church basement, in New York any numbers parlor or corner saloon, and ask the common man what he thinks about so-called gay people teaching in your public schools and you'll be lucky if you get out of there without your clipboard wrapped around your neck. That's how the people of this country, and *this city*, with all its vaunted liberalism, feel about this perversion of biology and nature. So Mayor Koch thinks he can *swish* his pen over a piece of Gracie Mansion letterhead and eliminate three thousand years of established sexual morality?

You know, it's personally quite ironic to me that the sob sisters going along with the gay rights bill are the same pinkish Democrats who back in the fifties tried to smear the McCarthy committee with suggestions that David Schine and myself, that we had some sort of . . . well, involvement, merely because we were both bachelors . . . suggestions about David and me that were completely ridiculous. David Schine went on and got married to Miss Universe and had eight children! And anybody who knows anything about Roy Cohn knows there is nothing . . . about me. Whatever! I'm not afraid of women. I like women! David Schine liked women and still likes women, and as for Joseph McCarthy, he married his secretary!

There's a moral argument to be made as well. Take this set of facts. For two thousand years Christianity has considered homosexuality an abomination in the eyes of God. It's condemned in Leviticus and in Deuteronomy. I don't recall the exact quotes, but the Bible is explicit in saying that if a man lieth with a man as if with a woman, he shall be put to death, period. End of story!

Then we turn to Jewish law. Again, in three thousand years of recorded Jewish teaching, Jewish practice, not one single instance of any provision, any exemption, any suggestion of the legitimacy of a single homosexual relationship. Homosexuality is condemned, pure and simple.

So in the moral code of the West, the Judeo-Christian code, we find absolutely no toleration of, or excuses for, homosexual behavior. It's licentious, it's venal, it's perverted, it's against nature.

You know, one person who was untiring in fighting this thing was Cardinal Spellman, God rest his soul. I had dinner with him last year in Provincetown, and he told me this homosexuality thing just broke his heart. They're sick, he told me, sick in spirit, sad people, and only Jesus himself can really free them from the chains of this perversion. And to see how many of them are turning their backs on Jesus just breaks the cardinal's heart. Now, this is a man of God talking, with all the compassion and wisdom of his cardinalship. He didn't hate the gays, far from it. Neither do I, I feel sorry

for them. I sincerely do. Kitty, uh, Cardinal Spellman, even coun-
seled these kids, troubled teenagers from broken homes who get
mixed up in child prostitution and so forth. Breaks your heart, the
way the old ones prey on the young and so on.

This gay lib business can be traced back—1951, the foundation
of an organization called the Mattachine Society. Interestingly,
and perhaps significantly, this first American homo organization
was founded by a Communist named Harry Hay.

June 1969. The vicious Stonewall riots, in which various transvestites, or female impersonators, upset over the death of Judy
Garland, threw garbage cans at the police and set police cars on
fire! Next, homosexual groups such as the Gay Liberation Front
made a relentless assault on the American Psychiatric Association,
to force them to drop homosexuality as a psychiatric disorder.
Which the APA officially did in 1973, after years of intimidation
and disruption of its annual meetings. This has to be the first and
only time in the history of medicine that a disease *disappeared*
through the demands of people suffering from it!

Next, gay radicals espoused a strategy called "coming out of
the closet," meaning to make a very dramatic public declaration
of their homosexuality, showing off what they do in private, with
the female names for men, the limp wrists, the swishery, the various signals by which homosexuals recognize each other, to say
nothing of the lezzie girls in their tuxedos and cigars, all the while
bringing a lot of pressure on people responsible for public policy.

I can hear the howls of protest from the radicals if they ever
heard me say this, but in fact, a homosexual who doesn't draw
attention to his private behavior in some obnoxious way is not
gonna encounter any discrimination. Now that idea comes straight
from the *Village Voice*, strange to say, by a writer named Jeff
Greenfield, who is way to the left of me or you but obviously still
has a shred or two of common sense. Gays are not the only people
condemned to behave one way in public and another way in private. All of us check some of our personal habits at the door when
we enter the public arena.

Isn't that the whole issue in a nutshell? A black person doesn't choose to be black, a woman is obviously a woman—all right. They can't hide what they are, or change it. So if people discriminate against them—well, it's wrong, a lot of the time. But a drug addict, on the other hand, very much like the gays, a drug addict indulges in behavior abhorred by the majority. So the gays have a responsibility. If they refuse to seek help to change their behavior, which is done, I'm told, with electrical shocks, the gays can be made normal, but okay. If they refuse, the least they can do is to act in a way that doesn't draw attention to themselves, or else bring down the wrath of the community.

New York is a melting pot, yes, but let's not forget, it's a melting pot of *families*. Of Italians and Irish and Jews and Catholics, of Puerto Ricans and Germans and . . . uh, Russians. I think we'd all agree that one place where unusual personal habits have to be checked at the door is in the classroom. And there, I really believe, the parents of America have *every right* to demand that *no* homosexual, if known to be such, should be allowed to teach and influence our kids, to serve as a role model, or in any way contaminate the classroom.

Psychologists say that all children go through a brief homosexual stage on their way to maturity. If the gays can get at our children when they're most susceptible to the virus of homosexuality, we risk an exponential increase of inversion in this country that will amount to a plaguelike epidemic.

Only people like you and me, ladies and gentlemen, can stop this obnoxious influence from spreading out and polluting our school systems, corrupting our young, and ruining the fabric of a great nation.

I'm a New Yorker by birth, and as long as there is a Roy Cohn, there's one New Yorker who intends to stand up for American values and American beliefs.

I know you all here feel the way I do, and I hope that now you'll join me in singing my favorite song. I hope it's your favorite song, too. Written by Irving Berlin. Let's all sing "God Bless America."

What's Underground About Marshmallows?
by Jack Smith

(RON VAWTER, DRESSED AS JACK SMITH WAS DRESSED FOR
ONE OF HIS PERFORMANCES, WALKS SLOWLY ONTO THE
DARK STAGE, TAKES OFF HIS HAT AND DIRTY OVERCOAT,
AND VERY SLOWLY ARRANGES HIMSELF AND HIS COSTUME
ON AN "ARABIAN" CHAISE. BEHIND HIM IS A SHEET BEING
USED AS A PROJECTION SCREEN ON WHICH WE SEE AN IMAGE
OF A PENGUIN DOLL, STANDING ON A CANAL IN AMSTER-
DAM. WE HEAR A LOUD TAPE OF A SCENE FROM AN OLD
JOAN CRAWFORD RECORDING, ENDING WITH "WHY DON'T
YOU DIE!" HE ARRANGES HIS SCRIPT, PLACES AN EARPHONE
IN HIS EAR, AND TURNS ON THE SMALL TAPE RECORDER
LYING AT HIS BARE FEET. LIGHTS UP ON HIS FACE, COV-
ERED IN JACK SMITH'S GLITTER MAKEUP, UNDERNEATH A
GOLD-AND-BLACK TURBAN. VERY SLOWLY HE BEGINS TO
SPEAK.)

Uh, I, I have to live in squalor all day long, playing hide and
seek with odors . . . I want to be uncommercial film personified.
That's the . . . oh, wait . . . I have to live in squalor all day long
playing hide and seek with odors. No kidding, folks, they love, they
love dead queers here. Still, it is very nice to be let out of the safe
every ten years or so, whenever there's some retrospective program.
We underground filmmakers are kept in the safe at night. We sleep
in the safe standing up. It's like a French Foreign Legion of inte-
rior decorators. Everybody there for some reason, some because
they've betrayed their fellow filmmakers. Actually, I don't like to
be fucked. Others, because this is their only chance and they know
it. Others to seek the certification of Uncle Artcrust.

Kindly old, kindly old Uncle Oldie. I, uh, remember how I first
became involved with Uncle Roach Crust. It was in the early sixties and I was, uh, Donald Flamingo, living at home, minding my
own business—my business card read "Everything from Ancient
Egypt to the 1940s." But I was getting old, or at least my muscles
were contracting. My hair was turning white and I had a sort of a . . .

sort of a grayish color, and I started naturally to think of retiring to an aloha community. Which I did. And one evening in the dining room, as I looked around the plastic palm trees with the mothers pushing the baby carriages among the plastic palm trees (COUGH) it seemed to me that the orchids were whispering *about me*. It seemed that they were saying: "He is the next to be sacrificed."

And uh, the, uh, the olive sun was blazing in the cream cheese sky. The gravy oozed down the side of the volcano of mashed potatoes. I felt the carbonated tide of Coca-Cola rising in my veins, closing off my pores. I woke up on the floor beside an empty box of Chips Ahoy. Later I found myself swaying, uh, to and fro in front of the window of, of, of a confectionery shop. Then I was hanging around the, the, uh, Art Crust archives and, uh, one day a kindly old man appeared on the steps and offered me a job as a sugar zombie and, uh, which I, uh, accepted. And every day I and the other sugar zombies would be marched out of the safe into the underground sugar beet pits. No, the underground sugar beet . . . no, no, the underground desert of sugar beets? Uh . . . and we had to toil in the, uh, oozing marshmallow paste all day long to harvest these enormous spoiling sugar beets like giant empurpled Andy Warhol noses, like machine guns, like huge, bloated, machine gun turnips that . . . out of the enlarged pores of which oozed a sugary, a sugar syrup. They putrefied immediately if you touched them. It was loathsome, loathsome, the foul, empurpled things. It was hellish. Well, anyway . . .

(PAUSE.)

Oh. (COUGH) Uh, this is an intermission. Let's take a ten-minute break, could we please? I was even in the middle of a story, but I'll remember where . . . I hope you don't mind. Because there is already, you know, been enough good stuff already to compare with even the new, latest, hit: "Penguins of Penzance."

(PAUSE.)

The door to the safe was open a bit, so I crept out and, uh, passed out into the corridor. The light hurt my eyes very much, I remember.

Then presently my eyes became used to this, and I noticed a small pointed doorway that was the doorway to the . . . uh, to Uncle Film-crust's Hollywood Underground Sugar Hell. And so I went through this doorway and down some circular stone stairs and at one end of a giant cavernous vault I saw among the giant, boiling, uh, uh . . . what are those things that, you know . . . uh, giant . . . I wish this roach would leave the stage. Please go away. Psst . . . meow . . . Here, kitty kitty . . . uh, giant vats of, uh, boiling sugar paste, and among these I saw Uncle Artcrust bending over a film duplicating machine, and I realized that this was the reason, or the means by which this operation could be understood, and he was duplicating the film left in the safe overnight by anyone he could succeed in having the characteristic two-evening engagement of (PAUSE) of, uh, the, uh, Lucky Landlord Underground Desert of Blue Glitter.

Because of these hellish experiences, uh, you see, sometimes my mind wanders, uh, let's see, where was I? (CONSULTS PAPER) "Desert of Blue Glitter." And then I realized that he was sucking the travel out of all the baby filmmakers. And the thought occurred to me of rushing at him and knocking him away from the machine, but then, you know, I hesitated for a few moments and then, un-fortunately, one of my rings fell on the floor. Cheap jewelry is always crumbling off of me. And, horrified, I saw that Uncle Pawn-shop had spun around, and I hardly had time to pick up the ring when he had gathered up the pile of film cans and darted out of the room, through another pointed doorway, and slammed the door, and turned the lock.

So I . . . I thought, I may as well go back into the safe, because he had escaped again. Escaped again. "So I may as well go back into the safe." Because that wasn't the worst of it, anyway. The worst part of all was that nobody thinks I'm acting, or that I'm not a great actor, or even an actor at all, or that, that this doesn't, isn't even acting. If you can't—if you couldn't move in your theater seats, if you couldn't tear your eyes off of the actor, then it *must* be good acting.

How can I get some coffee? Does anybody have any coffee . . . left over? Somebody . . . someone must go for coffee! I *need*—I need an exotic volunteer from the Desert of Cheerfulness. Come on! It has to be black. With one sugar.

Uh . . . one of the secrets of great acting is always to contrive to be chopping onions during some dramatic moment. So I think I'll start the onion soup now. The, uh . . . Phyllis Newman is dropping by for onion soup. You see, you can tell this really is one of the big moments of the play because I have four onions. Two large ones, one unusally large onion and two . . . oops. (DROPS ONION; BEGINS CHOPPING)

Oh . . . I just made a very good editing change. Uh, you didn't see the thing last night, did you? You see, I'm cutting onions because it helps, it would help you weep at a dramatic moment. (CHOPPING)

The contract of Maria Montez was not renewed and, and, and, uh, her husband, Jean-Pierre Aumont, was rented by the studio to make love . . . to make love to her *replacement*, Yvonne DeCarlo. She died in her bath. She died in her bathtub. Now we know her to be the only fit subject for adoration of modern man. The only movie goddess the world has longed for. Christ returned draped in chiffon and, and boiled like a lobster in her own bathtub. (COUGHING)

Now I think we have come to the reading of the film titles of Maria Montez. Or the Maria Montez film titles might be a better . . . How terrible. I couldn't weep at all . . . it was so . . . even with onions.

There's a whole chunk of stuff I somewhere . . . I, uh, it must be at home. (RON BEGINS TO DANCE TO MUSIC IN FRONT OF SCREEN)

CHICA (SMITH'S ASSISTANT)

(READING.)

Feature film appearances of Maria Montez: As the bathing beauty being interviewed in *Lucky Devils* (SHE SOUNDS A GONG), 1941. As Marie the model in *The Invisible Woman* (GONG), 1941. As Linda Calhoun in *Boss of Bullion City*, 1941. As Inez in *That Night in Rio*, 1941. As Zurwika in (GONG) *Raiders of the Desert*,

1941. As Melahi in *Moonlight in Hawaii* (GONG SOUNDED TWICE), 1941. As Melahi in *South of Tahiti*, 1941. As Sonja Dietrich Landers in *Bombay Clipper* (GONG), 1942. As Scheherazade in *Arabian Nights* (GONG), 1942. As Tahia (GONG) in *White Savage* (GONG), 1943. As Princess Amara in *Ali Baba and the Forty Thieves* (GONG), 1944. In dual roles as Talea/Nadja in *Cobra Woman* (GONG IS SOUNDED TWICE), 1944. As Carla in *Gypsy Wildcat* (GONG), 1944. As Marina in *Bowery to Broadway* (GONG), 1944. As Naila in (GONG) *Sudan* (GONG), 1945. As Rita in *Tangiers* (GONG SOUNDED TWICE), 1945. As the countess in (GONG) *The Exile*, 1947. As Margarita in *Pirates* (GONG) *of Monterey*, 1947. As Antimea in *The Siren of Atlantis* (GONG), 1948. As Dolores in *The Wicked City* (GONG), 1949. (RON FINISHES DANCE, LEAVES STAGE) As Lucienne in *Portraite d'Une Assasienne*, 19 (GONG) 49. As Tina in *Il Wardo de Venezia* (GONG), 1950. As Dolores in *Amore e Sangre* (GONG), 1951. As Consuela in *La Vendetta del Corsario* (GONG), 1951. (MUSIC FROM "GONE WITH THE WIND" COMES UP. CHICA RETURNS FROM THE CHAISE TO HER ORIGINAL POSITION SEATED STAGE LEFT. LIGHTS SLOWLY FADE TO BLACK.)

O Solo Homo: Why This Book?

HOLLY HUGHES:

Before I stumbled into the WOW Cafe I thought I might be a painter and I had good reason to believe I was a feminist. I hadn't painted much of anything in years except for once drinking several bottles of wine and painting my apartment—walls, floors, ceiling—aqua. But one day I volunteered to serve coffee and within minutes it seemed like I was on stage.

I didn't think of what I was doing as theater. Theater was something that happened in a different neighborhood and I thought that theater people all wore those little furry whatchamacallits— the fox stoles made out of the whole animal, head, legs and everything. They spoke in English accents they'd picked up at yard sales in the Hamptons.

What I thought I was doing was falling in love. With about twenty-five women at the same time. I did this theater thing because that's what they were all doing. If it had been skeet shooting I'd be out there screaming: "Pull!"

I kept doing this theater thing and didn't worry too much about what to call it until I got the bright idea of applying for grants. You need more in your artistic statement than: "I want to meet girls." You gotta flesh it out a bit.

So it's 1990, the debate about public funding of art is heating, and I get a grant. I had applied in two categories: Playwriting and

Performance Art and I'd been lucky enough to win in both. But now I had to choose which one. My friends all urged me to pick Playwriting. Performance Art was becoming a target of the right. Even Doonesbury made fun of it.

So of course I decided I *must* be a performance artist. I liked that no one could really define it, that it was up for grabs, that traditional theater people viewed performance art with disdain appealed to the part of me that is eternally thirteen. Who wanted Andrew Lloyd Webber's or Jesse Helms's respect? OK, so it was kind of upsetting about Garry Trudeau.

The places where performance art is presented are usually called "spaces," not theaters. They're like little cracks and holes in the culture where something wild and strange can take root and bloom.

And sometimes that feeling of falling in love comes back when I perform and this time it's the love that dare not stop saying its name.

DAVID ROMÁN:

I have never performed alone on stage. What am I saying? I've never performed on stage at all! I am a professor who studies and writes about performance. In addition, I serve as an advocate for performance, in this case, queer solo performance. I can trace my immersion in queer solo performance to two key events. The year I came out was the year of the 1979 march on Washington. Seeing thousands of lesbian, gay, and bisexual people marching on Washington provided me a sense of comfort and security that seemed to me the point of the march itself. As a queer teenager, I felt that the legacy of the lesbian and gay liberation movement had created a space for me to be out.

I did what most people seemed to do that weekend—if endless lines were the indication—I marched and rallied, danced and cruised. But I also attended a performance by Pat Bond, who was recreating her one-woman show as Gertrude Stein. She performed in this funky space with an audience of mostly lesbians in their thirties and a sprinkling of other gay men. I had never been to a queer performance before or, for that matter, a queer march on Washington. I linked the two as interdependent events that crucially informed and shaped one another. The combined force of queer performance and politics was mobilizing most of us that weekend in ways impossible to fully measure or ascertain.

About ten years later I attended a gay pride event in Minneapolis. After nearly a decade in the midwest, I was about to move to Los Angeles for a one-year teaching position. The night before the rally, I saw Tim Miller perform *Sex/Love/Stories* and the next night I saw Peggy Shaw and Lois Weaver in *Anniversary Waltz*. It was the first time I ever saw these artists on stage, and their work struck me as smart, political, provocative, and fresh. Their performances spoke to me directly, challenging the choices I had made in my own queer life. And afterwards, when I met the performers, they immediately welcomed me into their world. I remember thinking, queer performers are so friendly—and accessible!

A few weeks after seeing Tim Miller perform, he—along with Karen Finley, John Fleck, and Holly Hughes—was defunded by the NEA. A few months after that, I received my Ph.D. I remember wondering at the time why so few academics were writing on contemporary queer performance, especially now that it was under attack. While there already existed a strong tradition of lesbian performance scholarship, in 1990 not many gay male academics were writing on gay theater. So I decided to stop my complaining, ditch my dissertation on early modern theater, and spend my tenure-track years writing a book on AIDS and performance.

These two events—separated by over a decade—set the foundation for my belief that queer performance is tied to queer politics and that this link enables queer community. I'm glad I reached that insight before I began to write about queer performance. It motivates my work and allows me to position my scholarship within a larger cultural mission. "Ask not what queer performance can do for you, but what you can do for queer performance," if you will. Since then, I have been involved in various multiracial and cogendered collaborative performance projects. I now co-chair the board of directors of Highways Performance Space in Santa Monica with Danielle Brazell, one of the Sacred Naked Nature Girls. At Highways, we mainly develop and present community-based performance. We support artists who are concerned with social issues and the various communities they serve. Some of this work is queer but certainly not all of it. Sometimes I try to recreate my own 1979 D.C. experience by curating performance festivals for queer organizations, bringing different people together in support of our larger shared interests.

In 1994 Russ Gage and I pulled together a performance benefit for International Gay and Lesbian Human Rights Commission (IGLHRC) at the Knitting Factory in New York City with performances by three of the contributors included in this volume: Tanya Barfield, Holly Hughes, and Carmelita Tropicana, as well as performances by Justin Bond, a drag performer; Marga Gomez, the award-winning performer and stand-up comic, Babs Davy of the Five Lesbian Brothers, and Richard Elovich, a New York City AIDS activist and performer. In 1995, Ellie Covan (of Dixon Place) and I curated a weekend of performances for the Center for Lesbian and Gay Studies (CLAGS) at New York Theatre Workshop and the Public Theatre with others from this volume including Michael Kearns and Susan Miller, and a list too long to mention here: everyone from Brian Freeman and the Five Lesbian Brothers to the cast members of *Hundreds of Hats*, a musical review directed by Michael Mayer based on the work of Howard Ashman. And only a few months later, Ellie generously offered me her space for a benefit I organized to raise money for the AIDS Prevention Action League (APAL). Holly Hughes and Carmelita Tropicana performed once again, this time they were joined by Nicky Paraiso, a veteran East Village performer and singer; Michael Cunningham, the author of *Flesh and Blood* and *A Home at the End of the World*; Andie Montoya from School's Out, a queer youth performance ensemble; the dancer and choreographer, André Gingras; and Dustin Schell, a New York writer and actor. And just this year, I curated a benefit at Highways to raise money for artists with HIV/AIDS with performances by four of the contributors included in *O Solo Homo*, Luis Alfaro, Michael Kearns, Alec

Mapa, and Tim Miller, as well as performances by David Rousseve, the celebrated choreographer and dancer; and the playwright Chay Yew, the author of *Porcelain* and *A Language of Their Own*.

These benefits confirm my commitment to queer performance and queer politics and they also begin to signal the growing community of performers who are out there doing this work day in and day out. I have been tremendously moved by the generosity of these and other performers who work so frequently for these and other organizations and almost always for free. Now more than ever, with the shrinking budgets available to support the arts—especially queer arts—queer people need to find and establish means to support queer artists and the important work they do. We can no longer expect queer performers to work for free to raise money for our organizations without also helping them raise money for their own rent.

I have been very lucky to have found my niche in this world. And I am proud to be affiliated with these artists and am especially honored to have worked with Holly Hughes in bringing *O Solo Homo* to life. I urge you, too, to do what you can to support the work of these artists: encourage your local theater, campus, or community organization to sponsor them.* I guarantee that they will enrich your lives as they have mine.

*See copyright page for information on contacting contributors.

About the Editors

Holly Hughes is a performance artist and playwright. She is the author of *Clit Notes: A Sapphic Sampler* published by Grove Press.

David Román is assistant professor of English at the University of Southern California. He is the author of *Acts of Intervention: Performance, Gay Culture, and AIDS* published by Indiana University Press.